MA
HIGH SCHOOL

BOOK 0: TRACE'S CROSSING

J. SANDROCK

MARS HIGH SCHOOL BOOK 0: TRACE'S CROSSING

ISBN 978-1-963019-05-6 (hardcover)
ISBN 978-1-963019-06-3 (paperback)
ISBN 978-1-963019-07-0 (Kindle e-book)
ISBN 978-1-963019-08-7 (audio book)

Cover Design & Artwork: *Alexa Eliza,* via 'fiverr.com'
Chapter Artwork and '*Lucky Seven*' Schematic: *J. Sandrock*

Sign up for the **Mars High School** series newsletter: www.marshighschool.com

To correspond by mail with the author:

J. Sandrock
c/o Mariner Valley Publishing
P.O. Box 136
Sandy, UT 84091

MARS HIGH SCHOOL

BOOK 0: TRACE'S CROSSING

J. SANDROCK

MARINER VALLEY

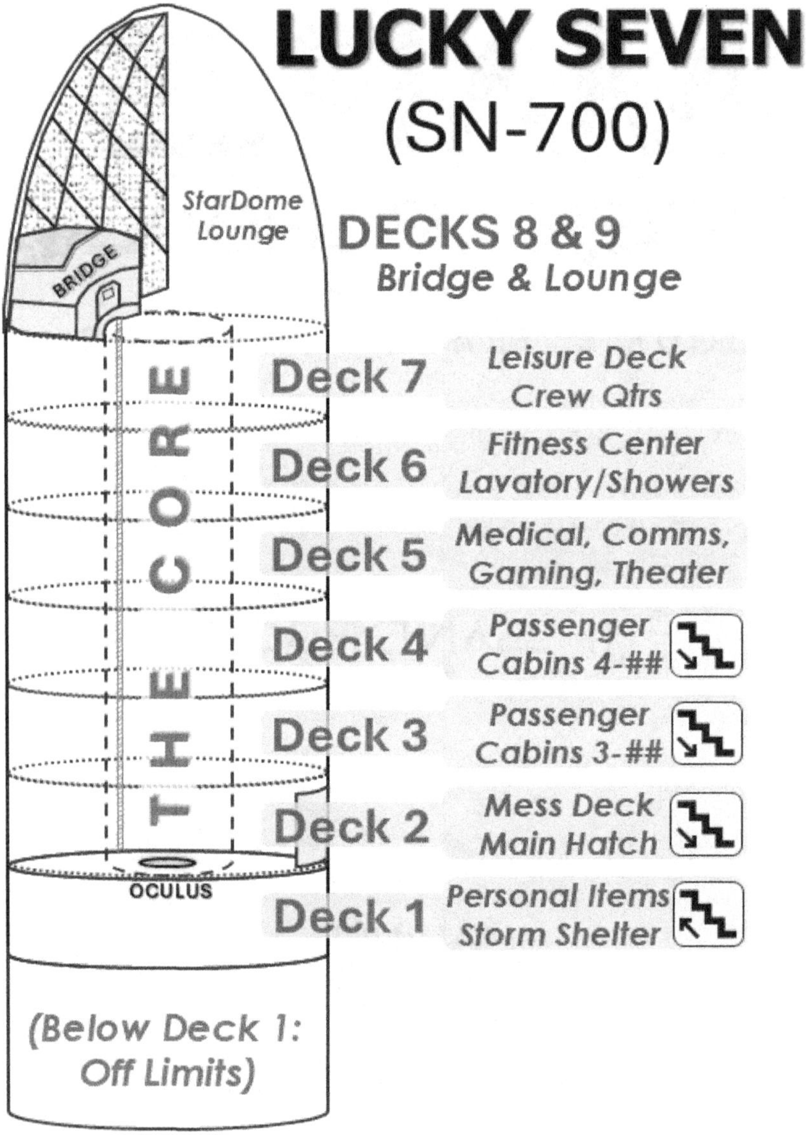

LUCKY SEVEN
(SN-700)
StarDome Lounge
BRIDGE
DECKS 8 & 9
Bridge & Lounge
THE CORE
Deck 7
Leisure Deck
Crew Qtrs
Deck 6
Fitness Center
Lavatory/Showers
Deck 5
Medical, Comms,
Gaming, Theater
Deck 4
Passenger
Cabins 4-##
Deck 3
Passenger
Cabins 3-##
Deck 2
Mess Deck
Main Hatch
OCULUS
Deck 1
Personal Items
Storm Shelter
(Below Deck 1:
Off Limits)

CONTENTS

to all A.E.S. Falcons
and Tigers
past, present, and future,
this story is respectfully dedicated

Introduction

Regarding Spaceflight

If you've never traveled to another planet, I invite you to read a few thoughts on the subject. If you *have* flown to Venus, Mars, an asteroid minesite, or the moons of Jupiter, I ask you to overlook any mistakes you find. As of 2025, I have not yet left the Earth to travel to Mars.

Making *the Crossing* to Mars is not easy—not by a long shot. Many challenges face us—some are physical, and others are mental or emotional. One challenge is utterly unforgiving.

Let's walk through the manageable ones first.

The greatest challenge of five months in space is not about air, food, or water—these, we pack a stockpile of, and filter, grow, and cleanse as much as possible. Thanks to our brilliant astronautical engineers, we produce and conserve resources in many ways, leaving us clean air, tasty food, and pure water to last the journey, with extra to spare.

Human companionship, social isolation, is also not the problem—up to 90 fellow passengers per Starship provide plenty of interaction. Lifelong friendships are forged between strangers, and regular video chats and DMs with friends back on Earth help too. Each passenger is assigned a *Mars Welcome Ambassador* who makes contact early in *the Crossing* and communicates often. Even holographic AI *gen-friends* are available, though most prefer real people over simulated ones. Even cape-wearing super extroverts have more social activity than they can hope for.

Okay, then . . . that insurmountable challenge must be sickness. *Motion sickness . . . homesickness . . . radiation sickness . . .* or *my-carry-on-bag-is-too-small sickness.*

Right?

Nope, nope, nope, and nope.

Motion sickness: Nausea was a huge problem in the early days of air travel, but we kept flying. Ginger ale was served; it calmed the stomach. Flights flew smoother as airframe technology improved; people got used to air travel. Now, it's Dramamine™ to the rescue, and Starships glide through space, smoother than a boat on a lake.

Homesickness: immersive, hi-def digital landscapes can be beamed directly into a person's VR headset, and there, conjure any world we can imagine. Earth environments, Martian environments, dungeon gaming, high flying, scuba diving . . . whole worlds await to transport you whatever you need to be. If that doesn't work, medicinal cocktails calm the nerves and help passengers cope. Your AI psychopharmacologist knows everything about you, and he will always take your calls. The Starship's counselor-medic, your 'Doc,' meets weekly with every passenger and crew member. In the rarest cases, a traveler who experiences a full-blown breakdown can be sedated and kept in an artificially-induced coma for the rest of the trip. Some volunteer for this procedure right after launch, but 'the deep sleep' has risks and is reserved for no-kidding emergencies.

Radiation sickness: Space does not play nice! The 1970s Apollo missions to Earth's moon, Luna, taught us all about radiation—shielding is key! Every idea tested, from outer hulls filled with a constantly-filtering water supply . . . to multiple thin layers of lead shielding, like Kevlar cloth, are employed to minimize the problem. Solar flares, like storms at sea, are particularly hazardous—a hardened fallout shelter is conveniently located on Deck 1. Don't miss your 'muster drill' right after launch—practicing a quick evac to Deck 1 may just save your life.

Carry-on containers: Your standard-issue carry-on box is small—it's an oversized safe-deposit box. You're allotted 5 kg/11 pounds at most. This forces you to prioritize! Starship Interplanetary recommends 5 items, each with a specific purpose.

Item #1: personal token—something to remind you who you are.

Item #2: personal gift—something given by a loved one or friend.

Item #3: passenger gift—optional; to give to someone on the way.

Item #4: clothing—jacket or hat; size waivers can be expensive.

Item #5: your little secret—as long as it passes screening, good to go.

The challenge of figuring out your specific five items makes the carry-on deposit box more of a fun challenge and less of a frustration.

All righty then, I can hear you say, the insurmountable challenge must be . . . *space*. A cramped little tin can rocket ship with restricted personal space, stuffed full of a hundred people making the mars Crossing. *Claustrophobia* is the greatest challenge, right?

Nope, that's not it either. Starships in the 2350s are much larger than just 300 years ago—there's more open space on every deck than a high school classroom, and each Starship has 8-10 decks, depending on configuration. You'll have open deck space to float around in to your heart's content, and each Starship is built around a large open central core, similar to an oversized elevator shaft. Plus, the *StarDome*, an array of windows fitted into the nose of the Starship allows you to look up at the stars and galaxies around the clock.

The hardest challenge, dear traveler, is not about your physical needs, missing home, or material possessions . . . and it's not space.

It's *time*.

Five months. 150 days is the best case for making a fast transfer from Earth to Mars. With no air in space, we can't accelerate the way air-breathing jet planes on Earth pull air in the front and blast it out the back. Further, we haven't mastered continuous acceleration, which could, in theory, reduce *the Crossing* to Mars from five months to one.

So, we have months to fill up and nothing pressing to do with all that time. On Earth, there's no limit to the number of things we *can* do . . . assign a huge list of chores or too much homework; deep down we're happy as a clam. Sure, we'll complain about how little we're being paid for that much work, or fuss about a single algebra problem that has seventeen steps, but deep down we're content to have more to do than we have time to do it.

Now flip that idea on its head . . . there is a seriously short fuse on the amount of nothing to do that we can handle. Kids on long car trips drive their parents crazy. Solitary confinement for prisoners does cruel things to the mind. Time, Stephen King observed, "can draw out like a blade."

A person can do horrible things, digging deeper and deeper to fill a hole in time they feel trapped in, without enough to do.

Starship Interplanetary (S.I.) takes this matter very seriously. Passengers and crew are required to follow a mental well-being program with goals and tasks day after day, week after week.

Teenagers and younger travelers will be recruited in Month #2 aboard the Starship to assist crew members with simple chores like routine Starship maintenance or growing and harvesting the garden salad greens in the on-board hydroponics labs. Young people especially, our teens and tweens, will be expected to roll up their sleeves and be as productive as they can. Adults may volunteer as well, but S.I. understands they have their own tasks for the work responsibilities that await them on Mars.

These measures keep travelers emotionally and mentally well-balanced for *the Crossing*, allowing them to boldly go where few have gone before, seeking a new life in a new civilization on a world far, far away.

S.I. now confirms you will be flying aboard SN-700 (*Lucky Seven*), a truly special starship with a distinguished service record. Please make sure your Mars immunizations are all up to date and carefully select the carry-on items you'll be taking with you for *the Crossing*. You are reminded to keep your total under 5 kg/11 pounds; one standard carry-on case will be provided to you at no weight penalty or cost.

Your first step in getting to Mars is traveling to the launch facility itself—Earth has several that service the Moon and Mars, but the most popular is at the United States Confederation's southernmost launch facility, *Starbase B-C.*

So please write your five items in the blanks below. Go on.

After you finish, per tradition, grab yourself a Mars bar if you can find one, and let's roll.

J. Sandrock
August 2025

My *Starship Interplanetary* approved carry-on list:

1. Personal Token: ______________________________

2. Self-Gift from a loved one: ______________________

3. Passenger Gift: ______________________________

4. Clothing Item: ______________________________

5. My Little Secret: ____________________________

TOTAL WEIGHT: ____________________

(Cannot exceed 5 kg / 11 pounds)

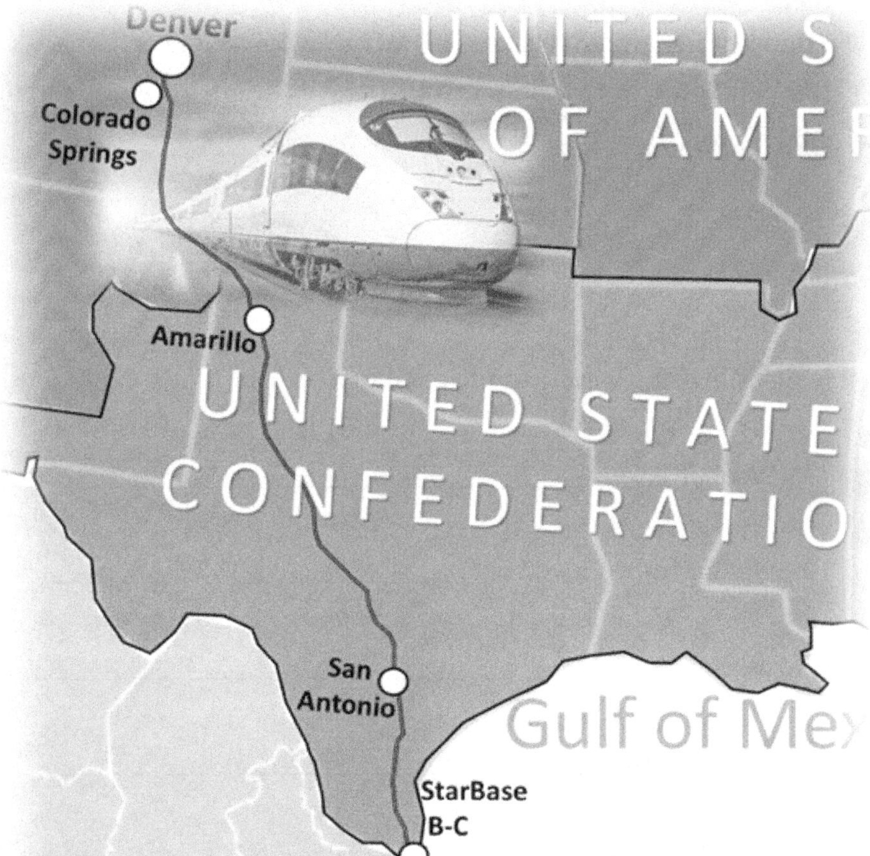
Denver
Colorado Springs
Amarillo
San Antonio
StarBase B-C
UNITED S
OF AMER
UNITED STATE
CONFEDERATIO
Gulf of Me

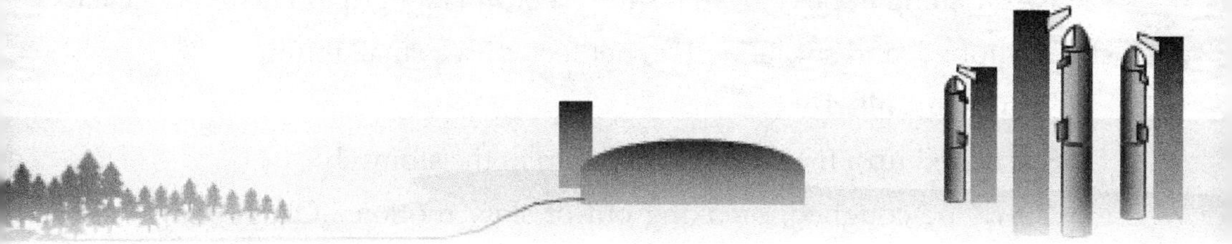

Chapter Twenty

Nothing to Take Along

"Gimme my bag, Trace!" Louise unbuckled her seat belt and looked up at her brother, who was standing in the train aisleway. He gripped the handle of Louise's purple roller bag, up in the overhead bin. They had reached the main launch complex—time to get off the *Starbase Zephyr*.

"You mean . . . this bag, ya goof?" Trace smiled, looking down at his little sister. She dropped her eyebrows down and parked her hands on her hips.

"You know I'm too short to reach that high. And don't call me a goof."

"Ohhhh noooooo . . . I'm stuck in slooooow-mo . . . can't break freeeeeee . . ." Trace moved her bag forward at a glacial pace on the luggage rack.

Tired from a twelve-hour train ride, Louise was all pouty lips and squinty eyes.

"Quit. Being. A punk," she said through gritted teeth. She jumped up and grabbed his arm, trying to pull it down. He held his arm up, leaving

Louise dangling in place from his flexed bicep. Her grip on his jeans jacket sleeve slipped, and she landed on her feet with a small thump.

"Ha." He smiled at her.

She balled up a fist and punched him in the stomach.

"Ow," he coughed, breaking out of slow motion. "Okay, okay, here you go."

He set her bag down on the aisle seat, and she snatched it away from him. He smiled and tousled her wavy brown hair. She batted his hand away and elbowed past him.

"Butt face," she muttered, setting the bag down and extending the handle to its full length. With dozens of passengers clogging the train's aisle, rummaging their own bags, she couldn't go anywhere. Arms crossed, she squinted up at him. In a low voice she said, "Wait til I'm taller. I'll pound you into the dirt."

"Mm hmm," Trace said, barely containing a laugh at her attempt to be menacing. "I'm sure you will."

He gripped his own faded green canvas backpack in the overhead bin, his smile fading. The bag's worn edges told of many adventures and a dozen or more times going through the wash. He brushed his wavy dark blond hair up over his forehead and looked at his pack. The welcome video they had watched half an hour before arriving made it crystal clear: no personal bags were going with them to Mars.

"They're not gonna let you keep it," Louise remarked, adding, "we have to use those standard carry-on crate thingys, remember?"

"Yeah, I know, Lou Lou, we all saw the same video."

Trace pursed his lips in frustration—he'd be throwing away an old friend. He felt the canvas, well softened by years of continuous and careful use while adventuring in the mountains above their Colorado Springs home.

Home, he mused.

Not anymore.

He felt other eyes upon him. From the seats behind Trace Worthington and his sister stood Mom and Dad. Dad smiled when he made eye contact with his son—Trace managed a small, forced nod. He turned back to his sister to take his mind off his daddy issues and shook his head in frustration.

"Lou Lou, what do . . ." his voice trailed off. Louise had turned forward and was looking straight up, out through the train's large overhead windows. A dozen steps ahead, the first passengers were starting to disembark.

"Look at the stars," Louise murmured.

Trace let his own gaze be drawn upward, soft hazel-green eyes noticing the time, 11:37 p.m., and the pitch-black night above.

He imagined Mars . . . somewhere up there, beyond the curtain of night, waiting . . . he gritted his teeth in frustration at the thought of the red planet.

Screw Mars.

More passengers started shuffling toward the exit. Trace and Louise took a few steps forward, following the trickle of people nearing the exit doors. He kept Louise safely in front of him. Mom and Dad followed.

As they turned to step down onto the platform, Trace glanced sideways into the Zephyr's main dining car. Recent memories flooded his mind—from the table where he sat several hours ago, trying to cope with the avalanche that had demolished his life.

* * *

The untouched soda sat before him, ice cubes long melted. The rocking of the train barely registered. Cool air of the window vent tickled his arm, raising goosebumps. It felt refreshing.

Trace stared out the window as the sun slipped behind the hills of Texahoma, casting long shadows across the western plains as they approached San Antonio.

His father walked into the dining car, adjusting his glasses on the bridge of his nose and looking down at his son, carefully studying Trace with the same hazel-green eyes.

A pregnant pause stretched out. Dad sat down, across the table.

"My son, I can see you're frustrated. We've talked about this."

"Dad, I heard you before. But Mars? Really? We'll hate it on Mars—it's dry, it's ugly, it's boring."

His father frowned.

"Young man, us going to Mars is not optional—the work opportunities for your mother and me are tremendous, and we stay together as a family. Plus, how can you not want to make *the Crossing*? You know how few people actual—"

"Yeah, Dad, you told me that too, once-in-a-lifetime, yadda, yadda, yadda. I just . . . I don't think you understand what you've done to me. To my life."

Trace looked at his father's hardened expression, noticing a few gray strands at his temples for the first time.

Dad said nothing, so Trace kept going.

"It's all cramped little caves, dry, irradiated deserts . . . that's not living, it's . . ."

Futility consumed him, and his hands flopped on the table.

"You could have left me in Colorado, you know. I had it all worked out." Trace held his exasperated expression, then looked out the window into the blinding light.

Dad cleared his throat. "Your mother wouldn't have that—it's your last couple years with us. In fact, in Mars time, it's one year." He reached across the narrow table and gripped Trace's upper arm. Trace smirked but did not shake Dad's hand away.

"And our journey . . ." Dad searched for the right words. "It's a new beginning—it's not what you predict; things like this never are."

"So, you're saying it's going to be amazing? Life in a dust bowl?"

"Not what I'm saying at all. It's . . ." He finally gave up searching for the right words.

Trace looked at him, waiting for Dad to finish.

"Look, you don't have to like it—you just have to do it. But try to keep an open mind, all right?"

"You're right. I won't like it. You've given me nothing to take along, not even hope."

Dad's shoulders slumped.

"Well . . . there's one thing I know you'll like."

"What's that?"

"Lucky Seven."

Trace exhaled a short sniff.

Jim gave Trace's shoulder a squeeze and leaned back to stand.

"I'll leave you to your . . ." Dad paused, noticing Trace's hand resting on his pack. Gripping his pack. Dad said nothing further, turned, and left. Trace watched him go.

The door slid open, the door slid shut.

"Lucky Seven," Trace murmured to the empty bench across from him. "Worst luck ever."

* * *

Louise hopped down onto the platform. Lost in his memories, Trace stumbled on the lip of the last step, nearly losing his balance. He caught himself, nodded to Louise, and they walked with Mom and Dad behind them, onward.

A crowd of two hundred disembarked the Zephyr, filling up the platform and pressing their way toward the launch complex and its overnight lodging.

Trace inhaled deeply as he walked along the platform. The salty night air, warm and humid, assaulted his senses. Colorado's crisp, dry mountain air belonged to another world.

With only intermittent sleep aboard the MagLev train, the exhausted crowd crossed a passenger drop-off zone with its ride-share stand, and entered the main complex. Doors whooshed open ahead of them under a lighted sign that proclaimed the Starbase Gateway Hotel.

Their meager personal possessions, properly tagged back in Denver, were dropped onto a small conveyor and auto-delivered via freight elevator up to their rooms. Trace hesitated, but plopped his trusty pack down, watching it vanish into the darkness of the scanner. The crowd shuffled on through the lobby.

Uniformed guides directed them through a series of simple security doors into the cafeteria where they would take their last meal on Earth. Six food service counters stood ahead, with a dazzling white dining area of simple round tables and chairs.

Dad picked a line at random. Eventually it was their turn at the front, where they found rows upon rows of soft plastic tubes just the right size for gripping.

Louise selected a white food-tube from the serving shelves, after considering several colors. She looked sideways, holding it up and catching Dad's gaze.

He shrugged, grabbing an orange one for himself.

"We're eating toothpaste." she said, scowling. She plunked it on her small tray, grabbed a soda can, and led on in search of an empty table. Trace grabbed a tube of his own, a red one, and followed his little sister, soda in hand.

They gathered at an empty table and took seats, stealing glances around at the other passengers, who were in various stages of eating their unusual meal.

"Which flavor did you pick, sweetie?" Mom asked, setting down her tray and pulling out a chair.

Louise turned hers over and read the label. "*Dreamy Mashed Potatoes,*" she said, reaching up to twist off the top.

"Mmm, sounds great," said Trace, watching her.

"It says here we can . . . close our eyes while we eat to better enjoy the experience? What does that mean?" She squeezed a bit of the tube's contents onto her fingertip—blue gel.

"Ewwwww, it *does* looks like toothpaste," Louise said, eyes flashing in mock alarm. She tasted the bit on her finger. "Mmm, but it tastes yummy."

She stuck the end in her mouth and squeezed, closing her eyes.

"What's yours, son?" Mom asked as Dad sat down.

Trace shrugged. "I just grabbed the red one. Says here . . . *Apple Pie Addiction.*"

He twisted the top open and squeezed out what looked like the same gel toothpaste, but in his case, a deep red.

Dad spoke up. "Kids, remember what they said in that last video aboard the Zephyr? You need to eat at least half the tube unless you want to be starving tomorrow morning when we board *Lucky Seven.* It's best if you eat the whole thing." He popped the top on his soda with a ptsss sound.

"And it prevents upset stomach for at least three days," Louise parroted from the same video, in a crisp announcer voice. She popped the top on her own soda can and took a sip. "Mmm, tastes like Sprite."

After their odd meal, which lasted a whopping eight minutes, they dumped the empty tubes and cans in the appropriate bins, stacked their trays, and joined the small clusters of guests heading up to their rooms. Trace yawned as they waited their turn at the elevator—then felt the buzz of his tablet. He pulled it from an inner jeans jacket pocket, tapped it awake, and read the notification.

A video message from Jeni awaited.

He hadn't heard from his girlfriend since their tearful goodbye on the Denver main terminal . . . fourteen thousand hours ago, it seemed. But that had been just this morning. Fourteen hours ago.

The Worthingtons stepped into the elevator and rode up, stopping several times for others to get out at their rooms. Trace drummed his fingers on his leg, eager to get to their room and watch Jeni's video. At last, the elevator doors chimed open at the top, the 11th floor.

Dad led down the left hallway toward their family suite, found it, and scanned his palm to open the door. Louise eagerly pushed in, dodging neatly around their luggage, which awaited them just inside the door.

Louise grabbed her roller bag and dragged it through a small sitting area into the bedroom with two twin beds, ignoring the other room with its single queen bed, clearly for Mom and Dad.

She pulled long curtains aside with a "oooooh, wooooow…"

The StarBase complex lay sprawled before them, the darkness of the Gulf of Mexico beyond. Trace followed, dropping his pack onto the bed next to the bedroom door. He took a moment at the windows next to Louise.

"Look, Starships," she said, indicating the launch towers. Far off, at least a half mile away, six towers stood unmistakable in the bright glow of floodlights. Among the six towers, two stood empty, and four towers held steady their gleaming starships, ready to launch.

This was really happening.

After a long, hard look, Trace walked back into the sitting area and pulled out his tablet. Louise stayed at the window, awed into silence for once.

Trace shrugged out of his jacket and dropped it on the seat next to him. He slipped ear pods in and sat, waking his tablet.

He scrolled past a series of pinned videos from the farewell party his parents had hosted in their home a week ago. One week? Felt like longer.

He opened the video clip from Jeni; her face filled his screen. He tapped the 'play' triangle.

She smiled, a tear already on her cheek.

"I miss you already," she smiled. "I'm about to get out of this car, go inside the station, and say goodbye to you, probably forever. It's not fair."

She wiped the tear from her cheek. He loved her freckles, her mousy brown hair, always perfectly straight . . . or up in a ponytail. He remembered from their goodbye that she had her hair up in a ponytail.

"I know we can't change things, but by all the gods, I wish we could. It just wasn't meant to be."

Trace felt a darkness descending on him . . . a foreboding.

"Hard to believe we just celebrated two years last month. Remember that little ice cream stand in Monument? Yeah. I'm not sure I can ever go back." She glanced off to the side, lost in the memory of their first meeting.

She shook it off and looked straight at Trace through his screen.

"By the time you get this, I'm guessing you'll be asleep at your hotel, and blasting off in the morning. Another world calls; you have to go. This is where fate is taking you, and my own path stays here in C-Springs." She put on a serious expression, lowering her head, a look he had hardly ever seen on her.

"I need you to get on that rocket and know that I can't try to keep you in my heart. The memories we've made . . . I will remember everything. I just can't keep trying to make new memories with you, since we are literal worlds apart now."

He felt his heart racing, his breathing faster.

"I have to let you go."

She wiped her eyes one more time.

"But I left something in your pocket last night, a gift, and I want you to wait until after you're on your way to Mars before you open it. It's in your top buttoned jacket pocket, the one you hardly ever use. I hope you like it—it was my grandfather's, and I want you to have it.

"And now I have to go inside and say goodbye to you."

"I love you. But I have to say goodbye."

Now Trace had tears welling up in his own eyes.

"So . . . goodbye."

Trace sat still as a statue as the video ended, the camera freezing on her face, her eyes blue and glistening.

"I love you too," he murmured, sucking in a deep breath and letting it go. "Jeni."

He wiped his eyes and reached for his jacket to find her gift. Sure enough, in the buttoned chest pocket, the one he never used, he removed a small package, neatly wrapped in black and held with a forest green ribbon, his favorite color. The package was no larger than an old-school matchbox, the kind he saw occasionally in classic holo films.

He eyed the wastebasket in the door of the bathroom and flexed his arm for a perfectly-aimed throw, and—

Dad walked into the room, stopping when he saw Trace's expression.

Trace dropped the small package in his lap and turned away.

"Are you all right, my son?"

"Uh . . . yeah, Dad, just . . . processing. I'll be fine."

"Okay." Dad looked into the kids' bedroom, speaking loud enough to be heard through the doorway. "Kids? It's getting late . . . well, early, actually. We should call it a night."

Trace looked at him, nodding. The lump in his throat stopped him from speaking.

Louise strutted out of the bedroom wearing her brand new shipsuit, a rugged canvas material in bright blue. "Check this out, Trace! It has my name on it and everything!"

"That's really cool," Trace croaked, smiling and nodding. Mom stood in her own bedroom doorway, smiling at Louise in her new outfit.

"Right? And hey, look—our carry-on boxes!" She grabbed one from its stand against the wall and lifted it. "Wow, it's . . . really light."

Dad took a step toward Trace, but the last thing Trace wanted right now was a pity hug from his dad. He stood up and went over to Louise to grab his own carry-on case.

Hefting one, he could see there was enough space for the things he wanted to take with him, Jeni's small wrapped package included. He'd throw it away some other time.

"My son, you won't be needing that case," Dad said as Trace scrutinized his carry-on box.

Trace cleared his throat. "What do you mean?"

Mom walked over. "Your father means he paid extra for you to be able to use your backpack as your carry-on."

Trace snapped his gaze to her face.

"You're keeping your pack. If that's what you want?"

"Seriously?" He smiled, setting the carry-on case down. "Uh, yes. Yes please."

Dad smiled. "Kids, we can go over it all later, and pack when our alarm goes off. Sleep fast, we have to be up in just six hours, and be heading downstairs in seven."

"Aye-firmative," Louise said, snapping a mock salute and getting bedtime hugs from parents before heading into the bedroom, carry-on case in hand.

"Good night," Trace said, rubbing his eyes like he was tired, and heading to the bedroom himself. Jeni's small gift was still clutched tight in his grip.

* * *

Five floors below, the operative pulled the needle out of the dock worker's neck. Eyes wide with shock, the worker's knees wobbled; his legs folded and he flopped heavily on the bed, barely managing to stay sitting up.

The operative put a gloved hand on the front of his coveralls and pushed him backwards. Tools on his work belt jangled as he bounced once then stayed flopped out on his back. Staring up in the ceiling, his eyes looked around in confusion.

Slurring his words heavily, the man said, "What did . . . you . . . give me?"

The operative shrugged. "Not the $750K you were expecting – that much is clear, yes?"

The worker twitched groggily, pawing in front of his face at demons that weren't even there. "You lyin' . . . sack – "

The operative grabbed his face under his chin, squeezing hard and cutting off what he was about to say. They locked eyes; he hissed in the man's face, eyes flashing.

"Torching one of the boss' prized possessions was not part of your job. For that, your life is forfeit."

"I . . . what?" Confusion washed over the worker's face.

"You smoked a $1.3 million cigar, you idiot! But of course, you have no memory of that. And surprise, you will not remember your time on Lucky Seven today either, thanks to my little friend here."

He set the needle back in its small case and slipped the case in a jacket pocket.

The worker made a weak swipe at the operative's face.

The operative batted it aside and in the same motion, pulled a large crescent wrench from the worker's tool belt. He flexed his hand, ensuring he had a good grip.

The last of his energy fading, the worker's hands flopped at his sides. His eyelids fluttered.

"Please, do not misunderstand," the operative said. "The corporation appreciates your usefulness. But . . . loose ends, not so much. And since I cannot have your blood all over me when I board the Starship tomorrow . . ."

He pulled a sheet down over the worker's face.

He raised the crescent wrench high above his head.

"Uhhhhh . . ." the worker murmured, then lay still.

Curious, the operative peeked under the sheet and saw the man had passed out.

"Hm, that works too," the operative said, shrugging and setting down the crescent wrench.

He poked a gloved finger in the man's eye, checking if he had truly passed out. The worker's head lolled sideways and stayed still.

"Sweet dreams." He slipped the wrench carefully back in the tool belt, facing it the right direction. He scanned the room for any forgotten objects. Satisfied, he returned to the sleeping man's side.

"We could not have done it without you . . . oh, and the clean-up crew will be here shortly to make certain you never wake up." He took a step back. "Enjoy oblivion."

He gave a small salute, turned, and crossed the room.

He paused, looking back from the door.

"We stand avenged."

He slipped out, leaving his victim in darkness.

* * *

Trace eased out of his bed. The wall display read 4:14 A.M.

Louise slept on in her bed, and presumably Mom and Dad were still asleep in their own room. Trace tiptoed over to the huge windows and pulled the curtain aside just as quietly.

The launch complex stood glowing, four towers holding Starships like falconers, ready to launch them into glorious flight.

A light blue glow from directly below caught his eye. The trapezoidal hotel swimming pool ran out to the property's edge. A happy couple splashed around, enjoying the morning sea breeze and one final dip before leaving such things behind. Beyond, the broad expanse of pitch black stretched out to an unseen horizon—the dark waters of the Gulf of Mexico.

The launch pads tugged at his attention once more and he scanned other buildings, sprawled in stillness on the verge of a very special event that only happened every 26 months. These were not routine rocket flights to and from Asia, Europe, or even the Moon . . . today was *interplanetary.*

"Which one is *Lucky Seven*?" Louise asked from right beside him. Trace jolted, then tousled her hair.

"Um, let me see," he said, grabbing his tablet from the bedside charging pad. He swiped up and tapped it a few times. "Looks like it has a green-and-yellow stripe running up the side.

Louise squinted out the window. "I can't tell from here."

"Yeah, me neither. Strange."

"Which ones are the others?"

Trace read from his listings. "Okay. Other starships in our flotilla are SN-485, the *Manitou,* SN-844, the *Bozeman,* and SN-154, the *Williamina Fleming.*"

"What's a flotilla?"

"Uh, a smaller part of the whole fleet, I guess? Eighteen starships, all launching today."

"Oh." Louise said simply. "There's only four."

Trace swiped his screen a few times.

"Mm, says here four starships launched from Taiwan . . . an hour ago, five are going soon from United Arab Emirates, and five are lifting off from the Florida island chain just an hour before it's our turn. Looks like we have . . . six hours and forty-five minutes until liftoff."

"Why are the take-off times so weird?"

"Taking turns to refuel maybe? You know, that ring thing up in orbit. And then we all take turns for a slingshot past the moon," Trace said, looking down.

Louise looked back out the window.

"Oh," she said again.

The first hints of daylight glowed on a distant watery horizon.

"Trace? Will we ever come back?" she murmured.

"I wonder that too, my Lou Lou."

They stayed, watching their last Earth sunrise.

* * *

Dawn broke the darkness, sunlight shimmering off the waters from higher and higher as the Earth turned. There was no breakfast in the room, just a small snack-pack to alleviate any last-minute hunger pangs. Down a disposal chute went their civilian clothes, 'civvies' as the Zephyr video had called them, and any other personal effects they couldn't take with.

Everyone had showered and cleaned up and donned their blue ship-suits, which zipped neatly up the front. Matching soft booties snugged over their feet; the overall look was something between nerdy and cool.

"I love it has my name on it—Louise Worthington, S-N-seven-zero-zero, reporting for duty sir," she announced, flopping a goofy salute at no one in particular.

Trace glanced at his own suit nametag and nodded. He stretched his arms, flexing his shoulders.

Loudspeakers throughout the entire facility sounded soft, pleasant chimes. A man's deep and gentle voice followed.

"Attention in the complex, travelers bound for all Mars destinations: this is your first call to proceed immediately to the lobby area and then to your designated departure gate. Again, please proceed immediately to the lobby to begin the boarding process. Thank you."

Dad peeked his head in the door. "You guys all set? It's time."

"Okay, Dad," Louise zipped her ship suit to the top and turned to grab her carry-on deposit box off the bed. She dropped her roller case down the chute. "Bye bye," she said as her purple pack vanished with a soft swish.

Trace shouldered his olive-green backpack.

"Dad. Thanks for getting a waiver to bring my pack as a personal item." He nodded his appreciation, patting his shoulder strap for emphasis.

Dad smiled and nodded. "Absolutely," he said, smiling. "So, I think we're all set."

Trace looked down at his sister. "You ready?"

Louise looked at the door, her face serious, focused.

"Let's do this thing." She marched out of the bedroom and straight toward the suite door, carry-on case in hand.

Trace smiled widely, and dad stifled a chuckle. Louise gripped the knob, and without so much as a look back, threw it open and stomped proudly out into the hallway.

Mom and Dad and Trace, carry-on burdens in hand, caught up near the elevator. Louise stabbed the button, and from the opposite hallway, another family group approached. Walking in front of two older passengers, presumably her parents, was the most beautiful teenage girl Trace had ever seen. Pageant-winner gorgeous. Designer baby gorgeous.

Trace's parents stepped through the open elevator doors, and Trace stood . . . captivated. This girl was stunning—wavy blonde hair fell in perfect curled tresses down past her shoulders in the front. Her bright blue eyes matched the intense royal blue of the ship-suits they all wore. No, Trace thought, they seemed a bit more of an icy blue. Definitely a designer baby, Trace thought.

Trace's family had stepped inside. He shook off his gaze and made to join them, but the blonde girl spoke.

"Ever heard of ladies first?" she asked.

It didn't sound like a question.

Trace, eyebrows raised, did not reply. He stepped aside to let the girl and her parents step onto the lift. He stepped in beside them, shifting over next to his own family. Dad and Mom seemed not to have noticed the brief exchange.

Before the girl could toss her hair over her shoulder, he noticed her nametag read *Dominique Van . . .* something. He didn't see which ship she was on but he couldn't help but notice how well the snug shipsuit fit her curvy, petite frame. It looked as though she had been poured into it.

"So . . . what Starship are you flying on today?" Trace asked.

"Are you addressing me?" the girl sniffed, still looking straight ahead at the doors.

"Mm-hmm."

"*Lucky Seven*, of course. Everyone who's anyone flies *Lucky Seven*. Don't you know that?"

Trace sighed. Great. His ship—he'd have to put up with her for five months.

"I guess," he said.

"What about you?" Dominique still had not made eye contact with Trace.

"It's—" The elevator slowed. Dominique cut him off.

"Can't always have what you want," she said, flipping her hair and striding out of the elevator. Dominique strode on ahead without looking back; her adults followed.

Trace shook his head. "I can't tell you how much you're *not* what I want," Trace muttered under his breath.

The Worthington family walked forward together, joining the sea of humanity that had swelled overnight from two hundred to nearly four hundred, pouring from every elevator into the assembly area.

Families intermingled with couples and the odd solo traveler. Nearly everyone clutched the same type of carry-on, like a boxy briefcase.

The blonde girl and her parents strode ahead into the crowd, her dad murmuring something to her mom about hoping 'the flying Dutchman' was all right before walking out of earshot.

People closed in from all around, shuffling through eight double-wide doorways and into a vast departure plaza. Overhead, a super-wide flatscreen, fifty feet wide at least, glowed with bright aqua letters:

THIS WAY PLEASE.

ALL DEPARTURES

WE WISH YOU A PLEASANT JOURNEY.

Trace held Louise's hand so they wouldn't be separated by the mingling people. Mom and Dad stayed close behind. Inside the departure plaza, the crowd slowed as passengers crossed paths and split into separate lines at the four active departure gates. Glowing above them, four widescreens showed:

GATE 1	GATE 3	GATE 4	GATE 6
MANITOU	BOZEMAN	Wma. FLEMING	LUCKY SEVEN

With no outside-looking windows to distract from boarding, passengers queued up in their respective lines, craning to peer ahead. Trace caught snippets of conversation all around him. The young man ahead of them in line mentioned even though it was his second time flying to Mars for their biotech company, he could never be bored with it. Clearly his companion, a woman with braided black hair and deeply tanned skin, had never flown in a Starship before—not a *MoonShip,* or even a *Continent-Hopper.* She sounded both nervous and excited, like a kid about to ride her first rollercoaster.

Trace looked between them, craning to see departure Gate 6.

Two company officials stood there while a platoon of armed security guards looked on, electro-stun sticks safely holstered.

Louise walked in front of Trace, his hands on her shoulders. He snugged up his backpack straps and kept calming contact with his sister. She strained to look around people blocking her view, and they finally arrived at the front of the line. A graying man in his 70s welcomed them.

"Hello friends," he said, smiling warmly. "Your palm please?"

Louise hesitated, glancing back up at Trace.

"Want me to go first?" he asked.

"Nope, I got this," Louise said, her voice cracking a little. Her hand print scanned, her picture popped up on a portrait display tablet. Her status changed from "Standby for Check-In" to "Ident Confirmed." The old man's much younger companion, a perky blonde woman, passed a drink pouch to Louise from a food cart.

Trace's turn. "Why so much security?" he asked as he pressed his palm to the touchscreen.

The blonde smiled. "To prevent stowaways," she said, passing Trace his own drink pouch.

"Stowaways? Has that ever even happened?" He accepted the pouch.

The older man answered. "Not for sixteen years now, I think. Seventeen maybe? We take it seriously."

The blonde gently instructed them both to "drink up." Again, the warm smile. She seemed a bit too eager. Creepy in her manner, almost.

"Oh, is this that calm-ya-down thing they told us about on the train?" Louise asked, stabbing the small straw into the top.

"Yes indeed," the man said. "But it won't stop you from enjoying or remembering the experience. You'll just feel all those calm, happy vibes."

"Mmmm, orangey," she said, after taking a sip.

"What if . . . someone doesn't drink up?" Trace asked, holding up the pouch.

"The health scanners will notice the compound is missing from your body, you'd be flagged, and they would watch you drink one before being allowed to board the Starship. Just one of those must-do things."

Trace shrugged and stabbed his straw into the pouch. He took a gulp and stepped forward with Louise so Mom and Dad could have their turn. Pleasantries exchanged, four pouches in hand, the Worthingtons pressed on, each still bearing a carry-on and taking sips.

"Wow, now that's a people-mover," Mom observed.

Shiny metal guide rails funneled them into a moving sidewalk, just wide enough for one person and stretching ahead as far as they could see.

"Aaaand, here we go." Trace murmured, stepping into one of the conveyor belt's yellow circles.

Chapter Nineteen

Travels & Leisure

Fifteen minutes passed in a blur.

Four moving sidewalks each led to a separate Starship launch pad. Louise waved at a boy roughly her own age in the next line over; he waved back until they lost sight of each other behind a divider wall.

Viewscreens played a recorded message describing what would happen next: first, a bin to toss their empty drink pouches, a health scan, a questionnaire, and final security. Then, after one last restroom break, they would ride the elevator up to the main hatch and board the Starship itself.

Louise's grin seemed fixed in place; she looked up and around at every little detail. Trace noticed he felt more relaxed, yet very alert. He allowed himself a smile. As the moving sidewalk rolled onward, they each chucked their empty pouches into the labeled bins.

"Yes, two points," Louise said proudly. "Do they have basketball on Mars?" She looked up at Trace.

"Yes, but the rims are like twenty-five feet high."

"Awww, I can't even reach the rims here," she pouted. "Not like you."

"You might, since you'll jump a lot higher on Mars."

"I'll jump higher? Oh yeah, less gravity. Duh." She looked up as the recorded voice spoke again.

"Will you each turn to the right and face the health check monitor, please?"

They rested their chins in a chinrest and breathed normally.

"After your portrait status changes from orange to aqua, please step back from the monitor."

Trace did as instructed, and after a few breaths, the bright orange border flipped to aqua. The screen display showed: *CLEARED. Thank you.*

He leaned back. The medical device swung away, but the monitor stayed in place. Five questions appeared. Louise carefully murmured hers aloud as Trace read his own.

*1. Are you < **Trace Worthington** > ?*	*< YES >*
2. Has any unknown person given you something to carry?	*< NO >*
3. Do you intend to sneak forbidden items onto your Starship?	*< NO >*
4. Do you feel well enough to board your Starship today?	*< YES >*
5. What is your final destination for this flight today?	*< MARS >*

Trace's screen showed *QUESTIONNAIRE COMPLETE, Thank you*. The tablet went blank. Trace frowned. Strange. He was not even tempted to tap "The Moon" or answer *No, he did not feel well enough to leave Earth today, thank you very much.* What was in that orange drink--some kind of truth serum? Weird.

The trundling sidewalk ended. Louise and Trace stepped off and stood in line at a clear cylinder, where people stood with arms raised. Security personnel watched from elevated computer stations, scrutinizing passengers and baggage monitors.

Trace and Louise set their carry-ons on a conveyor belt to be scanned, and took a turn inside the cylinder, standing in the footprints and raising their hands high above their heads. The machine whirred around them, and each stepped through without incident.

They retrieved their bags under the stern gaze of security guards and headed to the restrooms.

"I don't really have to go now, Dad," Louise said casually.

"Gotta go when you get the chance, kiddo—never know when your next chance will be," Dad said, leading the way. Each unisex bathroom had an "Occupied / Available" lighted sign.

A few moments later, they gathered once more after finishing their business. Through some turnstiles and in a waiting room, the elevator arrived almost immediately. The doors chimed open; the Worthingtons joined a dozen other passengers inside. The doors closed, and they felt the room begin to rise.

"Yay! It's finally happening!" Louise whispered with glee.

Trace took a deep cleansing breath as the elevator rose to the top. He exhaled, feeling momentarily light-headed. The doors opened.

Just ahead, an earlier group of passengers was finishing up their turn boarding. This time, Dad took the lead.

"Worthington family, present and accounted for," Dad said half-jokingly to the man standing where the gangway linked up with *Lucky Seven*. A stern woman frowned at them, her brown hair pulled up in a bun, and gestured to yet another hand-print ID screen.

Dad pressed his hand to the plate, and with a gentle 'ding' confirmation, a different attendant reached out to him. "Left or right, sir?" the man asked. "For your access ID bracelet."

"Oh, um, left, please," Jim replied. To this, the attendant clipped a silver bracelet on his wrist, which locked in place with an audible *click.*

Dad held it up and checked his name. "James Worthington. B-positive . . . and the social ident number . . . Looks good to me," he confirmed.

Mom stepped forward and performed the same actions. Louise took her turn, made 'oooh' and 'wooowww' noises at the shiny silver bracelet, then stepped aside for Trace.

He paused. He let go a breath he had been holding.

Pressing his hand to the pad, his picture popped up once more.

The screen displayed:

WELCOME ABOARD,
TRACE WORTHINGTON

STATUS:
ON BOARD / READY TO FLY

YOU ARE NOW A PASSENGER OF
***LUCKY SEVEN*.**
PLEASE ENJOY THE JOURNEY.

Without really thinking about it, Trace held out his right wrist, and felt the bracelet click into place. The attendant waved her hand in welcome, for him to board. He adjusted his backpack, squared his gaze ahead, and strode toward the hatch.

He slowed at the threshold, and stopped, resting his hand on the outer skin of the Starship. He closed his eyes, feeling the cool metal. It trembled slightly.

Louise tapped his arm.

"What are these?" Louise indicated three colored dots on her bracelet.

"Hm. They look like L-E-D's." Trace tried to make out the colors, but none of them glowed. "We'll figure it out later. Let's go."

Louise turned and walked inside, where another tower official guided them down the narrowest, steepest set of stairs Trace had ever seen, curving along inside the curving hull of the Starship as it descended. He adjusted the straps of his pack and gripped both handrails.

At the bottom, he passed under a "Deck 1" sign and joined a dozen passengers, carry-on deposit boxes in hand, some still admiring their bracelets. A uniformed crewman in a light gray shipsuit stood before the group at a closed door labeled "CREW ONLY."

Trace scanned the room as he shuffled sideways to stand with his family.

The curving wall here was fitted with dozens of rectangle lockers, most of which had their doors standing open. Trace did a quick mental calculation: nine high, twelve across . . . so 108 carry-on deposit boxes set into the wall. Thin gray carpeting covered every surface here—floor, walls, and ceiling. Carpet on the ceiling? Odd.

The man in the gray shipsuit cleared his throat to get their attention.

"Welcome, everyone!" He greeted the group with a warm smile. His bright eyes were as gray as his uniform, almost silver. Trace wondered briefly if the man had mechanical ocular implants or something.

"Now that you are all here, we need to get you settled in quickly. My name is Yeoman Daniels, your Starship steward and I will ensure all your every last need is taken care of during our journey." He made a little bow and smiled.

"The able crewman on my left here is our security officer, Sergeant First Class DeBrus. He handles all security matters on board, so please trust me, you do not want to get called to his office for any reason."

Passengers regarded the gruff-looking, bearded man standing by the lockers, arms crossed. He looked for all the world like one of Thorin's muscled kinsmen, straight out of a Tolkien novel. DeBrus said nothing, but after a few seconds spent scrutinizing the passengers, gave a terse nod.

Trace was intrigued; the Sergeant-at-Arms looked familiar somehow, but he couldn't place where. Daniels continued.

"Okay, we have two things to do quickly right now: get your personal items secured for liftoff and get you settled into your cabins. Everyone, please pick a locker, any locker, and slide your deposit box along the rails, until you hear it click into place at the back. Then, shut the door and scan your thumb as you would at any public fitness center. That locker is yours for the entire journey. After you have secured your box, please meet me at the stairs for cabin assignments. Please, go ahead."

Passengers shuffled over to the wall of lockers and started inserting their carry-on boxes. A middle-aged Latina woman, gray highlights in her jet black hair, turned to Sergeant DeBrus. "Senor? Can I just take one thing from the box, please?"

He cleared his throat, then spoke in a rough-and-tumble bass. "Unless it's medications you require immediately, I'm afraid not. We can't have loose objects floating about."

The lady hesitated, looking at the box and shaking her head. She hefted her box very carefully into the locker space, as if its contents were made of glass. She sealed it with her thumbprint, and a beep! confirmed it was secure. All along the wall, other lockers made the same sound as passengers locked up their carry-ons.

Trace, waiting his turn, thought about DeBrus' accent. Was that . . . Scottish? Or Irish? Trace stepped forward as the lady stepped away. He held up his pack to the Sergeant-at-Arms.

"Uh, Sergeant . . . DeBrus? Where should I put this, since it has no rails to guide it in?"

"The end row, just here, has padded lockers for personal effects like yours—pick one and fold your pack in as best ye can."

Trace murmured his thanks, picked one at random, locker #105, and folded his bundle inside. He squeezed the outer zipper pouch, feeling for

Jeni's small present, still unopened. It resisted his squeeze reassuringly. He clicked the door shut; it scanned his thumbprint and made the telltale beep.

DeBrus watched the remaining passengers as they finished up.

Daniels spoke up again. "Everyone finished? Good. This is Deck 1, with Engineering and the Emergency Muster Deck. Through the *oculus* you see here is the core of the ship, where you will be free to float around after we are at zero-gee. The core starts here and goes clear up to the *StarDome,* eight decks above us."

A few leaned to peek up through the round hole in the ceiling.

"But while we are on the ground, we use the staircases you came down a moment ago. Deck 2 is the Galley, where you get all your meals, and on Decks 3 or 4 you will find your cabin. Everything above Deck 4, we will tour together after leaving Earth orbit. Now, please check in with me before you head up the stairs, so we can get you into your cabins."

Louise wandered over to the open ceiling hatch where Daniels had given his little briefing, and looked up, straight up into the core of Starship.

"Trace, check it out!" she whispered, gesturing. He walked over and looked up through the *oculus*.

"Yikes, this thing seems . . . bigger on the inside?"

"Indeed, it does," DeBrus said, stepping up beside them. "Plenty o' time later for exploring. Now go on, join your folks over there for cabin assignments."

The passengers clustered around Daniels started vanishing up the stairs one by one.

"Mister and Missus Teagarden?" Daniels consulted a tablet. "We have you assigned to Cabin 3-17. So, two decks up and make your way around the circle balcony until you reach door seventeen. Your bracelet or thumbprint will open your door."

The couple thanked Daniels and trotted up the stairs.

"Worthington family, here you are." The steward smiled. "Jim and

Mary? You will be up on Deck Four, cabin 4-09 . . . and you two spacefarers will be right next door, cabin 4-10. So up three flights, and look for cabin number ten, where either of you can scan it open. All right?"

Louise nodded enthusiastically, grinning.

"Thank you, Mister Daniels," Mom said.

"My pleasure, dear lady," the Yeoman said with a bow, gesturing a hand toward the steep, curving stairs.

"Lead the way, my son," Dad said. Trace led.

He stepped up, hand on the side rail, with Louise right behind. He looked to the right, towards the main hatch as he reached Deck 2, and saw the next group of passengers, shiny new bracelets on and ready to board.

He climbed on, up to Deck 3, and noticed a ship diagram displaying all the levels. With Louise right behind him, urging him to keep going, he didn't catch any details.

When they reached Deck 4, Louise nudged past Trace and fast-walked ahead in search of cabin 10. Seeing the vast empty space next to them, she paused to look up then down.

"It's like standing in one of those tall hotels, you know, empty in the middle?" Trace nodded to her, and they walked on. They could hear voices, like murmurs, echoing up and down the core, but couldn't make out individual conversations. Trace thought he heard Dominique's voice mixed in for a second, but it faded and he couldn't be sure.

Louise walked her hands, one over the other along the rail, until she called out "Here it is!" and she scanned her ident bracelet eagerly.

The door slid open sideways with a gentle sigh.

"Yay!"

This comment was followed by her saying, "Oh. The room's kinda little."

She stepped in. "I call top bunk!" She scrambled up the end and lay back onto the gel-foam mattress, hands clasped behind her head. "Oooo,

I'm sinking in, Trace. And there's a TV screen above me!"

From the lower bunk, Trace nodded with satisfaction that he also had a large touchscreen display right above his foam-fit pillow, the underside of Louise's bunk.

From his spot sitting on the lower bunk, he reached out to open the drawers, four of them, against the wall. He found spare blue ship-suits and simple athletic gear in his and Louise's sizes, including extra booties with treaded soles. He closed the drawers and looked in the mirror.

Both bunk touchscreens glowed with a bright array of tropical fish swimming along a dazzling coral reef. Words in the lower right showed: *"Time to Launch: 35:37"* and *"Pre-Launch Briefing in 20:37,"* with the seconds counting down.

A moment later, a gentle chime at the door grabbed their attention. Trace rose and took two steps, opening the door at the touch of a shiny button. Mom and Dad stood there; Trace stepped back to let them in.

"All settled in, Jellybean?" Mom asked.

"This room is cool! I have my own TV and everything! Ooo, Picasso Triggerfish," Louise said, looking at the screen. "What's yours like, Mom?"

"Our room is just like yours," Mom said, nuzzling Louise. "Bunk beds for mommy and daddy too." Louise giggled.

A crisp, eloquent man's voice cut in, through the speakers overhead.

"Lucky Seven passengers, your attention please? This is the Bridge, Executive Officer Telore speaking. Captain Strahan has asked me to remind all of you that your Pre-Launch Briefing begins in twenty minutes, at which time you must be reclining in your bunks, ready for liftoff. Your viewscreens will show you how to get buckled up before the briefing begins. Again, in twenty minutes, please be lying in your bunks, buckled up and ready to tune in. That is all. Bridge, out."

* * *

"Thank you, X-O," Captain Strahan said from her Captain's chair, one leg folded in ladylike fashion that matched her fit, slender physique.

She drew up her Captain's tablet on its swivel arm, which parked in front of her like a college student's desk. She tucked a few locks of short, dark brown hair behind her ear and focused wide hazel eyes on the screens in front of her Executive Officer.

"How's our count?" the Captain asked.

Exec Officer Telore, a tall, handsome blond man wearing a lieutenant's twin silver bars, scanned his own screens before answering.

"Looks like the last few are on their way up the 'vator now, Captain. Full count in the area: 88 passengers. Last to board will be a solo traveler, Mr. Shin Kazama. After that, we can seal'er up."

"Very well. Our checklists?"

The lieutenant tapped open a different screen, tapped several systems acknowledgments, and spoke to her again in crisp tones. "Fueling for both the booster and the starship is complete, booster shows all 55 engines green. Ground personnel are clear and all accounted for. Meteorology reports winds are steady at three knots out of the West, no remarkable gusts. Ideal conditions for launch."

The Captain nodded. Telore paused and watched the camera feed from the main hatch. The outer door closed with a barely perceptible thud from six decks below.

"Main is now sealed, and we show *Murphy*, still sealed. Beginning our weight and balance calculations . . ."

A moment passed while the starship's computer measured and compared the actual mass aboard with expected values. The screen popped up the numbers.

Telore frowned. He unlocked his X-O's chair and swiveled around to face the captain, expression serious.

"Ma'am . . . we are heavy one-zero-five kilos."

"Say again? Plus one-oh-five?"

"Yes, ma'am," the Lieutenant said, turning back and swiping open a fresh screen filled with figures and status lights. The status of all critical Starship systems glowed green. "We're within launch, orbit, refuel, and cruise tolerances . . . and balance is good in all three axes."

The Captain tapped her earpiece.

"Mister DeBrus, re-run contraband checks, and ask ground to run a sardine scan of the entire starship, top to bottom. We may have a stowaway or a serious amount of contraband. Report back in three mike, please?"

"Three minutes, aye, Cap'n," the rough Scottish voice replied over the crew's dedicated intercom radio. She frowned, then gave a little head shake.

She tapped her earpiece again. "Doc, status please?"

The Starship's physician, P.A. Belvoire, radioed up from his small two-room clinic below. In his deep bass, the man said, "Captain, all passengers and crew show *Code One: stable & steady*. Wristband life signs ping 100 percent, pre-launch mood stabilizers 100 percent. Medical is ready to rock and roll."

"Thanks, doc. Mister Daniels, how are you coming along?"

"Briefing the last group now, Captain. No anomalies. Will radio back when all our guests are tucked into assigned quarters."

"You have five minutes." She clicked her headset again.

"Five minutes, aye."

"Engineering?"

"Yes, Captain?" came a different male voice over the channel.

"Mister Richter, anything you know of that could account for an extra hundred kilos? That's like an extra person aboard, a beefy one."

"I cannot account for this extra mass from the systems viewpoint," Richter replied in a clipped German accent. "The crawl spaces, engineering access points, and *Murphy* Door all show clear of people und foreign objects. Outer hull und skirt were both inspected four hours ago by myself and the port engineer—all are clean. Port logs show upgrades und installs we've known about for months, so no surprises there."

The Captain considered for a moment, in silence.

"Every Starship carries extra unexpected mass," the Engineer commented.

"But not a hundred kilos. What is the most you've ever seen before?"

"Never more than twenty-five. So, we could investigate during *the Crossing*," Richter offered.

"Of course we will. What is your *go/no-go* recommendation?"

"We go to Mars, Captain. I can use our final weight and balance data to isolate the parts of the Starship where the extra mass is most likely hidden—and there, we may begin the searching."

"Thank you, Mister Richter."

"Yes, Captain." He closed the channel.

"Ma'am? DeBrus here."

"Go."

"Gate security reports a few fumbled attempts to sneak contraband aboard, hip flasks and such. All the carry-on cases, for both passengers and crew, match their mass expectations perfectly. Hazmat scans at the main hatch show a clean ingress. Portside sardine scan shows no heartbeats and no motion outside of expected locations. If I had to guess, whatever extra mass we're carrying . . . was no' brought on board today, or in the last forty-eight hours."

"Please run a full swab of the entryway for chem analysis en route to the Moon."

"Aye, Captain. I can have full forensics for ye within twenty hours."

"Make it half that—this is top priority."

"Ten hours, aye."

"Thank you, Mister DeBrus."

"Ma'am." He clicked off the channel.

"Lieutenant, any reservations about flying today?"

"*Lucky Seven* will get us to Mars just fine, Captain." He turned to make eye contact. "And I'll find whoever's playing games."

The Captain nodded. Telore went back to his screens. Another moment passed before Daniels radioed in.

"Captain, Steward Section here."

"Go ahead, Stew."

"All 88 passengers in assigned quarters; bracelet locators confirm 100 percent. Six crew are at assigned stations. Ninety-four souls, ready to fly."

"Thank you, Mister Daniels." The steward clicked off the channel.

Captain Strahan turned again to the Exec. "Lieutenant, please complete your checklists, report the extra mass to Ground, and confirm Pad Control shows us ready to fly."

"Aye, Captain." Telore scrolled through the master Pre-Flight Checklist on one of his three control screens, watching step by step as they lit up green, good to go. Captain Strahan monitored his steps, watching each on her tablet as he completed them one by one. She listened for radio calls from the other three Starships of *Flotilla Four*. After a few moments, Telore turned around to address the Captain once again.

"Pre-launch checklists complete. I show *Lucky Seven* safe for launch, Captain."

"I agree, safe for launch." Captain Strahan tapped her tablet confirmation and watched the last few seconds tick away until the clock hit exactly 15:00.

She keyed her Starship's radio mike in the armrest.

"S.I. Launch Control, this is *Lucky Seven*, we are 15-minute go for launch. Confirm position four, please."

Telore smiled to himself. During his handful of crossings working for her, she always preferred to be the very last starship to leave the Earth.

"Roger, Lucky Seven, we confirm you are number four to launch and show you

as a 15-minute go."

In the minute that followed, the *Bozeman*, the *Williamina Fleming*, and the *Manitou* each made similar radio pronouncements. Captain Strahan nodded at hearing familiar voices, but her brow still showed agitation. She cleared her throat.

"Lieutenant, begin the briefing."

* * *

Trace followed the instructions on his screen to pull a thigh strap across, a hip belt, chest belt, and slipped both arms through shoulder straps, clicking shut a buckle on his chest. He heard Louise above him, rustling around as she did the same.

He tapped the flashing "All Buckled Up" confirmation, center screen above his face. He heard Louise tap her own a moment later.

The aquarium screen faded away, now replaced by the handsome face of their Executive Officer, with Captain Strahan partly off-screen in the background.

Then, in a strange vertigo screen moment, the view shifted. The Exec's entire background shifted up as he sat stationary. The Bridge crew seats had just rotated backward 90° into launch position. Rather than facing toward the horizon, the crew were now nose-to-the-sky, like all the passengers in their bunks.

"Attention passengers, this is the Exec. Your restraints all show green, thank you for buckling in properly. Now, before we tighten down your restraints, please reach into the pouch attached next to your left hand and grab out your ear-foamies. You just hold them by the blue tab and push them gently into your ear canals to protect your ears during launch. If they feel strange, just rotate them a bit until they are comfortable. Please do this now."

Trace and Louise, and everyone else on board, quickly complied. The countdown ticked on.

"Once you have finished this, please reach up and touch the green dot on your screen to confirm your ear protectors are in place and you are giving your full attention."

Trace saw that Telore's words started to flash in closed caption on the screen, but he could still make out the announcement, faintly.

Telore's voice continued, though it was muted.

"Thank you, we're nearly there. Now, just relax your arms in a comfortable position at your sides and please do not cross your legs. Your safety harnesses will snug down tightly in a few seconds, preventing you from shifting around or injuring yourself during launch."

A loud *bang* reverberated through the walls. Louise let out a surprised yelp.

Trace felt his shoulder straps zip down snug, almost to the point of cutting into his shoulders and across his hips and thighs—tight, but not quite painful. His arms were practically pinned to his sides.

"That sound you heard was ground control, popping the lockdown bolts. Like the sea-faring ships of old, we have raised the anchor and are ready to get under way. If you notice in the corner of your screen, our countdown to launch just reached ten minutes. All systems are in the green, and Lucky Seven is ready to fly. Now, your next task is to relax. Breathe normally. In through nose, out through mouth."

Trace looked at the wall next to him. A low rumble, a hum barely on the edge of their hearing, grew louder. A gentle breeze drifted across his body from some vent he couldn't see.

The lieutenant's face on the screen faded to an external view of *Lucky Seven*, then zoomed out, showing the entire complex. A cluster of towers gleamed brightly in the morning sun. Four starships, each well-spaced from its neighbors, pointed skyward in shining, eager anticipation.

The rumble came from . . . seemed like it was coming from everywhere. Trace tried to reach out to feel for vibrations, but the straps across his chest had his arms pinned to his sides above the elbow.

Louise mumbled something, barely audible.

"What?" Trace called back.

"What is that?" Louise asked loudly, her voice trembling.

"I don't know . . . the engines?" Trace guessed, not knowing the source of the hum-vibration. "But it's completely normal, I'm sure."

"Uh huh," Louise called back.

The seconds ticked past.

The countdown showed less than six minutes to go. Above the countdown clock, three previously hidden figures appeared:

Liftoff force:	**1.00 g**
Distance from Earth:	**0.027 km (MSL)**
Relative Velocity:	**00000 kph**

The image held, and the lieutenant's voice came back on, his words also on the screen. *"Passengers, we are now running on internal power. Once the counter reaches thirty seconds, we are committed and then we will be on our way up to orbit. Please relax. Keep breathing. Enjoy this amazing event."*

The hum rose louder in volume, a low pitch.

"Amazing event, is he kidding? Traaaace?"

"Yeah, Lou Lou?"

"I'm scared."

"*Lucky Seven* is a great Starship. We're going to be fine."

Two minutes remained on the countdown.

"You do know if anything goes wrong with a rocket ship, it's usually during launch?" Louise shouted above the hum.

Trace did not reply.

The clock passed through 1:30 remaining.

The first of the four Starships, the one with a red stripe, rumbled to life and began to lift off. Louise wriggled a hand free and reached over to feel the vibration in the wall.

The first starship cleared the tower and vanished out the top of the image.

At 1:00 remaining, a second starship, with a blue-and-orange stripe, lifted off and cleared the video feed.

Louise gripped her harness with both hands and squeezed the straps in her small fists. Trace breathed deeply, faster than before.

0:30 to go. The third ship, purple stripe, lifted off like the others and cleared the top of the screen.

The reverberation in their room seemed to be shaking the air itself.

A lone ship remained standing on the screen.

Twenty-one seconds.

Twenty.

A deep bass rumble from below accompanied the reverb from above, as nearly five dozen Raptor V rocket engines spun up, preparing to ignite.

Seventeen . . . sixteen . . . fifteen . . .

The rumble raised to deafening. "Traaaaace?" Louise called out. "I think my orangey thing stopped workiiiiiing . . ."

Trace could barely hear her voice over the din.

"I'm not feeling calm, I'm not feeling calm!" Louise cried out.

"We're fine, Lou Lou, just watch your screen!" Trace shouted over the blast of noise, not knowing if she could even hear him. The countdown continued.

Telore's voice, barely audible: *"Nine . . . eight . . . seven . . . six . . . Raptors start . . . four . . . three . . . two . . . one."*

The rumble escalated to a deafening avalanche of sound. The room shook.

A gentle push at first, then a weight . . . pressed them down, deeper into their beds.

The numbers above the countdown clock began to climb.

Louise closed her eyes and screamed, a long, piercing tone . . . though no one, not even Trace, could hear her.

At nine seconds on the clock, *Lucky Seven* cleared the tower.

Chapter Eighteen

Faster Than a Bullet

Trace's eyes darted around his screen, which was trembling and hard to focus on. The rumble continued.

His display flipped to a new feed. A digital continent, across the Gulf of Mexico replaced the Starship's external launch feed. Four curving tracks arced gently up and over the horizon to the right of the screen.

He recognized the Florida islands immediately, dominated by the broad main island *Osceola*. Their trajectory took them South of the abandoned, drowned cities Tampa and Miami, and out across the Atlantic. His gaze briefly glanced up the jagged coastline of the United States Confederation, up through U.S.C.'s biggest cities, New Orleans, Charleston, its capital Atlanta, and then above the border, the U.S.A.'s cities Washington-Plex, Boston, Philadelphia, and near the top, New York City.

Trace tried to take a deep breath but found he could only manage shallow breaths.

The three dots ahead of *Lucky Seven* showed their names, with the *Williamina Fleming* leading the way. The mission clock showed 40 seconds and climbing.

Trace felt like his eyeballs were being pressed back into his skull, but noticed he couldn't feel any real pain, no stabbing, no ache in his joints. These beds truly were amazi—oh wait . . . their orange powdered drink. It must also have powerful painkillers in it or something.

"Louuuieeese? Talk to me," he called out loudly.

Louise remained quiet. The thunder of the rockets rolled on in a steady wave.

He shook his head, banishing dark thoughts about his sister, and refocused on the screen.

The screen briefly flashed the words "MAX-Q" in green above the mission clock as it passed through the one-minute mark. The numbers:

Liftoff force: 3.7 g
Distance from Earth: 8 km (MSL)
Relative Velocity: 01288 kph

The velocity reading spun upward—the two smallest digits whipping along so fast he couldn't make out individual numbers.

"Already faster than a bullet." He couldn't hear his own voice.

The crush into his bunk persisted. The clock continued to climb. As it passed through 2:30 minutes, he felt the crushing force diminish. A mild tingling covered his face.

He tried lifting his hand up to touch his cheeks, but the restraints blocked that range of motion.

The words MECO flashed in green above the numbers and vanished. Many Engines Cut Off. That meant separation from the Super Heavy booster should be—boom! A loud thump reverberated from somewhere far below. He felt a kick in his back.

Seconds later, the grav-crush returned with a vengeance, heavier than before. The noise was deafening, right through his ear plugs. He felt like he might sink through his mattress and land heavily on whoever roomed in the cabin one deck below.

But the bunk held his weight in place.

He kept his gaze on the numbers:

Liftoff force: 4.2 g
Distance from Earth: 71 km (MSL)
Relative Velocity: 05193 kph

The next six minutes passed thunderously and quietly—not a peep from Louise. Trace reached up, arm heavy against the weight, and tapped the camera view to the nose camera. Straight ahead, small but unmistakable, a ring-like structure floated, panels reflecting sunlight.

Was that the *Wyndmark Holiday Space Station*? He squinted, hoping to see finer detail. He'd never actually seen ring-hotel from orbit, but this one looked different.

At just shy of nine minutes on the clock, the crush ceased.

Trace felt his stomach lurch.

Not a lurch like he was seasick, but more of the lurch at the first drop of an epic roller coaster. The sensation continued for a few seconds, then faded as his stomach caught up with the rest of him.

It was only then he noticed his hands, floating above the mattress. His feet felt light as well, and he lifted his head to look at his feet; they hovered a few inches above the mattress.

The screen showed:

Current g-force: 0.012 g
Distance from Earth: 279 km (MSL)
Relative Velocity: 28,104 kph (7.81 km/s)

The torus on-screen grew bigger, and he could see it was not a smooth circle, no lighted rooms, but rather a 16-sided figure, each section a tube itself. As they drew closer, he could make out an inner ring, also made up of the large metal tubes, eight sections on the inner ring. Between the two rings, huge sheets of solar cells powered the automated orbital station.

They had arrived at the refueling torus, or *'Rocket Ring'* as the world called it.

A wire diagram of the station appeared in the corner of his screen, showing colored dots where the four Starships in their flotilla would dock for refueling.

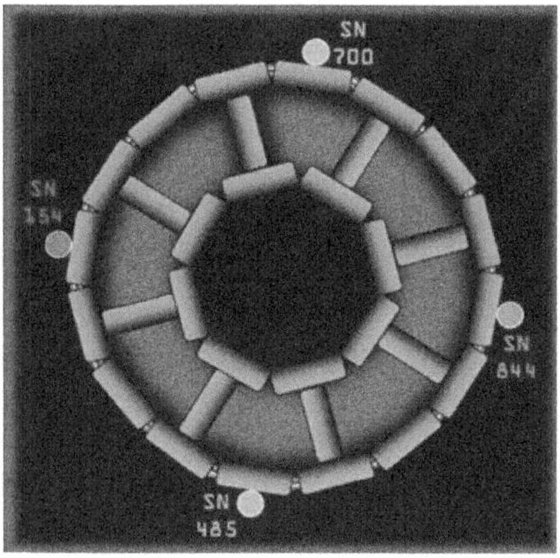

The rest of the screen went dark, to be replaced once again by the smiling, handsome face of Lieutenant Telore.

"Ladies and gentlemen, we are up! Any tingling sensation you may feel, as well as your stomach feeling like it's in your throat are both completely normal. The discomfort will pass shortly. I imagine for most of us, this is your first time experiencing microgravity. You're not weightless, it just feels that way. Technically, we are in freefall around the Earth, and we have reached our assigned refueling altitude of 280 kilometers above sea level. Our current velocity is just under 17,500 miles per hour."

"In-flight refueling is coming up quickly, so we need to stay buckled in. In the next ten minutes, Lucky Seven and our fellow Starships will all be docked with our assigned cybertanker pumps. You may notice we get pushed around a little as we get closer. Those are automated course corrections, using the orbital maneuvering jets, as we ease up to the refueling ring to dock for fuel transfer. We are required to stay strapped in until refueling is complete, and also the next rocket burn, which takes us out of Earth's orbit and on towards the moon. Once that rocket burn is complete, we will have nearly two full days on the way to our Moon slingshot, giving you all a chance to explore the Starship, grab a couple meals, meet your fellow passengers, and take in the magnificent views through the star-dome."

"Until then, please just relax, and choose whatever viewing option you wish on the touch screen above you. Your options include external views of Earth, our nose cameras for the docking procedure, or any of the other options on your in-flight screen menu. So please enjoy this special moment, and I'll check back in with you when IFR is complete."

The screen faded to a view of the Earth. Africa was passing underneath at astonishing speed.

Trace called out. "Louise?"

Quiet.

"Hey, Louise, are you all right up there? Talk to me."

Trace started to tug at his straps, fumbling around for a release, any release.

His room intercom crackled, and a black man's handsome face appeared on his screen. The man wore a crewman's shipsuit, a pale blue, like a doctor's scrubs almost. His deep brown eyes behind thin-rimmed glasses showed compassion, his expression gentle.

"Trace? Can you see me? This is the ship's Doc, P.A. Belvoire. I imagine you're concerned about your sister?" His deep bass voice, a soothing voice, came through.

"Is she all right?" Trace replied.

"She's just fine. She's in REM-state, asleep and dreaming. Looks like in the first minute of flight, she passed right out. She's fine, otherwise."

"Okay . . . how did that happen?"

"Happens every launch, my man. Several passengers pass out, that's just how it is. Her brain was trying to understand, experience, imagine, explain . . . everything happening. It was just too much. Too many circuits firing off all at once, our brains switch off as a protective measure."

Trace drew breath, saying, "how do I know you're not just telling me what I want to hear?"

"See for yourself."

Next to Doc's face, Trace's split-screen now showed a downward-view of Louise, peacefully slumbering. She looked completely relaxed, if pale, and her eyes were moving around under her eyelids, typical of an active dream. Her chest rose and fell with each breath.

"Look man, if she was in distress, we wouldn't be talking. We'd be face to face and I'd be in there with you, making sure she's all right. So I assure you, Louise is just fine."

Trace nodded, thinking Belvoire could see him on the Doc's own monitor.

"Okay, Doc. Thanks for letting me know. Will you let my parents know as well?"

"Will do. Now. I have others to attend to and make my rounds. If you need something later, just call out 'Hey Doc' and I'll reply just as soon as I can."

Trace nodded. The speaker beeped and the room fell silent.

Trace kept Louise's face on the left, and watched the refueling maneuver on the right. Nothing had really changed, so he flipped back to Earth-view. The Indian Ocean slipped past beneath them, with a dark shadow-line, the terminator, separating day from night. A few moments later, darkness enveloped the world below, and he could see the city labels floating near the splashes of light across Australia. Perth, Alice Springs, Adelaide, and the trio of Melbourne, Canberra, and Sydney all slipped past serenely beneath *Lucky Seven*.

He felt a mild jolt and flipped to the refueling view. Twin *Canada-Arms* had reached out from the *cybertanker* and locked on to the hard points of *Lucky Seven*, fore and aft. The arms retracted like someone doing a pull-up, elbows out to the side. *Lucky Seven* was drawn gently in to the outer ring, until Trace could see only a little bit of starry space in the camera feed between them.

A few small mechanical clunks in the walls behind his head, and he knew the hull had been locked into place. Trace strained to listen. A distant sound like flowing water . . . or was it hissing, like someone spraying a can of spray paint? Maybe it was his imagination.

The screen showed:

IFR Time Remaining: 23:12 minutes

The next twenty-five moments passed in quiet, with Trace flipping around between camera views and listening for any signs of consciousness from Louise.

She started snoring.

She even slept through the jolt that freed the Starship from its in-orbit gas station.

"Passengers, we've detached from the refueling torus and will be firing the rockets shortly, to set us on our slingshot trajectory that will take us out to the moon. Please keep your earplugs in as we approach the correct orbital position for our next engine burn. Stand by."

Ten minutes passed before the engines spun up again. When they re-ignited, the noise came crashing in once more, but the gravity crush was not quite as strong as before. The engines fired continuously for seven minutes, then, cut out as before, leaving Trace feeling the lurch in his stomach. Not as intense this time—it felt like the second drop of an epic roller coaster.

Again, the Exec's face appeared on the monitors.

"We've completed our escape burn and our Lunar trajectory is nominal. In forty-two hours' time, we will have to be strapped in once more for a gentle gravity slingshot around the moon. But for now, I am releasing your safety belt locks, so you may very carefully twist the buckle on your chest to release the straps. They will retract automatically, allowing you to float free. Please take it slowly."

Trace reached up and twisted his chest buckle, and his upper body straps retreated to their fittings. He slipped out of his shoulder straps and tucked his ear buds away in their pouch.

"Whenever you feel ready, try moving around, inside your cabin. Keep your movements gentle and note that the carpets have a light Velcro surface, which allows your shipsuit boots to adhere slightly. Try standing. Try taking a few steps, if you wish."

By now, Trace had unclipped his knee strap and ankle strap.

"Louise?"

He floated free of the mattress, reaching up to the viewscreen above him to keep from bumping his head.

Gripping the edge of the bunk, he tried to ease himself over the side. It was awkward going. His legs either went where he didn't want them to go, or they went exactly where he wanted but his torso and head were pointed the wrong way. His feet finally touched the floor, and he felt the gentle tug of the Velcro on the soles of his feet. He awkwardly stood up and turned to Louise.

"Hey," he said softly. No response. He pinched the tabs of her ear plugs and eased then out of her ears. She stirred slightly but went on sleeping. He stowed her ear plugs away, then nudged her shoulder.

"Lou Lou, wake up." She opened her eyes and immediately flailed in a spasm of panic. Her hand smacked Trace in the mouth and he tasted a drop of blood. A pair of small red droplets floated away, toward the door.

"Hey, hey, easy there," he said, putting one hand on her shoulder and making eye contact.

She looked around, eyes darting until they settled on Trace.

"What happened?"

"You split my lip."

"No, not that. *Urggh*. I meant what *happened*?"

"You fainted."

"No, I—*woah*." She had noticed her arms rising up in front of her.

"Yeah." He tucked his bottom lip under his top lip to stop other droplets of blood floating away.

"I missed the launch?"

Trace nodded, and he sighed deeply.

"I'm not sure exactly how to tell you this, but we're landing on Mars in two days."

"We're—what? I missed the whole trip?"

"'Fraid so."

"Well, why didn't you wake—oh."

"Gotcha."

"Trace, I'm gonna kill you!" She tried sitting up, but her harness yanked her right back down in the bed.

"Hey, take it easy. Let me get you free. One sec."

Once the harness and belts were retracted, Louise grasped Trace's hand and the side of her bunk. She eased over and floated next to him. She marveled at being the same height as him, his feet on the floor, but she, weightless next to him, not touching the floor at all.

"Ooo, can I stand on the ceiling?"

"I guess, but there's no Velcro." Trace pointed.

"Oh."

"Passengers, we will be unlocking your cabin doors momentarily. The Captain

asks everyone to gather at the railings in the core for our first All Hands meeting. Please steady yourselves along the handrails, whatever level you happen to be on, ready to give your undivided attention in three minutes.

A knock at the door.

Trace and Louise both instinctively said, "Come in."

The door's simple AI, hearing the proper voice command, slid open. Mom stood in the doorway, one foot stuck on the carpet, and both hands on the door frame.

"Hi Mom," Trace smiled as she awkwardly stepped through the door to embrace Louise.

"Mom, I slept through the launch, can you believe it?"

"Yeah, sweetie, that's what Doc told us."

"But what was it like? I don't want this doofus to tell me; he told me we were already at Mars."

"Oohhh," Mom said, wonder in her voice. "Well, it was intense, my sweetie."

"And I missed it. Dad! You're upside down?"

Dad's face appeared just below the top of the doorway.

"Or maybe it's you who's upside down?" Dad smiled.

Trace nodded to his dad. "That's . . . pretty cool." Trace scrutinized his dad's bold first step, making a mental note about the subjectivity of up and down in zero-gee.

"Not my first rodeo, kiddo," Dad said with a wink.

"Right, your time in the Fleet. So is there a Navy vessel escorting our . . . fleet? Group? Whatever you call it?"

"Our flotilla? Nope. We are entirely on our own, with seventeen other Starships, stretched out over several hundred miles in space."

Dad righted himself and lighted on the Velcro-carpeted walkway. Mom and Louise went next door to give Lou Lou a tour of the other room. Trace eased past his dad. He gripped the railing, leaned out over the rail and looked up, then down.

All around him on Deck Four, and down on Deck Three, people were emerging from their cabins. Almost directly across, he noticed a recessed ladder running from the bottom to the top. He looked left and saw an identical one much closer.

"One minute until All Hands meeting, please find yourself a place along the railing. One minute."

Nodding, he pulled himself over the railing, one hand gripping a rung of the ladder tightly. He fishtailed slightly, legs swinging out.

Glancing down, three stories of empty space below him, he felt a surge of adrenaline. Shaking it off, he righted himself to start a hand-over-hand climb up the ladder. He passed small aqua-colored lighted signs Deck 5, Deck 6, and Deck 7. Seeing no other levels with railings above him, he grabbed the Deck 8 railing beside the ladder and swung his body neatly over the railing, feet first.

"Ach, watch out!" a stern, clipped voice blurted out as an unseen hand slapped Trace's foot, redirecting him aside. He had nearly kicked a crew member in the face.

Trace, managing to keep a grip on the railing, retracted himself and twisted so he could see who he had nearly collided with. The crewman wore a shipsuit, olive drab, and briefly wore a look of annoyance until he saw Trace's surprise and flushed cheeks.

"I'm so terribly sorry," Trace managed to say.

"There is no harm done," the man said. He drifted over to join Trace at the railing.

The two 'stood' peering down over the rail. Rows of faces now lined the rails along Decks 3 and 4. The Captain, drifting down from above, had just positioned herself in the very center of the core. She floated in the middle where everyone could see her. She swirled her arms in the air in an artistic flourish, and began to rotate in place, very slowly.

Trace looked at the man he had nearly kicked. "My name's Trace, and—"

The man shushed him gently, "It's okay, we talk later, ja?" He held Trace's eye contact for a moment. Trace nodded.

The Captain tapped her earpiece, and her voice came through all the speakers up and down the core of the Starship.

"Ladies and gentlemen, thank you for assembling for the first of many All-Hands gatherings. As the Exec Officer briefed you moments ago, we're on our way to the moon, and have just under forty hours before we need to get all strapped in for the last gravity you'll feel for the next five months. But for now, we have time to learn how to get around, run a muster drill, tour the Starship, have a meal, and start some other tasks I'm assigning you."

She smiled as she spoke, her voice continuing to pour through all the speakers.

"So, first things first. You're weightless! There are a few critical skills for you to master as quickly as you can, the most important of those is moving about the Starship while avoiding injury or getting yourself stuck somewhere. Take a good look around. Familiarize yourself."

Trace watched as people looked in all directions, then he took a look around as well. Looking up, he was surprised to see the third-quarter moon, half-bright, half-dark, through the dome windows above.

The man in the olive shipsuit focused on the Captain, a red stress ball in one hand. He sipped his drink pouch, then twisted it shut and tucked it away in a pocket. The man hovered in place, perfectly still without steadying himself by any hand-hold—still as a statue . . . a gargoyle gazing down from the parapets of *Notre Dame* upon the citizens below.

Trace leaned over the rail, looking down to Deck 4, where Louise stood by Mom and Dad. Louise saw her brother and waved, grinning ear to ear. He matched her smile and waved back. Dad looked up at Trace, frowning, then back at *Lucky Seven*'s Captain. Mom was taking it all in.

Captain Strahan spoke into her lapel mike again.

"Now, take a closer look where I'm at – I've managed to get myself completely stuck. In theory, I could be trapped here for months. So I ask, what actions can I take to get myself un-stuck? Your ideas please."

One man raised his hand and spoke up from Deck 4, a few doors down from Trace's family. "Captain-san, could you ask someone to fly out? Give you a push?"

"Indeed, I could. What's your name, sir?"

"I am Kazama."

"Hello, Mr. Kazama. Shin, is it?"

The man bowed slightly, brushing long, wavy hair out of his face.

The Captain nodded back. *"That's a good answer. If done carefully, that could work without any injury. Now, someone else. What if I was alone and got myself stuck?"*

She paused to let the group consider.

"Um, Captain?" a piping feminine voice came from a few doors down from Trace's family. "Over here? I've seen, like, KlipToks of people swimming through the air."

It was the blonde from the hotel elevator. Trace shook his head slightly.

"You could try air-swimming for hours and make zero progress. But you'll get a great workout. Tell me your name?"

"I'm Dominique Van der Waal . . . of the Boston Van der Waals." She held her head high, chin stuck out over her petite, curvy frame.

"Well, we're not in Kansas anymore, miss Dominique."

"Um, Boston literally isn't in Kansas."

"They'll both be sharing the same pixel on our cameras pretty soon," the Captain smiled. She turned her head to scan the group. *"Who else has an idea how I can rescue myself?"*

No one spoke at first.

Then Trace spoke up. "Ma'am? Trace Worthington. Up here, hi." Trace smiled. "Could you take off your shoe or something and throw it?"

"Very good. Trace, you said? That's the answer exactly. But, a couple important considerations: be very careful what you throw, and where you throw it. You might hit someone, or worse, you could hit the dome, which would set off the proximity alarms and earn you a private chat with Sergeant DeBrus."

She swirled her arms again, leaving them extended, and stopped her gentle turning in mid-air. She looked from Trace to the man beside him.

"So, let's have a demonstration, for which I'll ask the help of our Starship's Engineer. Mister Richter, if you please?"

The Engineer in the olive drab green shipsuit gripped the railing with one hand and very gently tossed his bright red stress ball to her.

All eyes watched it slowly drift down toward her where she floated. It took many long seconds, all without falling any faster. Weird and cool at the same time.

She plucked it from the air and in one fluid motion, tossed back it upward, hard, toward the glass windows above. As it whipped up and away from her, she floated downward at a leisurely pace.

Richter launched himself like a caped crusader over the side, following the red ball upward. He grabbed a handgrip on the underside of Deck 8 and whiplashed around it, vanishing from view.

"See how that toss has gotten me moving in the opposite direction?"

The Captain drifted down toward the floor below as she continued.

"So, let this be your first flying lesson. Also . . ."

An alarm sounded from above the bridge. Two long seconds later, it switched off.

"That's your warning not to get too close to, or throw anything at, the dome. It's practically indestructible but we take no chances . . . which leads me to Lesson Two." She pointed upward.

At these words, Richter reappeared, red ball in hand, looking down from high above.

"You might have missed it – our Engineer never took his eyes off the ball. He knew exactly where it went, because he knows FOD checks can make the difference between all of us arriving safe and sound and risking the entire Starship. Now, can anyone tell me what a FOD check is?"

"Ma'am, Chief Jack Graves here," a fit-looking passenger in his seventies spoke up from Deck 3, holding hands with the lady at his side. In his thick, comforting Georgia accent, he continued.

"In the C.S.A.F., we do FOD checks on the flightline because foreign object damage sucked into an engine can bring down an entire aircraft. I'm guessing that might just be what FOD stands for here on a Starship?"

"Floating object damage, FOD, is exactly what we're trying to prevent while on board, Chief, thank you for your insight. And thank you for your service."

The Chief nodded.

"FOD is something we must be constantly aware of, yes, every one of you. In your cabins, here in the core, the mess deck, exercise rooms, the theater, everywhere. I need you each to be hyper-aware of people and objects around you. Never let that slide. Stay aware of every object, article of clothing, twist tie, bracelet, earring, stylus, and Ear Pod. If you misplace something, I guarantee it will not be wherever you last saw it. And if you see something, say something."

Captain Strahan's feet touched the deck below. Her Velcro shipsuit boots gave just enough grip to stop her bouncing back off the carpeted floor. She stood by the circular hatchway, the *oculus*. At this moment, it stood closed.

"Through this hatch, the oculus, are your carry-on lockers and Engineering, which is off limits to passengers. You can access your lockers using the stairs over there, or you can drop down through the oculus here, which will open for me now at the touch of that button."

She pointed but did not move otherwise.

At that moment, the stress ball Richter had retrieved from the dome whizzed past the Captain, smacking squarely on the red "Open" button for the *oculus*.

The ball rebounded and the Captain snatched it out of the air with barely a glance.

The *oculus* opened, four quarters of the hatch each receding back into the door's housing like the top hatch on the fabled *Millennium Falcon*.

A surprised chorus of 'ooo' and 'wow' filled the space.

"Did you see that?" Louise's piping voice came floating up through the surprised remarks of the passengers.

Trace looked aside at Engineer Richter, a surprised look on his face. Richter shrugged, winking. The Captain continued.

"My friends, before we begin a few practice exercises to train you how to control your movements for the next five months, let's have one final demonstration. I present your Master-at-Arms and Security Officer, Sergeant First Class DeBrus." She pointed straight up.

Standing at the very peak of the spacecraft, DeBrus held a fist up, arms' length above his head. He stood at the pinnacle of the observation, the very bow-point of the Starship, where the windows converged.

He squinted toward the Captain, adjusting his stance slightly. Then he flexed his knees slightly and pushed off, just a little push.

The result was staggering.

With his hand extended ahead of him, and his head bowed down, bearded chin brushing his chest, he drifted serenely down past the bridge, Deck 8.

The Captain narrated his fall through the core.

"I challenge you, each of you, to become as skilled as our Sergeant-at-Arms in zero-gee flying. Watch him as he goes."

DeBrus soared down through the core, past the fitness area, theater and entertainment deck, two levels of passenger cabins, the mess area . . . deck after deck.

His chin pressed to his chest the entire flight, he closed his eyes. A blind fall.

With fist clenched, he passed Deck 2 within arm's reach of the Captain. DeBrus sailed cleanly through the *oculus* without so much as a brushing of his sleeves on the sides.

"Swish," Trace muttered to himself, shaking his head in wonder.

The Captain led the applause. Within a second or two, everyone was cheering. Louise looked up at Mom and Dad in wonder as she clapped along with everyone else. Many peered down at the *oculus*, watching for DeBrus to reappear.

After the cheers died down, the Captain said, *"Friends, you could attempt that jump a hundred times and never hit that mark, and he just did it blind. I want all of you to make a passable flight, end to end, before we hit Transition. Aside from being fun, it's a skill you are expected to master very quickly. Should we experience a real emergency, there won't be time for learning to fly – your survival may depend on skills that you work at now."*

DeBrus' face reappeared through the *oculus*, and he emerged smoothly to float next to the Captain. A fresh wave of scattered applause greeted him; he bowed his head.

"Now, any questions?"

"Um, what's Transition?" Dominique called out.

Trace shook his head. "Did that dingbat skip all the pre-flight reading?" Trace muttered to himself.

"Transition is our half-way point to Mars, a big highlight of our journey. But there's more about that later. For now, I'll leave you in the capable hands of our Starship's Steward, Mister Daniels. Stew?"

The steward floated feet-first down from one of the side balconies and lit gently next to the Captain. He tapped his own earpiece-microphone. *"Friends, you heard the Captain, it is now your turn. Please find yourselves a partner."*

Captain Strahan, Sergeant DeBrus, and Engineer Richter all headed quietly upward as passengers paired off.

"Everyone good? Okay then. Our first flights will be no more than twenty feet, so let's spread out. Remember, there are decks above you and below you. Plenty of common area spaces."

Trace saw Louise waving both hands to get his attention. He eased over the side and started sliding down the ladder toward her, head down and feet pointed toward the nose of the Starship. He stopped himself on Deck five and leaned over the side to grasp her hand.

She climbed over the side, squeezing his hand tightly.

"Easy . . . leave a few fingers intact, will ya?"

"Sorry. It's a long fall."

"Nope. It's no fall."

"No fall?"

"Nope."

"Oh. Oh yeah, I can really fly here! Trace, I can fly!"

All around, people were spreading out. Passengers floated in all directions, with partner-pairs giving each other something to aim for. It was awkward and hilarious at the same time.

Louise and Trace found themselves floating upward, toward Deck 6, the fitness center, to get some separation from other passengers. Curious, Trace floated from one piece of fitness equipment to the next, seeing them all bolted to floors, walls, and ceiling.

"Lou Lou, see if you can thread between these machines and come straight to me."

"Okay, I'll try . . ." she pushed off gently and floated between two bench-press machines and over a rowing machine. She missed Trace, but managed to grab a stationary bike by the handlebars, her legs swinging around near to the fitness center's wall, by a large air handler.

"Woah, close one," she said.

"Get away from there," a man hissed in a stern voice from the railing.

Trace remembered this man from the elevator ride down from their hotel room—it was Dominique's father, Mister Van der Waal.

Trace looked him in the eye and said, "I'm sorry, what?"

"I said keep away from the . . . walls of the ship."

"She stopped herself before she even touched anything. What's the worry?"

"Um, yes, um . . . but that's the outer wall, see? Damage to that could, um, risk us all."

"She's hardly big enough to do any real damage."

"Just keep her clear of—"

"Ohhhhh . . . I know--did your orangey drink stop working too?" Louise asked him. "Mine did not keep me calm at all." Louise said innocently.

His face contorted in confusion and frustration. "No, I . . . my—what?" and whatever he was about to say next was drowned out by Daniels' voice over the speakers.

"Ladies and gentlemen, just ten more minutes until we divide up into four tour groups. Ten minutes."

Mister Van der Waal turned and pulled himself away, shaking his head.

"Jeez, what was that guy's problem?" Trace asked.

"Having a bad day, I guess?"

Trace glanced around at the wall where Louise almost bumped it—looked solid, perfect, unblemished. The vents pushed cool air as vents do.

"I don't get it."

"His orangey drink totally stopped working."

"Like yours?"

"Like mine."

"C'mon Lou Lou, let's get outta here." Trace winked at her as they floated together back toward the Core. Mister Van der Waal had vanished, presumably rejoining his wife and daughter.

"Hey, let's practice a few more minutes before we have to do tour groups."

"I wanna fly straight across to the other side, Trace. Will you catch me? Please?"

"Why don't we fly together?"

"Okay." She scrunched up her face in a serious look and gently pushed off. Trace flew right beside her, like Superman with Lois Lane.

* * *

Up on the Bridge, DeBrus addressed the Captain and Lieutenant Telore.

"I swabbed the entryway, full forensics, while we were refueling. There were traces of cleaning chemicals, a few drops of sweat, and two unidentified chemical compounds. The scanner's working on them now—we should have results shortly."

"Let me know as soon as you can."

"Aye, Captain. I also checked the air filters, newly installed one week ago. They contained traces of tobacco."

"So . . . someone on a cleaning crew took a smoke break?"

"Unlikely—that'll get ye sacked if you're caught smoking aboard a Starship, even while she's docked. No, this was something else. Likely someone was celebrating sommat."

"How can you be sure?"

"It was a cigar, an expensive one at that—Cuban or perhaps Dominican. The sample I distilled is unmistakable, even to an amateur like me."

"Keep me informed."

DeBrus nodded and left to take his place as one of the four tour guides.

* * *

The Worthingtons joined more than a dozen other passengers floating down awkwardly to their tour stop #1, gathering at the *oculus* on Deck 2 with a few minutes to spare.

"I see I was right—you're enjoying *Lucky Seven*?" Dad asked Trace, a knowing look on his face.

"Okay, don't rub it in. Yes, it's extremely cool."

"I'm just glad you're feeling more at ease, being in a Starship."

"Rather be flying one than riding in it as a passenger."

"So? Nothing's stopping you—you have time to pursue those dreams of flying."

"Nothing's stopping me? Dad, you didn't even consider my plan for staying behind, remember? Pete and his family were all set to put me up my last two years of high school . . . I could've graduated with my friends, where I *belong* . . . done my time at the Academy, gotten my pilot's license, joined the Spacers' Corps . . . That was my jolt, my fire. You killed it without a second thought."

A few other passengers were now tuning in to the exchange, their own conversations fading.

Trace looked down in frustration. "Can we talk about this later?"

Dad persisted. "But what about on Mars? There's flight opportunities there. They have their own fleet of Starships too, you know."

"Dad, they have ninety. For two million people. That's probably about three hundred pilots, maybe four hundred, max. What do you think my odds are of even getting into the Nerus Flight Academy? They accept like ten new trainees a year, if that."

"I see you did some research."

"Of course I . . . and another thing—I'm an Earthling; what are the odds they even pick me over a local-born Martian? It's ridiculous to even—"

Trace cut himself off when he noticed Daniels landing gently among the assembled passengers. The tour was about to begin.

"Let's talk more later, all right?" Dad asked.

"Talking won't change reality." Trace muttered.

Chapter Seventeen

Than Ever Before

Yeoman Daniels watched Trace and his Dad's conversation end, though he was out of earshot. The other passenger conversations quieted. The tour group gathered around, twenty strong.

Lieutenant Telore's voice poured out of all the Starship's speakers once more.

"Ladies and gentlemen, you should now be joining your tour group's first station. Please assemble around the crew member there and give them your undivided. Bridge, out."

Trace, now annoyed at both Daniels and his dad, kept his expression blank.

"Welcome to Deck 2, I am glad to have you here." Daniels held his arms wide in welcome. "Can everyone see me? All right. Below us, Deck 1, you've already seen; so I will be giving you a tour of Deck 2's main attraction, the mess area. Please follow me."

He floated through the crowd toward the railing and pulled himself over to stand facing the group in the core.

The tour group made an awkward clump, while trying to stand up straight on the Velcro carpeting and shuffle toward the mess area—a waddle of penguins, complete with Velcro steps and bobbling left to right.

When they reached the railing, Louise pointed up. "Look, Trace, there's tables and chairs stuck to the ceiling. Hee hee, that's funny."

"And the bulkheads too." Daniels smiled, then noticed Louise's confused look. "Oh, that's just our fancy word for the walls."

Louise nodded, looking at the tables mounted . . . all over the place here.

On the far bulkheads, floor to ceiling, they could see mounted food dispensers, drink dispensers, more tables, chairs, and recycling bins. Every bit of available space on the far wall had its own device or dispenser, all neatly labeled.

Daniels waited for the group to get settled. Everyone tried to be where they could get a clear view of the man, some leaning awkwardly. One man stood above the group, able to see better, his hands gripping his husband's shoulders below him.

Daniels cleared his throat and beamed at them. "Welcome! We met just before liftoff. My name is Yeoman Morn Daniels. Please, familiarize yourself with this deck, where you will take all your meals, keep up with news and events, and pass the time with your fellow passengers."

"Over there, across the core, you see the main hatchway where you boarded, and next to that, running up and down the outer hull, the staircases that connect Decks 1 through 4. Down on Deck 1, where you stowed your carry-on cases, is our fallout shelter, where we will have our lovely muster evacuation drill in just a few hours. It is the most heavily-shielded part of the ship. The good news: for the next five months, you are free to ignore staircases entirely, that is your call to make. The ocu—"

"How did—" Trace started to ask. "Sorry, didn't mean to interrupt."

Daniels glanced at Trace's nametag. "No problem . . . Trace . . . please, go ahead."

"No stairs above Deck 4, right?"

"That is correct. It saves on space."

"So, how did the crew get up to the Bridge for takeoff? Is there another hatch up there?"

Daniels' eye twitched. "Fair question. As hatchways go, that one is the only one," he said, indicating the main entryway. "And to get up to the bridge while we are on the ground, crew members clip in using a safety line and they climb those two ladders, up four stories. It can be a little scary, especially on Earth."

"Trippy," Trace observed, eyeing the ladder leading clear up to Deck 8.

"Absolutely. Now, everyone, the *oculus*, just there, is your main accessway from here in the core down to Deck 1, but the staircases are still an option. Either way down can only handle two people at a time, maximum. When we are on a short fuse to evacuate to Deck 1, keep the staircase as an option. After roll call, the staircase door and the *oculus* both slam shut. So . . . as my ancestors would say, mind the gap." He smiled again, scanning faces.

"Now, please follow me." With that, he floated back, deeper into the open mess deck area. The rest followed, with the occasional 'sorry' and 'whups, my bad,' as people nudged or bumped into one another. They eventually untangled as a group and focused on Daniels. He swept his hand across the food service area.

"Snacks, electrolyte beverages, and coffee are available around the clock. Hot breakfast runs daily, 7 to 9 a.m.; lunch is 11 a.m. to 1 p.m., and dinner is from 6 to 8 p.m. Behind me, on this column, please notice the digital bulletin board. It cycles through important events, all-hands gatherings, journey milestones, and fun social activities. Another digital bulletin board is up on Deck 6, in the Fitness Center, and a third screen is way up on Deck 8, under the *StarDome*."

The screen next to Daniels showed:

Time to Lunar Slingshot:
41:34:59

Time to Secure Stations:
40:34:59

"To better orient yourselves, I invite you all to become familiar with the schematics throughout the Starship." He indicated a mounted sign at the railing.

Heads turned, looking at the diagram. Trace and Louise, being right next to it, took a closer look.

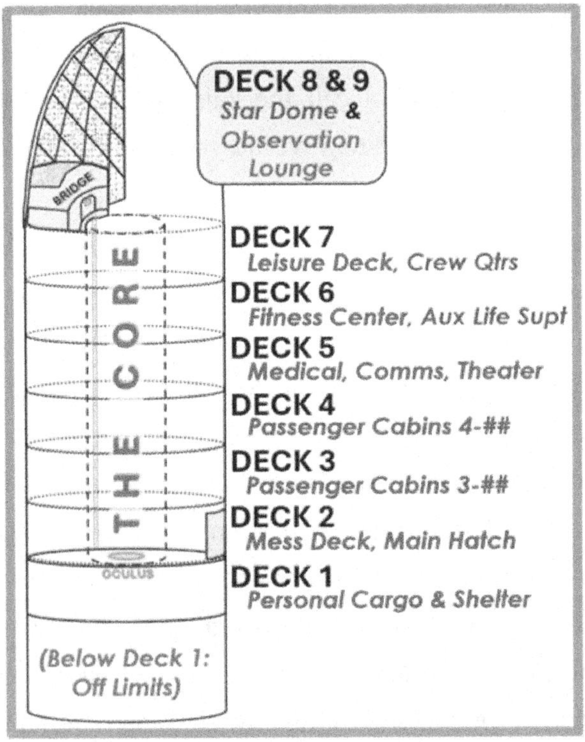

Daniels' watch beeped.

"Friends, that beep means our time here on Deck 2 is nearly up. Your next stop is up three decks, on Deck 5, where you will find medical, communications, and the theater. You'll find 'Doc' Belvoire waiting there for you. Please be careful heading up there; remember, the tour group up in the dome is coming down at the same time. Let us avoid those M-A-C's if we can."

"What's an M-A—" someone started to ask, but Telore's voice interrupted, pouring through all the Starship's speakers.

"All hands, your attention please? It's time to change tour locations. Your crew member will tell you where to go next. Please take it slowly and carefully. Bridge, out."

"C'mon, Louise, race ya there," Trace whispered, then pushed himself off diagonally toward Deck 5, eyeing his chosen target up three decks and across.

"Last one there's a stale tater!" as Louise pushed off too.

"Kids, that's not such a . . . good . . ." Mom started to say, but her kids were already gone, floating up and away. She shook her head and muttered, "they get it from your side, you know."

Dad wisely kept his mouth shut. "Mm hmm."

They exchanged a smile and followed, taking a safer path along the core inner walls—bulkheads Daniels had called them—pawing and pulling their way carefully up to Deck 5. People were already sailing down through the center of the core, and the occasional 'look out!' and 'dangit, sorry!' echoed around as people ran into each other, mid-float.

Daniels, looking up from Deck 2, silently counted mid-air collisions. "Five . . . six . . . seven, eight . . . come on, ten," he whispered under his breath.

DeBrus caught his eye from far above, where he stood, looking small six stories above him. The Security officer was counting mid-air collisions as well.

It was as good a thing to bet on as any.

* * *

Louise beat Trace over the rails, narrowly avoiding a collision near the end of her flight. Others arrived from different angles, including several who overshot entirely and had to carefully work their way back down to Deck 5.

Trace recognized 'Doc' Belvoire from his bunk's viewscreen during launch, when Louise passed out. They both exchanged smiles and a brief wave. The handsome black man, wearing his perfectly pressed, off-white shipsuit, stood at the railing, nodding at people as they arrived, his bright white smile making them all feel at ease. He ducked under Jack Graves' wife as she misjudged the leap and sailed past his head, her husband floating along with her, keeping a grip on her ankle.

The couple righted themselves and carefully managed their way back to the gathering area at the railing. Doc watched them, a bemused expression on his face.

"I'm sure sorry about that, Doc—we blew by you faster than a dog with a pork chop and a five-yard head start." Jack smiled.

Trace liked Jack Graves immediately. He had that way of expressing himself—made you want to just listen to whatever he might say next. Doc accepted Chief Graves's handshake, smiling back. "Don't you worry about it, Chief, no harm done. Good having you on board."

Chief Graves smiled back. More passengers filtered in to get settled, the occasional 'look out!' and 'my bad' still echoing in from the core.

After a few moments, all twenty got settled—some upright, others upside down. People were starting to take risks, letting go of their gravity norms.

"Hey everyone, welcome to Deck 5," he said in deep, comforting tones. "I'm Physician's Assistant Burke Belvoir, but as Starship's medical officer, you can just call me 'Doc.' So, we'll start with that hatchway across the core, that's the medical suite. It's where I spend most of the voyage, and you'll be visiting me there every week so I can keep close tabs on all your physical, mental, and emotional health needs."

The group craned around, noting his door, white with a large red cross painted on it.

"If you are bleeding, barfing, or burning, please come see me. If you're lost, disoriented, or homesick, please come see me. If you're bored out of your mind, definitely come see me. If your husband is drivin' you crazy and you just hit him to see how far he'll go . . . come see Sergeant DeBrus."

Chuckles rippled through the group. Couples eyed each other.

"Then send your husband to come see me."

A few more laughs.

He carefully made eye contact with every person in the group as he continued, running one hand over his shaved-bald cranium.

"First, a bit about me. I am a licensed therapist and UNMA-certified in minor surgeries, as all Starship PA's are. So no matter what creative injury or illness you come up with, odds are I've helped people get through it before. A prime example: the calloused, hardened skin on your heels might flake right off in a matter of months, leaving brand-new baby soft skin underneath. Your feet will be tender, but that's nothing to worry about—come see me anyway. Motion sickness is managed by the electrolyte additives you'll be drinking every day, so don't worry about that either."

"Aside from certifications and my seven crossings aboard three Starships, I'm told I am an excellent listener. Whatever you have to say, we enjoy doctor-patient confidentiality. None of what we say in private is recorded, ever. Questions so far?"

No one spoke.

"Good. Catch me later if you think of something. That reminds me, I'm the one person on the ship that you enjoy a constant, uninterrupted connection with, no matter what. Just say the words 'Hey, Doc' and the nearest communicator box will connect us immediately."

Doc's pocket communicator pinged, his keyword prompt having been picked up at a communicator box on a nearby bulkhead.

"Hello, self? And what can I do for you?"

One second later, the speaker on the wall nearby said "Hello self? And what can I do for you?"

People smiled, a few chuckled. He canceled the call with the tap of his thumb.

"Okay, let's show you the movie theater. Every day, Yeoman Daniels runs a PG or PG-13 feature at 4 PM and at 7 PM. Friday and Saturday's evening showtimes, however, may occasionally be rated "R," and it is up to parents to manage their children's watching privileges. Full 3-D goggles are right there, in the UV-storage case, and of course all showings are free. If you get to the theater before those daily showings, and nothing's on, you're free to watch any movie ever released; just use that tablet mounted right over there. The theater's capacity is thirty . . . unless you feel like sitting on the ceiling and watching upside down."

"Over on your right, we have six gaming cubicles that have every *Atari, PlayStation, Nintendo, Sega, Xbox, Origin, Sony, Nooma, Blasto,* and *ZoMedia* game ever released. You could play continuously for ten thousand years and get about halfway through the list, so please try those out. Most games are also playable using your bunk screens or with 3-D visors as well, if you find all the gaming stations are occupied."

"And finally, the most important part of Deck 5: the communications center. Please, follow me."

Doc pushed himself off, above the group, putting a half-twist in his effort, and started hand-walking across the ceiling past the theater and gaming cubes. He did a graceful pike-flip and landed standing next to a dozen pivoting seats that faced semi-private cubby screens, mounted on the curving outer hull. He pulled one swing chair out, sat down, and swiveled around to face the group.

"The Captain expects each of us, myself included, to communicate with contacts on Earth, Mars, or even aboard the Starship *at least* daily. Your tablets can do the job as well. Text messages, voice-chats, video-chats, it's up to you how you choose to reach out. The general rule is: live, real-time chats with Earth work for the next two weeks, and with Mars the last two weeks. For most of *the Crossing*, it's recorded messages or DMs, because of the time lag."

Dad raised his hand. "Doc? Are we supposed to communicate more with Earth or more with Mars? And are our messages being recorded or tracked?"

"The recommended amount is 60-40 Earth these first two months, then a 50-50 split between Earth and Mars during Transition, then 60-40 split, favoring Mars the last two months. No one is listening or watching your conversations; the log keeps only your start-time and end-time, the link to your recipient, and the duration of your call. That's it."

Doc checked his watch.

"So, any other questions, please just ask me individually at our first appointment, which is required in the next twenty-four hours, before the *lunar slingshot*. Watch for my first meeting invite, and don't you be late. You're free to DM me any time."

With that, he ended his presentation. A few conversations started bubbling up within the group as people looked closer at the comm desks and gaming cubes.

Louise nudged Trace. "Are you gonna try out their gaming cubbies? Those look so boss."

"Yeah, totally. I wanna finish *Days Gone: M-B-M*. I just hope they have it—I ran out of time before we left C-Springs."

"Is that your game with the motorcycles and zombies?"

"Yep. This chapter takes place on the moon."

"Cool."

Doc spoke loudly, for all to hear. "Good friends, your third stop on our tour is up just one deck, where—"

"Ladies and gentlemen, your attention please? It's time to proceed to the third stop of your tour. Your crew member will guide you where to go next. Again, please take it slow. Bridge, out."

"Your next stop is up just one deck, where our Starship's Engineer, Mister Richter, will show you around Deck 6. I'll be seein' you real soon." He smiled and gave everyone a little wave.

The group poured over the rail, climbing and floating carefully up one deck.

Dad leaned in to confide in Trace, "I'd given up any hope of us keeping up our strength on this trip, but here we are, a pretty full gym."

"Right? Check out all this gear. I hope they show us how to use it."

Trace recognized Engineer Richter, from the zero-gee demonstration at their first All Hands gathering. He stood in the middle of a group of exercise machines, carefully spaced out across the floor and ceiling. He gestured for everyone to intersperse themselves among the equipment for his presentation.

He quietly counted to himself before speaking up. "Neunzehn . . . und, Zwanzig. Gut."

"Good afternoon, ladies and gentlemen, my name is Engineer Konrad Richter, and I am the keeper of all our on-board systems. The engines, life support, communications, power plant, fuel system, and so forth."

"Welcome to Deck 6, where you will be visiting every day to keep up your physical strength and mental well-being. Across, just there, is the hydroponics lab, where some of our green salads are grown for the entire trip. As far as the Fitness Center, you can see, we are nearly one hundred souls on board, and this room cannot hold more than twenty-five."

The tour group people looked around, clearly interested in the equipment.

"So, each of us has an allotted time during which you are required to do twenty minutes of cardio on either the rowing, running, or bicycling machines on my left, and also fifteen minutes of strength training, resistance training, or yoga. The zero-gee yoga is very challenging; I do not even try."

"I have found the best plan is to do as many different routines as possible, letting your tablet's *StarShip App* create a workout plan for you. I hope you will mix it up as much as you can."

"The *Lucky Seven* computer randomly assigns everyone a one-hour time slot that is yours every day. If you wish to switch times with someone else, this is also fine. Six days out of seven, stick to your routine. The computer automatically tracks completion and reports your progress to Doc Belvoire. One day each week, you are free to do a much lighter workout, or take a rest day, or to use the sauna, those two small rooms behind you. These only allow two people at a time, so please limit your use to ten minutes if others are waiting. Towels are dispensed here, and showers are around the back. Questions so far?"

"Um Mister Engineer, sir?" a young girl with mousy brown hair, Louise's age, raised her hand.

"Hello, yes, and what's your name?"

"I'm Kasia."

"And let me see your nametag; okay, K-A-S-I-A. And you pronounce it Kaja? Like Raja, king of the tigers?"

"No, *Ka-sha*, with a *shh* sound."

"Okay. Nice meeting you, Ka-sha, tell me your question."

"You know those showers in space? I heard they're . . . weird."

Louise tugged Trace's sleeve. "That's what I was gonna ask," she whispered.

"They are very weird indeed." The Engineer smiled. "I want you to think of a shower like a two-minute race, to preserve water. You wear a small air mask over your nose and mouth, and the warm water comes from three mist sprayers here, here, and here. The spray hits your body then is pulled out by your feet with a vacuum. A timer on the wall screen shows your time remaining, and beeps when you have fifteen seconds left. You push the "pause" or the "finished" button any time you wish, and a high-speed air fan blasts remaining water mist away. Five seconds later, the door latch releases and you can use your towel and put on your clean ship-suit. Okay?"

"O-kay." Kasia caught Louise's glance and smiled.

Louise waved back, smiling.

"She's gonna be my friend," Louise whispered excitedly. Trace nodded, imagining how he would use the water and scrub clean while floating around freely inside a shower.

"So, any other questions?"

A pause, no questions at first.

"Yes, Mister . . . Richter?" The Engineer nodded to Kasia's father. He asked, "How do we learn these machines? The treadmills and bikes look familiar, but the others look different from back home."

"You will find upon returning to your cabin, a list of tasks that must be completed in the next 36 hours. One of these is a tutorial on how to properly use the fitness center. After completing this tutorial, the computer unlocks the machines for you to use them."

"Can we start today?" Trace asked.

"Ja, after our tours of the Starship are complete, you will be able to do anything on your checklist. You may also watch a movie, visit the Stardome, and so on. Just keep in mind you have 36 hours only to finish your task list, which is right now more important than anything else."

"Than anything?"

"We have ways of knowing if you have finished the list," Richter flashed his eyes and tapped his fingertips together, looking maniacal. Then his ominous expression broke into a smile.

Trace nodded. Richter seemed like a good guy.

The Engineer continued. "Also in the next 36 hours, please be sure to take a meal or two, and get a good sleep before the slingshot tomorrow. So . . . next, your final tour stop—you go up one more deck, and you will see where the Bridge is, some crew cabins, and the Stardome itself. See if you can find Mars, ja?" He winked at Kasia and smiled at Louise. The two girls looked at each other, grinning.

Right as he finished speaking, Telore's booming voice filled the Starship once again. Trace ignored it, finding himself eager to see Mars, then he thought about it.

"But we won't be able to see Mars, will we?"

"What makes you say this?" Richter asked.

"Well, aren't we aiming at the spot where Mars will be in five months? Not directly at where it is now?"

"Very good," the German observed. "But remember the slingshot? Perhaps we are facing Mars perfectly right now, but after going around the Moon, we face ahead of it. So, when you are up there, see for yourself. Test your hypothesis."

"I will." He nodded his thanks to Richter, who gave a brief nod back as Trace passed.

The next group was already on their way up, so Trace dodged around a couple and pulled himself up toward their final tour stop.

The last few in the group filtered out of the fitness area with him and over the railing.

On Deck 7, Sergeant DeBrus patiently awaited his final tour group, instructing them to line up along the railing. The Stardome was directly over their heads; six stories of empty space lay beneath them. Everyone got settled; DeBrus waited until he had everyone's attention.

"All right—shall we see what you're made of? Everyone, over the rail, if you please."

No one moved at first.

DeBrus stood impassively by the door to the Bridge.

"Go on—go on then, but keep a grip on the bar," he said firmly.

Everyone gently stepped or swung themselves over the side, ensuring they kept a grip on the rail. Mom slipped, lost her grip, but Dad caught her wrist and reeled her back in.

Louise, her body now suspended straight out, over the empty core, gripped the railing tightly. "Woah. It's SO trippy!" She looked straight down into the emptiness below.

From next to her, Kasia said "I know, right?"

Louise looked left to Trace and made a strange hissing sound through a wide smile of gritted teeth.

Trace looked back at her in confusion. Then he grinned, hissing back.

Like the rest, Trace hovered over the same six-story drop, lightly gripping the railing with one hand. The entire railing here was lined with floating people, looking straight down and then up over the railing at DeBrus, and back down again.

"All right, ye passed the test. Let's go across the way, please, and meet me among those folded seats."

Trace and the others turned, seeing a darkened section that climbed up the opposite wall, filled with folded seats in neat rows. He looked closely and saw the space was cleverly divided into two levels, with seats on both . . . again, climbing right up the walls and directly beneath a curving half-dome of windows.

A few awkward moments later, everyone was clinging to a chair or to their partner.

"Everyone here? Now then, stand up please, hands on the folded seats and feet on the floor. I'll tell ye about this very special Deck of *Lucky Seven*."

DeBrus swept his arm across the dome area. Everyone righted themselves quickly, taking in the view, mostly reflections of themselves in the windows above.

"Right! Welcome to the pointy end of the Starship. See those glass windows up there, just above us?"

Heads swiveled around; people nodded.

"That's our dorsal side, like the top of a shark, where his fin is. Never, and I mean never, touch the glass. And see this glowing red line, all the way 'round the perimeter here, right up and across?"

Passengers looked around, heads turning. Several nods.

"We call that the Bridge *sight line*. Don't let yourselves or any of your personal things break the *sight line*, please, because the bridge crew maintains direct visual contact with our fellow Starships around the clock."

"So that huge window behind you, that's the bridge's . . . windshield?" an older man asked.

"Aye, that's a good analogy, and you best no' be a bug on the windshield, all right?"

The man nodded, marveling at the large, curving sheet of glassite across the ceiling of the bridge.

"For the moment, we can take a closer look tho. Please follow me up to the nose cone. Gently now."

He pushed off, rising higher up the seated area, toward the point of the Starship but still below the Bridge sightline. He stood near the tip, where all the windows and their struts converged.

"This part, opposite the windows, is the ventral side, the underbelly of the shark. But instead of it being soft, like a shark, ours is covered with 23,000 heat tiles, to protect *Lucky Seven* during its re-entry at both Mars and Earth. Now, will everyone kindly keep a good grip on a seat, any seat?

Upper level or lower level, does no' matter."

The Worthingtons stood together on the lower level, their views only partially obscured by the upper deck. The design was quite clever, allowing the greatest number of seats here without compromising anyone's view through the Stardome windows.

"Do you see Mars?" Trace whispered to Mom.

"I don't. It's too bright inside—I can only see our reflections."

Heads craned around, looking from the bridge windshield to the stars beyond. Not many were visible, with the inside glare coming off the windows from several angles.

DeBrus cleared his throat for their attention.

"In—let's see," he checked his chronometer, "—just under forty-one hours' time, we'll be making our slingshot run around the moon and be on our way to Mars. We will feel gravity for that maneuver, and ye'll need to be strapped in. But ye'll all be oriented differently than we were for takeoff. Allow me to demonstrate."

He held up a foot-long, 3-D printed plastic model of the Starship.

"So, as you see here, when the Starship is blastin' off vertically, all the forces ye felt slamming ye back in your bunks are pulling you downward, no surprises there. But now we're no' moving straight up anymore, we're moving horizontal, towards the moon." He turned his model on its side and pointed his free hand toward the Stardome they were all facing. "If ye doubt me, just take a peek out there, through the Stardome."

DeBrus pressed a small dial on the wall. The internal lights dimmed to darkness.

The audience gasped, with *oooh's* and *ahhh's* at the starfield, suddenly visible through the windows. Dazzling bright ahead of them was the moon, already much larger than it appeared from the ground back on Earth.

He gave them a moment to take it in, before bringing the lights back up to a dim setting, so they could just make him out.

"So, our attitude is now horizontal as we fly toward the moon, and when we whip 'round the moon, which will technically be above us, the dorsal side, we will all have to be all strapped in differently from takeoff."

"Sergeant DeBrus?" A gruff-looking man with a full black beard, speckled with gray flecks got his attention. His voice sounded like a cartoon character's, raspy and rough.

"Aye, Mr. . . ."

"Haddock, Archie Haddock. Where will all the passengers sit for that moon slingshot? There's not enough seats here for all . . . eighty? Or ninety . . . of us."

"Ye're right, Mister Haddock. We've got eighty-eight passengers and six crew. So—the thirty-eight seats here are not nearly enough. Thirty will be belted into theater seats on Deck 5, and the rest are divided between fold-out seats in the fitness center and down on the mess deck."

Trace drifted far away in his thoughts, scanning the starfield for any hint of the red planet. He missed the rest of whatever DeBrus had to say, then Telore's crisp command voice snapped him back to reality.

"All passengers, your attention please? While you are free to chat with any crew member at their assigned tour locations for the next fifteen minutes, this does conclude our tour today. We hope you've enjoyed getting to know Lucky Seven a little better."

"Also, the Captain has asked me to advise you that when you return to your cabins, you will find a new task is added to your active to-do list, which is the Mars Ambassador Program questionnaire. The Mars Arrival Center uses your responses to assign your contact person on Mars. This is not optional, so please complete that questionnaire before you retire this evening. Answer the questions honestly, and you'll have a far better experience. That is all. Bridge, out."

"Trace?" Louise was tugging his sleeve. "Hey, you awake?"

"Sorry."

"C'mon, I wanna go see my *to do list* thingy."

"One sec." Then he turned to the Security Officer. "Can I ask you, Sergeant—"

"DeBrus. And you're Mister . . ."

"Trace Worthington. Hi. I just wanted to ask you how you did that dive during the Captain's speech. That was . . . epic."

"Well it's—no' easy, and takes a load o' practice. Tell ye what . . . I'll show ye, sometime after slingshot. We've got plenty o' time on our hands. All right?"

"I'd like that. Thanks."

DeBrus nodded, still looking stern, focused. Trace turned to Louise and swept his hand toward the Core. "After you, Lou Lou."

She pushed off, climbing hand-over-hand through the seating area.

Trace followed, pushing off with vigor, toward the core. A little too much vigor.

A little too much vigor . . . right toward Jack Graves, who had just launched, unseen, into his path.

* * *

Trace pulled himself into his lower bunk a few minutes later, groaning in pain. He tapped his viewscreen awake to distract himself.

A menu popped up, and from the available options, he selected "To-Do List," still wincing from the pain and groaning a bit.

A small clock appeared next to a task list, showing 'time remaining to completion' with the number 38:47:22 quietly counting down. His list showed six action items:

"Not a lot at all," he muttered.

He zoomed in on the action items, thinking about which one he might knock out first.

1. Watch Emergency Ship Muster Drill Tutorial (12:55 min)

< Tap HERE. >

2. Watch Lucky Seven Voyage Overview (4:30 min)

< Tap HERE. >

3. Watch Fitness Center Familiarization Tutorial (15:30 min)

< Tap HERE. >

4. Complete Mars Ambassador Questionnaire (3:00 min)

< Tap HERE. >

5. P.A. Belvoire Initial Visit (Day 2, 0900 hrs), Deck 5

< Tap HERE to set a Reminder. >

6. Optional: Get to know the Crew (Biographies) (12:00 min)

< Tap HERE. >

He had barely finished scanning the list when they heard a knock at the door.

"Come in," Louise called out. At her command, the door slid open.

Mom and Dad appeared in the doorway.

"Hey you two. Checking out your lists?" Mom asked.

"Yep, we have lots to do! And lots to watch, but I wanna explore first," Louise said.

Dad stepped lightly over and looked down at Trace in his bunk. "So, I saw you, ahem, met someone as we were finishing up the tour, my son?"

Trace's cheeks flushed. Louise spoke up before Trace could.

"Yeah, Trace tried to stop himself but you know that Air Force Chief guy, Mister Graves? They crashed, pretty good."

"Sounds rough."

"It wasn't that bad," Trace said, cheeks still red.

"He may be singing high notes for a while," Louise giggled.

"Louise—"

Mom's jaw dropped. "Oh no, so he got you—"

"Right in the naughty nuggets," Louise said, laughing hysterically.

"Louise!" Mom held her hand over her mouth.

"Whaaaat? It's true." She collapsed into a fit of giggles. "Plus, Mister Graves said something about bein' 'dumber 'n a box o' rocks," Louise added, snickering and looking down over the side of her bunk at Trace.

"He was referring to himself, Lou Lou, and we both apologized. He wasn't even—ugh, go away."

Trace looked around for something else they could all focus on.

"You're being a good sport about it," his Dad smiled.

"I'm fine," Trace said, easing out of the bunk and 'standing' up as straight as he could manage.

"Should I tell the Doc?" Louise asked. She took a breath. "Hey Do—"

"No, you little twit, we're going exploring, remember?"

"Oh yeah. See you, Mom & Dad."

She eased down out of the bunk and gave both parents hugs before pushing off through the open doorway. Mom and Dad watched them both go from the Deck 4 railing.

As their kids floated away, they heard Louise ask, "Can Kasia come too?"

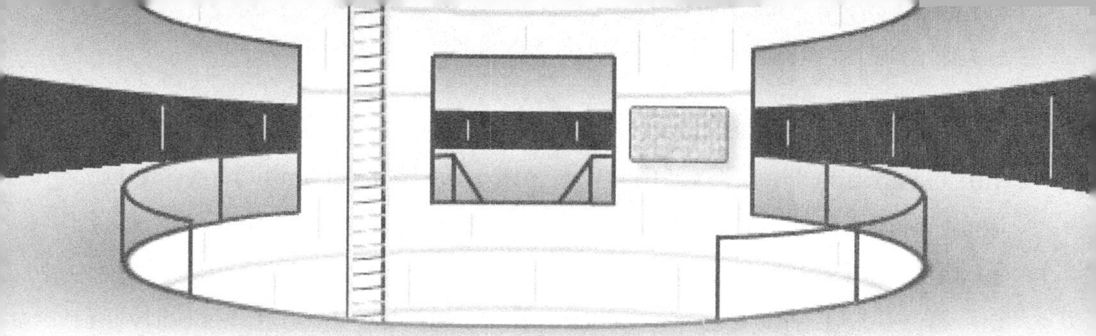

Chapter Sixteen

The Mark of a Pilot

The eight hours after launch zipped past. .

In that time, Louise and Kasia had explored every nook, cranny, and corner of every common area, right up to the edges of the off-limits parts of Decks 1, 2, 7, and 8. Trace accompanied them a while, but seeing they could manage themselves and keep tabs on each other, he peeled off the last several hours to pursue his own plans.

He felt better. After a few hours exploring, he and Louise had watched all their instruction vids with loads of time to spare, until all Trace had left was the Mars Ambassador Questionnaire, whatever that was.

He felt restless. Time to work off a little steam, get the blood flowing.

Early in the afternoon, Trace changed into a pair of boxers, a ship's T-shirt, and comfortable padded form-fit athletic socks from his cabin clothes drawers. He found the reinforced athletic footwear more flexible than the normal shipsuit Velcro booties—molded foot-pads seemed perfect for running on a treadmill and not slipping while lifting or doing squats.

He got his thirty minutes of cardio on a rowing machine, all strapped in, then did some resistance-lifting to isolate the five main upper body muscle groups. He noticed that the cardio machines actually harvested the rotational energy he generated and supplied it back to the Starship power plant—*that's pretty clever*, he mused.

Energized with feel-good endorphins coursing through his body and mind, he headed to face his next test—the shower.

His first zero-gee shower—a fun little challenge, that one—he started by following the simple instructions posted on the wall. Inside a private changing stall, he slipped out of his shorts, boxers, tee-shirt, and footwear, then stepped into the tiny shower space. With the door closed and sealed, it should have triggered his anxiety about tight spaces, but anticipating the shower itself, he found he wasn't nervous. First thing he noticed was the floor had small foot-loops to hook his toes under. Good, those would allow both hands to be free for the task at hand.

He slipped the air-tube mask on, snugged the stretchy band around the base of his skull, and dispensed some soap. A sign suggested applying 15 seconds of water, pausing it, and scrubbing all over. The soap, which turned out to be a laughably small amount, was still enough to do the trick when combined with a small amount of water. He scrubbed down, resumed the water, and rinsed off under what felt like a gentle mist sprayed over him from three angles.

At the end of the two minutes, he didn't feel quite finished, but several wind jets blasted the water and soap residue away, whether he felt finished or not. Clearly, this was another task he needed to get better at, if he was to clean up comfortably in under 2 minutes.

Richter's words to little Kasia during the tour replayed in his thoughts: this was a race against the clock.

As he stepped out, he noticed a temperature control for the air jets, making a mental note to turn them lower next time to help cool off from his workout. He dried off in the small changing stall, pulled on his shipsuit and booties, and returned the towel to the dispenser. That seemed to be all there was, so he stepped out and made his way back to his cabin.

Louise and Kasia were somewhere else, so he had the cabin to himself. He tapped open his to-do list.

Two items remained: the questionnaire and his meeting with Doc Belvoire, pre-scheduled for 9:00 a.m. tomorrow morning. He tapped the link to the questionnaire; his information auto-populated.

Name: **Trace Worthington (Born 03-Nov-2336, Age: 17)**

Occupation: **High School Student, Grade 11.0 [E], Term 5.0 [M]**

Employer/School: **Pine Creek H.S. (Colorado Springs, CO)**

Academic Emphasis/Track: **Science (CHEM / BIO)**

Extra-Curricular Interests: **Track & Field, Basketball, Strategy Gaming**

Career Interest/Focus: **Starship Pilot**

Is this information correct? __ Yes __ No

PART 1: YOUR IDEAL MARS WELCOME AMBASSADOR

1. What group would you prefer your Ambassador be assigned from?

__ Friend/Peer __ Mentor __Teacher __ Work Colleague

2. What gender Ambassador are you most comfortable engaging/ conversing with?

__ Masculine __ Feminine __Nonbinary __Other

3. What ethnic/language group do you most closely align with?

Ethnic Background:________________ Language: _______________

4. Have you been to Mars before?

__ No __ Yes (Location: _________ + Duration: _________)

5. Which city/settlement will you live in, after arriving?

__Mons-Plex	__Nerus/Mesa	__New Marrakech
__Skye/Uist	__ Libertas	__New Kyiv
__Hathorton	__Nooma Outpost	__Westdown
__Toschen	__Jupiter's Crossing	__Helfer Outpost
__Tycho Station	__Ceres Crossing	

Note: Mars Welcome Ambassadors are here to inform and welcome you. They are not travel agents, charity providers, or licensed therapists. Their role is to help you get through the Crossing. Be a decent human being and expect the same in return. Our Ambassadors compete for these positions and are carefully screened before training. They are paid for their work at a competitive rate. You may request a new Ambassador at any time, and your Ambassador has the same option. They are not obliged to meet you in person, nor are they required to communicate with you more than twice per week. Ask your questions. Expect direct, honest replies. Speak with your on-board Starship medical professional if you have any concerns.

I have read and understood the above. Thumbprint Scan: _________

Trace finished the survey and thumbed his confirmation. An automessage informed him his part was complete and whipped his replies off to the Mars Arrival Center for processing. He should have an assigned Welcome Ambassador within one week.

He stared at the screen for a moment, then snapped out of it as Louise walked in the door, Mom in tow.

"Hey you two. How was your appointment with the Doc, Lou Lou?"

"It was good, but Mom had to sit in the waiting area, on the other side of the glass. Doc asked me how the launch went, then he explained to me why I passed out. But he says I should focus on the trip, and on making friends! I told him about Kasia, and he gave me some homework."

"No kidding? What did he tell you to do?"

"I gotta send a video message back to my class at Edgemont Elementary, telling them how the launch went. I told him already sent two vids to Dr. LaClair and my friends, and Doc says I can wait to send another one after we go around the moon."

Trace nodded, but Louise wasn't finished. "When will we be at the moon?"

"Tomorrow afternoon, jellybean," Mom put in from the doorway.

"Hm." Louise pulled herself up onto the top bunk and started tapping the screen.

"Where's Kasia?" Trace asked.

"She had to meet with the Doc too, with her dad. I couldn't stay," Louise said casually.

"Okay. Wanna go grab some food?"

"I told Kasia I would meet her for dinner after she's done with the Doc. We're going soon. I hope it's soon. I'm starving."

"Well, don't wait too long," Mom said. "I'm off to find your father. See you both later on." Trace waved to her from the bottom bunk.

To pass the time, he panned through views of the Moon and Earth. The departure-angle camera showed Earth, still large enough to make out weather patterns and many bodies of water smaller than oceans. He could see India just entering sunrise, and the bright nighttime line of lights along the Nile, glowing brightly right up to the Mediterranean Sea. At the top of the world from this angle, he could see the lights of Turkey's cities, the many lands of stan, and on the left, the recognizable glowing coastlines of Greece, Italy, and northern Africa.

He felt a pang of regret, not having visited any of those places before leaving Earth. India he especially wanted to visit someday. He wasn't sure why.

A beep at the door interrupted his reverie.

"Come in?" The door slid open, and Lousie sat up upon seeing Kasia and her dad standing there.

"Kasia, yay! Wanna go eat? I'm starving."

"Me too! Let's go see what they have."

"Hello, I'm Kasia's dad. You must be Trace."

Trace stood and shook the man's hand.

"Trace Worthington."

"Derek Kowalski. Nice to meet you. Where you all from?"

"Colorado Springs, and yourself?"

"Ventura," Mister Kowalski said.

"California?"

"That's the one."

"We've got people from all over. There's that guy from Japan, the Doc's from Philly, and there's the *Van-der-hoozie-whatsits* from Boston," Trace said.

"The Boston that's not in Kansas?" Mister Kowalski grinned.

"Right, the one literally not in Kansas." Trace smiled back. "And I bumped into a guy from Georgia. Retired U.S.C. Air Force, I think."

"Interesting. In the cabin by ours, there's a family from Calgary, and before liftoff, we met two guys from Omaha—nice couple, super friendly."

"That's cool. It gets me thinking about the people where we're going. Did they have you fill out your Ambassador Questionnaire?"

"The one with like fifteen cities?"

"Right? I thought there were *Seven Cities,*" Trace mused.

"Seems that most are more like settlements, waystations, research outposts. Ours is Nooma Outpost." He looked down at his daughter with pride.

"Nooma. Like Nooma Games? I wonder which came first, the outpost, or the gaming company?"

"I'll have to look it up, I guess." The man smiled at Trace.

"Dad, I'm starving, can Louise and I go now?"

"Sure, you two go on. I've got to find your mom anyways. Have fun, girls."

"Bye dad!"

"See ya Trace!"

"I'm gonna go grab a bite too. It was nice meeting you, Mister—"

"Kowalski."

"Right. Nice meeting you."

"And yourself. I'm sure we'll see you around."

Trace let the handshake go, and both left the cabin. Trace watched the man leave, drifting down to Deck 3. From the rail, he caught sight of the girls as they floated into the mess area. He pushed off after them, and a moment later grabbed his meal as they were getting seated, jabbering constantly as energetic fourth graders do.

From his own small table several feet away, Trace kept an eye on the girls as they took in their first real meal aboard the Starship.

Breakfast and lunchtime had come and gone, but no one had been hungry. Now, with everyone's orange drink appetite suppressors worn off, hunger came on like a freight train. The mess deck was crowded; hardly any floor, wall, or ceiling tables had empty seats.

From the machines, several food choices presented themselves. Trace had picked a *Moo Goo Gai Pan Chicken* mixed with wild rice. It squeezed out hot and chewy like cookie dough through an oversized flip-top. Texture aside, it tasted delicious. Trace suspected there were probably taste-enhancers, vitamins, minerals, mood calmers, and loads of calories. Once he got over the odd way one had to eat in zero gee, he found the meal filling and satisfying. The drink pouches were a flat, sweet electrolyte similar to the lemon-lime soda they drank the night before liftoff.

After dinner, the girls floated their way up through the core with a "woo hoo, we're so high up!" toward the theater, to watch an ultra-hi-def augmented-reality Anime feature film that changed intensity according to the reactions of the audience.

Trace followed, but as the girls found their seats, he drifted past, heading for the gaming cubicles. He liked anime just fine, but he wanted to take a crack at the gaming list.

Four of the six stations were occupied, so he chose the middle-top position, swinging out a swivel seat, and settling in. Grabbing the corded game controller and a *Look-Listen* 3-D headset, he tapped open the games list. He jumped to the "D" part of the alphabet and looked among the dozen "Days Gone" titles.

"Dang it . . ."

The newest in the series, *Days Gone: Moon Base Meridiem,* in which zombies had overrun the moon's *Shackleton City* . . . wasn't on the list. Its predecessors were here, and he was tempted to play the O-G, *Days Gone,* set in twenty-first century Lost Lake and Belknap, Oregon . . . motorcycles and zombies—can't beat that. He flipped back to the index to scroll the other options.

The Starship's library really had basically every game ever made.

He scrolled back up to the "B" part of the alphabet, and quickly found another of his favorites, an RPG title that had been on the market for just under a year. He tapped it open.

The opening animation ran as Trace expected: a raiding party of dark elves stalked a displacer beast in the subterranean warrens near their cavern city, their uncanny ultravision giving them an advantage in the pitch-darkness. As an unseen, second displacer beast lunged straight at the gamer, jump-scare style, the title of the game appeared in shock-violet letters: *Baldur's Gate 27: Shades of the Underdark.*

The title menu appeared. He almost clicked on "Create Character," to generate the race/class combo he preferred: Duergar Dark Paladin. He liked the tough little tank-warrior, imbued with twisted chaos magic and limited healing. Then his eyes caught something he did not expect . . . *"Load Saved Adventure"* was available, not grayed out, as it should be when playing a game for the first time. He popped it open.

His dozens of saved games from Colorado stood neatly in a row.

"How in the—" and with that, a sudden pang for home, his own room, his view of the Rampart Range of the Rocky Mountains hit him, unexpectedly.

The Starship suddenly felt very small, isolated, floating away in the vastness of space.

"I miss the mountains . . . ." Then he snorted. "I miss my life."

He shook his head, throwing off thoughts of home, and scanned the saved games list.

"But seriously, how?" and then, his screen froze for a ship-wide announcement.

"All passengers, your attention please? We are now halfway to the moon, and it's time for us to announce your randomly-assigned seating locations for the moon slingshot."

"I would like to remind everyone that because of the centrifugal forces we will experience during the turn, no one is permitted to be in their cabins for the duration of the slingshot. The four seating areas are: under the StarDome, in the theater, the fitness center, and the mess deck. Trading seats is permitted, but only on a one-for-one basis, to maintain proper mass distribution throughout the Starship."

"Please direct your attention to any of the screens throughout the Starship . . . or simply look at your bracelet. Blue, you will be up in the StarDome viewing area. Green, you are in the theater. Red, you are in either on the Mess Deck or Fitness Center.

The common area screens filled up with 88 names, colors, and seat numbers.

Trace looked down at his bracelet, as if checking the time. The Blue LED glowed brightly.

"Aw, sweeet."

"With those seat assignments made, we also remind you that your first day aboard Lucky Seven has been a long and busy one. The time is now 17:45, that's a quarter til six p.m., ship's time, and you'll need a meal and to be well-rested for tomorrow's big events. At nine o'clock every evening, all Starship lights dim to night-time settings, and quiet hours begin. Please plan to be in your cabins no later than ten o'clock for lights out. That is all. Bridge, out."

Trace turned around in his gaming chair, wondering if Louise had been assigned blue for the Lunar turn as well. Gamers nearby were also processing the news, some bringing up diagrams of *Lucky Seven*'s layout or looking around for the common area screens.

* * *

DeBrus joined another private audience with the Captain and Executive Officer on the Bridge.

"You have the results?"

DeBrus nodded. "Aye, both samples. The first sample I found is harmless—a drop of saliva and Scotch Whisky. I've reviewed the camera footage and kinna' say who it was for certain, but clearly one of the passengers downed a hip flask before entering security, and he might've drooled a bit in the entryway. Bit 'o liquid courage perhaps? No one's been actin' disorderly; suggest we let that matter rest."

"And the other?"

DeBrus took a deep breath and ran his hand over the top of his crew-cut stubble.

"I suspect someone's brought an explosive on board."

"A bomb?" Telore asked.

"Aye, based on what's been found—but there's no knowing how much came aboard."

"Just tell me what you know," the Captain told him, taking a deep breath.

"The sample was barely enough to register, and it was long dried. The analyzer shows it to be one-half of a binary liquid explosive that has no other known industrial purpose but to be blended with its counterpart and then detonated. The chemicals are very different from plastique explosives but think of it as the destructive equivalent of liquid C-4."

"Even a thimble full could punch a hole in the hull, properly placed," Telore said.

"Aye."

"Find the rest, Mister DeBrus."

"I've already started scanning, mum," DeBrus replied. "But the Starship's bloody huge. It'll take time to search it alone . . . and if the whole crew conducts a massive search, we'd set off a panic."

The Captain considered this, nodding. "Your solution, Lieutenant?"

"Um . . . Captain . . . we activate the mentoring program a month early."

"You think teenagers and young people are the answer?"

DeBrus spoke up. "It might work, we instruct them to pay close attention to the details, report everything and everyone they see, anything out of the ordinary. I could teach the more mature ones to use hand scanners, since I have several in Security. We'd have extra eyes and I could get *Lucky Seven* scanned in half the time."

The Captain thought for another moment, weighing possibilities. The tension in the air was palpable.

"Do it."

* * *

Trace closed his gaming screen, making a mental note to return and play again soon, and pushed off in the direction of the nearby theater. He found Louise and Kasia discussing their seats, wondering how they could arrange to sit together for slingshot.

"I know, I'll get Trace to switch with you, he won't mind," Louise was saying to Kasia. "Oh, there you are," she said, seeing Trace standing in the theater doorway.

"Shhhhh," a theater-goer hissed from the back row. The girls joined Trace outside the theater door.

"Um, Trace?"

"Forget it, I'm not missing seeing the moon up close."

"Come onnnn . . ." Louise fussed.

"No." Trace said firmly. Then he noticed Kasia's bracelet also glowed blue.

"Hang on, you're both in the same section, blue."

"Yeah, but we're not next to each other, so I need you to switch."

"How about we go up to the window—*StarDome*—thingy, and see for ourselves where we're seated?"

"Okay. Coming, Kasia?"

"Yeah, I wanna see too."

The three floated to the rail, and pushed off, upward, toward the nose of the ship. They got to the seating section, seeing Daniels already there. He was extracting the folded seats and locking them into proper slingshot position. He looked up and saw he was not alone.

"Ah, there's our intrepid spacefarers! Would you three be willing to help me get these seats all squared away?" Daniels smiled, popping a chair up from its 'down & locked' position and clicking it into place.

"Uh, su—"

"You bet we do," Louise said with gusto.

"Okay, squeeze the headrest, this red button here, and press down gently with your feet on the carpet. It will unfold, like this, and when you hear a loud click, it has locked in place. You may want to start back there while I finish up front."

"Okay."

Trace, Louise, and Kasia got to work. Trace popped open chair #31, then went on to chair #32. From nearby, while on her third or fourth chair, Louise flexed her legs with too much force, and her grip on the chair slipped free. She floated up, free of the carpet. Fast, toward the red line.

"Uh, Trace? Help?" she said, arms flailing upward. She floated up toward the glass panes, right in front of the bridge. Trace pushed off, aiming for a spot near the underside of the bridge where he could grab a bar and snag Louise by her ankle before she ran into the *StarDome.*

He gripped the bar at the same time as he grabbed Louise's booted foot.

From inside the bridge area, both Telore and the Captain saw a little girl's face appear in the glass in front of them, wearing her shocked look, then vanish back below the Bridge's direct line of sight with the *StarDome.*

Telore snapped his head up with a 'what the heck?' expression, then chuckled to himself. "Good catch, whoever caught you." He refocused back on his screens. "Captain? Looks like our contraband is on either Deck 1 or Deck 2, according to this report from Mister Richter."

"Very well, we'll concentrate our searches there until it's all found," the Captain said, tapping a few notes into her tablet and sending messages to the crew.

On the other side of the glass, having heard none of their words inside the Bridge, Trace eased Louise back down to the seating area.

"That officer guy totally saw me, Trace."

"Ooooh, that's bad."

"What do you mean, bad?"

"I think they're gonna lock you up for the rest of the trip, Lou Lou."

"They—what?"

Trace smiled and started laughing.

"Oooooh, you." She squinted and turned away in an awkward, floating huff, to find the next seat to set up.

Daniels emerged from the front rows, having finished that section, and observed his helpers finish the last seats toward the back.

"Which seats are ours, Mister Daniels, sir?" Louise asked, proudly holding up her bracelet, with her blue LED still illuminated.

He smiled at her and consulted his tablet, Velcro-strapped to his thigh.

"Hm. Looks like you and Trace are in seats nineteen and twenty, over there, back half of the seating area. You scored some great spots," he said with a thumbs up. "Would you like to go try them out, see how they feel?"

"Yes, um, but first, where is Kasia's seat? We have to make a chair change, if it's okay."

After consulting his chart, he indicated a seat on the lower level. Kasia turned to Trace.

"Come on, Trace, that's not a bad seat. "Switch with her? Pretty pretty pretty pretty pleeeeze?" She batted her eyelashes.

Trace thought about it.

"All right. But you owe me, since you'll be ten feet closer to the Moon than I will."

Louise stuck out her tongue. Then she grabbed Kasia's hand.

"Come on, this way. Nineteen and twenty." They both grabbed chair back after chair back, floating across the rows toward their assigned seats.

"Thanks for the help, and I will see you both later."

"Mister Daniels, can you make the change for her please?"

He tapped a few times on his tablet. "Done, and . . . done." He smiled, showing Trace his new seat. "I'll see you later then."

Daniels turned away to chat with a few others who had managed to float up to the dome area, satisfying their own curiosity about the seating.

Trace pulled himself, gripping chair over chair, down to the lower seating area, and found his new spot, number 30. He took a seat, clipping the lap belt in and leaning back in the reclined position. His view up through the Stardome was indeed excellent.

Lucky Seven's lights dimmed an hour later. Trace barely noticed it, with the *StarDome* lights on their dimmest all the time. He scanned the Solar System beyond, imagining all the places humans had made settlements.

From Mars to the stars, he thought to himself.

As curfew approached, Trace reluctantly pulled himself away from the view and floated back down toward his cabin. He arrived a moment later, having had zero collisions on the way.

Louise and Kasia had already said their goodnights, and Louise was watching the tropical fish screen saver, the one she had seen back at the *StarBase* before launch.

Trace drifted in with a "heya, stink-brat."

"Butt face."

"Still cooler than you."

Louise ignored his last jab.

"Hey, I can't see the Picasso Triggerfish . . ." she murmured.

"He got eaten."

"You're a punk."

"Mm hmm."

Louise leaned over the side, looking at Trace.

"I think they aren't showing us everything. You know, the little hidden places on the Starship. You know, like they have on *Serenity*?"

"Can't stop the signal, Lou Lou."

"Can't stop the signal," she parroted back.

"Hey, how do *Reavers* clean their spears?"

"Too soon," Louise said without hesitating. "And we should search for hidden places."

"You should go to sleep."

"Ya, okay," Louise yawned, reaching up and dimming the room to darkness.

* * *

The operative ran a digital sniffer around his cabin, ensuring he was not being observed or listened to. No devices, no stray e-signatures. Good.

He opened the image that just arrived in his inbox from Earth. He saw it was supersaturated color version of Da Vinci's The Last Supper.

"How appropriate," he mused, slipping a thumb drive into the monitor. The image was filtered through a digital key that extracted a line of text from the pixels themselves. A chain of words appeared beneath the image as The Last Supper dulled to its original colors.

He read quickly, knowing he had just seconds to commit the details to memory.

Phase 2 begins. SN-485 O2 leak is no earlier than Mission Day 135; prepare now to incapacitate your crew. Memory crystal, location St. Denis, contains L-7 computer control worm. Upload the worm then leave it dormant. Wipe the crystal's memory. Bomb remote control is location Beaumont. Per contract, your clone will be awakened and receive your consciousness download only if Lucky Seven is destroyed before reaching Mars.

Be creative.

"Be creative? My dear filthy rich friends, I had this part worked out long before you recruited me." He snorted in disgust. Be creative.

The screen flashed the words

We stand Avenged.

Then it went dark.

He re-activated his thumb drive, superimposing the floor plan of the most famous Cathedral ever built on top of the schematics of Lucky Seven. He had a bomb remote control and a computer virus memory crystal to find.

* * *

Morning broke and Trace attended his first appointment with Doc, which went just as Louise had described hers. Lots of questions, a few observations, and the inevitable list of jobs he needed to get done. Doc seemed like he genuinely cared about everyone aboard, and Trace was eager not to let him down.

He had lost track of his sister and her new bestie, so he headed down for a snack instead. Coming up to the mess deck just as Trace floated down to it was Mister Richter, the Engineer. The man gestured ahead, indicating Trace had the right of way. They floated into the dining area. Not many passengers were here between meals; most seats stood empty.

"So. Trace, ja? I hope your meeting with Doc was productive?" Richter said as he grabbed a protein granola bar.

Trace nodded, grabbing a bar of his own and a lemon-lime drink. "Do you know anything about the mentoring program? Doc mentioned it."

Filling his personal drink pouch with black coffee from the dispenser, Richter replied, "the Captain told us this was beginning for all the young people on board. So. The way this works—we stay busy all the time."

"Okay, so, help me understand ranks and jobs aboard the Starship. Six crew, right?"

"Ja. The Captain, she's the big boss. The Executive officer, a Lieutenant or Ensign, is the next rank below hers. Our Exec, Lieutenant Telore, takes over if Captain Strahan is unable for any reason. They are technically our only two qualified pilots, and both are officers."

"So, pilots are always officers?"

"Always. To be an officer is the mark of a pilot."

"Okay, and the rest of the crew?" Trace took a bite of his bar, then moved aside for a thickly-bearded fellow he didn't recognize, reaching for the food dispenser.

"The Doc is a special case. He could be considered an officer, but he's more of a specialist, medically trained . . . but not a part of the Starship's decision-making chain of command."

"So that's three . . ."

"And the other three of us are the working crew. In a military sense, we might be considered enlisted, though our titles are tied to our functions aboard the Starship, and have nothing to do with military grades. It's a lot of tradition."

"Sergeant-at-Arms. Yeoman."

"Exactly."

"So who is next in line of authority?"

"It's not so simple. If an engineering problem arises, or if the survival of the Starship was threatened by a radiation surge or whatever, then the ship's Engineer has authority."

"Because as the Engineer, you know systems and how to handle . . . problems."

"Just so. And if there is a security problem, someone starts a fight, or someone steals, as an example, then the Sergeant-at-Arms asserts himself as the authority. But these situations aside, I am basically . . . um, equivalent to the Sergeant-at-Arms."

"And that man has arms."

"Like steel, ja."

"And that leaves the Steward."

"Yeoman, the junior position—his is an important task; he keeps the common areas and passengers organized, motivated, and able to perform their important functions. His hands are never idle, and yet his face, always he keeps it cheerful."

"But he's still just a yeoman."

Richter looked at Trace.

"Hm. Try not to let the rank or title determine the level of respect you feel, Mister Worthington . . . if you give great respect for the work someone does, or the duty burdens they bear, you will receive back at least some of that respect."

"I would say that your worthiness to the ship is more critical than his, that's all I'm saying."

"Worthiness of others is never a question. Focus only on being the best crew member you can, or in your case, passenger, and the rest takes care of itself."

Trace nodded.

"So, I have much work to complete before the slingshot, so I leave you now. Enjoy the show."

"Thanks, and I'll see you later."

"You can count on it." He nodded, then pushed off, down toward the *oculus*.

In the hours that followed, a noticeable rise in activity and tension picked up throughout the ship. It wasn't any one thing, just a busier atmosphere, a sense of urgency about everything.

All passengers were drafted as 'volunteers' to run FOD checks in every common area. Their highly detailed instructions: *look for things floating around freely and make them not float around freely*.

Each common area had at least a dozen or more people looking, making FOD-search lines unnecessary. DeBrus, who rarely would be heard on the all-call speakers, had this to add:

"Passengers, this is the Sergeant-at-Arms. If ye keep a keen eye out, there is a

pocket money card worth Ten Mars Credits stashed in one of the common areas. So as ye secure any floating items you find, snag that card if ye can, and bring it to me for activation. Now, let's get the FOD out o' here! Twenty minutes' search begins now."

Trace's assigned location, the fitness center, was an uneventful place to search. He found nothing more than a dust ball, a bit of lint really, stuck in a corner near the sauna. Trace noticed Dominique's parents also searching this level, hovering around and above a few machines near the wall, but he did not say anything to them. They ignored him completely.

Very few people found anything at all. One lady, searching inside the theater, found an ear-pod lodged up behind the movie screen with so much dust on it, it could have been there for three crossings.

No one found the ten-credit pocket money card; DeBrus probably made it up. He gathered everyone's FOD findings and thanked them all for participating.

The last free hour passed with many passengers, even those not assigned to *StarDome* seating, visiting to take in the magnificent moon—it loomed large, filling up nearly half the viewing space. Surface details were plain to see.

At half an hour before slingshot, the Bridge made a 30-minute heads up announcement, and directed everyone to proceed to their designated seating area to watch a special ten-minute video overview of the maneuver and the physics behind the idea. Mom and Dad were down in the Theater.

With ten minutes to go until buckle-up, the dome section was a buzz of activity as people edged past each other, found their seats, belted in, and leaned back, looking up in awe of the moon, which many had taken for granted all their lives. Not now.

"All hands, five minutes until secure stations. I repeat, please get strapped into your assigned seats immediately. As we fall into the moon's gravity well, the Starship may have to roll through the long axis to balance out gee-forces. If this

happens and you are not properly strapped in, you will be gravely injured as Lucky Seven adjusts her course. So please strap in immediately if you haven't already."

Trace found Louise, deliberately blocking her view of the moon.

"Need help with your harness? Or have you got it?"

"Yeah, yeah, I got it." She started clipping buckles into place. "Trace, moooove."

"Why? Think you might fall asleep?"

Louise punched Trace's arm.

He grinned at both girls and made his way between people to his own section. A lone unoccupied seat was there, and as expected, it was his.

Right next to Dominique Van der Waal.

"Oh boy," he muttered under his breath.

She looked up at him and *smiled.* He was so caught off guard, all he could do was awkwardly smile back. He couldn't see her parents anywhere nearby.

He eased himself into the seat, not an easy thing to do without pawing all the people nearby to guide him, and he got settled.

Clipping the buckles and shoulder straps, he eased back in the seat. He could tell this seat would be super comfortable, even under full gravity.

"I've always wanted to see the dark side of the moon," Dominique said, leaning into him a little as she said it.

"Hm. Fun fact—there's no 'dark side;' it's just the side we can't see from Earth. The back still gets sunlight half of every month."

"I meant far side. But I'm glad you're here to explain these things to me." Her eyes flashed, and she smiled, crinkling her nose.

"Wait, you knew there's no dark side?"

She said nothing, just raised her eyebrows.

Those royal-ice-blue eyes. So lovely. He wondered again how much nature had to do with her perfect face, and how much of her features were tweaked in a genetics lab before she was even born.

She must have been a very expensive baby.

The two broke eye contact at the same time to look up at the moon, which was closing awfully fast.

Chapter Fifteen

Speed Through the Core

Lucky Seven barreled straight at the Moon.

The viewing space through the windows was so filled with the moon, hardly any bits of space itself could be seen around the edges.

Trace could make out individual cities now, with their nearby dark squares of solar arrays, and radial highways and train lines, running up from the south polar region toward the lunar equator.

The craters were sharp and perfectly clear up close; their well-defined edges made them look almost too perfect, like a hi-def movie or video game.

"Ladies and Gentlemen, our path today takes us over Byrgius crater, Tycho city, and a host of smaller settlements under their domes. In a few moments, on the extreme left of your viewing space, you may just be able to glimpse Shackleton city."

Trace strained to look left. He couldn't see any skyscrapers, but one small bit of the rough edges on the moon's horizon . . . perfectly smooth. Shackleton City Dome, he thought. He imagined its array of skyscrapers standing under one of humanity's greatest engineering marvels. The dome had only been in place thirty standard years now, and it was on his bucket list of places to visit. Very high on the list.

The downward press into their chairs was getting stronger. Raising one's arm felt just like normal Earth gravity.

The lunar surface edged closer. Alarmingly close. Trace felt his heart race, like it might beat its way out of his chest. He breathed heavily, taking in deep lungfuls of air. The crowd hushed.

More features of the landscape rushed past, the closest starting to flash together in a blur instead of a moving landscape.

Trace redirected his focus downward, toward his feet and the pointy end of the dome, where everything seemed to be rushing directly toward them. The lunar horizon curved gracefully up on both left and right. He saw engineering and science stations, depots, industrial complexes, and yes, even more cities, smaller ones, under their broad and sweeping geodesic domes.

"Ooo, look at that," Dominique said, pointing at a series of flashing lights. Her breathing was fast as well. Trace kept his gaze upward. Occasionally, a splash of small flashes of light came from under the domes.

"Sunlight reflecting off the buildings or pools, maybe?" Trace guessed.

"No. Those are flashes from people taking pictures. A lot of people."

"That many? At this distance?"

"Trust me. I know what it looks like to have my picture taken by hundreds of camera flashes at a distance."

Trace didn't say anything but kept watching the domes roll past down on the surface. The gravity force started to lessen, then the drop became more noticeable.

Instinctively, everyone in the group strained to look higher, watching the moon rise up, above, and behind them, getting noticeably smaller as the seconds ticked by.

A few more of the smaller cities and dwellings, each under domes in smaller craters slipped past, the last little blips of light flashing sporadically, then fading into the gray background.

The lunar landscape began to rise up and away from them through the dome. The moon's horizon rounded out into a shape more circular with each passing second. Space itself reclaimed the bulk of the *StarDome* viewing area.

Then, over the course of a few more minutes, the moon slipped away behind them, lost to their view. A strange wave of vertigo hit the group, as full weightlessness washed over them. Arms that just a moment before rested on their armrests . . . suddenly floated free. A series of "oooo" and "woooahh" echoed through the group.

From nearby, Louise called out "woo hoo!" followed by a ripple of laughter through the audience. Stomachs lurched slightly. One man a few rows away reached for his sick bag.

Trace sat in silence, taking in the amazing moment. Dominique sat quietly as well. They made eye contact, still breathing fast.

"Oh my," she said, "wasn't that . . .

"It was," Trace nodded, feeling every bit as energized as she.

"It absolutely was."

* * *

"Ladies and gentlemen, it's time for us to gather briefly in the heart of the core, for our second All-Hands meeting. As before, please find a spot along any railing. We will begin in five minutes. Bridge, out."

Louise asked, "More flying lessons? Will they teach me how to do a triple backflip?"

"I doubt it, my Lou Lou; it's prolly about the slingshot or something."

This time, Louise joined Trace up along the railing of Deck 7. A minute before the appointed time, Kasia looked up from Deck 4, whispered excitedly to her mom and dad, who shrugged and nodded. Kasia pushed off gently to join her newest bestie.

As Kasia eased over the railing, the Captain emerged from the Bridge and floated down to hang motionless in the center of the core, as with their first mass gathering. She puffed a little hand-held canister of air to position herself just right, then swirled her arms to set herself rotating gently. She tapped her earpiece.

"Friends, welcome back. Did you enjoy the slingshot?"

A rousing cheer went up, most passengers clapping their hands.

"Was that amazing or what?" she beamed, eliciting a second round of cheers.

"I've always found that to be one of the great highlights of the Crossing. We were just two kilometers from the Lunar surface at our closest approach. That's about one and a half miles, so all that detail you saw, I imagine we gave the people of Tycho city quite a show. But imagine it from their perspective. Eighteen starships zipping by overhead, one after another, and Lucky Seven was their finale!"

Another round of applause and cheers greeted this.

"Yes, a truly special moment. Now, let's talk about the special moments we have still ahead of us, things to look forward to. First, something you may not have noticed earlier."

Curving display screens, which until this moment had matched the neutral tan or gray of whatever deck they were mounted to, blazed to life. Captain Strahan tapped her earpiece again, and spoke softly.

"X-O, departure angle on common area screens, please."

Trace did a quick count; each deck had its own screen, stair stepped up opposite sides of the core. If the ladders climbed up North and South inside the Core, the screens alternated East and West, six in total.

Every screen flipped to a live image, a hi-res view of the Earth, with the Moon at this moment appearing slightly larger than the Earth. As the

Earth barely diminished in the seconds that followed, the moon shrank noticeably as they cruised away. The effect was chilling.

Passengers gripped their handrails tighter without realizing it. The moon continued to shrink.

"Friends, there, you can see one of many options for your cabin viewscreens, tablets, handy-phones, and so forth. It's a good thing to keep tabs on Earth, don't get me wrong, but let's balance that with keeping tabs on Mars as well. Lieutenant?"

The screens cut to black. No, not entirely dark; a small dot floated on the right side of the image, barely brighter than the stars.

"Can you see that Pale Pink Dot? That's our objective. That's Mars. That's our future home. For ten thousand years, humans have looked up in wonder, at first thinking the planets were heavenly messengers, then eventually, the gods themselves. Now, that dot is our beacon of inspiration, our sanctuary for weary travelers, hope for our futures. Every culture has a place on Mars. With its 'seven cities' and a dozen smaller townships . . . with its hundreds of small waystations along the original highways, Mars appears to be no more than a rugged frontier."

As she spoke, the image zoomed in, bringing the dot into a much better resolution.

"Don't be fooled--it boasts Nerus, built to be the best of the Las Vegas playgrounds and old-world Venice . . . waterways for streets, five grand hotel-casinos, and all the high fashion and nightlife socialites could ask for – just imagine. New Marrakech, in the North, boasts the second-largest open market in the Solar System. The Mons-Plex is the largest underground city ever made, where a million people live out their lives with purpose and joy.

"Mars is home to three major league sports, twenty colleges and universities, more than thirty-five recognized cultural and art museums, and more than seventy performance spaces from the Capital Grand Opera to every corner comedy club . . . and how can we forget the tallest roller coaster ever built, dropping more than a mile down into the Night Labyrinth?"

The image reached the tightest part of its zoom, with the pale pink dot filling a quarter of the viewing space, fuzzy and without much detail. The image held for a few seconds longer, then faded to black.

"My point is, dear friends, this journey is not just about where we are headed. Neither is it just about where we departed yesterday morning. It's about where we are. We, the diverse, the explorers, the people of the Earth. So, look at those standing to your left. Now look to your right. Check out the decks above you and below you."

"We have here five dozen different cultures, races, and nations represented in the ninety-four souls aboard. There are seventeen distinct languages spoken among us. We hail from all the major continents, and half of the twenty-four time zones back on Earth. We do not have the luxury of isolating ourselves or allowing others around us to feel isolated. We represent too many good things for that."

She paused, ensuring everyone had their eyes on her.

"We are on too big a voyage to allow any among us to feel small."

She let that sink in.

"For your assignment today, I am directing each of you to meet at least ten other people you have not introduced yourselves to yet on our voyage. Share three facts with every person you meet: your name, where you lived back on Earth, and one talent or interesting fact about yourself. All right? Does anybody need me to repeat that?"

A few heads shook no. No one spoke.

"Before I leave you to your mix and mingle I have one final thing to unveil. Our three clocks."

She smiled and pressed the valve on her hand-held canister of air, propelling herself gently up and toward the Deck 6 railing. Gripping the railing with her left hand and pocketing the small air-jet, she turned to face the assembly. Trace and the two girls leaned over the railing, almost looking straight down at the Captain, one deck below.

Next to her, three displays lit up. Two had red digits, both displaying the same numbers, counting up together. A third display, showing the current time where they departed back on Earth, glowed bright aqua numerals.

"I hope you all like a good party. Any party animals in the house?"

A ragged cheer went up from many of the passengers.

"Arguably our biggest party aboard Lucky Seven . . . we call it Transition, the exact mid-point of the Crossing. So, if you notice, the Mission Clock, here, and the Voyage Clock, there, show the same time. They both count forward. However, at the exact mid-point of the Journey, the point of Transition, the Mission Clock will freeze. Then it will start counting backward – counting down, tracking the time remaining until we begin our final approach dive into the Martian atmosphere. So, I invite you to use these three clocks as a reference whenever you like, we will keep them running for the rest of our journey."

"That reminds me, everyone from ages 10 through seventeen, you have been selected for our S.I. Starship mentoring program, and each of you will have duties and responsibilities aboard our home here. You'll be in hydroponics, the fitness center, with security, in engineering, water and air filtration, and so forth. Lucky Seven needs you, and your adventure starts tomorrow. Now, everyone, to your meet and greet. Ten people in ten minutes. Three facts. Ready go!"

She lingered at the clocks, distracted for a moment. She rested a hand on one of them, as if connecting with something far away.

Then, after a long moment, she pressed the valve on her hand-held canister of air, propelling herself gently up and toward the Deck 6 railing. Trace watched her go, wishing he could just join her on the Bridge as a flight officer, and avoid all the *bumping elbows* with strangers. Ugh.

Someday.

Louise dragged Trace over the side, then when he held back, she abandoned him to go with Kasia to meet people with her new favorite wingman. Trace watched them go, holding hands, and he reluctantly joined the throng of enthusiastic people meeting each other as they gently met face-to-face . . . face-to-feet . . . face-to-elbow . . . and face-to-anything-else-you-can-imagine.

Trace collected his ten-count quickly, most of them Americans,

Canadians, and Asians, reaching ten with an articulate man named Pakal and his wife Ocoxochi, who pronounced it *Oh-ko-zo-shee.* Part of an interplanetary cultural exchange, they hailed from the small village *Amatlán,* near the Mexican city *Cuernavaca.* The man's interesting fact was that his village was the birthplace of the ancient god *Quetzalcoatl,* the Law Giver of meso-America before the conquistadors. Trace was intrigued; he abandoned his intentions to leave the party as quickly as possible. He chatted with the man and his wife for nearly an hour, until they drifted on to other things, mentally adding *Amatlán* to his list of places to go and show his respects to.

He ate dinner with his parents, and returned to his bunk afterwards to sift through several new messages from his buddies back on Earth, and send them his latest news.

* * *

Trace woke early on his own. He dressed and tried to slip out quietly, but bumped his knee on the bunk in the darkness. Louise stirred awake, but he reassured her it was still time for sleeping. Once she drifted back to sleep, he made his way down to Deck 2, searching in the low-light for a pouch of hazelnut coffee. The ship's clock read 4:47 A.M.

He squinted at the labels in the nighttime gloom. Occasionally a dispenser's blip or bleep sounded, but the only steady sound was the woosh of the air conditioners.

"Trouble sleeping, my young friend?"

Trace jumped.

With no gravity to oppose his startle-reflex, he jumped right off the deck and hit his head on a chair bolted to the ceiling.

Richter burst out laughing, a rich, baritone laugh.

'Aw, sonofa—" Trace said, pushing off the chair above with his right hand and rubbing a growing bruise with his left. His hazelnut coffee pouch floated nearby.

"Couldn't you have eased into that? I thought I was the only one awake."

"Ja, bruises are a mark of the engineer, I'm afraid." Richter stood nearby, sipping an orange drink mix pouch. "Also, sleeping very little."

"Hey, if you're looking for bruises . . ." Trace held up his arms like a boxer, making a few air jabs in the Engineer's direction and thumbing his nose like a 1920s movie pugilist. Richter chuckled.

"You will have to get in line behind Sergeant DeBrus to get to me, I'm afraid. So, you have difficulty sleeping?"

"I can only sleep four or five hours," Trace yawned. "Then my brain is awake." He sipped his coffee, found it too hot, and bit at a droplet that had escaped the pouch, floating just in front of his nose.

"Besides, if bruises are the mark of the Engineer, I think I'd rather be up on the Bridge. Aside from being an officer, what's the mark of a pilot?"

"For this answer, you must ask the Captain or the Lieutenant."

Trace yawned again, straightening out his mussed hair.

"Doc has all the fun pills, perhaps he has something to help you to sleep."

"Mister Richter, I was thinking, actually . . . is there something I can do to help you? I mean, I'm already awake and we have that mentoring thing we've been assigned to."

"So, as in, help me in Engineering?"

Trace nodded. "You're the only other one awake, and I don't feel like watching a movie by myself."

"They are going to assign you to work with me soon anyways. So let me think just a moment." He sipped his juice. "Ja, okay, there are checklist items that are easier with two, and one must be done this week. Have you ever performed a suit integrity inspection?"

"Sounds . . . scary. Are you pushing me out the main hatch?"

Richter laughed, again, his hearty German laugh. "Ach, no, that one is sealed, locked before takeoff and cannot be opened at all until we stand on Mars. No. This check is completed on the engineering deck, going outside is not required. Have you ever worn a space suit?"

"Just the practice suits in school for career day. That's when I knew I wanted to pilot a Starship."

Richter looked at him a moment, scrutinizing the teenager.

"Well, then there's no time like the present, ja? Follow me."

"Okay, but I'll probably need another cup of this heavenly hazelnut before too long."

"Okay, I buy you a coffee after one hour. This way."

The engineer stuck his orange drink pouch onto the outer Velcro of his engineer's vest and turned to the core of the ship. At the railing, he redirected himself toward the *oculus*.

Trace did his best to imitate the flight of Mr. Richter . . . but was a bit off in his execution, missing his target completely. He made another attempt, with less boost this time.

On his last push-off, he saw printed on the handgrips nearby "HAND GRIP HERE" as well as other places up and down the core. The words seemed to be everywhere.

"Question . . . why is there writing on everything? Don't they think we know a door from a hole in the ground?" He gestured at their feet.

"Ach, it's not a hole in the ground, it is the *oculus*. And if you ever see the writing on that door, this will be a very bad day."

"Why's that?"

"Aside from launch und landing or emergency drills, that *oculus* stays open the entire trip. It only closes if a, um, micrometeorite, ja? . . . has punched a hole in the hull and we are losing atmosphere. Or a radiation surge."

"What about our cabins? Would they go vacuum too?"

"So many questions. Nein."

"Nein?"

"Nein."

"The people are just . . . trapped? Or are there Exo-Suits hiding under the bunk beds?"

"No suits. There are procedures we train for if the core goes to vacuum, and passengers become trapped inside their rooms. Everyone shelters in place in their cabins, and a member of the crew finds the leak and repairs it. Then we dock with a sister Starship and receive some of their atmosphere. The procedure takes hours, and it can get very cold throughout the Starship."

"Have they ever had to do that?"

Richter nodded. "Two times. The first was very successful, and the air transfer to SN-148, the *Rodger Young*, was fine. But the second, there were two leaks, where the micrometeorite passed through one side of the hull and made another hole in the other side. So the transfer of atmosphere didn't work. The passengers rode out the last five days of the journey trapped inside their cabins."

"Which Starship was that?"

"I give you three guesses, but you only require one."

Trace's eyes widened. "You're kidding! *Lucky Seven*?"

"Before now, she was SN-504, *Hydros*. Many design changes were implemented after that voyage, and *Hydros* was the first to be modified. After her refit, she was re-christened SN-700, *Lucky Seven*."

"So . . . what happened to the people inside . . . *Hydros*?" He looked up, trying to imagine where the micrometeorite entered the hull, and where it exited.

"It was a routine Crossing, just like this one. Captain Manning and his Engineer, Mister Herschel, managed to save the ship, but they were both killed in the process. The junior-most flight officer, an Ensign barely out of flight training, was trapped alone on the bridge and could not reach any other compartment. She completed the final approach kick-flip and landed the ship single-handedly. Everyone else on board survived because of her."

"A trainee? She's a true hero then."

"Captain Strahan does not prefer the label . . . but ja, *hero.*"

Trace's jaw fell open. "Are you kiddi— . . . wow."

Trace stopped talking for a moment.

"If you ask her, she will tell you she was only in the right place at the right time, and simply did her duty." Trace looked at Richter, nodding his understanding.

"Which, of course, is all any of us can do." The engineer smiled. "So, let's put you into an EVA Suit and see if it will pass inspection." He pulled himself through the *oculus.*

Shaking his head, Trace followed Richter down to Deck 1.

"Bridge, this is Engineering."

"Go ahead mister Richter," Telore's crisp voice snapped out over the speaker.

"Please be advised we are conducting the departure leg pressure suit checks on both EVA suits, using the Engineering vacuum tube under low pressure. Non-crew personnel Trace Worthington is assisting."

"Bridge copies. Report when complete."

"Acknowledged. Engineering out."

Trace pointed at the small 'EVA' suit label on the nearest suit. "So what does this—"

"It stands for Extra-Vehicular Activity. It just means this suit is for going outside, like the *Exo-Suits* on Mars."

"Have you ever been . . . outside?"

"Only in simulation. It is extremely rare for Starships to be approved for EVA space walks, even if they request it. Only when there is a serious problem, ja?"

"Ja."

Richter smiled. "So, you have to slip into the legs first and seat your feet into the ankle stops. They automatically adjust."

Trace started to reach for the closest suit, the one on his right.

"Ach, nein, this one I will check. You put on the other one."

"Ah. What's the difference?"

"This one has my name. See? Pay attention to the details, Trace. As an Engineer, you must see every small thing, because the safety of the Starship may depend on some small, unnoticed detail."

"Like your shoelace being untied?" He pointed down at Richter's boots.

"Ha! Nice try."

"I'll get you back for earlier."

"No, I think not."

"A challenge? I accept. What are the stakes?"

Richter grimaced. *This kid had guts.*

"Crew should not make wagers with passengers. But perhaps I should take the vacuum tube down to zero pressure, just make completely sure the suit has full integrity. Hmm?"

"I am not a fan of that idea."

"Less talk, more suiting up. Are your feet nested in the boots? Good. Now, reach up, pull down the upper part, arms in first, ja, that is correct."

Trace wriggled and squirmed his arms up into the torso portion and managed to get his arms started in both sleeves. His head popped through the open neck and his arms reached the full length of the sleeves. His fingertips fumbled to find the individual gloved finger spaces, but after a moment, he had it. He flexed his hands in the attached gloves.

Connecting the two halves of the space suit was easier than he expected; he put his hands on the sides of the chest piece and pressed it down until the belt receiver clams clicked into place. Then he snapped both levers flush with the sides. They stayed locked together.

Richter nodded, the seal looked good.

"These gloves come off, right? I can see the fasteners. They twist off?"

"If you need them to, okay, they come off. But today, you do the helmet attachment and suit checks with the gloves in place."

"Sounds awkward."

Trace looked around for the helmet, found it hanging above his left shoulder, and he reached up for it. He gently pulled it loose from its hook and turned it over to slide over his head. He had a struggle getting the threads to line up. He twisted, and it kept missing the mark.

"This would be easier with bare hands, let me just—"

"You do it with your gloves on this time. In an emergency, you may not have all the time in the world. Also, pretend I am not here."

Trace gritted his teeth, feeling his frustration building.

"Close your eyes."

"Close my eyes? That would make this even harder."

Richter just looked back at him. No words, just expectation.

"All right, I'll give it a try."

Richter looked aside, gave his head a little shake, and then focused back on Trace.

The helmet found its threads a moment later. Trace twisted it until he felt it seat properly, a little *click*.

"Okay, I'm guessing now, the power."

Richter kept watching him, still a blank, deadpan look.

Trace looked back at his wrist and jabbed the main power button with his right index finger.

The screen stayed dark.

He held it up for Richter to see.

Richter just watched him, shrugging slightly.

Trace looked back down at his wrist. A few fine beads of sweat formed on his brow—the suit's insulation was starting to make it feel warm inside.

A couple awkward jabs later, still nothing.

Why isn't this stupid thing turning on?

He pressed gently, letting his finger stay in contact a full second, and was pleased to see the wrist touchscreen light up. Power / Air Pressure / Temperature all appeared on his display. And colors. Lots of colors.

"Yes!" he whispered to himself.

He heard a mild hissing, inside the suit. A very brief painful pressure spiked in his ears, which softened as the pressure equalized. A trickle of cool air flowed over his face and down his back.

His nose itched. The air in front of his face made his nose itch; he reached up to try to scratch it, but his glove bumped the helmet. Yikes. Awkward.

Richter gave him a quizzical look.

Trace tried ignoring the itch and looked back down at his wrist. His display showed three colored bars.

In bright green: *Power 100% - 4.02 hours*; in light blue: *ATM 1.0, 2.55 hrs*, and in orange: *Temp, 22° C* with the plus and minus buttons. Trace noticed a (*) pulldown menu in an upper corner, but he did not press it just yet.

He nodded at the readouts, and looked up at Richter, showing him the display.

Richter gave a thumbs up. Then Richter slipped a thin-wire headset radio over his left ear, microphone running down his cheek, gamer style, and spoke softly into it. Trace heard nothing.

Richter spoke again. Trace tapped his ears and shook his head. Richter shrugged and looked at him.

Ah, another test. Okay, he could do this. Find suit comms and turn them on.

He pushed the pulldown menu button on his wrist, and saw 'PWR MGT' on the display, with more options below it. He swiped up. 'PWR MGT' was replaced with 'AIR MGT,' then 'EMRGCY,' then 'SUIT ENVR,'

'CLOCK/TMR,' and then, 'RADIO.'

Out of curiosity, he scrolled past the radio without opening it, to see what his other options were. 'WI-FI,' appeared, followed by 'CODE BLK,' which had a lock symbol next to it.

That last one was odd; he'd ask about it later. He scrolled back up to 'RADIO' and tapped it open.

His options were 'CHNL,' 'VOL,' and 'OPEN MIC.'

He selected the Channel option.

'CMD-1' appeared first. As Trace was about to press the green mike button, Richter slapped his gloved hand away.

Richter wagged a finger no at him, then he spun his index finger around in a 'keep going' gesture.

Trace scrolled to the next channel option. 'CMD-2' appeared, and again, the Engineer shook his head no.

He scrolled past 'CMD-3,' 'MED-1,' 'MED-2,' 'EMERG,' and saw 'ENGR-1' appear.

"This one?" Trace asked, raising his voice slightly.

"Almost," came Richter's faint reply. Trace swiped through ENGR-2, and on 'ENGR-3,' the engineer gave him the thumbs-up.

He pressed the mike button.

"Uh, hello?"

"Radio check, how do you hear me, Trace?"

"Uh, you sound just fine, Mr. Richter."

"Okay, let's practice good radio decorum. If I am coming through strong and with no static, you can say 'five by five' or 'loud and clear.'"

"Loud and clear, I hear you loud and clear."

"And now you ask me the same."

"How do you read me?"

"Five by five also."

"Why is it five?"

"The first number is strength, second number is clarity. One through five is the scale from weak to strong, for example."

"I don't understand."

"A radio transmission can be loud, ja? But perhaps completely garbled or static. Understand? That would be five by one, but no one really uses these numbers, aside from five by five. You would say strong and unreadable, or strong and intermittent, or weak and garbled, whatever the case is."

"So five by five is . . ."

"Loud and clear, yes."

Trace nodded. "That makes sense. So why are we using Engineering channel . . . 3?"

"This training channel has a much lower signal strength, a few hundred meters only. If we use Engineering 1 or 2, other ships in our flotilla would hear us and ask if we are all right. So, we use number three. Even if they hear us, they know to ignore channel 3."

"Okay."

"Okay. Give me a suit report, please?"

"What do I say?"

"Follow your instincts."

"Okay." He looked at his wrist. "Mister Richter, I report suit power is full, air is 100 percent, and temperature is . . . comfortable."

"Ha ha, only give the power percent, pressure, and clean air supply time remaining. Your comfort is not reportable, unless there is a problem."

"My nose itches," he said, working his nose around. "It's distracting."

"So? Figure it out."

He held up a gloved hand. "But—oh. Another test." He tried to lean his chin forward to scratch his nose on the helmet seams and ran right into the attached brush inside his helmet for that exact purpose.

"Oh. Okay, cool. In that case, suit power is 99%, pressure is good, and air remaining is two point five hours."

"Very good. Now, we perform the suit integrity check. Please, step into the vacuum tube." He gestured to the vacuum tube against the wall, just big enough for one suited person to stand inside. Trace stood by it, and Richter spun the cylinder's door open using a simple twist handle.

He stopped at the threshold. "You're not going to go full vacuum, are you?"

"I think yes. Otherwise, how would you fully trust your equipment?"

"I don't think I want to test my trust that much . . ."

"Trace, you must be like Adidas, *just do it*."

"That's Nike."

"Nike, Adidas, doesn't matter. Just flip the switch in your mind. Commit. Sometimes you have no choice but to go forward."

Trace noticed the beads of sweat were forming on his brow again, and his nose itched again. He scratched it and stepped inside, shuffle-turning around as Richter closed the door.

The engineer nodded and pressed a few buttons on a nearby control pad.

Instinctively, Trace put both gloved hands against the thick plastic walls.

In under a minute, a small, powerful vacuum pump sucked the air out of the tube.

Chapter Fourteen

Of Course, It's Lucky

In the hour that followed, Trace switched roles with Richter to test the other suit. Trace's suit checked out just fine, and he stepped out of the chamber, powered down, and took the suit off in carefully-directed steps to avoid damaging it.

Richter showed him how to operate the simple vacuum chamber controls. The Engineer could operate the tube's controls from a similar pad inside, but he wanted to give Trace a go at it. In half the time, the second suit checked out perfectly as well.

"So, I think it's enough for one morning; you have your exercise and your Mars Ambassador contact to make today, I believe?"

"Oh yeah—that's today. Even this early in the trip, every day feels the same."

They left Engineering together, talking as they headed toward the *oculus*.

"And yet, you must never lose sight of where you are . . . and when you are, Mister Worthington. I want you to also work on your attention to detail. Too many critical details escape your notice, and we must train this out of you."

"Uh, okay, how do I do that?"

"Notice every detail all day long. Understand?"

"Not at all."

"You will take note of how many people you see and do not see. I want you to know which decks you visit all day, and which ones you do not. I want you to remember what people say and do, and report to me anything abnormal, all day long. We make this a nightly habit."

"Sounds like a lot."

"Also, just for today, add to your end-of-day message two photos from inside the Starship, after you locate both the micrometeorite entry and exit wounds from her *Hydros* days."

"The damage is all patched up by now, how can I possibly find them?"

"This is for you to figure out. Think of it as an Engineering challenge."

He just stared at Richter.

"The clock is ticking." With a final nod, Richter launched himself up, toward the Bridge, to file his EVA Suit Check report in the ship's log.

Trace just watched him go, then scanned around the core, as if *Lucky Seven* would spin the decks above him like a giant slot machine and just show him where a metallic meteorite the size of a pencil eraser had punched its way through the hull so many years ago.

The ship's clock read 6:59 A.M..

All the daytime lights up and down the core blazed to full daylight. Time to go send off a text message to his Mars Ambassador and check on his little sister.

* * *

The note to his Ambassador, whom he learned through the M.A.C.

system was named Chrissy (no last name provided), was short and sweet. He typed up a simple greeting and asked her to share with him her favorite thing about wherever she lived on Mars. He signed it 'Your friend, Trace' and sent it on its way.

Trace and Louise found seats at one of the few remaining bulkhead tables. Sitting at a chair at a small table stuck sideways on the wall still felt trippy, but in zero gee, conventions go right out the airlock.

Louise handled her scrambled eggs with cheese breakfast pouch delicately, gripping the hot pouch by the corners. From a nearby table, Trace heard Dominique admiring the latest gift her daddy had bestowed—clearly she wanted everyone to know about it.

"The diamonds just sparkle, Daddy! I love my new tennis bracelet!"

"Just wait 'til next week's present, princess."

"Mmmm. Is it a matching necklace? Or earrings? That'll be nice."

From his own table, Trace rolled his eyes and silently mimicked Dominique admiring an imaginary bracelet for his sister's entertainment. Louise giggled, crinkling her nose.

Dominique wasn't done though.

"Ugh, but I can't believe the Captain hasn't invited us up to the bridge yet for a tour. I mean, she doesn't even know Boston isn't in Kansas—they're not even in the same country, Daddy. She's, like, so dense."

"Now, sweetheart, she's the Captain." Mr. Van der Waal took a bite from the tube of his breakfast pouch.

"Doesn't mean she knows anything. Do you think she's just an expert in space, and not brilliant in geology like you?"

He shrugged.

In a low voice, Trace whispered, "Geology? I think she meant geography?" Louise giggled, covering her mouth, then looked up as Dominique turned around.

"Excuse me?" Dominique asked, whipping her perfect spray-tight blond waves behind her and glaring under thin-lined eyebrows. Her complexion was flawless.

For Trace, cheeks turning red, it was *damn the space torpedoes and full steam ahead.*

"What part didn't you understand? It's *geography*. Geography is about where things are and what they're named. Rocky Mountains, Gulf of Mexico, U.S.A., U.S.C., Greater Canada . . . what you said is about rocks and minerals and how they change."

"That's what I said, geography."

"Mm hmm. And the Captain's record is amazing, you should read about her before you go trashing her."

"Is she some sort of . . . space hero or something?"

Trace just looked at her, eyebrows raised.

"Well, whatever. She's probably never even been to Boston. Bet you haven't either." She turned back to face her father before Trace could answer.

Trace just looked at the back of Dominique's head, admiring her beauty and hating her arrogance in the same moment.

"Uh, come on Louise, let's go see what's showing on the big screen."

He finished off the last of his breakfast and the two stood and floated toward the core, dropping their pouches in the recycler as they left.

Trace glanced back and was surprised to see Dominique watching him go, a strange but curious expression on her face. He quickly broke eye contact.

He didn't speak until they cleared Deck 3, on the way to Deck 5.

"Good gravy, that girl's annoying."

"Yeah, she's not like Jeni. Jeni was nice to people."

"Yeah." He thought about Jeni's gift, still unopened down in his locker on Deck 1.

Trace grabbed the Deck 5 railing and swung himself over. As they floated past the open gaming pods toward the large, curved movie screen, Trace noticed one of the few solo travelers, Mr. Kazama, had opted for an old-school flight simulator, in which he flew an A-7 *Corsair II* combat jet out of a dusty desert region as a mercenary pilot. Mr. Kazama had set the high score and was about to set a new one—the man seemed to be a retro-gaming god.

Trace made a mental note to challenge him on a different game, his own favorite retro simulator—the first-gen arcade racing title Out Run—see if his racing skills were as boss as his air combat skills. Another day, perhaps.

They floated further on, passing the gaming spaces to see what was on the big screen.

"Doctor LaClair and my friends asked me if I opened their class gift from Palmer Lake Elementary yet. I told them I have to wait. Why do we have to wait?"

"It's only a couple weeks away—it'll be here soon enough."

"Why do we have to wait until week four to open it? It's worse than Christmas."

"Gives you something to look forward to."

"Did Jeni give you a gift?"

"Yeah. She gave me . . . something."

The theater was dark, with all its seats free.

"Ooo, we're first! What should we watch?"

"Um . . . you want a cartoon?"

"I wanna see explosions. Lots of explosions."

Trace tapped the menu and scrolled the action-adventure titles. "*Lethal Defender*? Or . . . one of the Phase-18 *Star Wars* titles?"

"*Total Devastation 4*."

"The one where entire Earth finally gets wiped out."

"Yesssss! C'mon, c'mon, launch that dude. I wish we had popcorn."

"They have that tube stuff, popcorn flavored."

"I'm pretending you didn't say that."

"Okay, here we go." Trace cued up the movie and they both sat in their felt seats, with just enough Velcro to stop a person from floating up and away.

In the opening scene, Paris is swallowed up in an exploding volcano, where no volcanoes exist of course, and our hero and her children barely escape aboard a plane she hardly knows how to fly.

"How can one volcano threaten a whole big city like Paris? That's not a thing."

"Actually it's happened a lot. *Vesuvius, Pelée, Krakatoa*. I think tens of thousands died in each of those."

"But Paris has a million people or something."

"Yeah. So, pretty far-fetched."

"I like it—woah! That surfer dude got totally washed by that tidal wave. Ooooo, impaled on a spike. Ouch."

A tsunami wiped out the entire French and Spanish riviera and was heading southward across the Mediterranean. The mother and her children raced through Marrakech to board the last high-speed train, heading East across Africa towards Egypt. The tsunami completely obliterated the city right behind them.

From the previews he had seen before leaving Earth, Trace predicted the three would board the very last Starship out of Cairo and eventually end up on the moon, watching the Earth devour itself in floods, volcanoes, hurricanes, tidal waves, and wildfires.

He remembered from social media that the studio had been unwilling to pay Starship Interplanetary for the rights to use *Lucky Seven* as that last escaping Lunar Starship—they wanted it for free. Nevermind *Lucky Seven* was an interplanetary Starship and not outfitted as a moon shuttle.

Richter's face popped around the corner.

"Trace, can I borrow you for a particular engineering maintenance task, please? It helps if I have a second pair of hands."

Trace pushed up and out of the chair with a soft Velcro separation sound. "Sure, I can help. Should I bring Louise along?"

"Hmmm, no, let her enjoy the film. Her work will be in *hydroponics*, I believe. Unless she wishes it?"

Louise waved her hand dismissively at Trace and Richter without taking her eyes off the screen. "Wow, that guy got *pancaked* under a *MagLev* train. Is that even possible? Woah."

"She's fine. We can go." He floated toward the gaming cubicle spaces and the exit.

"See you later Lou Lou."

"See ya." The screen light flashed in her face and her eyes popped and her mouth fell open. "Oh noooooo . . ."

Trace followed the Engineer out into the core.

"So where's the party?"

"No parties today, my friend."

"But later?"

Richter shrugged.

"So what about that thing the Captain mentioned earlier--a party at Transition?"

"Yes, there will be quite a celebration. A countdown, a few surprises the crew will reveal, decorations, costumes . . . it will feel like a New Year celebration."

"There isn't dancing at the party, is there? I don't do dancing."

"Ha, you don't do dancing, and I don't do parties. But of course, people try to dance—it's more fun with zero gee anyway. There is always excellent music, party lighting, a few nice drinks, some social media updates, and reaching out to both Earth and Mars in celebration. And we have two surprises our crew has invented that no other Starships will be doing."

"That's cool. So, you go every time, right?"

"Nein."

"Nein?"

"Not once have I gone; I have important systems updates to prepare as all the clocks switch over."

"I'll go if you go."

"Not for all the tea in Japan."

"China."

"What?"

"Not for all the tea in China."

"China, Japan. They both drink tea, yes? The answer is still no."

"Okay, so, when do you relax? For starters, how long do you plan to stay on Mars?"

"Two weeks."

"Two weeks . . . that's all?"

"This is shore leave, before *Lucky Seven* begins her refit then returns to Earth. We have a much longer transit back to Earth, eleven months, but it will still get us back before the next Hohman departure in 26 months."

"What will you do with your two weeks?"

"I have been wanting to visit the markets of New Marrakech, or even better, see the historic *Viking One* landing site. Then I report back for several weeks of station-keeping and pre-flight duties."

"Isn't *Viking One* on the other side of Mars? The side with . . . you know, no cities?"

"Ja, it is at the frontier—after one expensive train ticket to the last stop at Valley of the Gods, one must take a ground vehicle for three extra days just to get there. It is Lief Outpost."

"That's an adventure. And *Viking I* is still there?"

"Perfectly preserved. And yes, guaranteed *abenteuer*. They replaced the *Viking I* power supply and some wiring, allowing it to turn systems on and take actual photos of visitors. The photos are sent back to Earth, just like in

1970s, processed by the Mars Historical Offices, und beamed back to us, so the retro look and feel is completely authentic. That photo will be an amazing artefact to have, don't you think?"

"That's pretty impressive," Trace had to admit.

"And with a great cost."

"Okay, you said it's expensive. Then how about we make a little side bet? Imagine you had more Martian Credits to spend? You know, to use during your shore leave?"

They had arrived at the *oculus*. Just before pulling himself down through, Richter squinted at Trace.

"You are not going to get me back for jump-scaring you, young Mister Worthington."

"Then you risk nothing."

Richter looked down and kept talking as he slipped through to Deck One.

"Okay, fine. So. I agree, but you cannot borrow the money, or steal it, and you cannot get it from mummy or daddy, ja?"

"You want me to just magic up a hundred Martian credits out of thin air?"

"Three hundred. I travel with first class."

"But . . ."

"Come, we get to work now. And what will I be wagering if I lose?"

"You have to attend the celebrations, all of them. Be social with the rest of us."

Richter put on a look that fell somewhere between annoyed and hurt, then his cool, calm German mask of professionalism was back on.

"Ja, okay, I agree." Richter led the way through the locked door.

Trace followed, and noticed right away the cramped work spaces were more spacious. Then he saw the two suit racks, empty. No, even the racks were gone.

"Mister Richter? Where did the EVA suits go? Weren't they hanging right here before?"

"Ja . . . I put them away. We won't need them until the final weeks of the voyage, when the second round of checks are performed.

"Storage?" He looked around. "Where, below Deck 1?" He looked across the floor but saw no hatchways.

"It's not in this room, the storage space. They are . . . with life support, and that's restricted, crew only."

Trace decided to search later.

There was something the Engineer was not telling him.

"I've also been meaning to ask, remember how you said the main hatch cannot be opened for the entire voyage?"

"Yes, I remember."

"Okay, how does the crew do any repairs outside the Starship? You said it's been done twice before."

The Engineer looked at him directly, his ice blue eyes intense. "There are . . . methods of going outside. But these are for emergencies only. Now, come, we have work."

Trace rolled up his sleeves, donned a pair of thin rubber gloves, and started cleaning out the gummed-up blue-green algae canisters that processed the air they breathed, reintroducing the oxygen and absorbing CO2. It smelled funky, but Trace didn't mind. The nose plug helped.

He focused instead on Richter's careful word choice in their last exchange. He wondered what exactly it was that Mister Richter was hiding. He rolled up his sleeves and prepared to get slimed.

He thought of Dominique, how she'd never get her hands dirty, those perfectly-manicured nails, even if it meant the ultimate difference in saving the Starship.

"Yeah, there's no way she would," he muttered out loud.

"Hrm?"

"Nothing."

His handy phone pinged from his suit's chest pocket, and he hastily slipped out of one glove to pull the phone out.

"It's an invite from the bridge. So, we actually get a tour?"

"Each Captain's discretion. She usually tries to get a feel for the passengers, then makes the decision. So, you should get going if you want to make it."

"But I still have half a canister to go."

"The Captain summons; you go. Immediately. I will finish—set your canister down, just there."

"Thanks, Mister Richter. I'll see you in . . . however long it takes." He vanished through the Engineering hatch, up through the *oculus*, and onward to his surprise appointment. In under a minute, he had hand-vaulted over the railing next to the Bridge.

Mister Richter finished up his own canister, then reached down to pick up Trace's canister. Something caught his keen eye—a tiny bit of white, tape or paper perhaps, barely visible under the bottom lip of the air purifiers under where their metal feet were bolted to the deck. He set the canister down and got a better angle. Reaching underneath, he gripped a package, and tugged it until it came loose. With a tear of Velcro, he produced a tightly-wrapped box, double-sealed in brown paper and wrapped tight in multiple wraps of clear plastic tape.

"Contraband?" he shook the package slightly to see if there was anything loose inside. Something *had* shifted inside. He stared at the package, deciding his next step. He clicked his headset and spoke in rushed, precise tones.

* * *

Trace steadied himself, trying to stand at the threshold of this most important hatchway on *Lucky Seven*, but the carpeting here was well-worn, so he floated there awkwardly, hands bracing both sides as the door slid open.

Just a few feet in front of him, Captain Strahan herself stood, smiling.

"Glad to see you here this morning. Trace, right?" Captain Strahan said brightly.

"Yes, ma'am. And were you expecting my sister? If you were, I think she's running late, sorry about that."

Captain waved her hand, dismissing his apology. "She's fine—her visit is with your parents, later this afternoon. Ah, Miss Van der Waal, good morning to you as well."

Trace glanced right, over his shoulder, just now noticing Dominique was there.

"Well, don't just linger in doorways," Dominique snapped, her shiny, perfect pouty lips glossed, and her eyes wide open with expectation.

Trace didn't rush to get out of her way.

"I think it's tradition to ask permission before entering the Bridge, Dominique. Or wait until we're invited?" He emphasized the last word for Dominique's benefit.

Her cheeks flushed slightly. She was clearly not used to pushback. She looked from Trace to the Captain, placing one small, perfectly-manicured hand on her hip.

"Come in," Captain Strahan said, nodding to Trace as they entered.

"Let's show you both around. Rules first. As you might predict, please keep away from control panels, and try not to touch anything aside from hand grips, chairs, the walls, and floor.

Trace pulled himself into the room, using a handrail along the right wall to guide his movements. Dominique followed closely. When they both were in the room, the hatchway hissed shut behind them.

"Cleaning fingerprints from the windshield above us is an impossible chore in zero gee," Telore said, reclining in his station seat, monitoring multiple screens.

Both teens' eyes were drawn upward. The clear glass ceiling was perfectly aligned with the windows of the *StarDome*, giving the flight crew an unobstructed view of the skies in front of *Lucky Seven*. The two officers let the teens take it in for a moment in silence.

"It's an amazing view," Trace commented.

"Um, that's Mars, right? The bright pink dot?" Dominique asked.

"That's right," Telore confirmed.

"It seems to be off to the right, are we going to miss it?" she asked.

Trace thought the same thing, remembering his chat with DeBrus during the tour on this same topic.

"Mister Worthington, why don't you take a crack at Miss Van der Waal's question?"

Dominique snapped her head up slightly, leaning around Trace to address the First Officer.

"Him? How would he even know the ans—" and Dominique's grip on the railing slipped. She floated up, the railing out of reach. Instinctively, she grabbed Trace's shoulder to keep from bumping into the glass windshield above.

"Whups, sorry," she said, embarrassed at the unintended contact. He didn't flinch her away.

"You're fine," he said casually, not really looking over his shoulder. His cheeks flushed slightly as she held a firm grip on his shoulder, perfect fingernails gently digging into his Shipsuit to hold her position.

"Oh . . . strong . . ." she murmured under her breath, hand still gripping his shoulder as she pulled herself back down toward the carpeted floor.

Trace felt a surge in his nerves, very aware that Dominique had accidentally brushed his back as she pulled herself back down. She pushed away slightly, ship suit-boots reaching the floor and, thankfully, her feet stayed in place this time.

"Ya planning on keeping my shoulder?" Trace asked, looking down at her hand.

"Um, no . . . sorry," she whispered, her cheeks turning bright red. Her hand gripped the railing behind him instead.

Their faces close, he could smell her faint perfume. Sweet, fruity, the effect was . . . Trace shook his head.

The Captain watched this little exchange with mild amusement.

Trace cleared his throat. "So, um, Mars? Why it looks . . . off-center? Will you help us out on this one, sir? I don't think I could explain it very well." Trace gritted his teeth in a save me grimace. The Lieutenant explained.

"It's a solid question. Our Mars Insertion Trajectory has us pointing the Starship ahead of Mars as it runs its orbital track around the sun. If we pointed *Lucky Seven* at exactly where Mars is right now, it would move in its orbit out of the way by the time we got there. We'd pass behind it and miss completely. So, our path through space leads the target, so to speak."

"Oh. Makes sense," Dominique said.

The Exec continued the tour from his seat. "So. From here, I monitor *Lucky Seven*'s critical systems, passengers' status, and the position and condition of the three other Starships in our flotilla."

He tapped a few screens, making different status boards flash on the main central screen, to be replaced seconds later by other systems' status displays. He jammed through them too quickly to keep up. Trace tried to catch the details, whereas Dominique shook her head, looking out the *StarDome* instead.

"Wait, are those the other Starships?" she asked, eyes open in wonder.

"Yes. The one on the left is the *Manitou*, and on the right is the *Bozeman*.

"If you lean forward, you can see the *Williamina Fleming*, further off to the right."

"Williamina—she was one of the Harvard Computers, right?" Trace asked. "Early 1800s?"

"Very good! She published books, discovered the Horsehead Nebula, and thought up the first star classification system . . ."

"But . . . I thought Annie Jump Cannon gave us our Stellar System?" Trace asked the Captain. "My Astro teacher back in C-Springs really drilled that into us."

"True, but it was Williamina who came up with the first solid idea how to classify stars in the first place. Her *A-B-C-D-E-F-G* . . . was based on Hydrogen strength in their telescope photos. So, a couple years pass, she publishes her findings, and catalogues tens of thousands of stars. Then Annie joins the team, and using her Master's in Astronomy, she reasons that ranking stars by the intensity of those spectral lines in the photos, not just the hydrogen presence, was a better way to categorize stars. So rather than undo all Williamina's work, Annie took her *A-B-C-D-E-F-G* and re-ordered it into *O-B-A-F-G-K-M*."

"O-B-A—what?"

"*O-B-A-F-G-K-M*."

"How can you even remember that—it's so random."

The Captain and the Exec looked at each other, smiling.

Telore gave a rare chuckle. "Oh, be a fine girl, kiss me," he said.

"Um—wut?"

"That's no-kidding how astronomers remember it. The O's are the hottest, and the M's are the coolest."

"Seriously?" Trace said, picking up the acronym immediately.

"Can't make this stuff up," the Captain said.

Trace said nothing. Now his cheeks were turning red. He could feel Dominique looking at him. He glanced at her. After a second or two, she looked away.

The Captain broke the silence. "Let's keep it moving. Over here, these screens monitor the engines and our trajectory—that's our pathway through space—and we have limited radar ability to detect nearby objects and radiation waves, warning us of danger. Over there is where we communicate with Mars and Earth, and this is the Captain's chair."

"So . . . the radiation waves, is that when we have to evacuate to the . . . shelter deck? Down where our lockers are?"

"Correct, Miss Van der Waal. That makes our situational awareness the most critical job. That's why your mentors are going to drill you on noticing every detail; it's good practice."

Trace was starting to understand Richter's obsession with attention to every detail.

"So, we have another group arriving shortly, leaving us time for one or two questions."

Trace opened his mouth briefly, then decided against it.

"Nothing?"

"Well . . . can I ask about the history of the Starship, ma'am? Specifically, where the two most interesting entry and exit locations are, inside the Starship?"

Telore turned and looked at him, stunned to silence.

The Captain chuckled. "I don't know how you acquire information so quickly, Mister Worthington, but you are well-informed."

Trace shrugged, "I ask a lot of questions." He looked at her; surely he had just overstepped his bounds.

She smiled, a Mona Lisa smile. "Check the *time* if you want to know more."

"Oookay," Trace said, thinking he followed her meaning.

"Then, fly straight. Perfectly . . . straight."

"I understand," Trace said.

"Good. Any other burning questions?"

Teens both shook their heads.

"Thank you for the tour," Dominique said, beating Trace to the punch.

"We enjoyed having you both," the Captain said. "And if you—"

The bridge door hissed open, and the Security Officer stood in the doorway.

"Sorry—hope I'm no' intruding?" DeBrus asked.

"Not at all," the Captain said evenly. "Our guests were just finishing their tour."

"Aye, Cap'n. Miss Van der Waal, I believe Yeoman Daniels might have sommat interesting for ye to help with, down on Deck five," he said to Dominique. "And Mister Worthington, ye're with me."

"Uh, sure."

"Right this way, lad. Captain. Lieutenant."

DeBrus escorted Trace from the bridge, and Dominique followed them out.

The bridge door closed. DeBrus shuffled to the rail, gripped it, and spoke over his shoulder. "Let's go."

He pushed off gently, down and across. Trace turned to Dominique. "I guess I'll see you later?"

"Oh ye—I mean, sure, if you like." She brushed hair behind her ear, looking down, then back up to make eye contact before he left.

"Okay." He smiled and made to follow the Security Officer. Dominique stayed near the railing, watching Trace go. Then she looked around for Yeoman Daniels.

Back inside the Bridge, Telore turned to the Captain. "*O-B-A-F-G-K-M* . . . did we just give that poor boy an *in* with the Starship princess?"

The Captain shrugged. "Up to them both I suppose—Doc suggested they be put together for this Bridge tour, right? Diffuse the tension, maybe? Maybe we should call him Doc 'Amour' instead of Belvoir."

Telore laughed, whispering *O-B-A-F-G-K-M* and shaking his head as he turned back to his screens. He noticed on the Bridge door camera the Teagardens had arrived outside and were chatting with Dominique at the railing. "Our next two are here, Ma'am."

She floated to the door and opened it to greet them.

Dominique drifted down through the core, in search of Yeoman Daniels.

She also drifted through Trace's thoughts, living there rent-free.

Chapter Thirteen

Light and Dark

"What have you roped me into?" Trace muttered to himself, following DeBrus down and away from the Bridge. DeBrus heard him.

"I'd like your help with some security sweeps, are ye up for it?"

"What's involved?"

"We'll stop in at the security office and fetch up a hand-held scanner, then scan each deck, one by one. And since ye've got other tasks on your list, it'll be jus' one deck a day until we've scanned the entire Starship."

"Okay then," Trace said with a smile. X-Ray vision sounded pretty darn cool.

On Deck 2 opposite the dining area, the Security suite included a lockable inner room, which at this moment served as storage.

"Tha's the brig as well," DeBrus said, indicating the closet space.

"Does it get used often?"

"Rarely. Twice in all my crossings, just minor matters. Nothing criminal, just personal disagreements."

"Personal disagreements?"

"Vigorous personal disagreements."

DeBrus opened the small cell, extracted one hand-held scanner from its charging bay, and then grabbed the other. He re-sealed the brig's transparent door.

"Which deck should we start with? And mind, I'm expecting ye to keep track o' where we start and where we finish, so nothin's missed."

"We don't scan people's cabins, right?"

"Only with probable cause, on Captain's orders. Faking probable cause to search someone's personal space is a felony, so no."

Trace chose one at random. "Okay, then, how about Deck 6, the fitness center?"

"Deck 6 it is. Here, try not to let it get banged up as we go." He passed Trace one of the scanners and a holster, which trace belted around his waist. The scanner itself looked like a cross between a ray gun and a tricorder.

"Lead on, then." Trace pushed off, floating up and across, with DeBrus close behind.

They lighted on Deck 6, where DeBrus held his scanner for Trace to see its functions. He showed how to adjust brightness, focus, and penetration depth.

"Depending on the material, she can see inside a wall or a carry-on case, for example, up to about 30 centimeters, or one foot. At that depth though, the image on the screen here is a wee bit fuzzy. So I like to keep it at 15 cm."

Trace nodded.

"Hold out your hand."

"You're kidding?"

"It's harmless. I'd have to turn it to maximum and leave it scanning your brain continuously for six months before there's even a slight risk."

"Um, okay, if you're sure." He held out his hand. DeBrus dialed the depth to its best clarity, minimum penetration—3 cm.

DeBrus scanned Trace's right hand. Right on the screen, Trace could see a part of his own skeleton—the carpals and metacarpals just above his wrist, and his finger bones themselves, the *phalanges*.

"That is so cool." Trace said in awe, flexing his fingers. The bones moved on the screen.

"Wha's this, right there? Do ye not know how to throw a proper punch?"

"What do you m—oh, my index finger? No, I just jammed it trying to block my friend Peter on a rebound—a bad day shooting hoops. That was years ago, and I broke it across the growth plate . . . never grew straight again."

"Sounds like an intense game. Ye've got skills, then?"

"This white boy can jump, if that's what you're asking." DeBrus laughed, a deep belly laugh.

"So ye broke it, bu' not in a proper fight."

"I've never had to take a swing at anyone in my life."

"We shall have to remedy that, I reckon. Show ye a bit o' the rough and tumble."

Trace just looked at him, not sure what to say . . . his smile stayed pasted on.

"Yeeeahhh . . ."

"Anyways, scanning. Since there's few in here at the moment, it should go quickly. Just watch how I do the scan for one section, how I sweep, where I pause for a closer look. After I finish the theater, we can work side by side until the deck is cleared."

DeBrus scanned around a water dispenser, pointing out where the water lines and electrical lines came in.

"If ye see something that looks enclosed, or a line or bundle in purple or blue, flag it and let me know. Understand?"

"Right, get to it then."

They cut through the fitness center quickly, only interrupting a few passengers in their workout routine. They got out of the way with minimal fuss—it's not wise to mouth off to a guy who looked like Thor, the god of thunder, fathered a baby with a WWE Women's Grand Champion, who was probably born ripped with three percent body fat.

They stood and got out of DeBrus' way without having to be asked.

The man called Trace closer. "Okay now, did ye see how I adjusted the depth from 3.0 to 15.0 whenever I looked through an object mounted on the floor, or wherever metal was present?"

Trace nodded.

"I'd like ye to make the same adjustments when scanning over equipment, mounted screens, and so forth. We still need t' see into the walls a bit."

Trace got started, turning dials as the man watched.

"No, not like tha—yea, that's it," he said, and Trace quickly got the hang of it.

He felt like they were making good time; only the outer walls, showers, and saunas remained in the Fitness Center.

"Nothin' amiss, you take the walls over there and I'll tackle the showers and saunas while they're empty."

Trace nodded, eyeing the end of a tall, flat air duct that ran horizontally along the wall, midway between floor and ceiling. It ended in a low, wide grate pushing a steady stream of cool air into the area. As Trace lined up to scan along the air duct itself, the image showed a blank.

Pure metal, probably thin aluminum, he thought. He made to adjust the scanner's depth while holding his spot, but he fumbled the scanner, which slipped from his grasp.

He made a mad grab at the spinning instrument before it could whack anything, and thumped his elbow on the air duct near the vent, leaving it rattling slightly and nailing his funny bone, the ulnar nerve, as he learned in human physiology class in C-Springs. A weird tingling ran down his arm to his pinky, but thankfully the scanner was undamaged.

"Ow," he said, shaking his hand a bit for the tingling to wear off. Trace looked at his elbow, hoping his shipsuit had been damaged.

"All right there?"

"I'm fine, it's just . . . I think I knocked something loose inside this what's it called? The bulkhead, the vent."

"Knocked it loose? No, that can't be. Let's have a look." DeBrus squinted, popping open the long vent on its hinge where it was clamped in place. He peered in.

"Everything all right?" Trace asked.

"Hm. Oh aye, there's something must have knocked loose inside. I'm sure it's nothing to concern yourself over, and since we're just abou' finished here, why don't ye head to the mess deck and grab a bite. I'll finish up here."

"Um, okay," Trace hesitated. "But don't you wanna scan that location?"

"It's metal, I'll take a proper look. So, off with ye now. We'll meet same time tomorrow and have a look around the opposite side of Deck 6. You keep that scanner to practice with, but mind you don't use anywhere there's people or their personal spaces. Understand?"

"I understand. See you tomorrow." Trace left. Something was very off.

Watching him go, DeBrus turned and scanned the duct work, his screen showing more fuzz than actual detail. Something had been stuck inside the vent, but where he scanned it, he found a black section with *no return image*. Black screen.

He switched the scanner off and holstered it, peeking inside the vent. "All right . . . no wires, no pressure plates, no bolts . . . let's see what ye're all about."

He fumbled at the top and bottom inside the two-foot tall opening, and after a moment extracted a black case, very thin and shiny, like hard plastic. DeBrus looked around, then slapped the hinged air vent shut. He ran the scanner over the plastic case's smooth surface, and looked at the image.

Then he nearly dropped the scanner.

He reached up to his headset and flipped it to the Command Channel. Selecting a private, secure command link, he tapped the mike. He spoke in a low tone.

"Captain? DeBrus here."

"Go ahead."

"Cap'n, ye'll want t'be meeting me at your earliest opportunity. I've found sommat . . . interesting—regards our extra mass."

"Threat assessment?"

"No immediate danger, mum, but we've got quite an expert smuggler on our hands."

"My cabin, two mike. I'll bring the Lieutenant."

The channel beeped in their ears. Richter's voice.

"Captain, I also have just made a discovery," Richter said, breaking into their conversation.

"Very well. My cabin."

Both men acknowledged. DeBrus released the headset call button and gently held the case by its edges, hands visibly trembling for the first time in years.

He looked around, seeing only a couple passengers absorbed in their workouts, and he pushed off toward the core, cradling his cargo carefully with one hand.

What DeBrus didn't know was Trace had hidden himself just past the railing and was peeking through a small gap in the railing to discover why he had been acting so strangely.

Trace ducked out of sight until DeBrus disappeared over Deck 7's railing. The Captain's cabin door whooshed open, then shut.

* * *

With the scanning of Deck 6 cut short, Trace decided to use the time following the Captain's clues about the micrometeorite entry and exit wounds in the core. He floated over to the three clocks, thinking this might be what she meant by 'time.'

He searched around the Ship's Time display, peeking around and under where the clock was mounted. Nothing unusual there.

The other two, mounted extremely flat against the wall, he could not see under as easily. He rolled up a sleeve and slid his hand up under the Voyage Clock as far as he could. It was smooth everywhere he could reach. Then, the Mission clock. He swept his hand against the bulkhead and felt a small, raised bump in the otherwise smooth wall. He shined his handy phone light behind it and the patch was a slightly different color, as though it had been welded and re-painted. Entry wound located! He snapped a photo.

He turned around, and pointed himself directly across the core, as perfectly straight across as he could estimate. The line of sight led directly back into the fitness center, toward one of the rowing machines mounted upside down to the ceiling. He checked for other passengers nearby, then pushed off and crossed straight back into the fitness center. He slipped past some stationary cycles, only one of them occupied just below him, and then he saw it. Right beside several Velcro patches, one currently holding a workout towel, he saw a blemish—a small depression. The spot that had been filled in and repainted, a near-match with the bulkhead. He touched the spot gingerly; clearly, this was the exit. He snapped another photo with his handy phone.

Whatever had burst through where the Mission Clock now hung must have been super dense to have kept its shape for not one, but two kinetic impacts. He tried to visualize the line it had followed after punching through this spot, exiting into space and leaving the whole core in a vacuum. He inhaled deeply, feeling the momentary fear of trying to breathe in a vacuum.

"Um, that's my gym towel, is there something you need?" Mr. Teagarden asked him, not unkindly. Trace turned around.

"Oh, I, . . . was just looking for something, but I'm good now. Sorry to disturb you," Trace stammered.

Mr. Teagarden smiled and nodded, continuing his pedaling and running his fingertips across a sweaty brow.

Trace went to the rail, then dived down to visit Engineering. Richter would be surprised he had found the answer, he knew it . . . but the Engineer was nowhere to be found.

He shrugged and returned to his cabin, planning to message Richter about it later.

* * *

While Trace was fiddling around with clocks and fitness center walls, DeBrus and Richter both arrived at the Captain's quarters, each bearing a package.

She buzzed them in.

The X-O locked the door behind them, and the four sat around the Captain's small staff table.

"Gentlemen, what do you have?"

"After you?" Richter offered.

"Uh, no, this needs to be opened last," he said, hand resting on the 2½ -foot by 3-foot plastic case.

"As you wish." Richter peeled back the first layer of wrappings.

"Cigars, right? I can smell them," Lieutenant Telore mused, looking at the case as Richter peeled away the wrappings.

"Yes, correct. Captain, we have here some Himalayan Gurkha Kukri Reals, nearly a full case in this travel humidor. It was attached under the primary blue-green algae air scrubbers . . . perhaps to mask the smell." He set the case on her desk, gently holding it in place. "I had to look it up—each costs more than all of us earn, combined, for this Crossing."

"That's . . . millions of dollars. For each one?"

Richter nodded.

"Any indication who put them there?"

"I am not a forensics expert, maybe there are fingerprints inside? The humidor timer shows it is two months along already for the 8-month freshness rating."

"Someone stashed it long before any of us boarded. Standard smuggling, port to port," Captain Strahan guessed.

"Aye, it's unlikely whoever placed them is even aboard. Still, some are missing?"

"Two cigars missing, if I counted correctly."

"The air filters—at least one was smoked already. A port technician perhaps, probably unaware he was burning up a million dollars," DeBrus said, shaking his head. "Still, it's peanuts to this." He raised up the plastic case, perfectly smooth and reflective.

"Lieutenant, I'll steady the case if you'd prefer to do the honors. The pressure safety catch is . . . just here. If my hand scanner showed true . . . ye'll no' likely believe your eyes."

Telore reached out and touched the case with his fingertips.

"Hazardous?"

"Nay . . . but be careful," DeBrus advised. "What's inside is, well . . . ye'll see."

Telore examined the exquisite box, roughly 2.5 by 3 feet, and just three inches thick. He gave it a gentle wiggle, like a kid gently checking out a

Christmas gift.

"It has almost no mass." He looked the case over. "And a vacuum protection case this thin must be . . . ridiculously expensive."

"A custom piece, no doubt," DeBrus said.

Telore looked at the hinges, then turned it back over. A simple latch popped open with the flip of his finger. The barest hint of air escaping.

He lifted the lid, allowing the contents to float free.

Telore gasped.

The captain raised a hand to her mouth in shock.

A painting . . . a painting floated gently up, turning slowly as it rose. A painting that had been missing more than two hundred years, thought lost forever.

Streaks of oil on canvas contrasted with others in the background, a perfect blending of blues, cast in light and dark. Golden spheres and bright points glowed with impressionistic perfection of the night sky just before sunrise . . . the moon and Venus looked down on a small village in *Saint-Rémy-de-Provence,* France. Gently frayed edges at both sides of its frame gave the painting a . . . humble feel.

"This is . . . nein. *Unglaublich . . .*" Richter murmured in awe.

DeBrus broke the silence.

"May I present our eighty-ninth passenger, Vincent Van Gogh."

"*Starry Night,*" the captain murmured reverently.

No one spoke.

* * *

Trace rested back in his bunk, tapping his viewscreen through a few video messages from his fellow hooligans back in Colorado Springs. Nothing new from Jeni, despite his quiet hopes.

He scrolled through personal messages, and opened a few new DMs waiting for him—one, from the Doc, shared ideas about alleviating boredom by setting a challenge, difficult to overcome but not entirely impossible, like writing a book in the four months remaining.

"Yeah right," Trace muttered, but still holding the 'challenge' idea in his thoughts. Maybe he'd do something physical—a test of accuracy or some strength-based challenge. He'd rather perfect the *DeBrus Space Jump,* as he started imagining it.

Another DM contained a ship-wide reminder to always keep aware of one's location and know the fastest route to the Fallout Shelter. Nothing surprising there.

He tapped open a message that had an "M.A.C." sender generic address. It had a single line of text and a large video file attached. Trace put in his Ear Pods and played the video message. A very pretty brunette, girl-next-door type, with shoulder-length wavy hair appeared on the screen.

She smiled.

"Hi Trace? My name's Chrissy, and I've been assigned as your Mars Welcome Ambassador. And since I believe Ambassadors carry the honorary title of 'Your Excellency,' I expect all your vid-messages to start that way."

She giggled and crinkled her nose.

Trace sat up. This one had a sense of humor and . . . some sass to her.

"Anyways, it says here I should tell you a little bit about myself, and since I've never done this before, I don't really know what I'm doing. Ummmm . . . ."

"I'm in high school, just started 5.0. I think for you that's eleventh grade? Yeah, here they don't have full numbers for every high school year; instead we have Martian Standard Years, one through six, I think you'd call that K through 12? But we take extended breaks at every half-year. What year are you in school? Do you miss it? Were there mountains where you lived? Hmmm, what else . . ."

"I'm really into cosmetology, that's my focus, so I spend a lot of time in the Arts and Trades hallway of our school here. It's Mons High, and we're the Olympians. Olympus Mons, Mons Olympians, get it? You'll love this school, it's

one of three places here in the capital where we have real windows that look out across the landscape. From my Film Trades classroom, we can see the mountains to the North, they're on the horizon, and the desert plains below, pretty big solar fields . . ."

"Mmm, did you know they filmed the "Anchorhead" mini-series down on the plains right below our school? They used an old driving waystation. But the Beggar's Canyon parts were done in the Night Labyrinth, which is really, really far away. Oh, have you seen Anchorhead? I shouldn't assume."

"I'm sure they want me to share more, but I'll end my rambling. It also says here that I'm to invite you to video me back any time you like, but no more than once per day, three minutes max, to save on bandwidth or something. Anyways, vid me back! Nice to meet you! And in the words of the immortal Frank Herbert, tell me of your home world, Usul."

Chrissy's vid ended mid-smile, then faded to the Mars Arrival Center (M.A.C.) logo.

He watched Chrissy's video again, to try to get a read on the kind of person she was, whether she could hold her half of the conversation. So far, first impressions, yes. He knew he really liked her personality. Nice. Girl next door. Funny. And she had read *Dune*, his late grandfather's favorite novel.

* * *

"So, it's a start," Sergeant DeBrus said to the officers and engineer.

"Right, so there's definitely more contraband, correct?" Telore asked, gently closing the vacuum case with *Starry Night* safely nestled back inside.

"This is all nine kilos at the most, including the case. This leaves another eighty or ninety kilos somewhere on board."

The Captain pondered for a moment.

"Very well. Leave me *Starry Night*; the New York Metropolitan

Museum of Art will probably be wanting it back. I'll secure it in my safe, here in the Captain's locker.

Mister DeBrus, let's set a hidden camera watching the stash location—Deck 6 was it? Okay, Deck 6. Someone will want to keep tabs on it, make sure it's still there, undiscovered."

"Aye, mum. And we can set one on the algae matrix processors as well, see if someone comes back for another cigar."

The Captain nodded.

"Gentlemen, what do you think—theories so far?"

"Ma'am, it could not have been put there by a passenger on launch day. One of the crew, possible, bu' it's no likely. My money's on both these items having been put there by the ground crew or dock workers weeks before we lifted from Earth. A lot of technicians coming and going before we left."

"So someone will come to retrieve it in the days or weeks after we land." The captain turned to Telore. "Lieutenant, where are we slated to land?"

"*Nav Com* has us putting in at *Port Mons,* ma'am," Telore replied.

"The capital. Hmm, maybe this is our chance to catch at least this one. Let them try to come aboard after we land—catch them retrieving it."

Telore nodded appreciatively. "That would work."

"Double your efforts, gentlemen. Explosives are not as forgiving as I am."

* * *

Trace tabbed back to his unread messages. The last unread was a local user-to-user note, clearly not from Earth or Mars.

'StarParty' was the sender's nickname; he hovered over the nickname to show the person's first and last name, but it came back as private-blocked.

He smelled a rat; someone could be messing with him.

"Richter, what are you up to? Fool me once . . ."

He clicked the message open. It was a poem in fancy, lacy lettering.

She hides, without revealing
Suppresses all the feelings
He searches and finds
Like a private eye's mind

He read the message a few times, trying to understand it. The message was incomplete, and the three dots suggested more would follow. Confused, he tried to reply back, but the address was hidden and blocked. He had to wait. Someone was toying with him.

Sleep did not come easily.

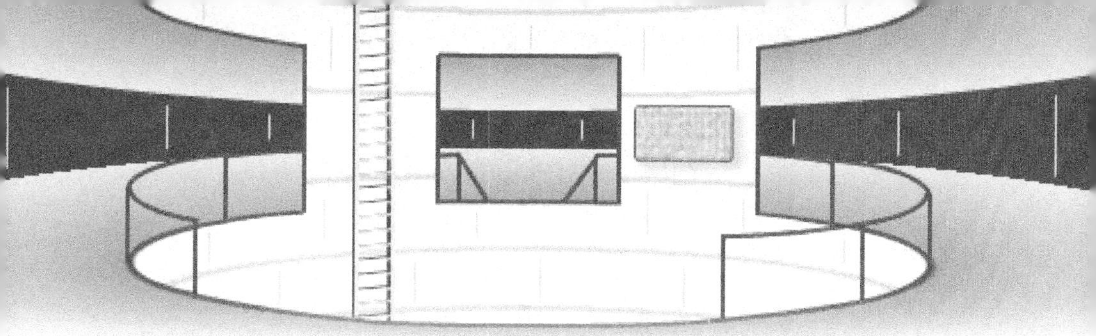

Chapter Twelve

With a Friend

“Next morning, his mind woke before 5:00 A.M. as before. No message waiting.

He slipped out quietly, heading down for coffee, wary for Richter in the low lighting of the Core before hours.

The coffee was tasty, he was getting used to it—almost looking forward to it now.

He opted to get in some gaming, logging in to one of the gaming stations and exploring the dangerous parts of the Dark Elf City with his Duergar Dwarf wandering around wearing a +3 *Ring of Disguising & Concealment* so they wouldn't slaughter him on sight. He was getting good at being stealthy.

Killing more than two hours this way, eventually his tablet buzzed in his shipsuit chest pocket. He got his character to a safe spot and saved his progress.

He tapped open the message waiting for him. “StarParty” had sent him another quartet of rhymes. It read:

Climb the boughs of the tree
After ten, meet with me
Where the moon was ours
And we count all the stars

Then it started falling into place—someone wanted to meet him at ten up under the *AstroDome.* After curfew? Seemed risky. And who did he share the moon with? His heart quickened at the thought.

"What's the punishment for being out after curfew, I wonder?" Trace mused, trying to sleep but failing utterly. Tonight could not come fast enough.

The day passed eventfully, but without any further intrigue. He watched a feature with his sister after they grabbed breakfast, he met up with DeBrus to finish scanning Deck 6, and he got an intense workout, doubling his aerobic time and spending ten minutes in the sauna after some strength training. Lunch and Dinner were tucked in there somewhere; parts of the day were a blur.

At last the lights dimmed in the Starship. An hour to go.

Trace sent a light-hearted reply to his Mars Ambassador, describing where he came from in Colorado, and asked her a few basic questions about the various places on mars worth visiting.

The clock read 9:37 P.M..

He checked and re-checked his messages, but nothing interesting showed up. Doc asked to meet with him for next week's appointment, which he acknowledged. Louise lounged up in her bunk, direct-video chatting with Kasia, who presumably was in her own bunk doing the same.

When the clock read 9:52 P.M., Trace eased out of his bunk.

"Where do you think you're going? It's curfew," Louise hissed from the top bunk.

"Not for another eight minutes," Trace said, holding up his handy phone for her to see, 9:52 PM displayed. "Go to sleep."

She hissed at him playfully, then lay back, resuming her chat with Kasia.

He stood in front of the cabin mirror, fixed his wavy hair in the front and straightened his shipsuit. If his suspicions were correct, he wanted to look good.

Six minutes to go. Better get up top and avoid being noticed along the way. He imagined having his character's ring of concealment—how handy that would come in right about now.

"Don't follow me, li'l brat," he said as the door hissed open.

"Yeah, yeah . . ." she kept her eyes on her screen.

The door slid shut behind him, and he floated to the rail, scanning up and down for anyone else out and about at this late hour. All the lights in the core were down to their night time setting, under the dim blue glow, with most common areas cast in shadow.

He eased around the Deck 4 walkway, going hand-over-hand along the railing, until he reached one of the two ladders running up and down the core. Satisfied no one else was about, he eased over the edge and gently pulled himself up the ladder, rung by rung.

Silence all along the way. He passed under a couple camera globes on the ceiling, hoping no one was monitoring at that exact moment.

He eased over the top of Deck 8. Deeper darkness. The stars above and a lone theater-seating light, set low on the wall under the Bridge sight line, were the only sources of light here. He found his chair in the dark, not seeing anyone else around.

Just as he was beginning to think it was a trick or a no-show, soft, delicate hands closed over his eyes.

"Guess who?" came a whisper, right in his ear. He could smell Dominique's perfume, just a hint stronger this time.

"Ohai," he said, a big smile on his face.

"You look like Brayden Redford in the dark, did anybody ever tell you that?"

"Ha ha, I could look like Brayden Jingle Heimer Schmitt in the dark just as easily."

She punched his arm. "So coy," she said.

She was just a silhouette as well, with the barest hint of light accenting the curve of her cheek and her cute little nose. Her eyes were cast in darkness, and he couldn't see much of the rest of her either. She eased into the seat beside him, the one she had sat in for the Lunar Slingshot.

"So, I was hoping that was you. Nice poetry, by the way."

"Thank you. I wanna be a writer someday, or even better, an artist. Maybe a runway fashion designer? I suppose we'll see." She shrugged. "Maybe daddy will just put me in charge of one of his hotels, who knows."

"So, I have to ask—I didn't think you liked me much before; I'm curious about what changed your mind?"

"I liked the way you stood up to me without being mean about it. I put on a princess act sometimes, I can admit that, but it's mostly to meet Daddy's expectations. I feel like with you, I can drop the act."

Trace nodded, not knowing if she wanted to share more. The light fabric covering their seats wasn't enough to stop them floating up, so lap belts did the trick.

"Feels like we're buckling in for a roller coaster ride, sitting side by side like this," Trace said, leaning in.

"I've never been on a roller coaster; they look really dangerous."

"It's the thrill that makes it so much fun," Trace said. "Remember what the Captain said? There's a roller coaster a mile tall on Mars."

"Ugh, that's terrifying. What if something went wrong?"

"Hm. It's lower gravity, so I guess you'd have a lot longer to panic about it as you fell?"

Her eyes wide, she said, "how awful."

"I've been on hundreds back on Earth with my buddies. They're pretty safe."

The backs of their hands touched, resting on the armrest. It felt like static electricity, with the hairs on the back of his wrist brushing her smooth, flawless skin.

On impulse, he brushed against her hand more deliberately, and she turned it over to interlace her fingers with his. He was glad his palm was not sweaty. Her hand felt smooth, slender, soft in his.

His breathing increased a little, but he held his breath to stop it from showing.

"So what kind of, um, art are you into?"

"I like the avant-garde stuff—the *decadence* movement is fascinating. *Cubist* and *post-impressionist* are close runners-up for me as well."

"I'm not too familiar."

"*Decadence* was all about excesses and extreme sensations. Think of it like the adrenaline rush of being at your favorite band's concert while they blast out your favorite hit song—captured in strokes of a brush. There are older *decadence* works that are far more . . . risqué."

"And the others? *Impressionist* and . . . "

"*Cubist*? Well, *impressionism* is a style where you can see every brush stroke, they don't fade into one another. Individually, up close, it looks rough, but if you step back, and let your eyes relax, you see not only what the artist saw, but actual depth and movement in the painting."

"Paintings move? Like, they feel animated?"

"Not literally. I just like that a 2-D impressionist master work can convey great depth, but only if we step back and keep a broader perspective." She stared through Trace, as though seeing something far away.

"Wow . . . that was . . . deep."

She snapped out of her faraway gaze. "Um, yeah, it's like so *topper*."

Trace smiled. He wasn't sure what caused her articulate, deep analysis of art concepts to flip back to a ditzy teenager persona. It was a jolt, and again he wasn't sure what he should say.

She gently played her fingertips in his palm.

"Look, Mars."

They both looked up at the pale pink dot, now un-missable in the sky. Mars cried out to be noticed, looked at.

"Our future home," he mused. When he looked at Mars, Chrissy's face floated through his thoughts. Dominique's feather-touch fingertips in his hand brought him back to her.

They talked about the constellations they could see, even imagined that some of the smudgy dots outside might be entire galaxies. At times they stared up through the windows, not saying anything, just sharing the view of the Universe ahead of them.

At length, she unbuckled herself and stood, booties adhering to the carpet. He stood and faced her.

"So . . . midnight. We should probably wrap up our . . ."

"Uh, yeah," Trace said. "I get the feeling breaking curfew this much might be frowned upon . . . I had fun."

"Me too," she said, running a finger across his chest, and poking him gently in the name badge. "Mister . . . Worthington." She smiled up at him. He started to lean in just a little.

"Oh hey, that reminds me, do you have anyone to hang with at the Party?" she asked.

"Um, which party?"

"*Transition*, silly boy. It's still weeks away, but it is the biggest social event of the entire Crossing." She smiled again, eyes bright.

"I, uh, haven't thought about that part—I'm not really a dancing in public kind of guy."

"Well, maybe you should . . think about it." She turned away. He reluctantly let her hand go, and she floated over to the Deck 8 railing, looking down into the core. She turned to face him, leaning against the rail as he approached her.

There at the railing, he gave her a hug good night, a snug full-body embrace with her arms up around his neck. He kept his hands gently around her back. She gave him a peck on the cheek and let the hug go.

She slipped gracefully over the railing. Turning to face him, she dropped herself down into the core, giving him a little wave as she floated down and out of sight.

Trace lingered at the railing, a jumble of emotions. She was nice and fun to chat with when she wasn't posturing for attention or acting superior to everyone else.

When he could no longer see her, it occurred to Trace—Dominique had asked him nothing about himself, his background, his interests, his future; not one question. He had explored all these things with her.

Benefit of the doubt, he thought. Maybe she was too shy to ask.

He returned to his cabin as stealthily as he could, easing into his bunk while Louise breathed softly above him. He set an early alarm—he was expected to help DeBrus scan a different deck in the morning. Then he had to keep messaging Chrissy. Early start.

* * *

"When ye finish scanning that bulkhead, we'll be done with Deck 7."

Trace nodded.

"Then we'll put the gear away and I've got sommat' to show ye."

"We're not scanning those rooms over there?"

"That's crew quarters and life support. So no."

"Gotcha. That's where exo-suits, uh, EVA-suits, are stowed, correct?"

"No exo-suits in there. They're all kept below."

"So you saw no Exo-suits hanging up inside?"

"I scanned it thoroughly yesterday—I think I'd have noticed them in m'way, when I scanned."

Trace nodded once, confused. Richter had said . . .

"Speaking of lasses and late night . . ." DeBrus raised his eyebrows and looked at Trace. "Did a bit o' stargazing, did we?"

"Oh, that. You saw? Um—it was . . . nothing."

"I know. I know it was a nothin'. If it had been a somethin', we'd be having a different sort o' chat right now."

"Are you talking about curfew?"

"There's no right punishment for breaking curfew, but don't tell anyone I told ye that. No. It's getting frisky with a lady in common area that'll land ye in a heap o' trouble. Keep that in private spaces, all right?"

"All I did was hold her hand."

"Then ye're a gentleman. Never sacrifice your gentleman's ways for some cheap thrill . . . and remember that aboard a Starship, ye're watched all the time."

Murmuring to himself, "handy to know." Trace finished his last sweep with the scanner; DeBrus inspected his screen and nodded approval.

"All right, this way then."

DeBrus led the way out of the fitness area toward the Deck 2 Security Suite.

He nodded a hello to Mr. Richter as the man passed them, headed down toward the *oculus* from the Bridge. Richter gave them both a short wave back, sipping his drink pouch as he floated downward.

DeBrus opened his office on Deck 2, and stowed both scanners, locking them safely in the brig-closet.

"Now, let's go out near the *oculus* and have a look about."

They righted themselves a few feet aside of the *oculus*, soft boots adhering to the Velcro-carpeted floor here.

"Whups, 'scuse me," Yeoman Daniels said as he passed by, disappearing down through the *oculus* after DeBrus gave way. Trace nodded a hello as Daniels passed by.

"Ye asked me a few weeks ago how I perfected my flying technique. Well, today I'll show ye the biggest part. Try not to think of it as the entire distance, as ye see from 'ere. In fact, let's go jus' halfway up between top and bottom."

DeBrus launched himself off the carpeted Deck 2 toward the dorsal-side ladder. He grabbed the rungs, one-handed, right at Deck 5.

Trace gripped the Deck 5 railing a few feet right of DeBrus, stopping his momentum. The man sipped at his coffee. Pausing his drinking, he casually tossed the half-full pouch upward as he pointed across and down.

"So, take a look down and visualize the last half of your dive. From this mid-point, ye can plan your dive and un-crouch at this point to properly manage your rotation and your pathway."

Trace looked down for a moment, visualizing how he would come out of a tumble or a roll as he fell toward the *oculus*, four floors below. Then he looked across, estimating they were slightly above halfway. "So those three screens straight across, are they halfway? And why are two of them counting the same number again? Seems unnecessary."

Trace referred to twin flatscreens on either side of the opposite ladder, both showing the same display in bright red numbers: **51:14:44:45**. The seconds were ticking upward on both, as one might expect. A third screen showed Earth time, the Julian Date and GMT, in blue digits.

"That screen on the right, the one labeled "Voyage" . . . that one is our voyage clock."

"No kidding," Trace said, with typical teenage snottiness.

"All right, young pup. That's the clock that at our exact mid-point in the journey . . . stops, freezes for a full second, then begins running in reverse, basically a countdown until our landing on Mars."

"Oh, that's right, I remember the Captain mentioning," Trace said, looking at the right clock. "So I'm guessing the other clock is our Mission clock?" he asked, reading the obvious label.

"Aye, and it'll keep counting up, tracking the total mission time for the entire Crossing."

"So, like a big stopwatch."

"Indeed. Like a bloody big stopwatch. And matching your cheeky little attitude this morning, I've got two tasks for ye, and I'll be wanting them both done by midday today, ship's time."

Trace instinctively glanced at an aqua-colored screen, mounted and centered above the twin red *Voyage* and *Mission* digits. Ship's time showed 06:41 (L).

"Okay, what two things am I doing before noon?"

"If we're set to land in Martian month number 15, the 6th day, at 7:53:09 in the morning local time at Port Mons . . . and we departed Earth on Saturday, November 7th, 2353, at 8:03 in the morning local time, then at exactly what time, displayed on the mission clock, will it stop and then begin to count down?"

At the mention of Earth, Trace's mind jumped to Jeni.

He shook her face free in his mind, trying to stay focused. He grabbed his handy phone out of its pocket and started entering the numbers.

"Okay, you said the 15th Martian month, 6th day . . . wait, Mars has how many months?"

"Twenty-four. All are 28 days, with two weeks extra tacked on for the New Year."

"And the landing time you said . . . was?"

"At 7:53:09 in the morning."

"Sounds simple enough." Trace finished entering the numbers for later use and stuck the device back in the shipsuit pocket.

"Did I mention you won't be using AI to predict your answer?"

"Now wait, that's not fa—"

"No' fair, is it? I'm challenging you to use your brain, young Worthington, not some bloody AI to do all your thinkin' for ye."

Trace just looked at DeBrus, annoyed at the request.

"It's a man who knows how to think analytically who is able to keep his wits. And a man who keeps his wits in a crisis, when all others are losing theirs . . . that's the man who'll live out the day. Think of it as giving your brain some much-needed exercise. How much of a workout do you give your mind day-to-day, eh?"

"Not a lot, I guess. Just input-output all day long, I guess?"

"Aye, and people who don't work at it can never stretch. So if a crisis comes on them, they'll run in panicky little circles until it's too late to think of a solution. So, use your brain, ye'll be right as rain."

Trace thought about it. "If you're taking away my best instruments for accuracy, then we need a prize for when I nail it . . . perfectly."

"Prize? What're ye on abou' now?"

"If I'm within one minute of the actual clock stop, then you pay Richter . . . 400 Martian creds."

"He'll ne'er agree to it. And that's a lot of money. Say 50. And ye'll be within thirty seconds to earn that amount."

"I'm sure you'll win it back from him. 300 credits, and I have to be within ten seconds. Oh, and one more thing—if I am within ten seconds . . . the only way Richter can collect it, is he must receive it at the party. Or he gets nothing."

"Oh, you're making this far too simple for me—he loathes parties. Plus, ye'll ne'er be so accurate."

"Then there's no real risk, is there? Okay, if I lose, say I'm more than ten minutes off the mark, above or below, then . . . I'll clean the security workspaces and the brig every day for the rest half of the voyage."

DeBrus thought about it. "Five minutes off. Any more than five either way, an' I'll have ye working like a dog."

Trace thought for a moment. "Agreed."

"Very well; 300 credits, aye."

They shook hands to seal the bet. DeBrus held the handshake until Trace looked him in the eye. Then he let the handshake go.

Trace rubbed his sore hand.

"Okay, now that's settled, what's the second thing?"

"Right. Remember our first All Hands meeting, what the Captain told us?"

"She said a lot of things."

"Do ye recall her telling you to never take your eyes off of objects floating loose abou' the Starship?"

"I remember."

"Well, ye just took your eyes off coffee pouch that was in my hand not two moments ago. Find where it went. Bring that to me before noon as well. And your calculation better be within thirty seconds of reality."

"But what about the perfect jum—"

"More abou' that, another time. For now, use your head."

"Um—"

But before Trace could utter another word, DeBrus launched across the core towards the bridge, muttering something about *bloody edjits* and parties.

Trace watched him go, then looked beyond, scanning the levels above the bridge, up, under the dome, wondering where DeBrus' coffee pouch might have floated off to.

He muttered a short obscenity under his breath and pushed off, trying to visualize the direction the Sergeant-at-Arms had flung his coffee pouch. He scanned ahead, all directions as he floated upward, head on a swivel. No sign of the pouch.

* * *

"Lieutenant, I have an update on the Van Gogh. Well, the case."

"You tracked down who it was made for?"

"Not a person, but the organization, aye. The manufacturer refused to divulge the client, which we expected. But given this is Interplanetary and concerns an act of smuggling connected with the safety and security of an active Starship *en route*, our request got shoved to the front of the line for a warrant with the Justice Department."

"Well, don't keep me in suspense," Telore said.

"The *Wyvern Corporation*. Well, one of its phony subsidiaries."

"And who do we have on board who's part of tha—"

"One mister Statler Van der Waal."

"Van der Waal? That rich gent who never engages with anyone?"

"Aye. You can bet your Crossing's paycheck they'll have layers of protection, culpable deniability, and lawyers a plenty," DeBrus said. "He may be a ring leader, he may be a patsy . . . who knows?"

"So they will likely never see the inside of a court room."

"Perhaps losing the *Starry Night* is punishment enough. Let *the Met* sort it out; it is their painting, after all."

"You left the empty case back in the air handler?"

"Aye sir, and it's been visited once since then, after curfew and by someone who concealed his face rather well."

"We'd best continue gathering evidence."

"I've got an extensive file," DeBrus said. "We'll have the proper authorities handle it when we get to Mars."

"We're liable to make a few enemies along the way though."

DeBrus shrugged. "We're so very prettier than they are, so yeah."

* * *

A half-hour had gone by, with Trace searching all the decks above the three clocks.

FOD first. Numbers later.

Trace knew he had to search upwards—that's the direction DeBrus had tossed the pouch, that much he was sure of. He floated up to the railing of Deck 7 and held himself there, trying to logically reason out where it might have ended up.

"Okay, what do I know? It blends perfectly with the starry background, if it's stuck up against one of the triangle windows of the *StarDome*. Oh, and I can't search them all without breaking the Bridge Sightline or setting off that blasting alarm. Lovely."

He scanned all the triangles he could easily float near, without getting too close, and without breaking the Bridge Sightline. Scanning methodically, he looked up one row, then down the next, following the curving lines of the struts holding all the *StarDome* windows in place.

Nothing.

He floated to the periphery, and searched the corners, where detritus might gather, or the air handlers might cause loose objects to drift.

Even more nothing. Then he stopped himself.

"Hang on—DeBrus wouldn't have done anything to risk the *StarDome*'s integrity, even something as flimsy as a coffee pouch. And the prox alarm never sounded, right? So the pouch never got close to the *StarDome*. So . . . so, what?

Trace racked his brain some more.

"Oh . . . you sneaky man. You must have had someone up there, a catcher. But who?"

There had to be somebody waiting, patiently waiting above him when he let the pouch go.

Richter? No, he was down in Engineering. Telore? No, he passed them at the *oculus* as Trace and DeBrus headed upward. That left the Captain, the Exec, and the Doc.

Doc started his day early, meeting with patients starting at 8 a.m., sometimes earlier. Logically, it probably wasn't the Doc. And these . . . shenanigans . . . seemed beneath the Captain. So that left one person. . . he knew who he had to speak with.

But how in the name of Zeus' butthole, would he get Lieutenant Telore to talk with him, one on one? The man practically lived on the Bridge, and that part of the Starship was restricted, off-limits to passengers except for an invited tour.

Could he just knock? Ya right.

Excuse me, Officers of the Watch? Are you secretly holding a coffee pouch hostage in here? He'd never hear the end of it.

So Trace parked himself across from the Bridge. He watched, he waited.

To pass the time, he pulled out his tablet and started his calculations for *Transition*. He flipped back and forth between a Notepad app and his Scientific Calculator, making sure the "AI" option was off. Every so often, he looked up and across at the Bridge hatchway.

No traffic, in or out; he waited.

Skipping breakfast, he waited.

He ran and re-ran his calculations, first using Earth dates and times, then in Mars dates and times. He referenced the moment of launch using Mars years, months, days, hours, minutes. He even remembered to factor in the length of a standard Martian day: 24 hours, 37 minutes.

One challenge was not as clear-cut: *Sidereal time* versus *normal time*. Over the course of one day, there was no real difference between the two. But over the course of half an Earth year, they differed by a lot. *Sidereal time,* which uses stars as a reference for a planet's full rotation, does not actually match the sunrise and sunset. For example, *Orion* (the hunter), from where Trace lived in Colorado, appears in the night sky in Winter, not year-round.

Orion rises over Pike's Peak at a different time in January than it does in June, so from the stars' perspective, a day in January is different from a day in June. Sidereal time.

The day people actually feel, however, is *normal time,* and scientifically labeled as *tropical time.* Normal time is strictly based on the sun rising at a certain time each day, and even that changes season to season because of the tilt of the Earth as it revolves around the sun. June, longer days. January, shorter days. These are not hard things to grasp, but what would the ship's clock use? His one clue was his personal devices—they were still rocking Texahoma time, which also still coincided with 'Ship's time' on the blue clock.

He chose to go with normal time in his calculations—if picked wrong, he'd be cleaning security offices for the next three months. Ugh.

He ran his calculations until the mid-point numbers matched, from both Earth's and Mars' viewpoints.

He jotted down his answer and circled it in the NotePad app: 76:19:15:02.

11:29 A.M. (L).

After an interminable stretch, he checked the clock again.

11:33 A.M. (L).

The pouch was still nowhere to be found, and noon, ship's time, was fast approaching.

11:40 A.M. (L).

No Lieutenant Telore sightings.

Did the man just live up there?

At 11:42 A.M. (L), Trace caught movement across the core. Yes! The Exec finally emerged from the Bridge. Trace pushed off in his direction.

"Excuse, me, Lieutenant, do you have a moment?"

The man nodded, righting himself at the railing so he could look at Trace face to face.

"What's on your mind, Mister Worthington?"

"This may seem strange, but do you have a . . . coffee pouch for me?"

A rare, broad smile split the man's face.

"Oh, that. Well done. Here you go." And from a thigh cargo pocket, he produced a cold, sealed, half-consumed pouch of Hazlenut #4.

Trace accepted it happily. "Thank you."

Telore just smirked, and floated away, off to whatever business drew him out of the Bridge.

Trace brought up the Starship's *OnBoard* app. He opened the messaging function, and searched for DeBrus' name. Finding it immediately, he opened a new direct chat window and typed in his best-guess calculation for the Transition moment: days, hours, minutes, and seconds.

76:19:15:02.

Before sending, he attached a photo of the coffee pouch, held in his hand, with his own bracelet clearly visible to prove it was him.

He confirmed in the 'To' blank: *Sergeant First Class Arthur DeBrus, SN-700(U).*

Arthur? He had never heard the man's first name before, but DeBrus didn't seem like an 'Arthur.' The man seemed more of an 'Angus' or a 'Duncan' or a 'Connor.'

He shrugged and tapped <send> with four minutes remaining before his noon deadline.

Now, food. His belly rumbled and he craved sustenance. He had also missed his allotted window for getting today's workout. He wondered if there would be consequences and made a mental note to visit the gym soon—maybe he could find a treadmill free . . . or that stationary bike next to the puncture spot. Thoughts swirled in his mind.

Food first.

* * *

A few days later, in a long overdue gladiator's match of brute strength versus wits and cunning, Trace came face to face with DeBrus again.

The two gladiators faced off, across the ring from each other, a tiger facing down a kitten. A group of spectators had gathered to watch, some fifteen or twenty people already around the railings.

"Think you'll enjoy receiving a proper punch, sir?"

"Ye've got the strength of a baby . . . do your worst, young pup."

Trace crouched at the dorsal ladder, assuming a Spider-Man pose on the wall, leaving one hand free, extended. He tensed, flexing his knees, bouncing slightly.

DeBrus flexed both legs on either side of the opposite ladder, gripping railings on either side with his ham fists. He looked as though he might rip both railings loose from their mounts and beat Trace with them.

DeBrus cracked his neck left, then right. He gritted his teeth and eyed Trace.

Trace gulped.

"Time fer a bit o' the rough and tumble," the man growled, loud enough for everyone to hear.

DeBrus launched himself right at Trace, hands outstretched.

Trace, having seen how fast the man could move, anticipated the attack and pushed off with his feet, up and across the core. His feet barely cleared DeBrus' grasp and the man swiped tree-trunk arms up at Trace as he passed over his head.

Trace grabbed the railing two decks up and turned to see where his opponent was. DeBrus had already launched himself at Trace and was right behind him.

Trace gripped the railing tight, and rolled his body right, pushing off with his left. His body basically swung aside like a swinging door.

DeBrus wrapped his fist around Trace's right hand on the railing, gripping his fingers down to lock Trace's hand in place, but Trace slipped his fingers free and managed a push-off with his left hand.

He spun in a twisting, drifting motion across the core.

A few more people had gathered at the rails to watch. A few encouraging cheers went up. Trace ignored them.

DeBrus caught up with Trace from behind, one hand gripping Trace's left elbow, the other arm snaking quickly around Trace's neck as they bounced off the deck railing panels.

"Your zero-gee agility isn't bad," DeBrus said, arms locked around Trace's neck gently, not crushing though. "But ye're thinking only in terms of side to side. All your moves are both defensive and predictable."

Trace ran his legs up the bulkhead under the three clocks. He bent his legs, flexing for a push-off, and pulled his left arm free to distract DeBrus. He shoved off the wall, taking them both across and away from the clocks. DeBrus had to use his left arm to stop himself from smacking the ladder on the far side. His right arm still snugged tight under Trace's chin.

"There comes a time when you've got t'take the offensive, surprise your opponent or even capitalize on a mistake he makes. And I don't see ye doing that any time soon."

Trace turned his chin into the crook of DeBrus' inner elbow and lifted on the muscled arm with both hands. Trace's arms flexed with the effort; he slipped down through the man's grasp.

As Trace's head came free, he momentarily let go his left hand's grip on the railing, and he grabbed for Trace's shoulders.

"You talk a lot," Trace said.

Trace swung his right arm in an arc as he drifted downward, connecting his forearm with DeBrus' right knee, setting the man tumbling forward and over Trace's head before he could steady himself.

"And it's not distractin' ye as I believed it would," DeBrus said, arriving across the core at the Deck 6 railing.

Trace shook his head, looking up from the Deck 4 railing. He glanced over DeBrus' shoulder.

"Louise, don't worry, we're just—" and as DeBrus turned to look over his shoulder, Trace launched himself right at DeBrus. Louise wasn't there; it had been a ruse.

DeBrus hadn't fallen for it. He snapped his head back around right after Trace had pushed off, and the man pulled himself straight down by a few feet. Trace's momentum carried him over the railing, past his opponent toward the fitness center machines.

Several people stopped their workout and came to see what was happening.

DeBrus reached up as he passed over, wrapping one beefy hand in a crushing grip around Trace's right ankle. He stopped the teen's momentum, and started to reel Trace back in.

"Zero-gee grappling is chaos. Ye've got to feel the fight. Don't think abou' where it will go. Move in ways your opponent can't predict."

Trace's ankle burned with stabbing pain where DeBrus gripped it, the blood vessels constricted shut where they crossed bone. Trace kicked his free foot down on top of the other, aiming for the crushing hand where DeBrus gripped it. DeBrus let his ankle go, to keep his hand from being stomped, and Trace's kick slipped past his foot and thumped DeBrus' shoulder. The man barely grunted, and the contact started DeBrus slowly drifting away, turning as he went.

Trace found a grip on the rail and steadied his feet, but only one foot found purchase.

When DeBrus' back was to him, Trace pushed off. He smacked both hands against DeBrus' back, shoving the man ahead of him at arm's length. They floated across the core, and as they reached the center, Trace grabbed the man's shipsuit by the fabric on his shoulders, not an easy thing given the snug fit, and Trace somersaulted his body gently over the top, stealing the man's momentum.

"Wha—no ye don't!" DeBrus grabbed for his ankle again, but both hands grabbed empty air. Trace had kicked both feet wide, not quite doing the splits, but beyond DeBrus' reach as Trace rotated over top of him.

Trace, having stolen DeBrus' momentum for himself, flew faster across the core than he intended, somersaulting over and slamming his back against the flat panel of the railing one deck above.

"Ungh," Trace grunted, his back spasming in pain.

Fearing DeBrus was right behind him, His hands fumbled and he managed to grip a rung on of one the ladders. He stopped his tumbling roll and righted himself, but in an upside-down posture. He looked 'up' at DeBrus, who was flailing and kicking, but floating, stationary in the core.

A few chuckles around the railing, and a handful of cheers went up. The crowd had gotten larger, now including Mom and Dad. She wore the expected expression of holy terror, and Dad looked on with pride. He gave Trace a solid nod. Trace smiled back then looked at DeBrus.

The Security Officer had folded his arms over his chest, looking at Trace through his eyebrows.

"Well isn' that jost beginner's luck."

Trace took an opportunity.

"Ladies, gentlemen," he called out. "I give you . . . Sergeant DeBrus."

The cheers and applause rose up, bringing even more people to the railing.

After a moment glowering at Trace, the man's stern resolve cracked, and he gave a chuckle in spite of himself. The cheers rose up even higher.

"All right, ye've had your laugh at my expense." He pointed at Trace. "No', get me the bloody 'ell outta here."

DeBrus slapped his own shoulder twice, tapping out.

Trace nodded. He gently pushed off, reaching out for DeBrus' shoulder, even as the man gripped Trace's shoulder in turn, something like a full-arm handshake. The two floated across to the Deck 5 railing, opposite. They both found a grip on the railing and pulled themselves over.

He looked Trace in the eye.

"Didn't even work up a proper sweat," DeBrus complained. "Bloody well done indeed."

"Still want me to take a 'proper swing' at you?"

"Oh aye, if ye fancy waking up on Mars."

Trace held up both hands in surrender, then started to head up to Medical, hoping Doc might give him some pain meds for the thirteen new aches he could feel at this moment.

DeBrus slapped Trace hard on the back in congratulations as he passed.

Fourteen new aches he could feel at this moment.

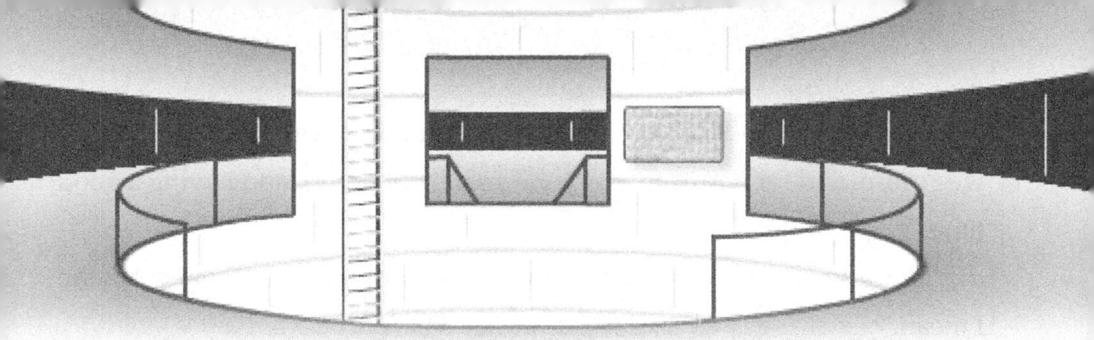

Chapter Eleven

The Party

"Transition is next week, right?" Trace asked. Several days had passed since their battle of strength and wits.

"Aye. Ten days. Less talk, more focus," DeBrus replied. Trace scrubbed at the bulkheads in and around hydroponics, where some leafy greens grew to help augment their food rations down on Deck 2.

DeBrus sipped at an unmarked beverage pouch while Trace scrubbed with one hand and twisted with the other, ensuring everything was properly bolted down.

The Starship, filled with sleeping passengers and those preparing to bed down for the night, drifted on serenely toward Mars, seventeen other Starships still ahead of her.

Trace knew he was almost out of time to finish his task. He checked the bolts' snugness on the devices and plant trays attached to the bulkhead, careful not to touch any delicate parts or sensitive components as he wiggled at each mounted location.

"Transition—it's the midpoint, is that all?"

"It's a bit more than just that. It's a time for a party, toasting with a wee dram, and for ensuring everyone's safe and sound, and having a good time."

"And what day do you predict will that happen? The actual moment, I mean."

"Should be about supper time this Thursday."

Trace ran a quick bit of mental math. "That's day 76, right? Any regrets making that bet?" Trace smiled as he gripped and checked the last bolted tray of greens, this one a half-grown leafy romaine. "There, all finished. All secure, and pretty clean."

DeBrus nodded. The 'salad lab,' as some called it, did indeed look shipshape.

"All right, get a move on, I need to meet with Engineer Richter abou' scanning parts of the Starship as require two crewmen."

"Can I chat with you both before I leave though? It's about the Mission Clock—then I'll be out of your way."

"Perhaps, but just for a moment."

They didn't have to wait long. Mister Richter arrived at Hydroponics to receive a hand-held scanner he would use for their inspection.

Trace stood back after nodding a hello to Mister Richter.

DeBrus pulled a scanner from his leg holster, checked its battery, and handed it over to Richter with its clip-on Shipsuit holster. Then he checked an identical scanner on his hip, read its power level readout, and re-holstered it.

"'Afore we head to life support, Mister Richter, young Worthington here had a question for us both, I believe?"

"Yes. Mister Richter? Can I ask you to have the ship's AI predict the exact digits displayed on the clock when we hit Transition?"

"We do not have to ask the computer, I have these numbers already, which I calculated a few days ago."

"Already? As in . . ."

"Ja, I need them to schedule the engineering processes that begin at the Transition moment itself. This is more than just a party, you see."

"I understand. Sergeant DeBrus and I have a little . . . challenge between us to see if I can stick the landing on the moment of Transition, so to speak."

"I do not follow."

DeBrus cut in. "What he's saying is, I gave him the challenge of using his brain, and he goes and turns it into a fool's bet. He seems to think his estimate will be within ten seconds, and that I'd lose a friendly wager between gentlemen."

DeBrus pulled out his own tablet, slightly beat up on the edges but shiny like it had just been cleaned and sterilized. He swiped to Trace's recent DM, the one with the coffee pouch attached image and Trace's predicted digits for Transition: **76:19:15:02**

Richter held up his own calculated time: **76:19:15:05**

"By your arse and parsley. . . three seconds off? Three bloody seconds?"

Trace stood stunned. "Wait, really? Can I see?"

They both turned their tablets around to let him see predicted results.

"Oh boy. Oh yeahhhh. Boom."

"I kinna believe that. Did he put you up ta' this?" DeBrus looked at Richter.

"Of course not, that would have been dishonest of us both."

DeBrus looked at Trace for few seconds.

"Well, take ye at your word then." He looked at Richter. "Come on, we've got work to do . . ."

Both men started to turn away from the locker; DeBrus reached out, about to close up hydroponics.

"Just one more moment, if I may?"

"Eh?"

"Our arrangement was for you to transfer it in a certain time and place, if I remember correctly?"

"Aye, so?"

"So in order for the good Engineer to collect . . ." Trace prompted.

"I have to be at the . . . oh, verdammt . . ." Richter muttered.

"See you at the party, Richter," Trace muttered, turning himself around and winking as he went over the railing.

The Engineer rolled his eyes, and the DeBrus burst out laughing.

"That alone made it almost worth losin' three hundred creds. Almost." Then he laughed some more. The two headed off to *Lucky Seven*'s most restricted spaces.

Trace floated back to his cabin, curious if any messages from Mars had come through. The door slipped silently open, and he floated through the door, allowing it to slide shut with a quiet *whoosh* behind him. Louise, in her top bunk, had a dark-screen sleep ambiance playing on her touchscreen, one of steady gentle waves lapping the shore under a crescent moon. Palm trees flexed gently in an offshore breeze, as if yearning to dive in.

Trace eased into the lower bunk, tapped the screen and slipped his ear pods in.

Two new video messages, origin Mars, were waiting for him, but neither was from his Martian Ambassador Chrissy.

"Aw man," Trace said out loud.

He heard an intake of breath above him.

"Be quiet, Trace . . ." came a murmured voice from under the covers.

"Sorry Louise," he replied automatically, feeling an odd sensation of déjà vu.

She went back to sleep. Trace set his Ear Pods in and tapped the first message open.

A handsome, bearded face filled half the screen, frozen, and before he pressed 'play,' Trace looked at the man's surroundings. A central plaza at the heart of some European city back on Earth, apparently. Cobblestones, buildings gently curving around an open courtyard. It even had a fountain, frozen in mid-splash from multiple jets around Neptune, where he held court with stone-carved fish and other eldritch creatures.

Nice use of A.I., Teach.

He tapped the triangle 'play' button.

"Hello Trace Worthington! I'm Mr. Steinheiser, geology and astronomy teacher here at *Mons High School*. My colleague, Mr. Chuumock, and your dad are old friends from their fleet days, and he suggested I reach out, since science is your focus. Congrats on making *the Crossing*, by the way--*Lucky Seven*, very cool! I imagine final approach will be exciting."

He smiled broadly, a genuine friendliness many teachers possessed. Pedestrians walked in the background, and the light in the plaza gave off a sunrise feel. A cup of coffee, not a pouch, sat before the teacher on a small, black wrought-iron table, gentle wisps of steam rising.

"Couple things for you to consider before you make landfall—since we can predict you'll have at least one class here with me, I can invite you now to our upcoming Geo-Symposium. Now, that's still a few months away, about two weeks after you arrive. You get to meet scientists like Dr. Holm, who you may remember hosted the most recent Cosmos series."

He took a small sip of coffee before continuing.

"Schools from all the Seven Cities are sending students as well: Nerus High, James Robinson High, Portree High, The New Kyiv *Lycaeum*, High Hedge Academy, and others, to discuss recent events. Then Homecoming and Cultural Convention will follow. *HoCo* is a blast, and this year, Mons High is hosting students from all over the planet. I know it's a lot to think about, but you can attend all these events, or just some, or none. Totally your call."

Trace paused the video. Dry, ugly, and boring is what he *knew*. This didn't look dry, ugly, or boring. It sounded interesting and . . . borderline *cool*. Also . . . a city square? Open spaces? And where were the crowds, fighting for resources? He resumed the video.

"So, by that time, you'll have finished quarantine and be getting settled into your family's new home—we'd enjoy having your Earth man's perspective, where you'd surely make some friends in the process. Think of it . . . heh, I mean, if you find a group of six friends, you'd be their *Lucky Seven*th friend."

Trace shook his head, smiling at the teacher's dorky joke. Against all his instincts about Mars and its people . . . this guy seemed all right. Then something unbelievable happened.

Stein scooped up the camera while it was still recording, stuck it on a short stick, hefted it above him, and started walking. He kept the camera pointed at him, selfie-style. The background shifted, and Trace could see this was not AI. That plaza was real. Huge and real.

That meant large groups of students from many high schools, he had counted at least five mentioned by the teacher . . . also real.

"Are you kidding m—" he squinted as the teacher continued.

"Anyways, I'll attach a link for you to decide if you're in for Symposium. So check that out and maybe discuss it with your folks."

The teacher's grip on the camera slipped but he caught himself. Briefly, the camera pointed upward, capturing a wide-open space and well-lit cavern ceiling above—far above. It looked like a sky back on Earth, complete with puffy clouds. That city cavern had to be . . . vast.

Vast?

No.

Way.

The teacher refocused the camera on his face.

"Sorry, trying to balance my *Mons Mountain Brew* and a CamStick, not the best idea. So, regarding my offer, shoot me a message, let me know. Cheers."

The teacher finished mid-smile. The image froze and faded to the Mars

Communications Services logo: twin red mountain peaks between which glowed a blue sunset above the letters M-C-S.

Trace re-watched the message. The fountain, colored buildings, shop fronts, second-story windows, people walking . . . all looked so convincing. Could Mars be . . . not what he expected? His dad's words from the Zephyr's restaurant car floated across the table in his memory: *"it's not what you predict; things like this never are."*

He shook his head and shoved the memory aside. Dad couldn't be right. Not a freaking chance.

The screen timed out and dimmed to power-saving mode. Through the darkness of the room, Louise's soft sleep sounds continued, along with the gentle crash of waves.

No way was Dad right about Mars.

Trace popped open the other message, a generic welcome message from the Mars Emergent Response Force (M.E.R.F.) Deputy Director, some old guy named Jackson. The man warned of recent events, minor tremors, and asked arriving passengers to be ready to make a positive difference in the lives of all people. He seemed optimistic, but . . . tired around the edges.

Trace switched off his screen. He wasn't sure what to believe.

* * *

Transition was an important event for all aboard the Starship for many reasons—it marked the midpoint of the journey, so they could celebrate fewer days ahead than behind, and it gave an excuse to throw a wild party. The party started late afternoon with a special surprise meal brought out of the food stores below Deck 1 . . . because nothing beats celebrating with food.

Word quickly spread that pizza, real pizza, was being served. The crowd gathered on the mess deck, growing by the minute. The smell alone was as ephemeral as it was inviting. Forming a makeshift line, passengers took steaming re-hydrated slices in twos and threes from smiling crew members and trickled back out into the core as party music poured from every speaker.

Festive scenes of people celebrating were piped in from other Starships as they broadcasted their own celebrations. Every time the feed jumped from one Starship to the next, the name in the corner changed as well. The *Anjiro*, the *Gilgamesh*, the *Bozeman*, the *Mark Watney*, the *Stirling*, the *Anansi*, the *Manitou*.

Lucky Seven's clock continued counting upward. The passengers knew they must be near the precise mid-point of their journey. A general rumble in the crowd, a rising murmur, filled the space, giving it more than a festive feel—a court of miracles celebratory vibe permeated their very own gypsy enclave.

Trace looked around for Dominique but couldn't see her. Maybe she was already up on Deck 8? He'd head up in a moment. For now, he stood by his family, enjoying a slice of pepperoni.

Some people bleeted small party horns, others donned sparkly colored party hats. Trace saw the occasional hip flask, sipped and hastily stashed away. Grins and smiles all around.

The group watched with excitement, growing quieter as the seconds ticked past.

The two clocks ticked upward as clocks normally do.

76:19:13:37

76:19:14:10

76:19:14:45

76:19:14:58

At fifteen minutes, zero seconds, the Voyage Clock *froze* for a full second . . . then started to count *down*.

"And there it is!" Jack Graves enthusiastically put in, and wild cheering erupted from all over the core. Couples kissed, kids clapped their hands, more party horns squeaked and blared.

Recorded fireworks played on all ship's flatscreens. The lights in the core started flashing and dimming then brightening with the beat of the music.

With a huge grin plastered on, Trace looked around for Dominique again. Still no sign. Where was that girl? He couldn't even spot her stoic, aristocratic parents around the rails. The classic 'Cool & the Gang' hit single "Celebration" blasted out from all ship's speakers. Couples started to spill over the rails, eager to attempt zero-gee dancing.

"Ladies and Gentlemen, we've hit Transition!" Telore's voice came through, loud and proud, over the speakers. More hip flasks magically appeared, then disappeared, and the music pounded on. Trace nodded his head to the music and noticed both Richter and DeBrus had left the food service area and were lingering on Deck 6. He saw DeBrus hand Richter a Pocket Money card and knew the wager had been settled. DeBrus tapped Richter, pointed out Trace, who clapped his hands enthusiastically across the way from them.

Richter smiled, held up the card, visibly rolled his eyes, then made his way back down to Engineering.

Small steps, my introverted friend, he thought, smiling as he watched him go. *You still have so much to teach me.*

Dancing in zero gee took some getting used to, but many couples tried it. Trace popped a breath mint in his mouth, just in case. He floated upward along one of the ladders, searching the throng of people, scanning over railings, searching all up and down, for that splash of perfectly-curled, platinum blonde hair.

No sign.

No sign, until she was right in front of him.

At Deck 7, he leaned forward to look up into the *StarDome,* and she popped up in front of him, her shipsuit tied off in the small of her back.

"Ohai!" she said over the railing.

"Hel-lo," he said back, smiling and catching her at the shoulders so she wouldn't drift on past.

"Happy Transition," she said with a dazzling white smile.

"Happy Transition to you too. Wow, you look . . ."

"Mmmmm," she purred. "Thanks."

He hesitated.

"So?" she asked.

"So . . .?"

"So, are you gonna be an oh-so fine boy and kiss me, or not?" Her eyes flashed.

"That's not how it goes."

"I know, but y—"

Trace pulled her into his arms, a super easy thing to do in zero gee, given his cut physique and her slender, hundred-pound frame. He cut her words off with a long, passionate kiss.

She stiffened at first, not expecting his sudden move.

Then she melted into his arms, her left hand going up to the back of his head. He kept his hands gently on her hips where they belonged. Her breathing was fast and deep, and he kissed her even more passionately. Her lip gloss was smooth and sweet like candy.

She pulled away from him.

"Come on, not here," she said, nodding up to the *StarDome,* where there would be fewer people. She shoved off first, and he followed.

When they had arrived at the darkest, most secluded spot under the *StarDome,* Trace asked her "Now, where were we?"

"Right about here, I think," she replied, arms going up behind his head again, and parting her lips for a delicious kiss that went on for a long time. A good half-hour passed that way before an all-call announcement cut their make-out session short.

"May I have your attention please?" the Captain said, her voice barely audible through the speakers above the din of the party.

A moment passed before laughter, conversation, and party hits faded.

Trace and Dominique floated over to the *StarDome*'s closest railing and watched the crowd from far above.

"Friends, we've got two special surprises for you – one will have to wait for tomorrow morning, but for now, we'd like to unveil something special for tonight only: our three-story, zero-gee trampoline. Please make way for our Engineer and Sergeant-at-Arms as they pass by to install . . . not one, but two full crash-nets across Decks 4 and 7."

"This will allow you access to the mess deck, your cabins, and so forth, using the Deck 4 staircase."

The two crewmen were quick and efficient at setting up the two stretchy-nets. Anyone above Deck 7, aside from Trace and Dominique, slipped past before the nets blocked them off from accessing the decks below.

Trace and Dominique watched as the first few passengers tried out two-sided trampoline jumping, the sheer novelty of it all.

"Looks like we're trapped up here," Dominique said, her voice barely above a whisper.

"Darn," Trace murmured back.

"Darn," she nodded, pulling Trace in for another delicious kiss.

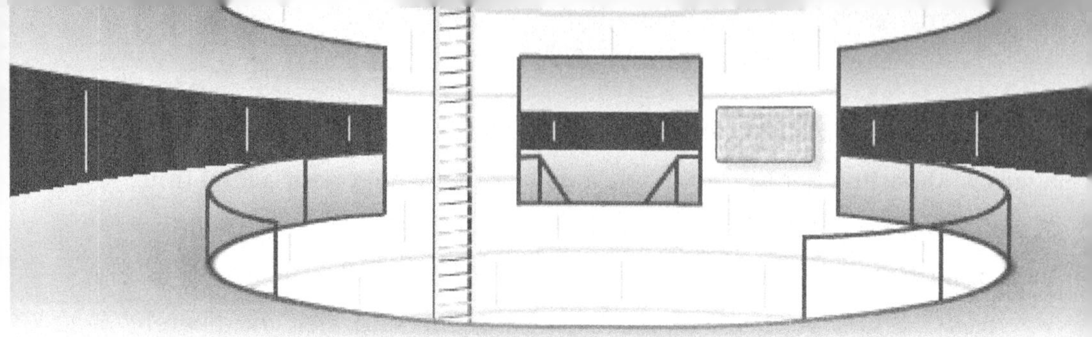

Chapter Ten

Possible Futures

Louise roused her sleeping brother from a deep sleep and a fun dream.

"Hey, c'mon, we're gonna miss breakfast."

"Wha—what time is it?" He blinked his eyes open, and the dream slipped away.

He squinted under the bright cabin lights.

"Almost 9."

"How—" he was at a loss for words. He shook his head groggily, rubbing his eyes.

"Okay, let me get dressed." As he floated up vertically to pull on a shipsuit, Louise slipped out the door to give him privacy.

Trace emerged from the cabin a few moments later to find Louise still nearby, chatting with Mom and Dad about last night's party. He ran a hand brush through his hair, straightening it out a bit.

"How long were you on the trampoline last night?" Mom asked.

"I was on it for almost an hour, bouncing between the up and down was so much fun," Louise said with the early-morning enthusiasm of a fourth grader. Or a Shih Tzu puppy.

Trace looked over the side and up into the core. Both trampolines had already been detached and put away. Momentary regret slipped into his thoughts, but then he remembered making out with Dominique under the *StarDome*. He had remembered what DeBrus had told him about cameras being everywhere; he was a gentleman.

Definitely time better spent than jumping around in the biggest eighty-thousand-miles-an-hour bouncy castle ever constructed.

"Okay. Food now?"

"Yes, I'm hungry," Louise said.

Mom and Dad were ready to go grab a meal as well, and Trace reached for the rail to jump over.

"Trace, hold on—" Dad reached out to grab Trace by the arm, but he had already pushed off over the rail.

Someone shouted down from two decks above.

"Oi, game in progress," came a voice from overhead.

"So-sorry, look out," another voice said.

A round, fuzzy object whizzed past his head. Trace flinched.

Loose objects tossed about in the core? What tomfoolery was this?

Mister Kazama, the solo Japanese businessman, had just tossed a Velcro-nerf ball from a few decks up. Trace looked down under his arm to watch the ball fall downward, even as he floated across the core.

The ball, a bright neon green, stuck to the Deck 2 flooring, a few feet aside of the *oculus*. The ball had stayed in place just inches from a bright red dot, a harmless red laser dot, the kind a cat likes to chase.

Trace heard a distant series of beeps and boops, reminiscent of an early-Nintendo racecar game driver driving through a power-up.

Trace looked back upward. "Uh, sorry . . . Mister Kazama," he called out.

Shin waved back to him and smiled.

Trace looked around for his family and noticed several dozen people had gathered along the rails of Decks 2 through four, observing the game. He spotted his family, making their way around behind him toward the stairs, to avoid interfering in whatever this new fascination was.

Louise caught up to Trace at the food tube dispenser, where they each grabbed a passenger favorite, the breakfast burrito in a tube, before seeking out a table for four. Louise pointed up.

"Up, on the ceiling," she said, and gently pushed off along a path that avoided other diners.

When they had settled into their ceiling seats, Mom and Dad joined them a moment later. Louise launched straight into explaining the new game.

"Zero-gee Bocce . . . can you believe it? *Space Bocce.*" She leaned forward, "Like we played in our backyard. Remember? But they don't have our usual colors, green-red-blue-yellow. And instead of a small white target ball, you aim at that little red laser dot. That way, the target doesn't get knocked around or bounce away or something."

Trace listened as he chewed then took a sip of his wild blueberry drink pouch.

"And there's an app; the computer keeps score," she added, squeezing and taking a bite . . . then fanning a free hand in front of her mouth. "Ooo, that's hot."

"So . . . how do we get up to the upper decks if we can't use the core?"

Mom spoke up. "The teams play from the railing behind Deck 5 and 6, but always on the dorsal side, under the Bridge. They told us to use the stairs up to Deck 4, then float up or use the ladder under the *StarDome*, to stay out of the line of fire. That's how Steward Daniels explained it."

"I like him, he's always happy," Louise said.

A burst of ragged applause and cheers broke out in the core. Evidently somebody had just scored a great throw. Trace turned back to his folks.

"How do players know which deck to throw from?"

Dad answered. "In most games, it's player's option—deck 6 shots earn extra points. In come games, the computer chooses the deck for the whole game. Plus, there's all these other interesting rules, like if you throw it too hard, and it bounces off that new fuzzy carpet down there surrounding the *oculus*, your team loses points. That way it doesn't get too aggressive."

"Some play in teams, others play alone," Louise added. "I wanna play with Kasia as my teammate, but there's a waiting list."

They finished up the meal, pondering. Dad scrolled incoming messages from Mars, frowning.

"Plus, I think they're doing a tournament with prizes," Mom said, keeping her eyes on the core. "Everyone's practicing."

Trace barely listened. He wondered if Dominique had any noteworthy athletic skill. His phone pinged with a request for assistance from the Security Office, meeting clear up on Deck 8.

"Gotta go you guys," Trace said, squeezing the last of his tube into his mouth and heading for the recycler. "Duty calls."

Dad nodded and smiled. "Have fun."

"Yeah . . . fun." Trace turned and left.

Trace glanced up, scanning the railings around and above as he neared the core but couldn't see Dominique. Maybe she was a late sleeper.

He floated up to Deck 8, careful to stay clear of the *Space Bocce* game in progress. Seeing the seating area was empty, he looked up and around the *StarDome* itself, spotting DeBrus up on the Bridge's glass shielding, the windshield as it were, polishing down the last of it and leaving it sparkling.

DeBrus saw him out of the corner of his eye and greeted him.

"Thanks for coming up so quickly."

Trace nodded. "Are we scanning another deck today?"

"No' this time, come on." DeBrus stowed his cleaning supplies in a small locker and headed to the railing.

The game was nearly complete, but DeBrus opted not to wait for the gap between games. He pushed off over the rail and down the Ventral half of the Starship core toward the Deck 4 staircase. Trace followed, looking around at the passengers holding back for the next game to start.

Trace managed to get his hand up an instant before smacking his head on the Deck 4 railing.

"Woah, that's a close one," DeBrus said. "Wee bit distracted, are ye?"

"Nope. So . . . I've never asked, how is it you came to be the Sergeant-at-Arms aboard a Starship?"

"I did it by never closing any doors. Keep every possible future open, no matter how dismal it may seem."

"When you considered your . . . possible futures, did you see yourself going a different direction?"

DeBrus scratched under his chin. "Never thought I'd be leaving Scotland, to be telling it true; the family had an estate to look after, the ancestral home *Broomhall*."

He headed down the Deck 4 stairs, carefully watching for anyone coming up. Trace followed.

"Any ancestors I might have heard of?"

"I'm one of many descended from King Robert, if family records and DNA markers are true."

"Robert the Bruce, of course! Why didn't I put it together before?"

"That's the one."

"Wow. What was he like--do we know what he was like?"

They passed Deck 2 and headed carefully down the narrowest staircase to Deck 1.

"Our family tells of a warrior-king, selfless leader, a patriot, all right? But critics say he was a bloodthirsty, power-hungry opportunist who burned castles even after winning his battles, and he took special care to ensure his enemies suffered. But those claims are well-refuted."

"What do you think?"

"History is written by the victors. But I know this much: he fought not just against something, he fought *for* something—Scottish freedom from the Kings of England, be they malevolent or benign. So, I rather think the truth was between those two ends; he was a good man, who loved his country with his whole chest, but had his flaws, like us all."

They lighted on the floor of Deck 1, beside the rows of carry-on lockers and the *oculus* above them.

"And what do you think are your flaws?" Trace asked, cheeks turning red, even as he blurted out such a personal question without stopping himself.

"My flaws? Hm. I suppose, like my ancestors, I've go' precious little patience for wanna-be kings, power-hungry trillionaires, their political corruptions... blast 'em all, if I could—they've got no redeeming humanity."

Trace considered DeBrus' words, briefly glancing up through the *oculus*.

"So what's your flaws, young Worthington?"

"Me? I . . . um," Trace stumbled. "I hate my dad."

"For what, exactly?"

"For dragging me up here. He ripped me away from a good life, a solid future. Now that's all gone."

DeBrus nodded. He looked thoughtful a moment before speaking.

"My last words to my father were spoken in anger. Take them back if I could, but he's gone, see?"

"So . . . how do I deal?"

"Ye make peace."

"Peace with my dad?"

"No, any fool can see he's proud o' you. The one ye've got to make peace with is yourself. And that's no' likely to happen until it's too late."

"Too late for what? Is something going to happen?"

DeBrus stared at Trace, hard. "I'm only tellin' ye, look within, and first forgive yourself for your anger. You'll know when ye're ready. Look him in the eye and speak with him as a man. No' as an angry boy."

Trace's cheeks flushed. He was righteously indignant. Not an angry . . . boy.

DeBrus clapped him on the shoulder and turned away. Trace followed him across Deck 1, into the Security offices.

There, DeBrus had him scrubbing down dust from the Closet/Brig, a second high-security space he had not seen before, and the outer office. Trace had won his bet, but he still wanted to help out, keep busy—scrubbing was not beneath him.

The only part he didn't like was how small the brig spaces were—half the height and length of his cabin with Louise. The walls started feeling like they were suffocating him. He scrubbed quickly, trying to finish up as fast as he could.

He wondered when he would see Dominique again. He imagined her in her snug-fitting shipsuit; it helped distract him as he finished wiping down the tight spaces.

He moved on to the outer office, where DeBrus had a simple desk, display screen, and two chairs, one on either side of the table.

"What's that?" He pointed at a small, black metal box, recessed into the middle of the table.

"I'll show ye." DeBrus popped it open, revealing a pair of handcuffs, which floated up on short chains until they reached their limit, eight or ten inches above the desk surface.

"For when I fancy an undistracted conversation." DeBrus looked stern.

"Have you ever had to chain up a . . . subject?"

"Once. The man was drunk and disorderly. He downed a hip flask in a low moment and lashed out, violent at his cabin mate. Had to secure him here to let the Doc sober 'im up a bit."

"So what happened?"

"He set off a medical alert with his wrist band, abnormal high heart rate and adrenaline. That, and his roommate came flying out the cabin door backwards, clear across the core."

"Was the guy all right?"

"A few bruises. But I arrived on scene just as the drunken man reached him, still wi' a head full o' steam, ready to pummel him some more."

"How did you handle that?"

"I grabbed his ankle and . . . separated them. Poor bugger made the mistake o' tryin' to kick me in my pretty face."

"And?"

"He woke up several hours later, chained to this desk."

DeBrus stowed the handcuffs and closed the black case.

Trace nodded.

"Okay then, cleanin' complete, I've got nothing else for ye. Have ye got other things to do?"

"Yes, I need to go get my workout in, before my window closes."

"Work up a good sweat. I'll see ye later then."

He thanked the Engineer and headed up to the Fitness Center, like before, sticking to the stairs up to Deck 4. His fitness center window had forty minutes left; just long enough to get a good workout in.

He looked for Dominique in the fitness area, but she wasn't there.

* * *

Arriving back at his cabin after grabbing a shower, Trace tapped his screen to check what tasks he needed to do today. Three messages were waiting: one from Earth—his buddy Pete—and two from Mars—his Mars Ambassador, Chrissy, and Mr. Steinheiser, that Mons High science teacher.

He tapped the message from Stein first, wanting to take his time with the other two. "Veggies before dessert," he mused.

The vid's still-frame showed the man seated in his classroom, with a fedora and a satchel hanging on a peg behind him. The fedora reminded him of some film action hero from the golden age of cinema, but he couldn't place where. He tapped the triangle play button.

"Hello Trace! Thanks for your response earlier, and I hope *the Crossing* continues to be uneventful and exciting."

Trace paused the video and squinted at the still image. So, clearly not in a public place over a cup of coffee, but in his classroom. He murmured, "is that sunlight?"

The cabin door slid open, and Louise entered, alone.

"Whatcha doin, Trace?"

She floated down next to him. He moved over so she could fit comfortably.

"It's a vid-cap from my science teacher, but the background might be AI, I mean, look."

"Your teacher from back at Pine Creek?"

"No, this one's at a Mars High School, the one in *Olympus Mons*. He seems pretty cool."

"Lemme see," Louise said, reaching for the resume button. She hesitated, seeing what Trace had noticed.

"Looks like a teacher's desk in a classroom. Is that a window?"

She backed up the vid and pressed play. They watched as Stein repeated the greeting part, and as the teacher spoke and gestured, the shadows moved correctly, so yes, real sunlight in the classroom.

"Wait, what is that?" The swish of something fuzzy and orange flipped onto the screen and then off again.

"He has a cat! Wait, Mars has cats? I want one," Louise blurted out.

Steinheiser continued.

"So, you'll be finishing up your 5.0 and 5.5 school seasons here as an *Olympian*—and with all these events coming up, you'll meet a lot of students from high schools from all over."

Off camera, Trace and Louise heard a girl's voice say *"Make us proud, you little punk. Lead the Rat Force on to victory!"* The teacher briefly looked off to the side.

"Bye Mister Stein," the same girl's voice said.

"You ladies have an excellent weekend," he said, then turned back to the camera.

Interesting. Mars has weekends. Have an excellent *weekend,* he had said.

But what the heck was this 'Rat Force?'

"Sorry. Andie and Aiya are a couple of my best students," Stein said, tapping at his keyboard briefly. "Now Trace, I want you to know the invitation stands, to join Symposium and Homecoming—we'd love to have your voice in the conversation, you'd bring an Earth man's perspective. I'll make sure you have an invite, DM you the details."

As Stein said this, the cat made his appearance on camera. The tall, bright orange tabby stood on Stein's lap, flipping his tail up in Stein's face. The cat's bright orange eyes briefly looked straight at the camera, and Trace had the strange sensation the cat was looking at him. Weird.

"Ugh, Ares, not now," the teacher said, setting him aside. "So anyways, Trace, think about it, and we wish you a safe rest of your trip."

As Stein ended the video, the cat jumped onto the windowsill behind the teacher and slipped out, through his own little sliding cat door.

"Ha!" Louise blurted out. "He has his own door. What was his name again?" The video froze and the words "End of Message" appeared on the screen with the M.C.S. logo.

"Ares," Trace said. "As in . . . Greek god of war. As in . . . Mars."

"He's kinda cute for the god of war."

Trace nodded.

He flashed his screen over to the nose camera view, where all three Starships were clearly visible in the camera frame. He would watch his other two personal messages later, when his sister wasn't around.

"I'm hungry," Louise said.

* * *

Pete's message was a field vid note from somewhere along the Rampart Range. His buddies were hiking a trail in the shadow of one of the peaks to do some camping—behind Mount Herman or Eagle Peak, probably. He had been up there many times; the view of it caught him off guard and he felt a pang of homesickness. He did not watch the video a second time.

The message from Chrissy was lovely as always. He got a charge out of hearing her talk—she had a way of balancing the latest exciting things in her life and roping him into her positive moment by asking him related questions. Whether this was Ambassador training or she was truly into him, she was extremely relatable and Trace looked forward to meeting her. She seemed like she might be an excellent person to spend time with.

He thought of Dominique; he messaged her at her "StarParty" address, and around lights out, he saw she messaged him back, agreeing to meet him the following night, 9:00 PM up in the usual place.

He smiled, thoughts swirling between his buds hiking his favorite mountains, his lovely Ambassador whom he looked forward to meeting, and the beauty queen who wanted him as her . . . he had no idea what.

Maybe he'd ask tomorrow night what *she* thought they were.

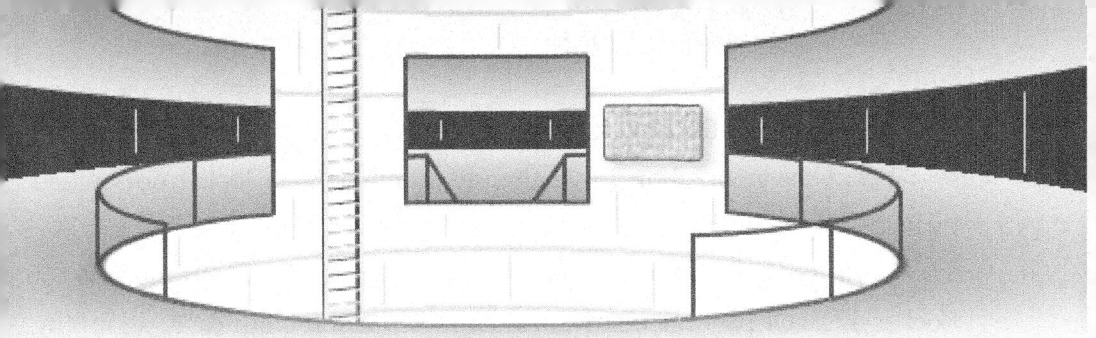

Chapter Nine

Exception to the Rule

“What in the blessed name of Saint Andrew have ye done in here, Daniels?”

DeBrus looked around at the chaos. It wasn’t even mid-day, and this mess to clean up, while passengers were coming and going was the last thing he wanted to deal with.

“I found a cache of smuggled goods,” Daniels proclaimed proudly. Deck 1’s wall of 108 carry-on locker slots now showed at least fifteen locker doors standing wide open, most of these with their cases pulled out and piled on the floor.

Daniels smiled, hands on his hips as he surveyed the rows of lockers. “Pretty clever of whoever—hiding contraband right here in plain sight.”

“We don’t open lockers without express permission from the Captain. That’s basic on-board protocol.”

“Lockers owned by passengers, of course. But the unassigned ones remain under the purview of the deck steward—I just wanted to lend a hand where I could, nothing more. And look.”

He gestured at the obvious.

"What are ye on abou'? I've already scanned every locker not owned by a passenger, and they showed completely empty and clear."

"Well, you missed a few. Take a look." He reached into the back of Locker 47, well past his elbow, and extracted a soft cloth case, wrapping something very solid, shaped like a brick.

DeBrus pulled his scanner out and let it play over the cloth. The image showed . . . bright colors; scintillating colors. Like a disco ball, but spots playing out in every color of the rainbow. "What on Earth . . .? It's pure crystal, has to be."

DeBrus turned off the scanner, making no move to touch anything else.

"These lockers—ye can't just go yankin' 'em open like this. There is a chain of evidence custody to be preserved, and it's all gone now. You've just severed any chance of legally connecting contraband with whoever put it there."

"I assure you, I took nothing from this room; everything is exactly where I found it just now," Daniels said.

"Think abou' it for just a moment. Every locker only holds the ident of the most recent person to open it. Now, they'll all show it was you, opening them today. Every last one. Whoever stowed that contraband in the first place, now there's no record of that person in any of the affected lockers."

"Oh . . . oh no. I had no idea. Drat." Daniels lost his smile for the first time DeBrus could remember.

"Daniels, security is my purview, and I've already used a hand-scanner on all the unassigned lockers. Clean and empty, the lot. Nothing inside."

"My name is Yeoman Daniels, if you please, and I am happy to carry on this discussion with the Captain if you wish, Sergeant DeBrus. Unless you have something to hide?"

"Of course we're involving the Captain, Daniels. I'll ask ye kindly not to touch anything else. Understand?" He leaned in, emphasizing his point.

"Absolutely. Your show. Captain told us all in our first meeting after liftoff to be on the lookout for contraband, remember? And it is regulation, standard procedure during every Crossing to do random security sweeps."

"Except the security sweeps are under the purview of the security officer. It's in the bloody title, see?"

"Are you calling the Captain, *sir*, or should I?"

DeBrus cued his mike on the discreet command channel. "Captain, will either you or the Lieutenant join me please? We've found more contraband. Risk level appears low—inert goods."

"What's your 20?" the Captain asked.

"Deck 1, passenger lockers."

"On my way."

The channel clicked off.

DeBrus turned back to Daniels. "So as I said, I scanned every one of these a few hours after launch, and once weekly since then."

Daniels held up one finger, as if using his finger to conduct his own thoughts.

"But hand-scanners have their limits, correct? I mean, how do you explain this?" Daniels held up the cloth sleeve case in his hand.

DeBrus floated closer, nodding to him to unzip the pouch. Daniels unzipped the sleeve, and peeled the cloth away from the top half, like peeling a square banana.

A brick of clear crystal, with a pair of gold-plated electrical leads on one end, glittered and refracted the light in the room, casting rainbow dots and splashes that danced across the walls, floors, and ceiling as he moved it in his hand.

"From what I can see, there are seven other—"

Right then, the Captain floated feet-first down through the *oculus*, landing lightly next to her Sergeant-at-Arms. "Oh, my, what have you got there?"

Daniels cut DeBrus off. "Ma'am, I have a friend who is really into this tech. This a crystalline memory brick, the kind that stores information holographically. I have never seen one this big before, though—pretty cutting-edge. Fetch a huge score on the black market . . . New Marrakech, or Hathorton, maybe? I don't know where, or how much, but it must be enough to be worth breaking the law for."

"I thought crystalline memory modules were tiny, maxing out at the size of a dice or a marble."

She reached out and took the crystal brick, careful not to touch the clear surface directly. "One this size must be able to store . . . what? All the TV shows and movies filmed in the last . . . four hundred years?"

"Probably one brick could store all the knowledge attained by humanity throughout our entire history. Or several fully-formed, self-aware AI personalities? Whatever gets put on this brick may be pretty darn devastating."

"What if one of those AIs is on there already?" the Captain asked.

"I have to guess these are blank, Captain, the data is complete gibberish, no matter what may have been on there before. Any movement at all while they are not plugged in to a continual, highly-conditioned power feed, renders the crystal's memory unreadable. That's how easy all those little zeroes and ones flip back and forth in each little space in the lattice."

"Even the slightest jostle, say a pigeon taking a dump on a Cadillac three states away, would reset the data randomly throughout the crystal, and any information on there would instantly become as disordered and unreadable . . . interstellar radio static."

"So they are completely vulnerable to any movement at all?"

"And photons passing randomly through the crystal," Daniels said. "They require perfect darkness and a highly-regulated low-level current to hold their data stable."

She admired it for a moment. "Look, the cloth sleeve has a symbol stamped into it, very faint. Looks like a flower."

Sergeant DeBrus spoke up. "That looks more like a lily, one of those French *fleur de lis* symbols."

"So it's the French royalty? Not likely. We'll have to let the proper authorities, those MERF people in Mons-Plex, do their investigations."

"How many did you find here?"

"I'll have to do a complete scan of all 108 lockers, with your permission, ma'am, and measure the mass of the whole group. I'll let you—"

"Eight," Daniels interjected. "There are eight. And my estimate is they are two kilos each. So maybe fifteen kilos total. But of course, Sergeant DeBrus can get you better numbers."

The tension in the air ratcheted up a notch.

DeBrus seethed at Daniels but held his tongue.

"Please scan them all, Sergeant DeBrus, right to the back of each and every locker, passenger boxes included, and report to me when finished. Nicely done, Mister Daniels."

"Cap'n."

"Thank you, Captain."

She passed the cloth-covered crystal brick back to Sergeant DeBrus, then launched herself up and through the *oculus*.

"So, how can I help—" Daniels began.

"Just go, let me do my job here without ye distracting me," DeBrus said, keeping his voice even.

"If you change your mind, you know where to find me," Daniels said, heading up the stairs.

DeBrus shook his head, looked around, and pulled his tablet from a thigh pocket, accessing the security checklist that governed processing compromised contraband. He waited for the device to connect, which took a few minutes longer than usual. He set the camera in the corner to begin recording his evidence-gathering process for the record.

* * *

Right as DeBrus was dismissing Daniels to let him work in peace, Engineer Richter was finishing up their latest Engineering deck work with Trace.

"Wait, really? We've got walkie talkies on board? These are so retro . . ." He turned one over in his hand.

"This is the engineer's prerogative. You remember Engineering Channel 3 from the suit tests?"

"Yes, the short-range one."

"Correct. The engineer must be able to speak with his teammates constantly whenever two or more are working a maintenance task from separate locations."

"And you trust me to be on the other end of this connection?"

"You can of course give it back, or we can see if you earn the trust of having the radio, in case I require your help."

"We should run a radio test," Trace said, starting to like his role as Richter's 'apprentice' more and more.

"Remember, when you accept this, you accept the obligation to be on call around the clock. Understand?"

"Yes, sure, I'll keep it on me."

"So, let's review what we talked about before. What does a leader do?"

"He inspires."

"Gut. And what does the follower do?"

"Obeys."

"There may be hope for you yet. So, we take two days off while I tend to tasks that don't require your assistance. But keep that radio near at all times. Understand?"

"How do you say 'I understand' in German?"

"Verstanden."

"Fer-sh—?"

"Verstanden."

"Got it. Verstanden."

"Good. Until next time." Richter turned back to his terminal.

Trace left, heading up to grab a bite and then, after his food settled, do his daily workout. Both went fine, no issues, and he didn't see Dominique all afternoon. But tonight, he had another date meet-up with Dominique, which he was looking forward to. Trace had learned as long as he kept the conversation on her interests or something they could see or share before them, it had yet to get awkward. There were, naturally, whole chunks of time when words would have gotten in the way.

Late in the afternoon, he claimed one of the vacant gaming terminals, to keep his mind from obsessing. He ran through every possible ending in the driving classic, *Out Run*, and then he knocked out several missions from the OG *Days Gone*, upgrading weapons and the motorcycle of the game's protagonist, a drifter named *Deacon St. John*, all while taking down hordes of zombies across the Oregon wilderness.

Night fell. The lights dimmed. Time to go meet Dominique . . . 'girlfriend' seemed overstating it. Maybe after they arrived on Mars, they'd figure out what they were exactly. He made his way up to the *StarDome* and she joined him, fashionably late.

The two teens sat once again in their assigned seats from the Moon slingshot, under the *StarDome*. The Starship internal lighting had faded to night-time low light conditions a few minutes before. Very romantic.

He held her hand as they looked up at the stars together, Mars more visible now than before, on the right of their view. She sighed contentedly, crossing her legs daintily at the knees.

He squeezed her hand as an idea occurred to him.

"Hey, so what do you want to do together once we reach Mars? You'll be living in Nerus, but traveling often enough to where I am in Mons-Plex, right?"

"I mean yeah, but it's not like we'll be seeing a lot of each other after we land."

"What do you mean?" He looked sideways at her.

"Come on, we both know I'm a bit out of your . . . circle. You went to public school back in Kansas, right? And you probably will again once we get to Mars. I'll be at the High Hedge Academy."

"Colorado. But what difference does tha—"

"And my dad is the CEO of the corporation that owns Caesar's Terraz'zo Grand Hotel and Casino, and half a dozen other leisure properties in the *Mons-Plex, Nerus,* and *Libertas.* And what does your dad do? He's ex-military, right? Some kind of manager now?"

Trace just looked at her.

"Look, I'm not judging, it's just facts, right? Not personal. So let's enjoy the time we have left aboard the ship. I mean, don't you want to kiss me again? Kiss me like you did at Transition?" She bit her bottom lip and dipped her head sideways.

He looked at Dominique, agonizing on the inside, a turmoil of emotions.

Chrissy's face popped up in his mind—her down-to-earth nature, her genuine goodness. Her inner beauty. Whether he ended up with Chrissy or not, it didn't matter—she proved there were far better people, those with compassion and real fire, to spend his time with. Jeni had been one, Chrissy was clearly one, and he would meet and get to know others.

It became clear to him all at once, just how hollow and sad this devastatingly beautiful woman in front of him actually was. Dominique was a shell of a person, manipulating him with her physical attributes. He was just a piece of meat to her, a diversion to pass the time. She would manipulate him until she no longer needed him.

"I think I wanna kiss you less and less actually."

"Excuse m—"

He let go her hand.

She tried to grab it before he drew away, but he was faster. He stood up.

"I should go." His hand brushed his radio, and he remembered he had it on him.

She looked stunned.

"Um, Richter's expecting me." He made a show of looking at his silver wristband, knowing full well it did not display the time.

"At this time of night?" she folded her arms and pursed her lips in disbelief.

Trace grabbed the walkie off his belt, angling himself with his free hand to float away.

"Mister Richter, Trace here. Uh, sorry I'm running . . . very late for our end-of-shift tasks. I'm on my way to Engineering now."

After a few long seconds, Richter's voice crackled back over the walkie.

Dominique stayed seated, watching Trace as he drifted away.

Trace gritted his teeth, praying Richter wouldn't ruin his alibi.

"Ach . . . again, you've kept me waiting, Mister Worthington. You had better have a good reason. Why are you so late?"

"No excuse, sir," he muttered into the mike. "On my way."

With one last look at Dominique from where he stood at the rail, he clipped the walkie back on his belt. He grabbed the railing and soared neatly over and down through the core.

Dominique sat in stunned silence, not quite believing what had just happened.

Chapter Eight

Of Their Own Accord

"What was that all about?" Richter asked as Trace came through the open hatch to Engineering. The door slid shut behind him.

"Thank you for going along with it. You helped me . . . um, dodge a bullet."

"Ach, so, with the Starship princess?"

Trace nodded. "Ja."

Richter snickered. "So, we have each other's backs, this is a good thing."

"She is just so self-centered, why did I even think she could change? Urgh."

"So, it's not my business. But since you are here now . . ."

"Algae canisters?"

"Algae canisters."

Trace sighed. "Sure, why not." He reached for a pair of rubber gloves from their drawer. He laughed, feeling better already.

Richter turned on a vintage *Rammstein* playlist for them to jam to while they worked, an artist in a metal sub-genre Trace had never heard before. He liked it, occasionally asking Richter what the lyrics meant.

Half an hour later, Trace had worked off whatever inconvenience he owed Richter for saving him, and the Engineer bid him good night.

"And tomorrow, we explore propulsion, the engines and how they work with the final approach maneuver."

"Sounds good," Trace had said before taking his leave. He was starting to enjoy his time learning the Engineering functions of a Starship, knowing he hoped to fly one, someday.

"And, we must not forget to take a closer look at Life Support, the auxiliary section down on Deck 2." Richter had said as they prepared to go their separate ways.

"Not Life Support up on Deck 6, where the E-V-A suits are stored?"

"Uh, no, not that one. That part is on permanent lock, given the components are so critical. We can explore the hydroponics lab; I believe your sister and little Kasia help Yeoman Daniels out in the hydroponics lab sometimes, yes?"

"That's right, the way I work with you and sometimes Sergeant DeBrus. So, I've been meaning to ask, how does a plant even grow without gravity? Doesn't life need an up and a down to grow from a seed?"

"Yes, but we have many seedlings already, large ones to grow at first, and small ones to mature later, brought from Earth, do we not? The germination, the sprouting itself, happens all on its own, but it must be watched carefully. Like sometimes with people, certain things happen aboard the Starship of their own accord."

"What do you mean, '*of their own accord?*'"

"Plants grow in strange directions, people act in unusual ways, they cannot always help it."

"Wait, what is this 'unusual' thing people do on a Starship, of their own accord?"

"The greatest danger is time and not having enough to do to fill that time. This is why I give you so much work. Young adults are the most susceptible to long periods of time with little to do. Some very bad things can happen . . . of their own accord. We keep you busy."

Trace nodded; Richter made a few taps on his tablet.

"I have sent you a short video clip describing the toe-flip, I want you to watch before tomorrow morning. So, see you tomorrow morning at 8:30, ja? We meet for coffee then get an early start."

* * *

Trace slept, then awakened early to watch Richter's brief video overview on re-entry. He still had some time, so he recorded a vid-message to Chrissy. By then, Louise had awakened and said goodbye, heading out to team up with Kasia for breakfast and some early-morning Space Bocce.

Trace turned on the camera, put a smile on, and pushed <RECORD>.

"Good morning, your Excellency, I hope this vid finds you having a great day, and school isn't too crazy for y—."

Louise walked back in, maybe having forgotten something. She saw Trace recording, and promptly stuck her own face down into Trace's camera view.

"Oooo, hi! You're Chrissy. I'm Louise, Trace's superior officer. He can't do a thing right, I hope you can figure him out. Pip, pip, warp factor six, Major Worthington! Gotta go!" She bounced back out of the cabin before Trace could even object.

He stared at the door as it shut, still recording, then looked back at the camera dot.

He closed his mouth.

"My sister. Yeah, she's . . . yeah. Can't rein her in, no matter how hard I try. Anyways, I've got about 30 days left, can you believe that? The time has blasted by so quickly . . . our Engineer, Mister Richter, is having me research this weird toe-flip thing we'll be doing for re-entry. Rather than flying straight in with the nose up and the engines down right from the start, he says we'll be nose . . . down? Then we're doing a weird somersault thing near the ground. The jets will lift *Lucky Seven*'s pointy end all the way up and *then* the ship's standing up straight. Three rockets fire; we touch down. Whups, I'm at my time limit. DM me back in a text if you wanna keep talking today, I'll read anything you feel like sharing."

He saved it and clicked <SEND>. Then he pulled on his full shipsuit and headed out to meet up with Richter. The two met at the Deck 2 coffee dispenser a few minutes before 8:30, and after a brief nod, sipped the first few sips without any conversation.

Morning java first, pleasantries after.

Trace followed his mentor down to the engineering spaces, where Richter needed to run a brief check of the Engines. The routine scan of all sensor components served to triple-check for any damage or concerns that had gone unnoticed during blastoff and the slingshot.

Every sensor and external camera check, from the Raptor V engine manifolds to the engine bells, the nozzles at the business end of *Lucky Seven*, checked out just fine.

Richter ran through the checklists, letting Trace watch and ask questions, then gave Trace the honor of pushing the <EXECUTE> button that pulsed the engines for 1/20th of a second, marking the successful test in the Starship daily log. He closed out that checklist, and for the last part of the scheduled hour, they chatted about innocuous things.

Trace asked him about other near-disasters in space, mainly from the early days of space flight. Richter proved to be an encyclopedia of interesting facts, anecdotes, and right-to-the-point storytelling. Richter wrapped up their chat though Trace still had questions; they could wait, Richter had work on the Bridge to tend to. Trace accepted this and returned to his room to see if Chrissy had replied.

She had.

Trace grinned, finding he learned something new about Mars every time they batted notes back and forth. He tapped open the message waiting, finding it was a text message, a DM, that Chrissy had sent between classes at her school.

Chrissy: Hi Trace! Your sister's super cute! I bet she's an excellent Commander. Something you said about 'reining her in' got me thinking—would you feel up for a horseback ride after you get here? The herd has a handful of mares and geldings tame enough for trail riding through the forest. I've only done it a couple times, but I'd go again if you are interested? LMK!

"Wait . . . whaaaat?" Trace said out loud. "Horses? Forests?" Trace started dictating a voice-to-text message.

Trace: Wait, hold on right there. Mars has horses? For serious? How do they even live in the rocky city caves? Don't they need open spaces to run? Grass to eat? This makes no sense to me... surely you jest.

He fired off his note, and was surprised to find her reply just over a half-hour later.

Chrissy: Nay, good sir, I don't jest about horses. And don't call me Shirley. ;-) You silly—of course they can run, there's a huge field in between the forest and Silver Lake. They graze all day, and they're fed alfalfa, I think, that's grown in the greenhouse domes up on top of The Mountain. Take a look, I have a few stills I took the last time I went to the shoreline to feed the ducks. I think the herd was in the background. Hmmm . . . yeah, here you go. See for yourself!!

Trace tapped open her attached images, and aside from being distracted by a beautiful, smiling brunette, sure enough—slightly out of focus in the background stood a half-dozen horses, grazing along a three-board white fence.

Trace: I'm . . . blown away. Horses, fields, a lake? Next you're going to tell me people go fishing and wind surfing . . .

Trace waited a half hour, but her reply didn't come right away. He filled the time getting a late workout and grabbing some lunch. By the time he returned to his Cabin, her reply was waiting.

Chrissy: Trace, you're so funny! Wind surfing? Nope, there's no wind in the cavern; and it never really rains either. Sometimes it does. But fishing? Yes - anything caught from the dock, usually tilapia, they measure it and sell it at market, or they release it back into the lake for breeding. There's a team of divers here that look after the lake, and I think they use real SCUBA gear—I know a girl, Andie, whose dad is one of the marine biologists. You'd like her, she's really smart. What I'm saying is there is soo much for you to do after you get here! But save the horseback ride for me, I wanna do that again. Anyways, gotta run do some stuff; hope the rest of your day is good! Vid me tomorrow!

Trace leaned back, processing all this. Mars was starting to seem . . . likeable. Who knew?

* * *

Eight hours later, in her dedicated cabin under the Bridge, Captain Strahan woke early. She sat in athletic gear at her small desk, reading through last night's dispatches and the daily Starship's log. A couple men had gotten into what amounted to a shoving match, nothing too serious. Aside from the doc's entry that the two involved were counseled, patched up, and released, everything looked nominal, no worries, no discrepancies.

Her eyes darted over to her wall safe, knowing the precious cargo that rested inside. She shook her head in wonder, still not quite believing that someone had managed to sneak it aboard.

Her tablet pinged, and she tapped her DMs open.

An audio message had just arrived, but TO: was blank. FROM: was also blank.

The file scanned clean of viruses or malware, so she tapped the voice message icon, letting it play in her earpiece. The voice came through digitally distorted, deepened. Ominous. Like something straight out of those AI-takes-over-the-world movies.

You do not know us. This is not personal. Your Starship was doomed the moment you launched. Nothing you can do will stop what is coming. You chose to leave Earth, knowing you carry extra mass—your arrogance is your downfall. We have already destroyed your precious Lucky Seven and will rain your scattered remains down on Mars. Tick tock, you cannot stop the clock. You . . . your crew . . . your passengers . . . already dead, you just do not know it yet. We. Stand. Avenged.

The voice stopped speaking. Then, a ticking sound, very faint.

The ticking faded away to silence.

Chapter Seven

Bad Intentions

Captain Strahan hit the replay button, but the audio file was already gone, self-erased. The message sender ID tag, "avenged.7z," flickered briefly on the screen before it, too, self-deleted.

On a digital tablet, she wrote down as many details as she could remember. Her stylus poured out details about the message. Then she pulled up the Bridge Events Log, reading it line by line.line.

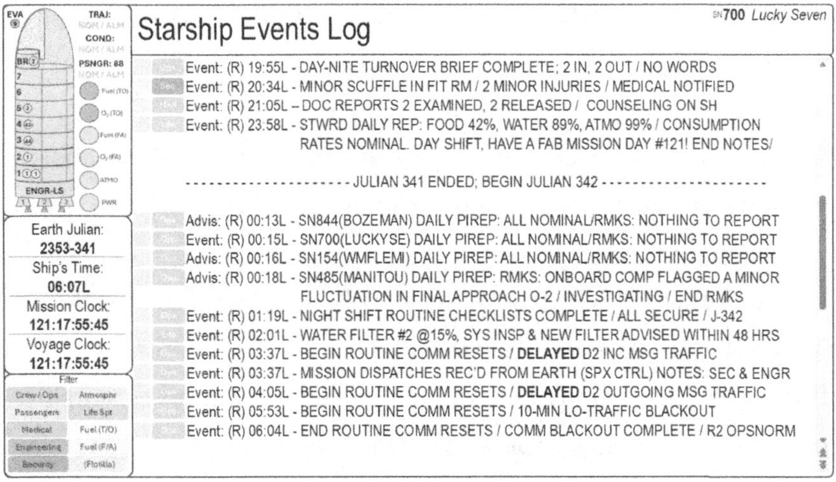

Starship Events Log

SN700 *Lucky Seven*

EVA

TRAJ: NOM / ALM

COND: NOM / ALM

PSNGR: 88 NOM / ALM

BR 7 6 5 4 3 2 1 ENGR-LS

Fuel (T/O) · O_2 (T/O) · Fuel (F/A) · O_2 (F/A) · ATMO · PWR

Earth Julian: **2353-341**

Ship's Time: **06:07L**

Mission Clock: **121:17:55:45**

Voyage Clock: **121:17:55:45**

Filter: Crew / Ops · Atmosphr · Passengers · Life Spt · Medical · Fuel (T/O) · Engineering · Fuel (F/A) · Security · (Flotilla)

Event: (R) 19:55L - DAY-NITE TURNOVER BRIEF COMPLETE; 2 IN, 2 OUT / NO WORDS
Event: (R) 20:34L - MINOR SCUFFLE IN FIT RM / 2 MINOR INJURIES / MEDICAL NOTIFIED
Event: (R) 21:05L – DOC REPORTS 2 EXAMINED, 2 RELEASED / COUNSELING ON SH
Event: (R) 23:58L - STWRD DAILY REP: FOOD 42%, WATER 89%, ATMO 99% / CONSUMPTION RATES NOMINAL. DAY SHIFT, HAVE A FAB MISSION DAY #121! END NOTES/

--------------------- JULIAN 341 ENDED; BEGIN JULIAN 342 ---------------------

Advis: (R) 00:13L - SN844(BOZEMAN) DAILY PIREP: ALL NOMINAL/RMKS: NOTHING TO REPORT
Event: (R) 00:15L - SN700(LUCKYSE) DAILY PIREP: ALL NOMINAL/RMKS: NOTHING TO REPORT
Advis: (R) 00:16L - SN154(WMFLEMI) DAILY PIREP: ALL NOMINAL/RMKS: NOTHING TO REPORT
Advis: (R) 00:18L - SN485(MANITOU) DAILY PIREP: RMKS: ONBOARD COMP FLAGGED A MINOR FLUCTUATION IN FINAL APPROACH O-2 / INVESTIGATING / END RMKS
Event: (R) 01:19L - NIGHT SHIFT ROUTINE CHECKLISTS COMPLETE / ALL SECURE / J-342
Event: (R) 02:01L - WATER FILTER #2 @15%, SYS INSP & NEW FILTER ADVISED WITHIN 48 HRS
Event: (R) 03:37L - BEGIN ROUTINE COMM RESETS / **DELAYED** D2 INC MSG TRAFFIC
Event: (R) 03:37L - MISSION DISPATCHES REC'D FROM EARTH (SPX CTRL) NOTES: SEC & ENGR
Event: (R) 04:05L - BEGIN ROUTINE COMM RESETS / **DELAYED** D2 OUTGOING MSG TRAFFIC
Event: (R) 05:53L - BEGIN ROUTINE COMM RESETS / 10-MIN LO-TRAFFIC BLACKOUT
Event: (R) 06:04L - END ROUTINE COMM RESETS / COMM BLACKOUT COMPLETE / R2 OPSNORM

She tapped her voice comms app and selected two recipients: Telore and DeBrus. After a moment's thought, she added a third person, Richter, and cued the mike.

"Gentlemen, get up here, now. My quarters. Stat."

Three acknowledgments came in immediately.

She pulled the ear pod out of her ear and magnet-stuck it to her small worktable, thoughts swirling. A moment later came a knock at the door. The three entered at her invitation. She stood and turned to the door, closing and locking it after the three entered.

"Take a seat please."

As before, Exec Officer Telore, Security Officer DeBrus, and Engineer Richter all sat down around her small work space table. She stepped past the three the table, her muffled Velcro steps the only sound in the room. She stood facing them.

"Someone has directly threatened to kill us all and destroy *Lucky Seven*."

Stunned silence followed. She eyed them, gauging their reactions.

The men waited for her to continue without commenting.

She looked from one face to the next.

"The voice message I just received said it isn't personal, and there's nothing we can do to stop it. Then something about us all arriving at Mars dead on arrival, nothing left to chance, we brought this on ourselves, knowingly carrying the extra mass along, the pieces of *Lucky Seven* would rain down on Mars and . . . they would stand avenged."

Richter murmured, "Mein Gott… perhaps there are multiple saboteurs aboard? You heard the voice say 'we' would stand avenged?"

The Captain nodded.

Telore spoke first. "Stand? No one stands on a Starship, we float. So maybe he's not even aboard?" Telore asked.

DeBrus spoke up. "It may be radio-controlled from another Starship in our flotilla. And . . . avenged for what? Mars has no oppression, no wars, no fascism—being oppressed is a problem for Earthlings, not Martians, Ma'am."

"So, a group of people, an organization. Maybe the *Free Mars Movement*?" Richter suggested.

Telore shook his head. "Those guys are hippies, not terrorists. They don't believe in violence."

DeBrus cut in. "Captain, before we speculate on who the bad guys are, we should nail down a few more details, if ye please. Did he say when this would happen?"

"Only that we'd get to Mars. DOA, in pieces."

"Okay, that narrows it doon ta sometime between today and final approach. Not much to go on. What about mannerisms? Inflection in his voice? Was he young or old?"

She shook her head. "The voice was heavily modulated."

"Did he identify himself in any way at all? This mister . . . bad intentions?"

"No. And I'm not certain we're dealing with a 'mister.'"

"What aboot—" but the Captain held up a hand, stopping DeBrus for a moment.

"Strange thing, now that I think on it—the voice didn't use contractions." She thought for a second, then shook her head. "Mmmm . . . nope, not one contraction. Almost awkward grammar."

"So maybe this voice was an AI-gen?" Richter suggested.

"I don't think so. It sounded like he's . . . looking forward to it? Like a birthday. Eagerly anticipated but inevitable. *Tick tock, cannot stop the clock,* the voice said."

Richter nodded. "AI doesn't have any concept of the future, it just mimics our human understanding of time."

The four sat lost in thought for a moment.

"This git's got nerve, thinkin' we'll take this lying down," DeBrus said.

"He started off saying 'You don't know us . . .' so it sounds like it's not personal."

Telore broke in. "Well then, these people *definitely* know you. Someone wanting you to overlook someone we either know very well, or someone from our past."

"So, someone trying to take Earth's political crap to Mars?"

"The colonies were more than 250 years ago—they'd have done that long before now."

"Well, what then?"

"A wise man once said, 'some men just want to watch the world burn."

A few nods.

"But who?" Richter asked. "This is a question, ja, but I'm more concerned with how they plan to do it. The 'who' is a coward and a crazy person, we can deal with later. We must learn how they intend to destroy *Lucky Seven*."

Richter looked at her in silence. After a moment, she exhaled.

"The extra mass. Eighty kilos."

"Ja, exactly."

"X-O, you're on background checks, and you're responsible for keeping the bridge secured around the clock. No more passenger visits; keep traffic to a minimum. Run scans of all ship-to-shore communications and have ship-board AI take a run at cracking any codes embedded in routine messaging and vid-chats. Someone is getting their instructions."

"Copy that."

"That's not all. I want you on assessment as well. We know our weakest points, inside and out. Prioritize the top twenty scenarios that result in our unpreventable deaths, and list the actions that could cause the greatest damage or cripple us in a way we can't fix before final approach. Then narrow it down to single actions that could accomplish multiple results from your top twenty. Think in terms of *location* but also in terms of *time*.

Where and when in this voyage are we weakest?"

"Yes, ma'am."

"DeBrus, be devious. Get inside the head of our bad guy. Think of all the ways you would sabotage the ship and explore what may have been required before we launched. Then search those areas, see what you can find."

"Yes, mum."

"Mister Richter, you are on immediate action; your movements around key parts of the Starship won't rouse any suspicion. Search without planning it all out, act on instinct. Think four-dimensionally. Look where you've looked before and then go look again. Search top to bottom, and everything in between. Use one of Mister DeBrus' spare scanners if you have to. Consider life support and our fuel tanks, but also ingress and egress points."

Richter nodded his agreement, brow furrowed.

"And keep in mind, where is the best place to hide something?"

"Right before your eyes?"

"Yes, in plain sight."

He started to rise.

"Oh, and get that apprentice kid to help you, Worthington, but don't tell him why—keep it routine. That'll help keep things looking normal for others."

"We have completed propulsion section and I was about to take him through life support sections for his orientation."

"Change it up for a less critical part of the ship then."

"Of course, captain."

She looked at each officer in turn. "Our lives depend on your actions and your judgment, gentlemen."

No one spoke.

"Dismissed."

All three men rose to leave.

"X-O, just a moment."

Richter and DeBrus left the Captain's quarters, closing the door behind them. The Captain tapped a fingernail on her teeth, her focus far away. "There's something I'm missing here . . ." she said simply.

Telore waited.

"By Uncle Mark's beard!" she exclaimed.

"What is it, Captain?"

She turned and locked eye contact. "I'll tell you later. But the call definitely came from inside the house," she said, bringing up the log again, and snapped a screenshot of it on her tablet.

"How can you be certain?"

"The audio file executed during the nightly comms reset blackout."

"Right, it's usually between 3 and 4 A.M."

"Yes—and this morning's reset came late because passengers and a couple crew were messaging Mars and a big dispatch came in from Earth. That's when the message flashed to me. During the Comms reset."

"So . . . a lucky break, that reset being delayed."

"It proves the message was either sent from one of our on-board tablets or terminals, or that it was set to go on a timer, pre-programmed to be delivered at that time from aboard *Lucky Seven*. Either way, that message was generated, or pre-packaged, aboard this ship."

"Then it self-deleted."

The Captain nodded.

"Gone. And nearly all the passengers were in their quarters, likely sound asleep. See?"

She showed him the log screenshot, and in the corner, a schematic of the Starship showed all passengers in their quarters, except one, down in Engineering.

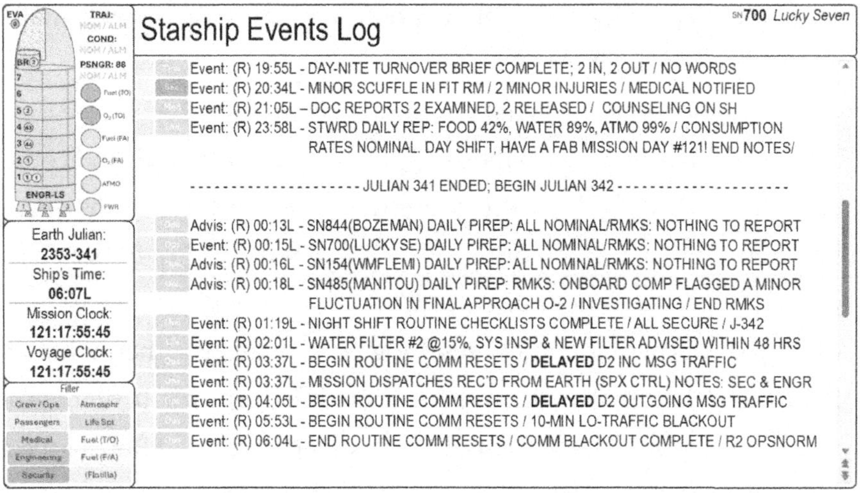

"Look, just here. One pax awake, down in Engineering. Probably Worthington again, or Kazama; I've seen them both up early."

He looked sharply at the Captain, awareness dawning on his face.

"That boy's always in the midst of something. But you don't think it was a passenger though. You suspect a crew member – one of us?"

"Crew have greater access to sensitive areas than passengers do. Think in terms of stashing a two-hundred-pound explosive. Plus, crew members have a more intimate knowledge of times to avoid, such as the 3-4 A.M. comms reset."

"A crew member, I can't believe it. Daniels?"

"No. That guy thinks every day is Disneyland. He's not the type."

"Belvoire then?"

"That would be ironic. It is the perfect cover, being a caretaker who heals and protects . . . right up to the moment he kills us all."

"So . . . you suspect Richter? Or DeBrus? But they've been Seven crew for multiple crossings now. I can't believe it. I won't believe it."

She looked at Telore, eyes boring into him. "Can we afford to take that chance, Brad?"

"Of course not. But you just invited them both to this briefing."

"Mm hmm. But neither one thinks I have any crew suspicions at all. I also set a hook, to see if either one bites."

Telore thought about it. "What you didn't mention before . . . the log."

"Exactly. If either man reads those logs, as they both should, and comes forward to tell us external comms were down at the time of the threat message, then that man is pointing out it's likely a crew member. Then we'd know that person is not our culprit."

"And if that particular comms-reset log entry vanishes, then whoever is logged in to delete that will leave his digital fingerprints behind. And who on the ship would know how best to doctor the log after it's been closed out each day?"

"The Starship's Engineer or its Security Officer."

"Yep. Aside from those two, only you and I have edit rights to the log."

"So we just restrict access to the logs from everyone else, myself included." Telore said, a serious tone.

"Brad, you are the last man in the world I suspect. I don't need to lock you out of the log."

"Captain, we can't just ignore the least obvious people. That includes all crew."

"How do you mean?"

"It's always the last one you expect who, in hindsight, was the most obvious, right?"

"You're thinking it might be a passenger."

"Someone with nothing left to lose, or no one left to lose. At least it's a possibility."

"As in a solo traveler? A political extremist?"

"Or a *Bonnie & Clyde*."

"Okay, point taken. During your shifts, start combing through passenger profiles. Solo travelers first. Report anything that looks a hair out of place."

"Yes ma'am. I'll get back to the Bridge then."

Captain Strahan nodded, watching him go.

Chapter Six

News from Mars

"A Marsquake!" the smiling face on the screen proclaimed.

Trace grinned at Chrissy's enthusiasm, which came spilling out through her video message. He had no idea if Chrissy had any other contacts in her role as Mars Welcome Ambassador, but surely this was not a level of enthusiasm for a story she had told several times.

She was a breath of fresh air.

"I mean, no one thought the volcano was still, you know, moving? But they're saying it's just deep rock layers shifting. So . . . they're not predicting any severe events; so that was here in the *Mons-Megaplex*, that's our capital city, and it was a 5.6, 40 clicks away, I think. Anyways, no one in the other cities, *Nerus* or *New Marrakech*, felt it. They're pretty darn far away."

Speaking of *darn pretty*, Trace thought. Chrissy smiled, and she glowed like sunshine. He liked that she didn't cake herself up with makeup but kept it light. There were times she showed up on screen without any makeup, or maybe it was just a few touches.

She glowed with a radiance he couldn't explain. Her eyes, perhaps. Or the way she kept tossing flyaways out of her face without getting annoyed at them. Her smile.

"Oh, and here's a thing," she continued, "I think that soon, we'll be close enough to have an actual conversation. It may be several seconds of delay on either side, but that's almost like having a conversation, right?"

"I'm excited to have you join our school, Trace, and I can't wait to meet you when you land. It's not expected for Mars Ambassadors to meet new arrivals, but . . . since you're landing near us at Port Mons, I can meet you, if you'd like that?"

"Um, yes please," he murmured as he listened to the rest of her message. He wished he could respond, have a real two-way convo. Maybe just a week or two.

"Tell me more about Transition, did your Starship have a big party? And have you had any other fun things since then? Okay, so, I guess that's it from this end," she said. "Vid me back soon, okay? Okay. See ya."

She reached out and the screen defaulted back to the Mars Arrival Center's red three-peak logo with a stylized starship, orbiting above.

Her smile stayed in Trace's mind.

He sat up, propped his tablet on a small shelf, and turned on the camera to start a video reply. He pushed record.

"Hey there, o Ambassador Extraordinaire, I just wanna let you know that when I get there, we—"

The door chimed. Dad poked his head in.

"Family meeting, parents' cabin. Shouldn't take long, I think."

Trace turned off his recording and deleted it without sending.

The four gathered. Louise must have already been in their room, waiting.

Dad stood along the narrow gap alongside the bunk beds. Mom and Louise sat above his eye level, legs flopped over the top bunk, curled under to prevent floating up and away.

Trace reclined above them, stuck upside down on the ceiling, his legs folded one over the other.

"Trace, you funny," Louise giggled, swatting a hand at him and missing. She stayed seated next to Mom on the top bunk, Mom's arm wrapped around her shoulders.

Dad cleared his throat.

"I have news from Mars—there's been a change in plans. My boss contacted me, and the company is restructuring, expanding into a new market in the city of Nerus. They've already coordinated both your mother's job and mine to be relocated there."

"Wait—so we're still landing at Port Mons, but then we're moving to Nerus right away?"

"After our week in quarantine at the Mars Welcome Center, yes. That's the plan."

Louise spoke up. "So . . . we'll be driving across the desert? How many weeks will that take?"

"There's trains, honey. Really really fast ones, faster than on Earth even," Mom said.

"Oooo I love trains. Like the one we were on when we left Colorado?"

"Even faster. No wind resistance to slow us down, so they really zip," Dad put in.

"What's Nerus gonna be like?" Trace was having a hard time liking this news.

Mom spoke up. "Remember what the Captain said? It's kind of like a cross between Venice and Las Vegas—it has Broadway and West End musicals, the flooded part of the city, some of those huge hotels and concert venues, and several Universities, I think?

"And they have this really large lake you can walk around, that glows at night time," Dad put in.

"Sounds great," Trace said, thinking quickly through the implications of once city over the other.

The Flight Academy is at Port Nerus. Nerus good.

Chrissy lives in Mons-Plex. Nerus bad.

Dominique lives in Nerus, I think? That's . . . not sure. Prolly Nerus bad,

Nexus is smaller than Mons, so living like sardines in a can . . . Nerus bad.

Tartarus does regular concerts in Nerus, right? Nerus good.

I won't be in that cool science teacher's class. Nerus bad . . . sort of bad . . . whatever.

Nerus is party central, while Mons is government jobs and serious. So . . . Nerus good?

Fate seemed to be choosing the people he might end up staying connected with. Trace tried to picture the city in his mind, but all he could conjure was people shuffling past each other, fighting for scant resources like power, water, and food. Not enough space.

Nerus.

He thought he might record another message, to take the place of the one Dad had interrupted. He tapped the M.A.C. messaging app open.

The right words did not come.

His thumb, hovering over the 'record' red circle, then floated a couple seconds later over to the blue "X." Trace closed the app and his tablet too.

* * *

He woke early, as always, and opened his MAC app to try again to send Chrissy a reply. He couldn't put it off forever, and bad news does not improve with age.

Since this one would feel mainly like bad news, he decided to make this vid different. After quietly slipping out of his cabin and floating down to Deck 2, he held his tablet at arm's length and stood, ready to record as he prepared to launch upward from where he stood by the *oculus*.

He pressed the red 'Record' dot.

"Hi Chrissy, hope you're having an excellent morning. Evening. Whatever. Hope you're having an excellent whatever." He smiled.

"So, it's early. I'm awake before everyone else . . . but a morning person isn't all that bad, right? Listen, I have some . . . news. My dad and mom's company reassigned them both to jobs in Nerus, so that's where I'll be finishing up high school. But we're still landing in Port Mons, I'm pretty sure that part won't change. So we can still meet when *Lucky Seven* lands, right? I'd really like to meet you, you know, in person. You're really fun to talk to."

He smiled, letting the recording continue.

"But let me show you the fun way I start every day—I do this every morning, to earn my first java of the day."

He gently pushed off the padded carpeting, adding a slight twist as he went.

Even though he knew right away he had misjudged the push-off, he kept the recording going. He held the tablet at arm's length, then set it in a flat-plate spin that went opposite the direction he twisted up through the Core. He hoped the effect would be nothing short of epic.

"So this is the Core, the center that's in every Starship, like an elevator shaft with no elevator. Just all this empty space to float around in. I'm trying to get better at my high-dive skills, because in just a few weeks, I'll never really be able to do this again. So here's my—ouch."

The tablet tumbled away from him as his head bumped the underside of Deck 7. He righted himself, and pushed off after the tablet to grab it, and caught up with it quickly before it hit anything.

"Woah, sorry," he called out, knowing it was still recording his message to Chrissy.

He gripped the tablet and leaned back into the camera's field of view, but upside-down.

"That was crazy."

He kept recording, upside down. "Anyways, I'll have more news soon. I think we're coming up on four weeks. Is that right? I'll be sure to send you a highlights reel. Write me back, tell me all about your day."

"Oh, whups, my bad." He spun the tablet around so he would be right-side up once more.

"DM me back, and we might be able to have a real two-way conversation in a week or two? See ya." He smiled, but despite his goofiness, he didn't feel happy.

Louise and Kasia came out a short time later and asked if he wanted to join them at breakfast, but he did the polite-pass, saying he wasn't hungry.

* * *

Telore swiveled his chair around to face the Captain. The two had the bridge to themselves at this late evening hour.

"Ma'am, that marks twenty-four hours since you noted the log entries, and neither Richter nor DeBrus has reported anything to me about it."

She shook her head. "Same. And we know both must have reviewed the log by now. Let's take a peek here . . ."

She punched a series of tap-commands on her tablet, and the large central screen flashed the current log. She scrolled back to the threat audio time frame. Telore turned back around to watch the big screen as she scrolled.

She scrolled a bit, and then a bit more. Finally . . . there. She located the time and innocuous events aboard the ship at the time the threat audio message was digitally delivered to her quarters.

She swiped the log up onto the large screen.

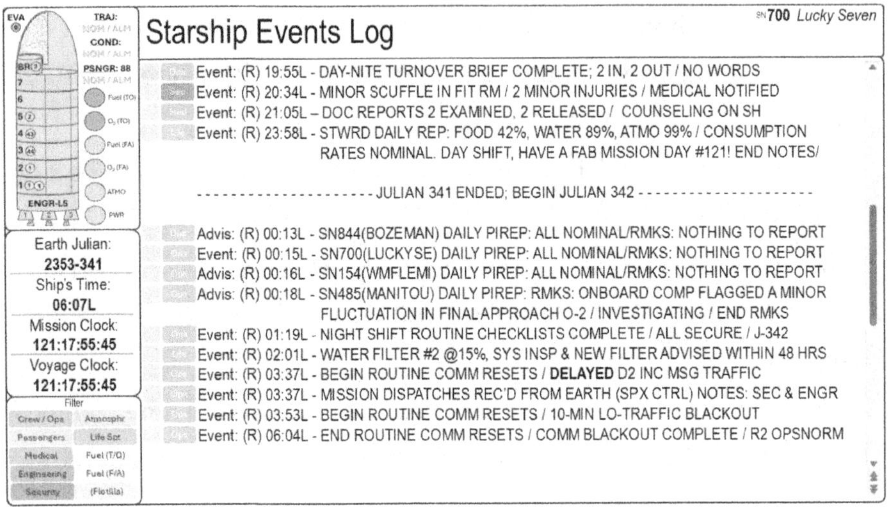

"Wait, what the . . . ?" Telore scrutinized the entries. "It's gone. The comm blackout entry's gone?"

The Captain scrolled back further. At 03:53, the log showed the Comms Reset and blackout, which she knew to have been executed by the computer several hours later; 05:53, ship's time, to be exact. Now it showed 03:53, a single-digit change to the time stamp on the comms blackout.

"Someone altered the log and we didn't notice? How?"

"I was anticipating this. Let's see who was logged in at the time the deletion and changes were made. Oh dang. Look."

"Wait, so they were both logged in at the time these changes were made? That's . . ."

"Exactly. But the key-logger shows neither of them made any changes. Weird."

"And yet clearly, one of them did."

"That's what it looks like, ma'am."

"So one of them turned off the keystroke logger? I thought that was impossible after liftoff. Preservation of critical mission records, or some such."

"It is impossible. Whoever it was found a way of bypassing a core control wall."

"How long a time?"

"Richter was logged in for seven minutes and thirty seconds, DeBrus slightly longer, at nearly eight minutes."

"Ooo, look here, looks like DeBrus corrected a typo as he was reviewing some previous log entry, um, three days before. That change was made during his eight minutes in the log, whereas Richter appears to have made no changes."

"Could be that leaving that edit visible was a distractor, to cover his tracks?"

"I trust Mister DeBrus with my life."

"I know I do too. Richter as well."

"So either we're both extremely poor judges of character, or we've been barking up the wrong tree all this time. But either way, . . ."

The Captain finished his thought. "Someone has set up a damn good smoke screen and is one step closer to killing us all."

* * *

At that same time, under the *StarDome,* Trace and his little sister sat in two random chairs, taking in the Mars view, as it grew ever larger by the hour.

He tried to imagine how far apart Nerus and Mons-Plex were. He had estimated it as basically more than the width of the United States, but no direct train route existed between them. His mind drifted . . . he wondered where they would live, and would it be in the same part of town as Dominique? Would they cross paths ever?

Why the heck did Mom and Dad's job locations have to switch? It was just so frustrating, the way fate had pulled him away from good things. Again.

But Dominique, in the mean time, he would actively avoid. Odds are he was safer up here than in other common areas, regardless. Louise interrupted his thoughts of avoiding Dominique when she leaned forward, pointing through the windows.

"Um, Trace? Is that what I think it is?"

"Where?"

"There, just above the one with the purple stripe."

Trace squinted in the direction she was pointing. At first, he saw nothing.

Then, a small fuzzy patch caught his eye. From halfway along the length of her hull, a puff of white vapors was escaping into space, like spray from a fine-mist lawn sprinkler.

"Oh . . ."

One of the starships was venting some gas into space.

"Come on, Louise. Let's go."

Trace pushed off, heading around the seating area toward the bridge entryway.

Chapter Five

Which Cause to Choose?

Lucky Seven's twin swivel-mounted external cameras had already spun left and zoomed in on *Manitou*, where the gas was starting to form a small cloud above her hull.

Just as Telore was tweaking the camera views toward *Manitou*'s hull, there came a beep at the Bridge Door call button, as well as a thump on the door. He brought the Bridge door camera up and pressed the call button.

"What can I do for you, Mister Worthington?"

Trace seemed out of breath on the small monitor.

"Um yeah, hi, my little sister noticed one of the Starships is losing gas into space, and we thought you should know."

"Yes, we are aware and looking into what's going on—we should know more shortly. So thanks for acting on your observation, but we've got it from here."

"Okay. Anything I can do to support?"

"No—actually yes, there is. Stay there, just outside the Bridge hatchway, in case others feel the need to report the same thing—let them know we're aware and

they don't need to push that call button. Don't speculate and don't start rumors. Got it?"

"Yes, sir."

"We'll make an announcement as soon as we know something. In the meantime, stand your post. Understood?"

"Understood. Uh, Trace out."

Telore smiled briefly. On his screen, he saw Trace nod and turn back to his sister, say something to her, and she nodded. The two remained at the Bridge railing by the hatch.

Telore minimized the Bridge door feed and returned to adjusting the external camera on the largest, central screen. The view showed a fine, narrow jet spouting out into space, pure white.

Captain Strahan flipped her radio feed to the bridge speakers. Captain Bolton's voice, a gravelly bass, poured out of the speakers.

"–ay again, *Manitou* to *Flotilla Four*, we are declaring an IFE, that is an in-flight emergency Code 3, venting into space. Engineer McMann is suiting up for his E-V-A through our *Murphy* door to isolate and seal the leak. Please stand by."

The venting continued. A figure could just be seen emerging, above the edge of the starship. Telore zoomed the view to maximum and locked on the lone figure, clipped to his Starship on a tether.

The gas venting out into space was just ahead of him as he maneuvered himself using the suit's built-in gas jets, canister of sealant in his free hand. A moment later he was next to the leak itself, where the jet of white gas continued, unabated. He let the canister of sealant drift beside him, floating tethered to his belt on a clip.

He seemed to be picking at something on the hull with his gloves, but the camera couldn't see exactly what.

Agonizing moments dragged on.

The spray of escaping gases diminished . . . and then a few seconds later, stopped completely.

"They sealed it off!" Telore cried out, uncharacteristically emotional.

Captain Strahan cued her mike. "*Manitou,* this is *Lucky Seven*. We see your venting is no longer visible. Your engineer is closing a panel and . . . is now turning aft toward your *Murphy* door."

"Thank you *Lucky Seven,* our status displays show the same, with tanks holding at current levels. Life support nominal, no losses. Fuel system O-2 is . . . standby, *Flotilla Four*." The channel fell silent.

The camera followed the engineer until he performed a brief visual inspection of the surrounding area before pulling himself back inside his starship and closing the outer door. Another few moments passed before *Manitou*'s Captain Bolton spoke again.

"*Flotilla Four, Manitou*. Here's our situation. We've maintained full pressure inside the living spaces, life support atmo is 100%. Engineering reports the breach was in our fuel tank O-2 reserve, in the external vent line, between outer valves one and two. The leak seemed isolated to the line itself, between the two valves. Engineer McMann closed the valve above the leak and that solved the problem. A simple fix, thank all the gods."

Captain Kilmer of the *Williamina Fleming* spoke up again. "*Manitou, Fleming*. Was it a micrometeor strike? Or mechanical fault?"

Again, a pause before Captain Bolton replied.

"Captains, take me off speaker, please."

Telore looked around at Captain Strahan, watching her intently as she flipped back to the private captains' channel. The conversation continued.

"Okay. We replayed the external camera feeds and captured a hull plate buckling from the inside, coincident with the start of the leak. It came from under the plate, just below the external vent release #1. McMann didn't even have to unscrew any hull side panels . . . the venting came from under the access panel, right by its hinges. He reset the shutoff valve to full open, then back to closed, and the leak stopped immediately."

"That's a lucky break," *Fleming's* Captain Kilmer noted.

"A little too lucky. Six inches higher and it would have vented above both shutoff valves. Pure luck it happened between the two cutoff valves."

"But you still have your shutoff directly at the tank."

"That's the disturbing part—the valve on the tank itself seems to be stuck in the open position, and as you well know, there's no way to get at that while we are underway. The internal feeds down to the Raptor landing rockets are fine, but it's this external vent line that's been compromised. So we've gone from three stops to one. If our one remaining valve fails, we'll be venting our landing O-2 into space all the way to Mars, and we'd have to leave *Manitou* in Orbit until she can be repaired."

"And shuttle passengers in small groups down to the surface," Captain Merrit, Starship *Bozeman*, finished for him.

"Exactly. And I would very much like to not be the first Starship to test such a thing."

Another pause in the conversation.

Captain Strahan cleared her throat. "Captains, *Lucky Seven*. May I suggest our engineers confer while we sort out this puzzle? In the meantime, what are your O-2 levels for the landing burn, *Manitou*?"

"Bad news; we're barely above red-line for landing. At these levels, we'd be giving *Neil Armstrong* a run for his money for *emptiest* tank upon landing. I have no intention of cutting it that close. If one of you is up for a docking and transfer, we'd be much obliged."

"You could transfer O2 from life support," Captain Merritt suggested.

"It's never been done in space before. Hell, it's never been tested in space before. And given our main landing tank valve is frozen in the open position, I'd rather not risk any of the other internal valves with just nine days before we flip and land. An external refill is our best option."

"So an I-S-R transfer then? That's what you have in mind?"

"That's what I'm asking you for. Something else for our engineers to discuss. I'll be asking for a volunteer Starship to do that docking and transfer. Can we re-convene in 30 minutes?"

All the Captains acknowledged then let the channel go silent.

Captain Strahan called Richter to report to the bridge as soon as his own Engineers' conference concluded; he acknowledged.

Fifteen minutes later, he and Telore and the Captain met gathered the Bridge to discuss.

"So, Captain, you consider now going to the rescue with a propellant O-2 transfer?" Richter prompted.

She shook her head. "I don't like it."

He persisted. "This is just a routine transfer, a re-filling of the propellant tanks, we do this every time we depart Earth with the main tanks. I could handle the controls easily and leave us plenty of extra for landing."

"I know it's feasible, and I know you are more than equal to the challenge. Something just feels . . . off about this whole situation."

"If the Captain requires it, I could run the numbers, down to the liter."

"It's not that. There's something else . . . elusive."

Richter stayed quiet, unsure what to say.

At length, she looked up at him. "Thank you, mister Richter. Stations, please. It's going to be a long night."

"Aye, Captain." He left the Bridge.

Telore turned to face her. "Captain, what do you want to tell our own passengers? Undoubtedly word has spread and rumors will fly."

"Right. Make an all-call telling them a leak has been contained and all our Starships remain on course.

"Ma'am." He turned back to his screen and cued his camera and microphone.

"Ladies and gentlemen, your attention please? You may have heard or seen that our flotilla-mate, the Manitou, has vented some gases into space. We've watched Manitou's Engineer stop the leak and there's no immediate danger to any of us in

Flotilla Four. We'll know more by morning, so please put aside any concerns you have and get a good night's sleep. It's just under ten minutes to lights out, so we bid you a pleasant rest, and we'll see you in the morning."

Then, as an afterthought, Telore brought up the Bridge door camera.

"Trace, can you hear me?" To which, Trace floated over, his sister close by.

"I'm here."

"Thanks for helping out, and as you heard, all's well for now. Please feel free to go turn in, and we'll see you tomorrow."

"I understand. Good night." Trace turned away from the camera feed and he and Louise left over the railing.

Telore and Captain Strahan focused ahead, eyeing the *Manitou* and *Bozeman.*

"X-O, am I going mad, or are those two Starships closer to each other than usual?"

Telore ran a few numbers and checked camera angles to be certain.

"Yes ma'am, they're about a hundred meters closer than they were this time yesterday. Separation . . . still more than a click between them."

"The venting. It's pushing them together." She lapsed into silence, and brought up *Manitou*'s design schematics on her tablet. Time ticked on.

Ten minutes later, Captain Bolton re-convened the Captains' conversation on their secure channel.

"*Flotilla Four*, moment of truth—who's going to pull my fat out of the fire?"

Captain Strahan opened her mouth to speak, then paused.

No. Something wasn't right.

After a long moment, Captain Merritt spoke up. "*Bozeman* volunteers."

Silence on the line for a moment.

"*Manitou* thanks you, *Bozeman*. Let's add our Engineers to the channel in five, please."

The line went quiet, though it was still active. Captain Strahan keyed her on-board comms again. "Mister Richter, from your station, will you please join the Command Channel for another conference in three minutes?"

"Of course, Captain."

He clicked off the channel.

A few moments later, the engineers' conference convened.

Manitou's own Engineer McMann reported that their stuck open valve was likely due to misapplied maintenance before takeoff, that showed green (open) and gave no cause for concern in the hours before launch.

"Nine days to orbit. Why couldn't this leak have happened months ago? We could have had all the time in the world to fix it."

Others on the channel ignored the comment as unproductive.

Richter spoke over the shared channel. "May I suggest we do the docking und transfer during this night? Fewer passengers' prying eyes, less chance of distraction or problems inside the Starships while they are all sleeping."

Captain Kilmer, aboard the Fleming, spoke up. "Sound logic. *Manitou*? When would be ideal?"

Captain Bolton addressed his Engineer. "It's a six-hour procedure, from burn to burn, but we can shave it to five, right, Mac?"

McMann, from the background: "Yeah, I can do it in five."

"Okay, *Bozeman*, shall we say 0100 maneuvering for 0200 docking? We both run a mock final approach in the meantime, to get everyone's head in the game before we fire up maneuvering jets."

"0200 docking works. Let's get our prep work done now, friends. I want everything checked and re-checked between all four engineers."

"Agreed."

"*Seven . . . Fleming* . . . will you please confirm observational status and record everything you see?"

"*Williamina Fleming* confirms."

"*Lucky Seven* . . . confirms."

The channel clicked off.

Many minutes passed before Captain Strahan spoke or even moved. She took a moment to return to her cabin and collect her thoughts, letting Telore know she'd be back in ten.

He acknowledged without looking away from his screens. He gritted his teeth at not being the Starship coming to the rescue, but the Captain's orders stood. He updated the log that *Lucky Seven* would remain in standby and observation mode, then stabbed the < ENTER > key a bit harder than necessary.

Captain Inara Strahan, in the privacy of her own cabin, screamed into a pillow.

"Why didn't I come to the rescue? They all expected it. Why did I hold back? Am I scared? Do I not trust my people? Am I more scared for my own ship, when *Manitou* clearly needs help? Which cause is more important? Which cause should I have chosen?"

She finally shook her head, downed a pouch of cold water, wiped her face with a damp cool towel, and left her cabin.

"Snap out of it," she commanded herself. "Stand up and stand strong."

She left her cabin, floated down and across the core to the three screens

She reached behind the Mission Clock to feel for the telltale bump that only a select few knew was there.

She murmured softly to herself, holding that spot, almost like a little prayer. "Uncle Mark . . . what am I supposed to—"

"Captain?"

She jolted around, the voice startling her.

Richter.

"Um, Mister Richter, I'm just . . ."

"Remembering," he finished for her.

"I thought I would find you here, sooner or later." He put on a serious, penetrating look she hadn't seen on him before. Intense. "You will do the right thing. You always have. Now is not the time to have doubts."

She nodded, not wanting to let this conversation play out any longer. "Stations, please."

"Yes, ma'am." He turned and pushed off downward, toward his post in Engineering.

With that, and doubting herself more than ever, she returned to the Bridge.

Four decks below, Trace and Louise had settled in for the night. Ten minutes before, when they entered their cabin, the core had been abandoned.

Trace lay back on his pillow, clipped his sleeping elastic belt into place, and tapped his screen awake. There was a message from "StarParty" asking him to meet up under the *StarDome*. He swiped it over to the trash without opening it.

He tapped his screen, put in some Ear Pods, and watched a historical short about *Viking One* and *Viking Two*, the landers that sent back the first images of Mars' surface.

After twenty minutes or so, he paused the vid, pulled one ear pod out, and listened for Louise. She snored softly from the bunk above him. He yawned.

He was about to sleep his screen and watch the rest in the morning, when a pop-up notification flashed in the corner of his screen, a live-message call. Live?

He opened the notification before it could be dumped to voice mail. It was Chrissy. He tapped the 'Connect' button eagerly, and her face filled his screen. Her smile was pure warmth and her eyes danced, looking down at her screen or keyboard and not directly at the camera.

He lay his head back on the pillow and smiled at her in his own camera.

"Hi, you," he said, grinning.

Several seconds passed. Her face lit up in surprise and she smiled back at him.

"Oh Trace, you're here! So cool. I'm just getting ready to get some sleep, and the rumor mill here in Mons-Plex is cranking out some real goodies, so I thought I'd check in. You've got just over a week left, you must be so excited. What's the latest?"

Trace replied right away.

"The craziest thing just happened, and my sister was the first one to see it, out the windows. One of our sister ships, ahead of us, was actually venting some gas into space, can you believe it? After a short time, they shut the leak off, and our Bridge said it's been contained, no more danger, blah blah blah. I don't know if they said that just to keep us calm, or what . . . um, so what are people saying on your end?"

"That's nuts, about that other ship. But here, there's this crazy rumor floated that one of the Starships is in some kind of danger—but apparently those rumors get started during every Crossing. In fact, I'm not supposed to even talk about it. So, somebody starts up some dumb idea that one of the . . . eighteen Starships on the way . . . is being sabotaged or something. But it's been almost ten years, Martian standard, since anything bad happened during *the Crossing*. Did you know that? I think that's like, twenty of your years."

A pause, then trace replied.

"I have heard that, and I think I know the time you're talking about. If it's the same one my Engineer told me about, it was the Hydros, which, get this, used to be my own Starship Lucky Seven, before she was re-named or whatever. A micrometeorite punched two holes in the hull, and two crew members died saving the ship. Can you believe that?"

Chrissy's eyes went wide, even before he finished.

"Wait. Wait. Did you say Hydros?"

"Yeah, why?"

"The rumor mentioned Hydros."

"You're kidding."

"No, I'm not." Chrissy shook her head. *"What I heard was something about Hydros sinking for good this time. But since Hydros isn't flying any more, everyone assumed it's an empty threat or like one of those lame killer clown hoaxes."*

She paused, then looked straight at Trace's face in the image. *"Oh my gosh . . . you don't think . . ."*

"Oh," Trace said. "That's freaky. Okay, I'm awake now." Trace shifted in his bunk a little. "But the leak was aboard *Manitou*. And *Lucky Seven* is fine, right? I could hear it in the Lieutenant's voice. He sounded almost . . . bored, in his last announcement. I think he would have sounded more urgent or something. Like, more stressed, if we were in real trouble."

He paused, looking off-screen in thought.

"So whe– "

"You cou—"

"Sorry."

"No, you go first. Ladies first." Trace smiled.

"He he, okay. What I was thinking is you could ask your Engineer if he needs help with anything. How he replies could tell you if he's concerned. Didn't you message me a month ago about those little walkie-talkie radios?"

"Yeah I do have it, but nah, he's been acting weird lately . . . it started when he told me he hung up the Exo-Suits in Life Support but the Security Officer says they're stored below that, down on Deck 1 or 2. Plus, it's after curfew, and I think they're serious about it this time."

"Oh. Okay. But if you find out what this is all about, tell me, all right? I wanna know you're okay."

Trace smiled. "I'm great, now that we're talking."

"I really like talking to you too. You're easy to talk to. So . . . what are you looking forward to the most after you arrive?"

Trace blurted out, "Ha—now you're slow-pitching to me. I want to meet you, of course. I just hope you can be there when we land. Will you be there?"

"It's a half-hour train ride to Port Mons, and they'll keep us behind glass from each other until you finish quarantine . . . but yes, I'll be there with bells on. I really want to meet you too."

Trace's cheeks flushed. He liked the balance of the conversation, and he found Chrissy stunning. She wasn't a supermodel, the fake kind grown in a genetics-mutation lab, but more of the pure, wholesome, girl next door, the kind boys are inexplicably scared to talk to.

It was another hour before exhaustion took them both and they finally said their good nights.

Chapter Four

Obeys and Inspires

Trace was going down with the ship.

He dreamt of *Hydros*, an imaginary tall ship of the line, three-masts. Her shredded sails flapped in the black skies under pounding rain, with sheets of lightning arcing overhead. She was going down by the head, her bow already under the water . . . the waves crashed over the middle of the ship and swept him over the side, headfirst into the black waters—he snapped awake, gasping for air.

The room was dark; after a moment, his breathing calmed. The clock showed 03:39 AM.

Eight days until flip-turn and re-entry. *Just eight days*, he told himself. *You can make it.*

He set an alpha-rhythm-inducing white noise called *Tibetan Singing Bowl*. He wiped the sweat off his face with his T-shirt sleeve and flopped back in the soft mattress.

No sleep came.

He tried counting electric sheep. But since he wasn't an android, that didn't work either.

He swiped up his display, showing the nose camera view of Mars, with the trip clock overlay. Two Starships ahead of *Lucky Seven* had joined together, looking like they were actually *touching*; he wondered if that was on purpose or some trick of the camera angle as they neared Mars.

By now, the pale pink dot was fist-sized on his display—dark shades and lighter shades easily seen, but still with no clear surface details.

He stared *through* the screen, mind spinning through different thought threads on high speed. Girls, his future, *Hydros*, changing cities, girls, burning up on re-entry, his next workout, *Lucky Seven*, girls, *Hydros* . . .

Giving up on sleep, he pulled the light blanket aside and unclipped his sleep belt. He eased his legs over the side of his bunk and pulled on his blue shipsuit. Louise slept on.

He grabbed the walkie-talkie Richter had given him, slipped it into a thigh pocket, and zipped it shut.

Clearing his cabin, the core at night lighting was pleasing, just a few blue lights on each level. What time was it? He looked across and up at the clocks. Pushing 4 AM. Maybe he would rest up in the *StarDome*, clear his mind.

In near darkness, he pulled himself over the level four railing and launched himself gently upward . . .

And crashed right into Richter. The Engineer was flying downward at high speed toward the lower decks; Trace was knocked toward the opposite side, flailing his arms around, disoriented with the head-over-heels, equal-but-opposite reaction of their collision.

"Hey, watch out!" the engineer said gruffly, grabbing a nearby ladder.

Trace flailed around and managed to grab the railing up on Deck 6. He turned himself toward the engineer, who was now passing level four and still descending. "Sorry Mister Richter, I didn't see—"

"Ach, forget it. Just watch where you are going, okay? And get back in your cabin, now." The engineer shook his head and seconds later, pulled himself through the *oculus* to Deck 1.

Trace noticed the man's coffee drink pouch floating away, tumbling slowly as it went.

"Hey, Mister Richter, you forgot your—" but the *oculus* door had twisted itself shut with a dull thump.

Wait. That door never shut. Not unless . . .

The pouch drifted further away, spinning and tumbling over the railing, leaving a trail of small droplets behind it. It bumped the wall over the railing on Deck 5, then rebounded and slipped out of sight.

Trace sighed and pushed to fetch and return it to the Engineer. He could ask about the *oculus* as well. Then follow orders to go back to his cabin.

* * *

"Stew, what are you doing up here on the bridge?" Telore asked. "Thought you'd be watching the docking from the dome all this time."

Daniels smiled. "Yes, all very exciting stuff, right? But with all the chaos on board *Manitou*, I knew you would be stuck up here and might be able to use a . . . good old cup 'o joe," he said, passing the Exec Officer a full sippy pouch of *Mountaintop Blend #4*.

"Hm. Hazelnut, my favorite. Kind of you." Telore smiled, accepting the drink and taking a big sip through the straw. He turned back to his station, blinking sore, red eyes and sticking the drink down on a desktop Velcro pad. He adjusted the camera angle and watched the transfer operation in progress. They were halfway done and looking good.

Daniels looked over the lieutenant's shoulder. "I have to say, I kind of hoped we'd be the ones coming to the rescue."

Telore shrugged. "Captain felt we were too far out of position—*Manitou*'s venting nudged her closer to the *Bozeman*."

"Uh huh," Daniels replied. "Where is she, anyway?"

"Below, in her cabin, meeting with Sergeant DeBrus," Telore said without looking away from the screen.

"I see. Well, enjoy that coffee, it's the last hazelnut on board."

Telore murmured his thanks and watched the screen for signs of trouble. He took another sip.

Daniels nodded and left the bridge, grinning as always.

Below, Trace had found Richter's lost pouch and was just turning to head back down to Engineering. From his spot in the shadows, he saw movement above him. Not wanting another midair collision, he held back.

Daniels' back was to him as the Steward zipped past, heading downward.

"What is going on down there?" Trace muttered under his breath. He peered carefully over the edge to watch Daniels go. While he watched, he twisted the pouch's end-cap tightly shut to prevent any leaks and slid the coffee into a vest pocket. It was warm, but not uncomfortable. He kept his eyes locked on Daniels.

The Steward didn't follow Richter through the Engineering *oculus*, which remained shut. Daniels stopped his fall one level above the *oculus*, Deck 2, and tugged himself over the rails toward the dead-end space Trace and Louise had noticed their first week aboard.

Curious, Trace turned himself upside down and gently eased himself head-first down the portside ladder, hand over hand. He moved slowly, so as not to rouse the steward's attention. He gripped the rung at the floor level of Deck 3, and peeked under the ceiling of Deck 2. He looked toward the Deck 2 dead end—there it was, plain as day in a soft orange light.

But no Daniels.

"Wha—?" He breathed, pulling himself further as he rotated himself feet-down. He drifted into the dead end, an empty space as always. Solid wall ahead of him, above, below, and on the sides. It was as though Daniels had vanished into thin air.

Gripping a ceiling water feed pipe for stability, he pressed his ear to the wall to listen—an awkward chore, but he managed.

A few mild bumps came through the wall, and what sounded like a faint, distant hiss, which then cut out.

Silence.

After a few moments, he heard a gentle thump directly in front of him, through the side wall, just adjacent to the surface he was listening to.

With a surge of adrenaline, he pushed off the dead-end wall, hard. He soared straight down Deck 2's walkway, walking the curving wall with his hands until he felt he was out of sight. He gripped a railing and spun around, just as a yellow light spilled into the L-2 space from a side door inside the dead end—an opening in the right bulkhead that did not exist, until now.

He peeked around the curve of the low wall, watching, waiting from shadow.

Daniels' face was silhouetted in the light, looking around in all directions from behind the cracked-open hidden door, but he gave no sign of seeing Trace where he skulked.

Daniels had a rectangular block in one hand, smaller than a brick but similar in shape. He pulled himself through the lighted doorway with his free hand, and once through, pushed the fake wall panel back shut with a click.

Trace could barely make out his movements in the low orange light—Daniels stuck the small gray brick to the wall, then gripped it with both hands briefly from either end. Then he wiggled at the brick with one hand, where it remained, stuck in place.

Daniels looked down the hall. Trace snapped back from his line of sight, certain Daniels had seen him. But no, the steward looked down, floating in place for a moment as he drew a tablet from his cargo pants pocket.

Trace dared another peek around the curving wall.

A few lights flashed on the screen, soft red colors reflected in Daniels' face, then the screen went dark. The steward pushed himself over to the core and launched himself sharply up, gracefully floating away. As he passed near, Trace ducked down under the panel railing.

Daniels floated up and away, pushing off the opposite wall and landing back at the bridge hatch.

Trace saw a light of the hatchway open, then go dark. He floated himself towards the Deck 2 dead end, curious about whatever Daniels had attached to the secret door.

Having no pen-light of his own, he squinted at the brick-like object. Then he saw it, behind the brick—the hairline seam of the secret door, and a small indentation of a thumb-press, nearly invisible in the wall itself. He pushed the hidden button, and a small latch popped up, which he gave a gentle tug . . . the door wiggled only slightly. The brick, set over the seam between the doorway and the bulkhead, had effectively sealed the secret door shut.

"Weeeeird . . ." his whisper trailed off.

He was about to reach up and grab at the brick, when he heard a strange noise behind him, one he had never heard before. He reached the rail and peered over just in time to see the blue *oculus* door light turn red, indicating a hard seal, a lock down. Then a flash grabbed his attention from above. Deck 3 and Deck 4 lights, all the blue access panels of every passenger's cabin door, now showed a locked-down red.

The running lights all up and down the core, now red. All red lights.

The on-board vacuum warning.

The spaced-out wall displays flashed silent emergency warnings and Trace noticed the time on all three displays showed red digits as well. 04:17 AM.

Trace gripped the rail, fine beads of sweat starting to form on his brow.

He looked up, across, and down.

"Think, Trace, think!" he muttered to himself. "Everything's in a vacuum lockdown. Where's it safe?"

Were the toilets up in the fitness deck sealed against a vacuum? He wasn't sure. Probably not.

What about the Bridge? That would be the most important place to keep sealed during a lockdown, and they probably wouldn't open up. The *StarDome*? Nothing enclosed there at all. Passenger cabins were already locked up tight.

"Think!" he breathed one more time, then the answer became obvious. He turned in desperation back to the secret door. The brick Daniels had placed. Was it a safety device? A security measure?

He looked at the brick for instructions--blank, no writing at all. The color of the rectangular block matched the color of the wall paint nearly perfectly. This object was meant to blend in, be stealthy.

He had to make it move. He grabbed it with his right hand and pulled—no budge. He braced his left arm against the wall and pulled as hard as he could with his right. Nothing.

"Okay, it has to come off somehow, cold welds only happen in a vacuum," he told himself.

Was the core about to go full vacuum? He listened for any hissing, felt the air for any movement, any wind. More sweat formed on his brow, and he picked up his breathing.

Deep breaths, he felt he couldn't get quite enough air in his lungs.

He thought about Daniels. Now what was Daniels doing when he attached this thing?

He gripped it from both ends, thumbs below the corners and fingers above. He tried to wrench it loose, prying it up with his thumbs. Nope. No movement.

Then he squeezed his fingers and thumbs as if mashing down a double cheeseburger before a giant hungry bite.

Success. The brick released its magnetic grip on the wall.

He moved it just aside the hairline seam and let it re-attach itself. Then he pressed the thumb release.

One tug of the latch and the secret door swung open, just large enough to accommodate one floating person. Inside, a soft yellow light shined down from above.

Trace pulled himself through the opening, then swung around to shut the door behind him, hearing it lock itself in place. His ears felt the pressure change. Good, this room was pressurized. He breathed a deep sigh of relief.

In the Deck 2 dead-end space he had just vacated, a ceiling camera turned toward the secret door and zoomed in to the spot he had just vacated.

* * *

As Trace had huddled, hidden in those Deck 2 shadows, Daniels had floated up and across to the bridge. The Steward pulled himself over the core railing and through the bridge doorway.

He closed the hatchway and tapped a few quick jabs at the door entry panel. It locked with a satisfying click. He turned to look at the lieutenant.

Telore was floating just above his seat, left hand up to his forehead as he tried to grab for his chair with the other, now just out of reach.

He shook his head as if trying to clear the cobwebs, then looked over at Daniels, who spoke to him in a jovial voice.

"Oy, Lieutenant, you do not look all right . . . how was your coffee, by the way?"

Finding a hand-hold overhead, the Executive Officer rounded on the Steward. He floated over to him and gripped Daniels by both shoulders, squeezing him in a viselike grip and shaking his head to rouse himself.

He glared into the smaller man's eyes and his head lolled a little.

"What . . . have you . . ." Telore gasped, his grip on Daniels' shoulders weakening by the second.

"What they said could never be done, fool," Daniels whispered into Telore's face, slapping the lieutenant's hands away. Telore's eyes sagged.

"Wha . . ." the lieutenant breathed.

Daniels reached out, gripping his superior officer by the lapels and pulling the nearly unconscious man close and again, whispering, "I have killed your precious *Lucky Seven*."

"You'll . . . never . . ." he trailed off and went silent. His eyes sagged closed and his arms flopped, floating out at his sides.

Daniels slapped him hard.

He yanked him close. Telore's head flopped forward.

"But sir, I already have. You are as good as dead. We . . . stand . . . avenged." The last word came out as a hiss.

Daniels shoved the Exec Officer away from him.

By reflex, Telore made a last vague swipe in front of him. His eyes stayed closed as he floated helplessly across the bridge. Telore thumped into the wall by the entry hatch and rebounded upward at an odd angle.

Daniels went after him, grabbing the beefy man and pulling his hands behind his back. He clicked steel manacles into place until they bit into Telore's wrists. Then he rotated Telore into the fold-down jump seat in the wall and locked the handcuffs to the seat itself. He tossed the keys aside, not caring where they floated off to, and brought himself nose to nose with Telore once more.

He grinned into his face for a long moment, licking his own lips. He sniffed once and turned away.

Easing into the captain's chair, he buckled the lap restraint in place.

"And now, my dear Exec, time for me to call the shots. Bet you never thought you would live to see a lowly deck steward take command in the Captain's seat, did you?" He shrugged. "I guess you won't live to see anything ever again. Hm."

He grinned and pressed a button on the chair, causing a swivel-arm to rotate neatly up.

"But back on Earth, my clone will live . . . forever." His eyes flashed as he tapped at the captain's oversized touchscreen tablet, glowing brightly before him. He accessed the login prompt and entered Captain Strahan's credentials.

"Time to lock everyone up—we cannot have any pesky interruptions to my final acts of service, can we?"

First, he locked out all access to the Bridge.

Then he tapped in a quick series of commands and opened a new master command prompt labeled "Vacuum Actions." Confirm? The screen asked him.

"Absolutely!" he said joyously, stabbing the green 'confirm' button.

Within seconds, the computer locked down all passengers' cabin doors, crew doors, common area doors, and the *oculus*. He watched with glee as the status board showed every door on the entire vessel now sealed tightly shut, including stairwell access down to Deck 1.

Richter was trapped; the Captain and DeBrus, also trapped. Doc was still in his quarters. Trapped.

The ship status board showed:

WARNING
CORE STATUS: VACUUM

"At least that's what they will think!"

He ran a quick personnel locator scan of the ship, squinting up at the large central screen. The screen filled with little green dots, all still in their quarters. The Captain and DeBrus were now trapped in her quarters, presumably engaged in some critical, yet now equally irrelevant, conversation. No matter. They were going nowhere.

"Well done, little worm!" he said gleefully to the tablet. "And thank you for looping all external crew commands!" *Lucky Seven*'s computer was now his alone.

He scanned down the Starship, level by level. Richter, that infuriating German, was standing directly beneath the *oculus*, no doubt frantically trying to get it open. Daniels activated the camera that viewed that area and saw Richter glaring back at him with a mixture of fear and frustration, trying in vain to override the *oculus* locally, to access the rest of the starship.

"Well look who is still awake," Daniels said, though Richter could not hear him. "No sir, you will not be opening the *oculus* while every door thinks the core has gone vacuum."

Daniels shook a fist at the camera, wishing he could just hit the German once. Just once. At least he was contained.

He tapped a few more controls, looking around the ship's scanning viewers, and saw only passengers sleeping. The Captain and DeBrus were now moving about her cabin frantically, clearly aware by now that things were very wrong aboard the Starship.

And they were trapped like rats.

"Let's see . . . all doors secure, and only one door is not hard-wired to the main computer . . . let's just put eyeballs on . . . that . . ." and he changed the main screen from personnel locator to a bank of several dozen common-area core camera feeds. Selecting Deck 2, he tapped the camera nearest to the secret hatch leading to the *Murphy Door*. That wonderful, perfectly hidden access, the one that led to the second airlock . . . the one they were to never reveal to passengers.

Lucky Seven's weakest spot.

He tapped the Deck 2 hallway camera and swiveled it around to look toward the dead end. As the camera turned, a hint of yellow light glowed briefly. But as the door came into view, he could see it was still shut tight.

To be certain, he zoomed the camera in on the magnetic door seal, the one he alone knew how to remove. A marvel of electro-magnetism and pressure-catch releases, he could see it was still stuck, immovably stuck, right where he had placed it.

"Delicious."

No one was getting through that door.

Daniels smiled. He laughed out loud.

"I've done it!" He smiled to himself another moment, taking it all in.

"And now . . . for my final report to the Captain." He opened a channel to the Captain's quarters, one deck below, and waited for her face to appear on screen.

"Telore, report!"

"Oh, I'm sorry, Captain, the Lieutenant won't be joining our little chat today," making sure the unconscious exec could be seen behind him, flopped out in the vid feed background.

"Mister Daniels, what have you done?"

"It is what I am about to do you should be freaking out about, Captain," he said, his voice condescending.

Letting the Captain see, he pulled out a remote control, looking like a smaller handy phone, and woke it. He tapped a blank corner of the display, watching a rudimentary digital interface appear.

"See this, o Captain, my Captain?" He held the device up to the camera feed and tapped the digits 20:00. He then tapped the red "commit" button.

Twenty turned to 19:59, with the seconds ticking away.

The Captain's eyes went wide with horror.

Then her expression hardened to steel.

* * *

After Trace had pulled the Deck 2 secret door hatch closed, he listened for any activity, any sound at all. The yellow light switched off.

No whisper of sound. Not a peep from any direction. No rush of air escaping. Nothing.

His eyes adjusted to the gloom, and he saw he was floating in a room just slightly larger than the cabin he shared with Louise. Aside from a few small red lights a dozen feet or so ahead of him, it was pitch black.

Trace shook his head. He patted his thigh pocket for the Engineer's walkie. Still there. He powered it on and keyed the mike button.

"Uh, Mister Richter? Trace here." Only a second passed before the man replied.

"Worthington! Where are you? Are you safe in your cabin?"

"No sir, um . . . actually, all the cabin doors locked while I was in the core."

"Was anyone else in the core?"

"Yes sir, Daniels. He set this weird magnetic lock on the Deck 2 wall before he shot past me up to . . . the bridge, I'm guessing. I don't think he saw me."

"That foul little weasel. Where are you? And is the core at a vacuum?"

"I don't think so, but all the red lights turned on. I'm in this weird hidden room on Deck 2, because all the other doors looked sealed. So when the vacuum warning lights turned on, I moved his block thingy out of the way and climbed in here."

"Stop . . . you went through the Deck 2 dead end panel?"

"That's the one."

"Ach, *Gott in Himmel* . . . okay, so, now just look around, tell me what you see."

"I see . . . the light above me turned off, and there are some blinking red lights ahead of me. Wait, is this a hatchway? There's a door . . . and it's . . . open."

"No. This is wrong. It should be . . . it should be closed. No red lights.

Trace, you are looking at an emergency hatch that leads outside, and only when it is activated does it have the red lights on. What does it look like?"

"I'm seeing a ring of red lights around the door frame, and three blinky red lights in the middle.

"Okay, forget the battery draining on your walkie, I want you to show me."

Trace turned on his walkie-talkie's camera, which auto-adjusted to the darkness. He pushed off gently from the entryway door, toward the red lights. On his left and his right, twin space suits hung in their racks, clear bubble domes glaring down at him, accusing him of entering their space.

So that's why Richter wasn't direct about where the suits had been stored. He couldn't talk about this place. This whole chamber was a secret. He felt ashamed for mistrusting Richter.

Trace reached up and tapped one helmet with his fingertips. Nothing happened.

"Point the camera toward the airlock, please?"

Trace complied. As he floated past the two suits, he reached the inner hatchway door, standing wide open. The blinking lights inside were on something bulky, a large metallic bundle set inside what looked like a small air lock.

"Mein Gott . . . the extra eighty kilos . . . you found it." Richter murmured.

"What? What is it?"

"Trace . . . this is a bomb. Someone is trying to destroy the *Lucky Seven*."

Trace turned the display around so he could see the engineer's face.

"Forget this, I'm out." Trace turned himself away and pushed off back toward the secret door.

"Trace!" Richter called out. "Stop. You have to go back."

"And what? Do what? That's a *bomb*."

"Yes, and you are the one in a place to do something about it."

Trace paused, having reached the door. He heard Richter's voice.

"Remember what a good trainee does. What does he do?"

"He obeys."

"And what does a good leader do?"

"He inspires."

"Correct. And right now, I'm telling you all our lives are in your hands. I cannot open the *oculus*, and the Captain is either incapacitated or locked out of the bridge. You can't get to any other part of the ship, and we have no clue when this bomb will detonate. So turn yourself around and do your duty. Right here, right now, Mister Worthington."

"Very inspiring."

"I know."

Trace snorted in disbelief and shook his head.

"Okay, boss. I'll try."

He took a deep breath and turned back toward the airlock. Then he held up the display so he could see the engineer's face.

"So who's doing this? Daniels?"

Richter shook his head. "Doesn't matter . . . all that matters is we have to dis . . . able . . . the device."

"Are you all right?"

"I'm tired, awake for forty-eight hours . . . it will pass."

Trace reached the airlock.

As if on cue, a new display on the device lit up with four digits.

Four digits, counting down.

20:00 glowed for a moment, then changed to 19:59, 19:58, and so on.

"Uhhh, Mister Richter? The clock on this eighty-kilo bomb is ticking."

* * *

"Mister Daniels, you will cease this—" at which, the Yeoman turned off the Captain's connection.

He sleeped his hand-held remote detonator and twisted the chair's harness release. Floating out of the seat, he pushed off toward the left to within arm's reach of the bulkhead, where several locker-cabinets were stacked, floor to ceiling. The screens on this side showed green status for air, food, and water, except for the false red vacuum indicators for the Core.

He found the cabinet with a wrench icon and twisted the handle. The door swung open and he pulled out a tool tray of simple chrome tools, each set into its own molded position. He tugged loose the largest set of cutters, very nearly bolt cutters.

He let the bomb remote control float in front of him while extending the handles on the cutters. After levering the tool open, he caught the remote control between the pincer blades.

A beep from his right caught his attention, and Daniels saw the Captain was trying to raise him on the tablet. He looked over to check on the lieutenant. The man remained motionless, still tied up in his chair. The Captain's tablet went on chirping. He ignored it.

He held both handles with the small remote control squeezed snug between the two sharp blades.

He brought his hands together in a smooth pincer motion. At first, the remote resisted. The display lit up, flickering and flashing wildly under the tremendous crushing pressure.

Then with a fresh surge of effort, Daniels forced the blades together until they touched.

Snap!

The two halves of the bomb's remote control drifted apart from each other.

Daniels grinned.

He noticed his own reflection in one of the cutter's chrome blades.

"For you," he said to himself.

Chapter Three

Its Crew is Its Family

"Trace. Trace, I need you to focus.".

"I'm here."

You have to push the explosive out the hatch into space. There is no other way I can imagine."

"Uh huh," Trace said.

"You completed your suit pressure test before. This is the same."

"That was months ago."

"So? It will come back to you."

"Right."

"We take it one step at a time. But please listen: if we lose connection, don't forget to clip a tether to your suit inside the air lock before you open the outer hatch. You understand?"

"Yes, but . . . don't these suits have some kind of maneuvering jets or something?"

"This requires weeks of training to master; we have no time. Please just use your tether. Quickly now."

"Okay."

He looked at the two space suits. The one had its name tag on it, *RICHTER*, and the other had no name tag. Out of respect for the engineer, he picked the non-Richter suit.

"Okay then, you remember? Legs first."

"I got it."

"Now, reach up inside, grip the neck of the upper half and pull it down over you."

"Wait, how can we keep in contact?"

"Ah yes, that's a problem. Okay, turn the volume up to maximum and drop it into your Shipsuit chest pocket. Maybe you will still hear me."

"Okay. Done. Can you hear me?"

"I can," came a muffled reply. "Okay, your top half. As soon as the upper half and lower half meet, use both hands to slide the . . . erm, hip locks, into place. Ja, now twist the locks to prevent them opening or catching on anything. They should be flat . . . with the side of . . . the . . . suit."

A few seconds later, "All set. They are locked and flush. Are you all right?"

"I'm not feeling so . . . let's do this quickly, power the suit on and tell me your wrist display. You see two green numbers, both 100%, yes? Your air supply, and suit pressure."

"Powering up . . . yes, two green, 100%. Suit power also shows full."

"Ah, yes, that also. Okay, the helmet. Pull it down, find the grooves, and twist it into place. You must hear a click."

The helmet twisted but missed the threads.

He tried again, and missed again.

Trace closed his eyes.

The threads found their groove and he twisted the helmet into place with a click. He tried to lift the helmet free by pressing straight up on both sides; it held firm, locked onto the rest of the suit.

"I think I'm ready," he said, looking up at the bomb. The clock passed through twelve minutes and continued.

"Okay, just check your suit vitals once more, please."

With fumbling hands, Trace rotated his left wrist over, tapping it awake with his right index finger.

"One hundred over one hundred, full power." Trace stepped inside the airlock. With the bomb already inside it was a very tight fit. Trace had no intention of making it angry, so he tried to climb in without touching the thing.

"Now, pull closed the inner door."

Trace reached back, carefully avoiding the bomb casing, and pulled the door shut. He twisted the locking handle until it stopped, and a green LED came on.

"Hatch closed."

"Now, your tether. On the right side, the box with two rings sticking out of it. The top tether is for 75 meters, and the bottom one is for 50. I suggest you choose the longer one."

"The bottom one says 75. I'm picking the bottom one." He slipped two gloved fingers through the ring and pulled the flexible cable from its reel inside the wall; the line reeled out with no resistance.

"Okay . . . that's good." Richter's voice was fading.

He clipped the carabiner ring into his belt anchor loop and yanked the loop in a couple directions to ensure it would not come loose.

"All hooked in."

"Good. And now, the fun begins. First . . . we purge the . . ."

"Air. Purge the air. On it." Trace saw just above the outer door, the "PURGE" button. Watching his wrist display, he jabbed the button. A hissing sound filled his ears, then it lowered in volume . . . until silence filled up the space once more. A red "VACUUM" light turned on.

"The vacuum light came on. Suit still good."

"Okay. Now, with one hand . . . I want you to twist open the outer door handle and use the other to hold the bomb so it does not drift away from you. You must keep . . . positive control . . . und throw it into space."

Trace set a hand on the hatch release handle, and the other on the bomb.

"Boss, I'm not . . . I can't . . ." Trace's voice trailed off.

"Trace . . ."

"Hrm?"

"Relax."

"Terrific." Trace muttered to himself. "I'm about to get killed a million miles from nowhere, and a gung-ho engineer tells me to relax."

"I heard that."

"Sorry."

"Try to focus."

"Be like Adidas?"

"Just so. Be like Adidas."

"Mister Richter?"

"Ja, I am here, but I feel I may be . . . unconscious . . . soon."

"Before today, I wanted to be a Starship pilot."

"I know this. And now?"

"I never want to go near one again."

The engineer chuckled. "You will."

"How do you know?"

The line was silent for a moment.

"Mister Richter?"

"Hm, ja?"

"How do you know I will want to board a Starship again?"

"Hmm . . . well, you see, Starship is a home, a home worth fighting for."

"But I'm just a passenger, a guest. I'm along for the ride—it's not *my* Starship." He let out a breath. "I just want to be with my family."

Richter's voice was a whisper.

"Trace, a Starship . . . its crew is its family. And today, you are . . . that . . . ffff . . ."

Trace nodded, looking at the red digits as they ticked away. Nine minutes.

"Okay. I'm ready."

The channel was silent.

"Mister Richter?"

Nothing, not even static.

"Hel-lo?" Trace looked up at the handle labeled EXIT. He set a hand on it and rested the other on the top of the bomb casing. He inhaled. He exhaled.

Bracing himself, steady with both booted feet, he twisted the handle. The door tugged him slightly, then he let it go, to open wide on its own.

Beyond, the stars—tens of thousands.

Trace nudged the bomb, which wiggled a little. He saw some Velcro tape holding it in place.

"Getting the bomb moving out the hatch now." Maybe Richter could still hear him?

Trace lifted the bomb. The two Velcro strips pulled loose with just a little effort, and he carefully pointed the bomb out the door, using just his toes to send him and the device floating smoothly through.

With his free hand, he grabbed at the edge of the airlock framing, and his hand found a handgrip. He pulled himself through the doorway, turning awkwardly as he exited, just like turning over a deck's handrail.

The bomb nearly slipped out of his other gloved hand, but he squeezed down, keeping a grip on it.

It was a challenge to turn himself the right way to stand on the hull and keep the device from bumping against *Lucky Seven*, but he managed.

"Okay, getting set up to make a big crazy jump," Trace said, now breathing a little heavier from the exertion of maneuvering the bomb around.

"I think I'm going to try to jump away and behind the Starship, before I throw it . . . I hope that's what you had in mind."

Trace looked up, above where he crouched. Into space.

Oh.

Wow.

He expected it to look like the curtain of night back on Earth, a wall of blackness that might seem to be just a few dozen miles away. But this was deep. He shuddered involuntarily. His whole body started shaking at the sight of . . . the Universe, laid bare before him.

"Okay, focus on the hull, Trace," he told himself. "What is in front of you. Never mind the Universe—relax."

After he had calmed down, he looked around behind him, forward.

"Where are the other starships?" He couldn't see them.

He looked down at the display. It showed just under 6 minutes remaining.

Trace knelt as best he could and yanked on his tether to ensure it was, in fact, still attached. Good.

"Okay, here goes nothing!"

He looked down at the black hexagon tiles of the Starship, in their rows just below him.

He pulled himself as low as he could, crouching.

He inhaled.

He exhaled.

In one motion, he pulled himself slightly aft, toward the rocket engines, released his grip on the handrail and tightly gripped the bomb on both sides of its casing.

He flexed his quads and leaped into space.

"Unghh," he grunted.

Trace floated away, upward and backward, toward the stern of the ship, rising away as *Lucky Seven* drifted out of view under his feet.

No matter which way he looked, just empty space. The stars moved in one large field, tiny dots of light, slowly crawling across his plane of view before him.

"Mister Richter, if you can hear this, I think I got a good launch, I'm not spinning too much. Starship is now beneath me, behind me."

Feeling a gentle tug at his waist anchor point, Trace noticed the slightest bit of resistance pull from his anchor line as it unspooled from the airlock.

It started him slowly turning left as he floated up and away.

In a moment he could see the Starship in all its beauty before him, and for the first time, he could see the entire hull, nose to nozzles.

The cable continued to reel out. His slow turn continued.

He waited until he could not see the Starship. He tried to imagine the direction that would be behind the Starship and second-guessed himself several times.

He gripped the sides of this thing tightly, this horrible thing on the verge of vaporizing him, or at least blasting him into little pieces. He could feel the cloth-metal mesh of the suit's gloves squeezing against the comforting reassurance of the edges of the bomb . . .

A new fear gripped him: What if he couldn't let go?

He tried flexing his fingers, relaxing his grip. It took some doing, but he managed to make a couple of his fingers loosen their grip. Okay. He could do this.

How close was he to the end of his tether, drifting away? Surely it must be close?

He looked around. None of the other Starships was visible.

Just blackness.

And stars.

Wait. Not just stars.

Over the top of the bomb, far ahead and left of *Lucky Seven*, he noticed a pale blue dot.

Earth.

He thought about Jeni and his buddies back in Greater Colorado.

The gift that he hadn't had the strength to open.

His high school. He felt his eyes welling up.

Then, unbidden, Chrissy's face filled his mind.

He looked down at the bomb and inhaled a deep breath, pulling the bomb against his chest.

Trace heaved.

The bomb, its smooth black surface barely visible in *Lucky Seven*'s fading dorsal running lights, drifted away slowly.

Trace had no sense of movement, and it occurred to him he had no idea where *Lucky Seven* was either. At the other end of this tether, right?

He swept his arm around, left then right, searching for the tether. It seemed to still be behind him.

He should be floating back toward the Starship after tossing an object roughly his own mass away . . . right?

He breathed.

He licked his lips, but cottonmouth had gripped him, and he couldn't conjure up any saliva.

The only sound was his own breathing.

The bomb drifted beyond the glow of *Lucky Seven*'s running lights.

Having lost sight of the edges, Trace focused on the red digits of the countdown, the only part he could still see. The display was small now, too far away to read the numbers.

A moment later, the numbers had blobbed into a single red point, just visible.

The red light rotated out of sight as the bomb made its own slow turn.

"Mister Richter, can you hear me?"

Not silence, but a few strange clicks on the channel. They continued in a strange sequence Trace couldn't make sense of. It almost felt like a series of taps on his helmet, but he felt no vibration.

Then the radio channel went dead again.

Wham!

Trace smacked, back-first, into against something very solid, and it shocked him. He thought he had at least twenty more yards to go. His head thumped back against the back of his helmet. The impact rolled him around, and right away he could see *Lucky Seven*'s hull.

He flailed and fumbled, grabbing out at one of the handholds flat-nestled alongside the honeycomb row of heat tiles. He missed the grab by a wide margin and bounced up off the Starship at a slow floating pace.

His tether was briefly in front of him, then behind him again. His legs flailed around uselessly.

The momentum of throwing the bomb backward left him drifting forward, toward the nose-end of *Lucky Seven*. He drifted up, away from the Starship, thirty yards or more above the hull before his tether snapped taut, effectively pulling him back downward towards the hull. He floated past the green and yellow stripe and saw the dorsal-side windows of the *StarDome* ahead.

"Um, Mister Richter, I'm coming in hot," Trace called out. "What do I do?"

No reply.

His speed increased as the tether ran out of slack, wrapping itself up and around the hull. Frantically searching around the Starship surface for any hand-holds, he flexed his fingertips for a quick grab. At last, he was just close enough to make out the faint shadow of several recessed gripping bars running down the long axis of the Starship.

Eying one that seemed close to where his tether was pulling him, he held his left hand out toward the fast-approaching handgrip and brought his right hand up to absorb the impact of his helmet against the hull.

"Bossss?!?"

No reply.

The hull came right toward his face.

Adrenaline surged through him, making both hands tremble. The bar would be just below his waist level . . . he reached. He gripped something solid, he squeezed.

Trace smacked, full-body, chest and helmet, into the hull right below the Stardome windows. One gloved hand gripped the bar, and the other prevented his hard-plastic faceplate from smacking the hull.

His body bounced back up, but his left hand held on. He gritted his teeth, felt his bicep tense up inside his space suit as he turned, and slowed. He settled himself, floating against the Starship, a death grip on the bar.

He looked up and saw Mars, still as big as a fist in space.

He eased himself over to the closest window, hand over hand along the bar.

He looked down into the bridge to see if anyone was actually in charge of this catastrophe.

Fifteen feet, directly below him, Yeoman Daniels sat in the Captain's chair, leaning forward and looking up at him with a look of utter confusion on his face as he bit down on a cigar.

The prick was smoking a cigar.

Trace shook his head in disbelief. Daniels.

Daniels looked at the screens, quick-swiped through external camera views on the main screen and finally settled on the one that showed a wide-open *Murphy* hatch.

An open hatch with no bomb inside.

Trace thumped his free hand against the windows.

Daniels looked up once more, cheeks red with anger.

With his free hand, Trace held up the single-finger salute he had been holding back since the day his father told him he'd be leaving home forever.

Daniels slammed a fist down on the armrest. He spit his cigar across the room, leaving a small trail of smoke trailing in a corkscrew behind it.

He glared up at Trace, face contorted in anger.

The teenager couldn't stop himself—he grinned the second-biggest grin of his life.

As the bomb drifted on the other side of the Starship, the red digits continued their march.

00:20

00:19

00:18

00:17

Trace couldn't hear it, but Daniels was clearly screaming one long, drawn-out screech of rage and denial—he unbuckled himself and jumped up toward Trace, slamming both fists into the thick glass between them. He steadied himself with one hand and banged the other fist repeatedly on the glass, basically right near Trace's face, until small droplets of blood floated freely from his split knuckles.

Trace shook his head back at the deranged man. "Too much time in space, dude . . . you total psycho."

Daniels stopped punching the glass and noticed Trace's tether, stuck to his waist.

There was a cold look in his eye. He held up one hand and made a scissors motion with two fingers. Then he grinned a half-grin at Trace, eyes dark with rage.

Trace's smile vanished.

* * *

Unseen by human eyes or camera lenses, the bomb drifted peacefully away.

00:04

00:03

00:02

00:01

00:00

Chapter Two

Own the Moment

Darkness.

Pinpoints of light, distant stars, watched impassively.

A flash of white light, neon-blue glow at the center.

Fading rapidly.

Darkness.

Flotilla Four drifted onward toward Mars, with all eyes focused on the transfer operation between *Bozeman* and *Manitou*.

The flash of energy washed over *Lucky Seven*'s hull, grabbing Trace's attention away from Daniels. The length of the hull glowed with an odd fluorescence, then faded. Trace blinked the spots in his eyes away.

He looked back down at Daniels. The man was saying something, and clearly his temper was rising again. He was stabbing at the controls now. On the screen, six circles contained within one much larger circle popped up.

"What are you . . . oh jeez."

The engines.

Daniels was going to snap Trace right off the hull by lighting the engines. Then, presumably, crash *Lucky Seven* into Mars at high speed.

Trace gripped the handle with both hands, squeezing tightly. He looked up again at Daniels, and something over the lunatic's shoulder caught Trace's eye.

DeBrus' head eased up into view through a hatch on the Bridge Trace didn't know was there.

How many secret doors does a Starship have, anyway?

Daniels glared at Trace. He stabbed the override. A short countdown, a red screen with a two-minute timer appeared.

Daniels did not notice Trace was no longer making direct eye contact; he continued swearing whatever obscenities he felt Trace deserved.

Trace saw his mouth moving, but in utter silence.

From the Captain's hatch, DeBrus gripped the edges, bracing to launch himself at Daniels.

He cracked his neck left and right, then mumbled something to himself.

Trace could not read lips, but he knew exactly what the man had said.

"Bring on the rough and tumble, DeBrus," Trace murmured.

Daniels stabbed the beginning of the countdown. 2:00 became 1:59 and continued.

The Sergeant-at-Arms launched himself like a missile across the bridge.

Daniels realized, too late, he was no longer alone. Just as he started turning away from Trace, the burly man collided with him, slamming Daniels into the wall and cracking his nose. Blood gushed out and spurted around freely.

"Yes!" shouted Trace inside his helmet.

DeBrus grappled with Daniels from behind, pinning one arm. Daniels instinctively pushed off from the windows, launching them both down, heavily, onto the control consoles.

Trace was so distracted by the scuffle, he let go of his handhold.

Flailing, he grabbed the bar before it drifted out of arm's reach. He tightened his grip, again, with both hands. He watched.

DeBrus grappled Daniels into a cross-throat chokehold, his tattooed left arm bent back by his own ear, and his right arm wrapped tightly around the Yeoman's neck, crushing his windpipe. Daniels' face quickly turned an ugly shade of red.

Daniels brought his arm up, short blade from his belt in hand, and began stabbing at DeBrus' arm. Blood spritzed out, floating away as the two grappled. DeBrus clamped down harder, crushing his windpipe tighter.

Daniels panicked, letting go of the blade. He clawed at the choking tree-trunk arms while his legs kicked the air helplessly.

Trace had a strange thought—*this would be so much better with popcorn.*

"Own it, DeBrus! Own your moment! Yes!"

Daniels' kicking legs weakened, his arms fell lax.

DeBrus relaxed the chokehold but did not let him go.

"Yess!" Trace shouted again.

Still holding Daniels snugly, DeBrus looked up at Trace and winked. His arm continued sprinkling droplets of blood outward, and Daniels likewise spritzed blood from his broken nose.

He made to turn away, though it was awkward keeping Daniels snug in his grip. Trace kept watching.

Captain Strahan had just come up through the small hatchway and launched herself over to Telore, still bound in his chair, head lolling. She shook him and held two fingers to his neck to feel for the life beat. Then he saw her face visibly relax as she nodded to DeBrus and said something.

Trace thumped the window. Both the Captain and DeBrus looked up at him.

He pointed to the main screen.

0:24 remained, next to a visual of the three vacuum engines, pulsing on the screen.

The Captain waked her tablet and hurriedly tapped a series of access commands. The screen stayed red. The countdown continued.

She rapid-tapped some more commands and the tablet turned a pleasant light blue.

She canceled the engine relight.

Trace looked at the screen. Wouldn't you know it . . .

0:07 remained, the timer stopped.

Groaning at his own pun, and thankful no one was listening, he shouted "Luckeeeee! Go Lucky! Woo!"

Captain Strahan swiped the engine controls panel closed. She tapped her earpiece and spoke hurriedly. She paused. Then she tapped it again, repeating herself.

DeBrus had been tying up Daniels; Captain Strahan settled into her Captain's seat.

She tapped some more and looked up at Trace. She spoke.

Trace, now figuring out what she was doing, shook his head.

She tapped the tablet again.

" – ace, can you hear me?"

"Uh, yes Captain, I can now."

"Engineers and their discreet channels." She shook her head. *"Trace? We saw the flash on my cabin monitors and can only assume the ship is safe for the moment."*

Trace nodded, exhaling. "That's good, ma'am. Mister—"

"Nope, just listen. The bomb would have ejected some small shrapnel, but given you threw it several kilometers clear, we may have gotten lucky. Still, we cannot assume your tether, or the ventral hull haven't been compromised. Do you have contact with Mister Richter?"

"I did, ma'am, but he went unconscious. Fifteen minutes ago, I think. Can you please make sure he's all right?"

The Captain turned to DeBrus, who had finished tying up Daniels, both still trailing blood droplets as DeBrus moved about. He wrapped a cloth around his bleeding arm.

She jerked her head toward the hatch, and he nodded knowingly.

He headed for the door, tried to exit. The door remained stubbornly sealed.

Captain Strahan shook her head in annoyance and tapped at a few controls, performed a retinal scan and palm scan to bypass Daniels' worm program, and canceled the false vacuum warning.

She re-enabled the fail-safe, allowing all the doors on the Starship to be unlocked. DeBrus saw the locks disengage, and quickly vanished through the doorway, which closed behind him.

Captain Strahan looked back up at Trace. *"Okay. Trace. I need you to do something while you're outside. Are you up for extending your little spacewalk juuust a bit longer?"*

"Uh, I guess . . . I mean, yes, ma'am, what do you need?"

"Good. First, you'll have to go hand over hand, aft along the hull to the Murphy door, checking your cable as you go. When you're amidships, you'll find the recessed grips to make your way around the curve of the ship to the ventral side, the underbelly. But look sharp, you're no good for the next task if you let yourself float away."

Trace nodded.

"Okay then, get moving. Slow and steady please. Keep a grip on Lucky Seven no matter what. I'll talk you through the next part after you radio me from the hatchway. Go."

"Got it." He reached for a handhold to his left. The cable did not go slack or flop away free of the hull. Good; it might be still intact.

He looked up through the top of his helmet dome as he turned himself and tugged hand over hand along the recessed bars that ran the length of the Starship's dorsal side. He thought he would feel terrified, but having an important task to perform, whatever it was the Captain needed him to do, overrode his fears for the moment.

He moved . . . hand over hand, sliding down the longer bars, with both hands gently gripping as he floated down along the hull. He glimpsed the word "Midline" in small letters at the meeting point of four handgrips, one in each direction, and nearly slipped passed it.

Tightening his grip, he stopped his progress and turned himself sideways. He made the right turn and headed around the curve of the hull toward the *Murphy* hatchway.

He paused to feed his line, now floating slack in large loops above him, through one hand, inspecting the cable for any damage. It shined in his helmet lights, looking like a brand new cable.

He looked up and was surprised to see he could just glimpse two Starships above *Lucky Seven*'s hull, a mile or two away. They were still locked together, nearly finished with the O2 transfer that would ultimately save the *Manitou*.

A horrible thought occurred to him. What if it had been *Lucky Seven* doing the O2 transfer when the bomb went off? Holy hell . . .

"Uh, Captain, can you hear me?"

A pause.

"Trace, stand by please."

He kept silent, not knowing how one replies when directed to stand by.

Another moment passed.

"Okay, Trace, what's your status?"

"My cable looks good, Ma'am; I'm almost at the door. It's still open, and I did not see any damage along the way."

"That's good. Now, since you're already out there, and we have no Engineer available to suit up, I need you to perform a very important task. I need you to inspect the hull for visible damage, especially any heat shield tiles that look cracked or dislodged.

"Uh, how do I do that?"

"You'll be floating free in straight lines, running up and back, along the length of Lucky Seven's underbelly."

"I'll be what?"

"Look around the heat shield tiles. Do you see any hand-holds?"

"Um . . . no . . . there's none except along the long edge."

"Exactly. So you're performing a true spacewalk, floating the length of the Starship, but it must be done slowly, to avoid whiplashing into the hull at the end of your tether."

"I think I got it."

"Put your morning ritual of jumping around in the core to good use. I want four passes down and back, if your air supply allows for it."

"Um, ma'am? How's Engineer Richter?"

"Don't you worry about him. Just focus on your task."

Trace exhaled heavily. "Uh, okay."

"What's your air time remaining?"

"I have . . . an hour and eighteen minutes left."

"I want you done, four laps, down and back, and safe inside the Murphy hatch in under forty minutes. So, ten minutes per length of the Starship, scanning your eyes back and forth for any damage. Understood?"

"Yes, ma'am."

"Check in with me when you're done with each length of the Starship. Get moving."

The channel clicked off. Trace took a deep breath in, and exhaled, turning himself toward the engine bells for his first sweep.

Then Captain Strahan cued the mike again.

"Trace, one more thing."

"Yes ma'am?"

"When you're up near the nose cone, do not go anywhere near the Stardome, understand? We, um, can't risk windows being damaged or scratched."

Trace scrunched his face in confusion, thoughts racing: how was that even—hang on, those windows could probably withstand a jackhammer banging away at them for an hour before they even took a scratch . . . whatever. Orders are orders.

Then it occurred to him why he couldn't go near the windows.

He'd be seen--he'd be noticed by any of the early risers aboard the Starship, and they'd raise the alarm or start asking questions.

The Captain wanted things handled quietly. He tapped his mike button on his wrist again.

"I won't allow myself to be seen, ma'am. And I think the cameras out here might still be on. Trace out."

Trace closed the channel.

Inside the Bridge, the Captain looked at DeBrus, who just looked back at her.

"Boy's smarter than ye thought, Cap'n," he murmured.

She panned one of the dorsal cameras in its glass bubble to look Trace right in his face. She saw him notice the camera move. He gave a salute and a thumbs up.

"Smarter indeed."

"Trace . . . thank all the gods for you," she whispered to herself.

She allowed herself a private grin of gleeful joy at their good fortune. So far.

From the left seat, DeBrus flipped all the Starship's external camera feeds to "Bridge Only," preventing anyone accidentally seeing Trace on their bunk screens or tablets.

Hopefully no one had already noticed a man in an EVA suit crawling around the hull of *Lucky Seven.*

Doc slipped back in through the Bridge doorway. Telore was waking up, thanks to an injection Doc had given him before heading down to find Richter. He shook his head quickly, as if slapped. He squinted up at the screen, trying to make sense of a teenager in a space suit, pawing around outside.

Still within the camera's viewing range, Captain Strahan and her Security Officer watched Trace take a deep breath, let it out, and pull himself slowly down the hull toward the engines and out of view. His shiny tether, trailing behind, slithered slowly across the view screen like some strange metallic cobra uncoiling.

Chapter One

Special Connection

Trace floated above the engine bells, wondering where he should grip the hull in order to inspect them. He settled on the metal housing just above the engine bells, reasoning the wall here must be less critical than the nozzles themselves.

The last thing he wanted to do at this point was break off a rocket engine.

He had already completed three lengths of the Starship, having been saved several times by his tether. That had taken longer than expected to get this far. Just one final length to go, starting with the rocket engines. His wrist showed 21:35 remaining for his usable air supply, and more time than that remaining on the other suit systems.

One by one, he shined his suit lights carefully over the three larger vacuum nozzles, and the three smaller atmospheric nozzles. No scars, no dings, as best he could see.

He rotated himself back around, ready to make one final sweep up the last section, along the tile rows right next to the unprotected part of the hull.

He had been outside much longer than he would have liked, but no one had complained at him yet over the radio. He must still be all right.

Floating slowly up, up, and along the divide between tile and no tile, he found small handholds every so often, just aside the tile line. He used these as often as he could.

A light reflected strangely off one of the tiles, catching his eye. One black hexagon, in the edge row of the Starship, stuck up at an odd angle. He stopped his progress, examined it closely, and saw it had a dent, clearly visible right near a clip underneath, barely still attached to the hull.

He gingerly touched it with a gloved finger, hoping he might press it back into place.

The tile snapped loose, floating free in front of him.

"Oh, sh—" and he grabbed it before it could float beyond his reach. He looked it over carefully, front, edges, and back. Seeing no sharp cutting edges, he tucked it into his suit's chest pouch, where it only partially fit.

The heat tile seemed a safe enough thing to bring inside; the Captain or Richter might want to see it. He finished the rest of his final lap along the length of the Starship. Nothing else looked damaged or out of place.

He turned back and made for the *Murphy* door without delay. His airtime remaining showed less than fifteen minutes—time to get back inside.

* * *

The Captain leaned over Telore's shoulder, reading all the recent radio messages from *Flotilla Four*.

All crew had assembled on the Bridge, aside from Daniels, who had been roughly stuffed into one of the brig's holding cells, unconscious but still breathing.

Richter was groggy, still at effect of the drugs, but Doc was here, helping him come out of it. Doc noted on his tablet passengers were starting to stir, but by the grace of the Cosmos, none appeared to have any clue what had happened in the last couple hours.

"So… am I reading this right?" The Captain asked. "None of the other Starships saw what happened here either?"

"Looks that way, ma'am. All eyes were focused on the *Manitou-Bozeman* docking. A couple cameras in our flotilla, and even one in Flotilla Three, caught a brief flash of light, but they're describing it like a halo glow, behind or above *Lucky Seven*. None of them caught any fragments . . . and none of them captured our space cowboy on camera."

The Captain stood, and looked around the bridge at her loyal four crew members in turn.

"Listen up. All of you are now sworn to secrecy. No one knows what happened here, and *we will keep it that way*. I'll inform Admiral Dixon at Mars Mission Control via secure-link, but until you hear otherwise from me directly, all the details of this incident are on hard lock. No messages, no chats, no log entries. Is that understood?"

Four nods around the bridge.

"Burke, please sedate that lunatic, and let me know when he's fully under."

P.A. Belvoire nodded and left, heading for the brig to visit Daniels.

"Mister DeBrus, bring Trace back inside at the *Murphy* lock. The minute Mister Worthington is safely through, please have a little chat with him about the merits of discretion. These events can*not* go beyond the few of us who know. Rumors will fly, and I will not have *Lucky Seven* become the dagger that guts public confidence in space travel."

"Can I count on you all?"

Nods all around.

"Can I count on you all?"

"Yes, ma'am!" came the unanimous, enthusiastic response from all four crewmates.

"Good. We are Ops-Normal from this moment on. Again, no log entries, no video playbacks. You've got to completely turn off your curiosity and continue to perform admirably. Dismissed."

Richter lingered with the Captain as DeBrus left. Telore resumed his station nearby, setting his coffee pouch into a sealed baggie as evidence, then securing it in a locker.

"Captain, I think we have a good option for how to convince young Worthington to never speak of this again. You see, more than anything, he wants to be a Starship pilot."

"Does he, now . . . that's interesting. Thank you, Mister Richter."

The Engineer nodded. He left to return to Engineering, shaking off the last of his grogginess as he went. He wanted to check every one of *Lucky Seven*'s systems one more time, and re-run pressure checks in both suits.

But more than that, he wanted to see if Trace was all right. He knew the Doc would want to check him out too. From his duty station in Engineering, he glanced up to his Deck 1 ceiling, imagining what was happening right above him at the *Murphy* door.

Trace pulled himself through the outer door, pressing a control to retract the cable back into its housing. It took a few long minutes. Then, he stabbed the button to close the outer door and restore airlock pressure.

As he turned to look through the small inner door window, he saw two eyes, glaring at him right up against the window. He jumped, bumping his helmet top against the airlock ceiling. DeBrus. Arg, the man was infuriating.

DeBrus laughed, a hearty bellow. Trace opened the inner door and twisted open his helmet. The tile floated free of his chest pouch, and DeBrus plucked it out of his way.

"That's some start-reflex ye've got there," he chuckled, reaching out to help Trace back inside the Starship.

"Permission to come aboard?" Trace said sarcastically, his voice cracking and tears welling up in his eyes.

"Get your scrawny arse in here," DeBrus said, pulling Trace into a bear hug. Trace just held on to him for a moment. DeBrus gripped Trace before him by his shoulders and looked at him, practically nose to nose.

"I was so scared," Trace said. "Thought I was gonna die out there." He wiped his eyes. A few small teardrops floated away from his gloved hand.

"*Bollocks*. That's the bravest thing anyone's seen in a hundred crossings."

Trace nodded, gasping for breath.

"Well done indeed." He clapped Trace on both arms, hard.

Trace felt the sting in both shoulders, right through his EVA suit.

"Ow."

"Let's get ye out of this suit, and then we'll have a little chat, hm?"

"How's the arm?"

"Meh," DeBrus shrugged, looking at his bloodied bandage.

Trace nodded, accepting DeBrus' help as the man fumbled at the suit's waist locks.

* * *

"The *Manitou* engineer reports their O-2 leak was clearly deliberate. Sabotage, ja? But long before we lifted off from Earth."

"A sabotage that was barely more than an annoyance? So easily fixed?" Telore asked. "But to what end? Unless—oh." Telore worked it out quickly in his mind. "If *Lucky Seven* had come to the rescue, as everyone rightly expected, and that bomb had gone off while the two Starships were docked . . ."

Richter nodded. No one spoke for a long moment.

"Ma'am, when Captain Bolton first reported his leak, what made you hold back?"

She looked at him. "Gut feel. We still didn't have our mass overage figured out, and the way he described his leak struck me as really odd. So I waited, to see if another Starship would come to the rescue. *Bozeman* was closest, and Captain Merritt made a brave call. The correct call."

No one spoke, leaving the Captain to finish her reflections.

"Gents, if something feels off, no matter what your logical mind tells you, or your emotional heart compels you . . . follow your gut, above all else."

Nods. No one added anything.

No one tried to mansplain her words.

She smiled in appreciation. "So, what else to report?"

Doc spoke up. "Daniels is in the sleeper box, Captain. We have sufficient pentobarbital to keep him under for the remainder of the flight, and several weeks after."

"Are you certain ye don't want me to just eject him, mum? It's the fate he had picked for us all."

The Captain smiled. "Tempting. But I'm sure they'll want him after they determine which court has jurisdiction."

"Glad we don't have to sort that part out, ma'am."

"You and me both, X-O. Anyone have anything else for the group?"

"Ja. This tile, Mister Worthington brought it back inside with him." Richter set it down before the Captain. "I have analyzed it and the damage is superficial. But even better, its location is well away from the red zone for re-entry, so going back outside to replace it is unnecessary. We will have no problems for kick-turn and final approach."

"That's excellent news."

"Ja. Also, I ran a routine pressure check of both EVA Suits. It seems Daniels punctured my suit with just a little hole, a pin-prick in the back, just below the tanks. It took him only seconds, and it would have seemed fine at first, until a few minutes out in the vacuum."

Again, silence in the room as the implications set in.

"So if Trace had grabbed your suit instead of the spare . . ."

"He would have asphyxiated long before having enough time to throw the bomb to a safe distance. And we would all die in an uncontrolled re-entry several days from now, somewhere in the deserts between *New Marrakech* and *Alba Patera*." Richter just shook his head in wonder.

Telore exhaled, exasperated. "That young man has some real luck on his side."

"He made good decisions, and he never quit." Captain nodded, a tear in her eye. "So, anything more for the group?" she asked, wiping the tear away. "Any other near-death close calls we managed to dodge on this trip?"

She scanned faces. No one spoke.

She nodded. "Very well. Bring the lad in."

DeBrus opened the cabin door, where Trace had been waiting, and gestured for him to come in. Trace floated over the threshold and steadied himself with an overhead hand grip.

"Everyone, please give us a moment." The four crew members turned to leave. "Mister DeBrus, please stay."

A chorus of 'yes, ma'am,' and the other crew members left in short order.

The door hissed shut.

The captain gestured for Trace to take a seat, where a soft Velcro-fiber cloth kept Trace, the Captain, and DeBrus from floating up out of their seats.

Captain Strahan looked at Trace for a long moment, then finally spoke.

"You. You saved the Starship, and everyone in it." It sounded almost like an accusation. She looked *through* him as much as she did *at* him.

Trace gulped.

"Mister DeBrus, Mister Richter, Doc, and you are the only ones who know, to my understanding. Unless you've told anyone else what happened, Trace?"

"Um, he said he'd eject me into space without a suit if I . . ."

DeBrus cleared his throat roughly.

"The Sergeant-at-Arms told me not to speak of it, ma'am. To anyone."

The captain smiled. "So your parents don't know? Your sister? And you haven't communicated any details of the explosion with anyone else at all? Not on Earth, not on Mars?"

"Um . . . no, none at all. I think I heard a few voices out in the Core, but I'm not even sure anyone's really awake yet."

The Captain leaned back in her chair, more at ease. She nodded, tapping painted nails on the armrests. "The Lieutenant tells me you might have the chops to become a flight officer."

Trace sat frozen. His cheeks turned red. He waited, wondering where this was going.

The silence drew out.

"Mister Worthington, this entire event buys you exactly zero points with the Nerus Flight Academy Admissions Office, which I presume will be your goal after graduating high school and finishing college. There is no *'Saved the Day'* section on the application."

She continued to hold Trace frozen in her gaze.

"What I can tell you is this: a flight officer must have both the proper training and the self-control to creatively apply all he has learned in every situation. You've either already mastered that . . . or you just got incredibly lucky. So which is it?"

Trace kept eye contact, considering.

She waited him out.

"Maybe it's a bit of both?" he suggested.

"Bit of both," she acknowledged.

Trace allowed himself the smallest smile.

"How badly do you want to fly a starship, Mister Worthington?"

"It's all I've ever wanted to do, ma'am." He kept eye contact.

She tapped her fingers on the armrest again.

"You don't fall under the Uniform Code of Space Corps Justice, so I can't threaten you with a court-martial or dismissal if you disobey my orders to keep silent. But I can reach you in terms you might be able to relate to."

"Ma'am, I won't talk about these events. Who would believe me?"

"No, you won't. Because not only would Daniels' act of insanity erode public confidence in the entire spaceflight industry . . . it would legitimize an extremist shadow group that advocates violence the likes of which we haven't seen since 2030's on Earth, when the old United States was carved in two. We can't let fear-driven fascism take root again. Not on Earth, not on Mars."

Trace sat silently, waiting for the other shoe to drop.

"So let me make this perfectly clear. If you blab so much as a hint or a whisper of the sabotage that nearly took place aboard *Lucky Seven* to anyone, including your family . . . I will personally see to it you *never* see the bridge of a starship again. Never. You have my word on this. Understood?"

Trace inhaled then exhaled. "Ma'am, the doom and gloom threats are . . . um, not needed. I said I won't talk—I won't talk." He stared into her eyes, resolve on his face. "And now, you have my word."

She raised her chin up, still looking him in the eye. "We'll see."

Without waiting to be dismissed, Trace stood up from his chair, trembling, and turned to leave. He made eye contact with DeBrus as he turned away.

The man nodded once to Trace, a man's nod of respect. He wore a strange little smile on his face.

"There's just one other thing, Trace," the Captain said.

"Ma'am?" He turned to face her.

"I can't pay you for saving *Lucky Seven*. There's no medals, no ceremonies—just the need for absolute secrecy. But there is one thing I can think of, to properly thank you in this moment—that lets you feel the sheer *gravitas* of your actions. You see, it wasn't just ninety-four lives and a Starship that you saved."

The Captain glanced at the Sergeant-at-Arms.

DeBrus nodded, the grin widening on his face.

The Captain turned toward her secure bulkhead compartment, her safe.

"There's something I'd like you to see."

She punched in the access code and scanned her thumb print.

"Are you a fan of art, Mister Worthington?"

* * *

Five minutes later, Trace let himself out of the Captain's quarters, his head reeling.

Oh. Em. Gee.

He barely heard the door slide shut behind him, and it occurred to him he hadn't eaten since the day before. He was ravenous.

He headed for the mess deck, and found Louise already there, waiting for him as she and Kasia munched on a breakfast burrito tube at their usual table.

Chapter Zero

Laws of Nature

Trace woke early, without using an alarm, per usual. Three days until the flip-turn and re-entry. He stared up through the pitch black of his bunk, wondering what the exact time was. Louise snoozed on, her soft little snores occasionally mixing it up in the darkness.

His mind was awake and swirling with images of the hull, empty space, and the bomb floating before him, of Jeni and her gift . . . the one he had *still not opened*. He wondered if he ever would.

He just had a feeling about today, maybe it would be a message from his new school. Maybe Chrissy had found some way to break away to Nerus after all, to meet him for landing. But, given their landing site had changed with so little notice and she lived several thousand miles away in the *Mons MegaPlex* . . . he had his doubts.

He didn't even know how to tell her how his day had gone. Above all others, he didn't want to lie to her or deceive her in any way. So he had backed off in his communications with her, and she, undoubtedly confused, had backed off as well.

He quietly turned sideways, floating and turning into a sitting-up posture, careful not to jostle Louise as she slept above him. Per usual, Mom and Dad, in their cabin, certainly wouldn't hear him slipping out.

He kept his ship's jumpsuit trousers on, slipped into a different shirt from the middle clothes drawer, and slid his feet into the shipsuit booties. Getting dressed in near-total darkness and zero gee–he had mastered that months ago.

He craved that first pouch of coffee, but he wanted to earn it today, really earn it. The cabin door hissed quietly shut behind him, and he floated out into familiar night-time low lighting of the core. Blue lights.

Blue lights, good.

Today, he would attempt the *triple lindy* of space jumps, the perfect single twist with one somersault, ending in a bullseye touch at the very tip of the dome, where the lines of all those viewing windows converged at the point of *Lucky Seven.* And he wanted to do it blind.

He just had a feeling nothing bad would come of it. He eased down through the *oculus* and planted his feet, looking up toward the *StarDome,* nine stories above.

"It's bigger on the inside," he murmured, thinking back to the first minutes he had been aboard.

Flexing his fingers just a bit out to his sides, he bent his legs ever so slightly, paused to do a slow exhale, and pushed up with just a tiny bit of force, toward that point on a ceiling far above him. He launched.

His rate of turn was agonizingly slow. Perfect.

As he passed through the *oculus,* he saw Doc Belvoire push off from the mess deck, presumably heading up to his medical suite.

Doc, having launched himself much faster, sailed ahead of Trace and went right over the rails by the Bridge, all without saying a word.

Trace floated slowly upward, rolling over in a smooth, twisting somersault. Past Deck 4, Deck 5 . . . up, up, and up . . . At Deck 6, he looked down, straight down, to the *oculus.*

He closed his eyes.

Floating up . . . levitating, but with all the sensory feeling of standing still.

He squeezed his eyes tight shut, gritting his teeth, to avoid the temptation to peek.

He reached out his left hand, sprawling his fingers apart.

His right arm, he kept pinned to his side.

Contact.

He opened his eyes and found his hand had touched just below and a few inches left of the confluence of *StarDome* window lines.

Nearly a bullseye . . . and no alarms had sounded.

He looked down; he had done just slightly more than one complete twist and exactly one flip. With only a couple days of zero-gee remaining, he wanted to nail a perfect jump before he was out of time. Goals were important.

He pushed off from the metal with just two fingers, slowly descending.

From the bridge, through the windshield hen saw three crew—the Doc, Engineer Richter, and Sergeant DeBrus—observing his progress, each offering a nod or a wave. Trace waved back.

He saw Richter tap the right-seat controls that re-engaged the *StarDome* proximity alarm.

As Trace turned and descended, he looked out, through the *StarDome* windows. Mars loomed large.

At first it had been just a pink dot on a distant cosmic horizon. Now, Mars' entire disc was clear and sharp, many features showing fine detail. He could see the Texahoma-sized ice cap at the north pole, as well as *Valles Marineris,* far to the South. The Mariner Valley made him think of the first grainy black and white images sent back by the planet's earliest visitors, *Mariner 4* and *Mariner 6* . . . nearly four hundred years ago.

He wondered briefly where *Mariner 4* might be now, a battered and worn X-shaped NASA derelict, adrift somewhere beyond Mars in heliocentric orbit.

Every day, the view of Mars improved. Every day, the *StarDome* had more visitors than the day before.

Trace tried to see lights of the city, any city, matching their locations in his mind from his Martian "Seven Cities" geography lessons, but no lights caught his eye—at the moment, all the cities were in daylight, the terminator just having passed over them, dawn breaking a short while ago.

His stomach rumbled. He needed coffee and breakfast. He had earned coffee and breakfast.

* * *

The last two days blasted by in a blur. Now, nearing final approach, time slipped away in uncontrolled free fall. After clinking pouches with Louise, toasting another 'exciting event,' they both sipped down their orangey drinks.

"Ooo, I remember the last time we drank this," Louise commented. "Hope mine works better this time."

Trace had a flashback to drinking this particular pouch concoction while riding that ridiculous moving sidewalk the morning he left Earth. He smiled and slurped the last of the drink gone.

"So what are those huge nets for?" Louise asked, noticing that DeBrus and Richter stretching a wide circular net, taut across the entire core at both Decks 3 and Deck 4. "More trampoline jumping?"

"Not sure, let's go ask."

"Mister Richter, what's this netting about? Catching—what did Chief Graves call it? FOD? Floating objects?"

"Just wait, young Worthington. You'll see. Or, mind sharp as yours, you can perhaps figure it out. Installing a pair of safety nets right before we land . . ."

He thought about it . . . "no idea. I got nothing," Trace said.

"Think of the staircases."

"How they only go to Deck 4? Noooo, are you serious right now?"

"How else can we get everyone safely down from all the upper decks after landing?"

"We're gonna jump?" Louise asked.

"Only if you wish," Richter shrugged, winking. "Many will choose the ladders, using clips and a safety harness, with the nets as a safety catch."

"Now I regret trading my seat," Trace murmured.

"You're not going up to the *StarDome*?" Louise asked.

"Nah, thought I'd give someone else the chance," he replied. "So tell Kasia I said hello."

"Okay," she said, giving him a hug.

"See you on Mars, my Lou Lou," he said confidently.

"Love you big brother."

"Love you too li'l bug."

She smiled, and pushed off hard for the *StarDome*, slipping past Richter before he netted off the space above them.

Trace watched her rise, until she nailed her landing, gripping the Deck 7 railing and swinging easily up over the bar, legs locked together like a seasoned gymnast.

From the other side of the Core, DeBrus gave a low whistle to get Richter's attention.

"Remember our bet. Upon disembarkation, right?"

"Mmmm. Five credits, ja?"

"Let's make it ten."

"Ten bucks. We have our wager." They fist-bumped in agreement, then went about finishing up anchoring the nets.

Back on the other side, Trace walked, hand-over-hand, up the side ladder to Deck 5, through small gaps in the netting the crewmen had left open until all hands were in assigned re-entry seats.

He floated past the gaming cubes and into the theater to find his seat. Mom and Dad were already here, seated in the back row. He gave each a hug as he passed by.

"Isn't this exciting?" Mom said, to which Trace nodded.

"It'll be good to feel gravity again."

"And have a real shower," Mom added.

"Dad? In the Quarantine Center, we'll have time to kill before they let us go, right?"

"Plenty. We might go more stir crazy than on this Starship."

"Heh heh, yeah. Could we . . . talk then? Like, without distractions and stuff?"

"Yes, I'd like that," Dad replied.

"Okay. Thanks."

He pushed away and drifted forward to the third row to find his seat. Out of the corner of his eye, he saw Mom whisper to Dad; he shrugged, then smiled.

Trace pulled himself down into seat C-5, which gave him a nice central view of the display. An entire galaxy filled the viewscreen, slowly rotating as a screen saver.

Trace had switched seats with Mister Kazama, who was all too pleased to get the offer of a real bird's-eye view for re-entry. Trace had never gotten around to challenging the man to a round of Out Run. . . oh well. In the Mars Arrival Center perhaps. Or their next life.

Trace just didn't want to deal with Dominique's manipulation, hot temper, or self-centered drama. He also wanted to experience his first planetary re-entry without distractions—after all, this might be a once-in-a-lifetime event if he ended up stuck on Mars.

All possible futures were open to him.

He clicked shoulder straps into the lap belt assembly buckle, grinning like a little kid, just like everyone around him.

A few moments later, all 30 theater seats reclined in unison.

Cool.

The speakers crackled to life, right on cue. Telore's face appeared on screen, and his voice rolled out of every speaker in perfect fidelity.

"Passengers, this is the very last time I will address you while we are in space. We've had quite a ride!"

"Understatement of the century, my guy," Trace said under his breath.

"The Bozeman and the Williamina Fleming have successfully touched down several hours ago at Port Mons, and we will be leaving our elliptical parking orbit momentarily.

The screen switched to a wire-model diagram of Mars, and the path they would be taking once the rockets fired.

"Our re-entry path will take us right over the top of the largest mountain in the whole Solar System, Olympus Mons, so be sure to watch for that. We may be able to glimpse other cities to the north, we'll see. We'll be passing through the night side, back into daylight as we descend, following the same path as the Manitou, toward our landing at Port Nerus."

"If you haven't already, please reach down with your left hand and find the small pouch mounted to the side of your seat. Grab out those ear plugs, and as before, rotate them until they are comfortable."

He paused, letting passengers do their thing.

Closed-captioning appeared on-screen when he spoke.

"As of right now, I'm happy to report that all seventeen other Starships for the 2353 Crossing have landed safely and are disembarking as we speak."

Wild applause broke out; people whooped and hollered enthusiastically. Someone tooted a party horn they saved from Transition.

"So, dear passengers, enjoy re-entry and landing, through our inverted flip-

turn, to the four gees of force we will all briefly feel when the engines re-ignite. Your seats will automatically rotate as the Starship turns and ignites for final landing burn. Then, the tower arms at Port Mons will pluck us right out of the air. Yes, Mars has very a thin atmosphere. After we're locked down, we will begin the disembarkation process. So just sit back, relax, and remember – breathe. See you on Mars."

The re-entry graphic cut away to a camera view, looking straight down. The Martian desert surface crawled past on screen. Trace could clearly see three massive volcanoes, marching their way up across the equator, along with vast rippling deserts, the longest canyon in the Solar System, and if he squinted, he could just glimpse thin lines crossing the desert here and there. MagLev train lines maybe? They looked too perfectly straight to be natural.

Lucky Seven crossed into the night side as the three smaller engines ignited, slowing the Starship's forward velocity and pushing her down toward the ground. The view lurched, the ship's nose pitched downward, and suddenly the view on screen was of the bright horizon behind them. The ground rose up and curved away, bottom of the screen to the top. Trace could see stars above the horizon. The sun was behind them.

The press into their seats was gentle for a long while.

The ground kept rushing up and curving away from them as they descended.

The curving horizon straightened out, looking less round and more flat. The ground below rushed by faster and faster. The camera image began to glow, fuzzy light around the edges at first, then brighter and brighter as the thin atmosphere turned to plasma across the camera's shield glass.

The camera view flipped to a dorsal camera, away from the flames licking all along the heat tiles.

The walls, screen, and seats they sat in began to vibrate, gently at first, then real shaking a moment later. Trace felt his stomach sink, then the direction flipped and the seats began to rotate. Then his stomach was up in his throat.

Lucky Seven flexed its four large landing fins in the thin air, beginning the skydiving part of re-entry.

The flickering flames settled into a strange, steady pink neon glow along both sides of the image.

As their chair rotation completed, the seats locked into a new place, parallel with the floor itself. Trace reached down and brushed the thin carpet with his fingertips.

Then the three engines kicked in fully, and the force slammed everyone deeply into their seats. The sound built its way up to the avalanche of constant noise he remembered from takeoff.

Trace concentrated on his breathing. The crush of sound and gravity went on for several minutes, and he felt some jostling as the three center rockets gimbaled around, steering *Lucky Seven* toward the tower for the last segment of final approach. Their seats adjusted into a sitting-up posture, with all the forces now pointing down, toward the engine bells.

The rumble continued another long moment. A bump-jolt hit the hull, knocking everyone sideways in their seats briefly. Heads swayed in unison.

Then, stillness; the rockets cut off.

All quiet.

The screen was filled with dust and haze.

Jack Graves's voice piped up from the front row. "Tell you what, I ain't never had a Mack Truck drivin' 'cross my chest before," he quipped, pulling his ear buds out. His neighbors laughed in agreement. A ripple of laughter passed through the small crowd, followed by wild cheering, the echo of which Trace could hear trickling in from other passenger areas of the Starship.

People cheered, people cried.

"You all right there, darlin'?" Jack said to his wife, who nodded and blinked.

"Look," she said, pointing up at the screen. Everyone followed her gaze.

The haze cleared quickly; a few last wisps of dust drifted down and out of the camera's view. Clearly visible, the metal of the catch-tower filled half the screen, and the other half . . . a dusty, tan sky. Near the bottom of the image, sunlight shined down the slopes of an extremely tall mountain, easily a dozen miles away.

"We're on Mars," someone said.

"Pavonis Mons," Trace whispered to himself. "I'm on Mars."

More ragged cheers, more tears, happy nods. Then lots of tears and happy nods, a few sideways hugs were exchanged between people, still secured in their seats.

"Whoa, feel that gravity?"

"I'm actually sinking into my seat."

"Gravity . . . laws of nature," Trace mused. "Now if only Chrissy makes it . . ."

The speakers dinged, a two-tone chime, like one hears aboard a passenger airliner.

The screen now showed a 'fasten seat belt sign' icon in the corner.

People noticed it and laughed all the more. Telore's face filled the screen.

"Welcome! You're on Mars!" he said happily.

"You'll notice the Captain has kept the Fasten Seat Belt sign illuminated, because it's just not yet time to let you jump up out of your seats. But soon. Please give your crew a moment to get to their assigned stations, so we can get you safely down to your cabin and then, down the stairs to Deck 1 to collect your belongings and disembark. If you feel dizzy or light-headed, I assure you, it will pass. This all takes time, so please be patient as we present you this welcome video.

The screen switched to the Mars Arrival Center logo, then faded to two officials standing inside what was, presumably, the Port Nerus spaceport. Several Starships were visible through the windows behind them.

The woman, in her perfectly-pressed red uniform spoke in rich, velvety tones.

"Allow us to be the first to welcome you to the Red Planet!"

Then, her companion, a tall man in his matching uniform:

"You've just spent more than five months cruising through space. You will feel disoriented, and Mars' constant gravity will make you feel like you are being dragged down. For that reason, we need you to take it easy these first couple days. No climbing stairs or strenuous exertion, your body and mind need some time to adjust.

The woman added:

"In a moment, your Starship crew members will instruct you on how you will get from the upper levels down to Deck 4 to reach your cabins and the stairwells. This graphic shows you your options."

"As you are well aware, there are no staircases above Deck 4. So, those nets you saw your crew members hooking up are one of your choices. You can do the trust-fall, where the net will gently catch you. Or you can take a side ladder down, wearing the simple harness and clipping in at the rails for safety. Those on Deck 5 are not required to use the harness on the ladder, since Mars' gravity is just one third of Earth's. Your landing will be very gentle."

Over the next hour, the 88 passengers made their way down, one way or the other, to Deck 4. Trace opted for the backward trust-fall, rather than climbing down a ladder just one story tall. Even that short distance felt like a huge drop with gravity present; he hit the net, bounced back up, and was guided to his feet with Doc's help.

Richter called the levels out like a lifeguard at those multi-platform swimming pools, getting everyone down safely.

Trace walked around to the Deck 4 railing near their Cabin, watching for Louise, who likewise opted for the quicker way down. Her piercing scream lasted all the way down to the nets, bringing both concern and laughter from onlookers.

In their cabin, Louise looked around, opening drawers and checking in nooks and crannies for anything they might have forgotten. She slipped her bundle of ship's clothing into the provided sack, considering it all to be well-earned souvenirs. Trace also left nothing behind.

Then, in groups, they were called by cabin number to visit Deck 1 to retrieve their carry-ons. During this process, Lieutenant Telore's voice quipped, *"Ladies and gents, please take extra special care that you leave none of your personal items behind, because it will be three years before we can return them to you."*

Trace shook his head. Dorky humor . . .

At the top of the narrow stairs, inevitably, Trace crossed paths with Dominique, who was coping up from below.

"Ladies first?" Trace said, stepping aside for Dominique to pass by. She paused, looked him in the eye, looking like she wanted to say something.

He nodded.

He knew whatever she had to say, she didn't have the strength to say it in front of her parents. So he said it.

"I'll see you . . . someday, I'm sure of it. Under the moons, maybe."

"Sure," Dominique said, turning to go. Her parents followed without so much as a word to Trace and his family. Mister Van der Waal looked livid, and he was barely containing it. Mrs. Van der Waal kept trying to reassure and comfort him, and he shook off her every attempt.

Apparently not everyone was overjoyed to be on the ground again.

The Worthingtons took their turn at the ladder down.

"Down ladder," Dad said, more out of habit than anything else.

Trace pulled his pack from locker F-105 under the watchful eye of Sergeant DeBrus. He stuffed his plastic ship's bag inside the faded green canvas backpack, with room to spare, zipped it up, and shouldered it. That simple motion felt . . . right. So right. Like coming home.

He looked around, half expecting Daniels to be standing there, grinning maniacally, but DeBrus stood alone, watching the passengers retrieve their belongings.

He caught DeBrus' eye. The man scrutinized him, no doubt curious what Trace would have to say on parting.

He walked over, risking one final handshake.

"Not as an angry boy," Trace said, keeping eye contact.

DeBrus nodded, smiling. "No' as an angry boy, indeed. Now go, and take a few good swings at life, will ye?"

"Aye, that I shall," he said, mimicking DeBrus' Scottish banter. "And seek out a bit o' the rough and tumble, right?"

DeBrus nodded, letting the handshake go. The smile never left his face.

Trace adjusted his pack and joined his family to take their turn at the staircase. They reached the top of the ladder, and Trace was surprised to see Richter standing over at the railing, wishing people well as they disembarked.

"Dad, could you give me just a minute, please?"

"Sure. Meet over there by the airlock." Mom looked up at her beloved Jim, and Louise impatiently tugged at her dad's hand, practically dragging him to the spot next to the Starship's exit.

"Mister Richter . . ." Trace's voice cracked. He knew might never see the Engineer again.

"I . . . hope you have an excellent trip out to the Frontier. Tell Viking 1 that I said hello, and that I'll be along some day."

"Trace." His both hands gripped Trace's handshake. "A true pleasure." The man nodded.

"I'll never forget you," Trace said.

"Ja. That's true."

Trace's jaw fell open, breaking into a laugh. Richter smiled back.

"Careful, I might kick you in the head." Richter's turn to laugh.

"So. It's time to go. Find your adventure, young Worthington. Your people await, and I'm sure there's a Starship with your name on it somewhere out there. Don't get lost, hm?"

"You neither. What's the German word for adventure?"

"Abenteuer."

"Abentooer?"

"Ah-ben-toy-air."

"Abenteuer."

"You say it better than me."

After another moment, Trace broke eye contact, turned away, and walked over to catch up with his family to disembark *Lucky Seven.*

Richter waited, watching where Trace and his family had headed down the gangway.

Chief Jack Graves fussed over his wife, carrying both her case and his as they left.

Finally, Mr. Shin Kazama walked past and stepped out of *Lucky Seven.* Before he had gone more than a few steps, Mr. Kazama turned, bowed the gentleman's show of respect, then went along his way.

Richter nodded, smiling.

Then he cocked his head sideways, listening.

A few seconds later, he heard the dull thud he was waiting for, followed by healthy cursing and swearing in a young man's voice.

"There's one every Crossing," Richter murmured, descending the stairs to Deck 1 and his Engineering suite.

He swiped his screen awake, smiling broadly.

DeBrus owed him ten bucks.

Epilogue

Trace pressed at his forehead; the bruise had faded somewhat in the weeks since landing—the spot was still tender and discolored. He had really clocked himself.

He found his seat on the *Zephyr,* in one of its rear passenger compartments. No, wait . . . this one wasn't called *Zephyr*. This was *The Thread*. Why do they call it that? Odd choice.

He slung his trusty pack up into the overhead bins and sat down in his aisle seat, nodding at the much older lady, a stranger, seated beside him. She went back to reading her tablet.

It was all too much, the sheer magnitude of changes he had seen these last several weeks—*Lucky Seven,* the landing, no Chrissy at the spaceport, having gravity back, finishing up quarantine, joining the new school, exploring only a couple places in Nerus, and filling in last-minute for a sick teammate on the Nerus High School *Academic Decathlon* team . . . except here they called it the *Knowledge Bowl*. Too much.

He needed something to remind him directly of where he was, when he was—something simple. Then he remembered Jeni's unopened gift.

Jeni, who had dumped him as he left Earth, never mind that it had probably been for the best. Jeni.

He extracted her small package from an inner jacket pocket. It wasn't the same jacket he had worn aboard the Zephyr back on Earth, but he had found a suitable substitute, a simulated denim, dark blue. A boss look.

Holding the package in one hand, he tugged at the small ribbon that wrapped it tight.

He hesitated. Why was this so difficult?

Muttering a short expletive under his breath, he tore the package open in one decisive motion.

Into his lap fell . . . a coin.

The front showed the word "Liberty" in caps, spaced out, all around its upper curve. In the center, a lady in a long, flowing dress, mid-stride, as she walked boldly toward the sun, shining over a range of mountain peaks. Just like the sunset he had watched from the train his last night on Earth.

Seeing the numbers beneath her feet, he gasped. The four-digit year on the coin showed 2031. Remembering his U.S.A. and U.S.C. history well enough, that was the last full year the United States had existed as one nation of fifty states, before a Constitutional crisis had torn the nation in two over a disputed, unresolved election. That would make this coin . . . 322 years old. Yikes.

The two nations had gotten along as well as anyone could hope for in the centuries since. Trace, a citizen of the North, the U.S.A., had nothing but profound respect for Chief Jack Graves, a military man from the U.S.C., the South. Everyone who knew Jack Graves respected him.

He turned the coin in his hand, wondering. Had Jeni been trying to tell him something? A metaphor? Getting back together some day? Or . . . this is it, it's over, we're separated forever but still friends, kind of? He shook his head, unsure of what embedded message was here. He squeezed the coin tight in his hand. He hoped he could ask her face-to-face someday.

A few passengers walked down the aisleway, and instinctively Trace stashed the coin back in his inner pocket and zipped it shut.

He reached for his seat belt, trying to calm swirling thoughts. Whole new planet, new apartment, new school, zero real friends (yet), and now, he had just boarded a train about to blast across a desert 17 times bigger than the largest back on Earth, at nearly double the speed of any bullet train back on Earth . . . all to attend a K-Bowl competition and eventually . . . a *Homecoming Dance*? Dancing in public . . . ugh, maybe he'd skip that part.

It was all too familiar and yet all too strange.

He slapped himself hard across the face, trying to dump his jumbled thoughts.

The gray-haired lady scrutinized him over her horn-rimmed glasses. He finally noticed her staring and turned to make eye contact. She smiled.

"This is very real, young sir, you aren't in a dream."

Trace didn't say anything. He smiled a smirk and nodded to her, grateful at least the slap had returned him to the *now*. To *this* moment. When Trace said nothing, the lady went back to her reading.

Trace knew his teammates, the *Legionnaires*, had been grouped together in some forward compartment with a contingent of thirty other students, a cheering section. He had been added to the roster so late in the planning that his seat was a solo way in the back of the train. Riding alone on a train. Again.

One of his teammates had raved about The Thread. A 3,000-mile non-stop from Nerus to the capital city, *Mons-MegaPlex*. Sounded a lot like his own *Denver MegaPlex*. He once again imagined a city in a cramped series of little connected caves, with a million people, all packed in a constant shuffle, pushing their way from here to there and fighting over limited resources. Then he remembered Stein's recorded message from months ago. Open plazas. Cavern ceilings so far above, you couldn't make out detail in the rock. What had looked like a bright sky above.

The train's overhead speakers crackled to life.

"Ladies and gentlemen, Julia here, your conductor for our journey today. On behalf of Maglev Interplanetary and our Chief Engineer, Driver Manny Ramirez, thank you for joining us aboard the Thread, with non-stop service to the Mons-MegaPlex, followed by New Marrakech, and our ultimate destination, Skye City. We remind you that due to recent seismic activity near the capital, safety restraints today include full harness. Please secure all loose articles for acceleration. We will depart in eight minutes."

Trace slipped into both shoulder straps, clicking the buckles into place. Grabbing out his tablet, he connected the train's Wi-Fi and opened the digital Welcome Package he had received the day before. The Mons High School logo popped up and started spinning as the rest of the package loaded. What was their mascot? Oh yes, the *Olympians*.

He liked his own Nerus High *Legionnaires* better, and hopefully his teammates would grow to be excellent friends. Maybe they'd be as good as the ones he had been ripped away from back in Colorado Springs.

"One solid friend," he murmured softly. "Then, Dad, I'll admit you might have been right about Mars."

"Did you say something?" the lady asked.

"Sorry. Thoughts out loud."

She nodded.

Trace slipped in his ear pods and cued up a playlist mixed by one of the more popular Martian DJs. He looked at the name . . . *DJ Ser.* Wondering what that referred to, the DJ's randomizer kicked out a 'brand new' tune that had topped the charts three months before he had left Earth. He knew it well. He nodded to the beat.

The train pulled forward and transited its air locks. After another pause, it pulled out from under Nerus city's mountain home, the extinct volcano Pavonis Mons. Trace and his fellow passengers were pressed back into their comfy seats as the Thread picked up speed through the open desert. It was a decent press into his seat, but nothing like blasting off aboard *Lucky Seven*.

He peeked down the aisleway after the train reached its cruising speed and the seat belt sign had been turned off . . . he thought of joining his new teammates.

But he held off, for now.

Little did Trace know that within just a few days, he would make not one new friend, but five . . . none of them *Legionnaires*.

One of these, he would eventually bond with like a sibling.

A kindred spirit.

But that . . . is another story.

----- THE END -----

MARS
HIGH SCHOOL
BOOK 1: THE OLYMPIANS
J. SANDROCK

Preview: Mars High School Book 1: The Olympians

Andie and Aiyana nudged their way through the rubble beyond the blue airlock door and stepped through. Though it was awkward in their *Exo-suits*, the two managed to move some larger rocks aside and pull the door closed, sliding the handle into its 'sealed' position.

The cat bounded gracefully across the tops of the larger rocks until he was clear of the pile. Ares squinted into the black tunnel ahead.

Andie turned her suit's headlamps up to maximum brightness and adjusted the cat's suit lamp settings as well. Aiyana did the same.

The tunnel on this side of the blue door was natural, not carved at all by machines. The floor had bumpy ridges, and the ceiling showed rivulets and frozen drips where some magma flow millions of years earlier had run through the tube then drained away to the deeper magma chambers far beneath *Olympus Mons*.

They continued on with Ares close by, carefully stepping over ridges and rough floor, occasionally stubbing a booted toe—but not enough to cause pain or compromise a suit.

The tunnel curved down, right, down, and left, no branches, no change in its diameter. Ares walked slightly faster, a few paces ahead of them. After another few minutes, he let out a low kitty growl and stopped.

"Rrrrrrr . . ." the cat's low growl lasted a few seconds before trailing off.

They had found another round room, but here, the floor simply fell away.

"Careful, there's a drop off," Aiyana put out a hand to stop Andie from walking right over the edge.

"Thanks," Andie whispered. Ares peered down over the edge.

"Look over there the wall curves side to side." The opposite wall also curved up to a rounded dome above, perfectly smooth.

"Why on Mars would someone cut a round room like this?"

"I . . . don't think this was the builders. They would probably have smoothed out the tunnels behind us, these rough magma tubes."

"Okay, then who?"

Andie shrugged. "Wow. Look, it's a complete sphere." The curving walls above, below, and on both sides had no flat surfaces, no sharp edges or angles, and no exit. Everything curved so perfectly it was tricky to look at. Andie swayed a bit; Aiyana kept hold of her shoulder.

"So . . . weird round room."

"Mr-reow."

"What's that he said?" Aiyana asked, looking down at Ares.

"That's the sound he makes when he wants me to do something. It's like . . . his call to action."

"Mew," Ares confirmed.

"Um, no thanks. We fall in there, we'd get stuck. So, nothing else to do here but go back, see?"

"Sadly, that sounds right. But something's bothering me. We're standing in a natural magma tube here, right?"

"I guess, yeah."

"So where is the rest of the tunnel? Magma tubes don't just . . . end. So this one just ends in this, what did you call it? Weird round room? It makes no sense--it should continue, straight across, right over there."

Aiyana looked down at the cat, who had just crouched.

"No, don't you even think abou—"

And the cat leaped over the edge.

Andie grabbed at him but caught nothing but vacuum.

Credit: TayandBay Studios, Inc. @tayandbaystudios

About the Author

J. Sandrock grew up traveling the world in an Air Force family, graduating from the American Embassy School in Delhi, India. Sandrock lives in Salt Lake City, Utah with his beloved bride Mindi. His three kiddos Jacob, Rachel, and Paige are his forever pride and joy.

Following in his father's and grandfather's footsteps, he served 24 years wearing Air Force Blue, with assignments in Germany, Italy, Guam, several U.S. states, and deployments to the Middle East. Upon retirement in 2014, he taught high school science for seven years (Earth Science & Astronomy) in one of Utah's largest high schools, where he expanded the Astro program to become one of the finest in the state.

Graduates of Granger High Astronomy are reminded of their two remaining homework assignments: the first is due when humanity sets foot on Mars, and the second, when Comet Halley returns in 2061.

To all who brave the unknown, question everything, and keep looking up. . . may you live long, and prosper.

Made in the USA
Las Vegas, NV
30 March 2026

44493273R00184